Extinction

By

Jay Korza

Table of Contents

Dedication and Forward	
Daria	1
Chapter 1	9
Chapter 2	15
Chapter 3	28
Seth	38
Chapter 4	53
Chapter 5	60
Chapter 6	68
The Warrior	80
Chapter 7	89
Chapter 8	92
Wilks	106
Chapter 9	116
Chapter 10	123
Chapter 11	130
Chapter 12	136
Chapter 13	145
Emily	146
Chapter 14	164
Chapter 15	169
Chapter 16	170
Scan	174
Chapter 17	189
Chapter 18	200
Chapter 19	202
Chapter 20	209

Chapter 21	213
Surgeon	224
Chapter 22	225
Chapter 23	234
Chapter 24	240
Chapter 25	244
Chapter 26	247
Chapter 27	248
Chapter 28	251
Chapter 29	254
Chapter 30	262
Davies	264
Chapter 31	279
Chapter 32	288
Chapter 33	291
Chapter 34	294
Chapter 35	298
Chapter 36	299
Chapter 37	303
Chapter 38	306
Chapter 39	313
Chapter 40	316
Chapter 41	317
Chapter 42	320
Chapter 43	332
Snake	351
Chapter 44	374
Bloom	391
Chapter 45	407
Reaper	412

Chapter 46	436
Chapter 47	461
Beast	499
Chapter 48	521
Chapter 49	545
Chapter 50	549
Chapter 51	587
Epilogue	603
About the Author	610

Dedication and Forward

Before the story starts, I'd like to take a moment to say thank you to a few people and make some observations about my writing.

First off, I started writing this book in 1998. It started with the intention of being a short story about two young people in love who were separated by military service. The first night I sat down to write, the story took off without me and left the two lovers in the dust and somehow ended up in space in the future. There is still a love story in there, actually several of them, but none are the centerpiece of the story.

I wrote fairly steadily for the first year but then moved to Massachusetts the next year and wrote much less. Over the years, I have picked it up and started writing again only to stop for some reason or another. Somewhere in the middle of 2012, I decided that I was going to start working on the book at least once a week, every week, until I was done.

During all of the starts and stops, my mother has been reading my drafts and encouraging me to continue writing. She told me the other day that she was my biggest fan and couldn't wait for the finished product. At the time of this writing, she is also my only fan, so I know I'll sell at least one copy! Thank you, Mom, for all of the encouragement you have given me since I started this endeavor and even more so for all you have given me throughout the rest of my life.

Over the years I've also had friends, girlfriends, and other family members who have read portions of the book and have given me encouragement and feedback. So there's maybe four or five more sales I can count on. Except (redacted). I don't think she'll be buying one, but thanks anyway for your input!

As I mentioned before, I started working on the book once a week. I would go every weekend to Starbucks at my local mall and set up shop in there for two to eight—or more—hours. A trente black iced tea with raspberry sweetener and a dash of cherry Mio, oh so very good. For less than four bucks a day with free refills from my Starbucks Gold Card, I had a great place to write with just enough distraction to give me plenty of micro-breaks to get through the day. Thanks to all of the baristas who were always so friendly and helpful, regardless of how much space I took up and how little money I spent.

Now about my writing style...yes, I know "anticlimacticness" isn't a word. Plenty of words in this book aren't accepted words. I wanted to write in a style that mimicked our true nature of communication. We make up words, we don't always use proper grammar, and we love slang.

I also know that there holes in the plot, not huge ones (*Prometheus*)—at least I hope there aren't. But if you think about it, there are holes in every plot, even in real life. Anyone can sit back and look at the story of what you did in your life and find holes, things that don't make sense, decisions that could've been better. So in the spirit of book reading and suspension of disbelief, just go with it and enjoy the story. And if any one from How It Should Have Ended or CinemaSins wants to make this the first book they spoof, I'd love that!

I would also like to thank Eric Schock who brought some of the characters to life with his fantastic art work. If you have a chance to look at his other work, I'm sure you'll be impressed. www.evilrobo.com

And last but definitely not least, I would like to thank Shannon and Maya for coming into my life and making this last year the best ever. Shannon was also a great resource while I finished the book and she was always eager to read the next chapter. Thank you for believing in me and thank you even more for putting up with me. I love you both.

There are plenty of other people to thank and comments to make but I think it's time to start the story. I really hope you enjoy reading this as much as I loved writing it..

Daria

NAME: DARIA O'CONNOR
SPECIES: HUMAN
MOS: HOSPITAL CORPSMAN
RANK: PO FIRST CLASS
AGE: 32 - EARTH STANDARD
SEX: FEMALE
HEIGHT: 5'6"
WEIGHT: 140 POUNDS

Daria was more excited than she had ever been in her nine years of life. She kept looking at her dad and squeezing his hand. The line was moving at a fairly constant rate but it wasn't fast enough for Daria.

In the hand not occupied by her father's, Daria held a raffle ticket, a winning raffle ticket. *THE* winning raffle ticket. Daria had used her allowance and some saved lunch money to buy five raffle tickets at her school's carnival fundraiser.

The first-place prize was a brand new digital-optical hybrid telescope that was the top of line in consumer electronics. Daria loved astronomy more than anything in all the worlds. And now, she stood in the customer service line of the store that had donated the prize to her school, waiting to redeem her winning ticket.

Daria and her family lived in a colony on the outermost planet of a Coalition co-op solar system. Their place in the system would make the views from the telescope the most wonderful sights Daria had ever seen. She already had every night for the next month planned out as to what she would be viewing. Tonight she would be mapping a system belonging to the Wordols with a name that loosely translated to "To Look Upon the Gods."

At the edge of Daria's periphery, she heard a commotion that grew to a point she could no longer ignore it. As she turned, she immediately saw two men, with handguns, pushing store patrons to the ground. At only nine, even Daria recognized the crazed look of someone high on Track Star.

The drug became popular when a galactic sports super star died during the last Olympics. The human sports hero was taking a new drug to help him compete against some of the Coalition species that had definite genetic advantages over humans. Daria didn't remember the Olympian's name but she did know her father would joke that he wasn't even in track events so the drug's name was kind of stupid.

The drug was a bad one, not the worst to be found but bad enough. It caused paranoia, aggression, a lack of grounding in reality, and a host of other issues that were common in a lot of drugs. What set this drug apart was that it had a synergistic effect with the neurotransmitters associated with the fight-or-flight response.

The synergistic effect astronomically enhanced the high experienced by the user. As a result, the user tended to perform acts to stimulate the response. Casual users, if there were such a thing, would typically take the drug before activities like planetary free-falling. Hard-core users didn't have the money for the extreme sports, so they tended to commit criminal acts to get their blood pumping and adrenaline up to enhance their high.

The two junkies were herding the customers and slapping them around, hoping someone would fight back. If a victim fought back, it would help stimulate the users' adrenal response and make their high better. Most people knew that being docile with the bastards would cause their high to wane and usually they would move on.

As Daria watched the scene unfolding and moving from the front of the store to the rear, she noticed there were two marines in uniform who had been shopping in the store. They were giving each other slight hand signals and head nods. Daria knew that they were making a plan of some sort.

Before the two marines could act, one of the junkies started to have a seizure, an inevitable side effect of prolonged use of Track Star. As the gunman fell, his convulsions caused him to pull the trigger on his automatic machine pistol. Bullets sprayed, people screamed, blood spilled and one maniacal drug user laughed and danced among the chaos as his adrenal glands kicked in and added to his high.

Daria stood in place and felt a bullet pass so close to her face that it actually caused her long hair to billow out behind her and a small clump of it fell away from the rest. When the hair drifted to her wrist, she glanced down at the odd sensation; her eyes were then drawn to the figure of her father lying on the ground with a pool of blood building around his body.

Daria dropped her coveted raffle ticket and knelt next to her father. She was still holding her father's hand and used her other hand to try to stop the blood pouring from his chest. She had learned basic first aid in school and she remembered enough to know that her efforts were in vain.

Daria felt a gentle touch on her shoulder and heard a soft voice in her ear, "Hey sweetie, let me help you with that." Daria looked and saw one of the marines kneeling beside her and slowly moved her aside so he could get to her father. Once she moved, he quickly went to work removing her father's shirt and examining the wound.

"Please help him."

"I'll do my best, sweetie."

"Daria."

"Huh?"

"Daria. My name is Daria. I don't like to be called sweetie. My mom used to call me that and she's dead now. So no one gets to call me sweetie anymore." Daria knew it was such a trivial thing to think of and complain about in this moment but she didn't know what else to say. "My mom is dead, so you have to help my father."

The marine looked at her. "I'll do my best, Daria, I promise." He turned back to her father and pulled out a pocketknife. "And my name is Bryce, but my friends call me Reaper."

Reaper was probing the wound with his finger and even though her father was mostly unconscious, he still went rigid and moaned as the finger went into the wound. "Shit", was all Reaper said as he pulled his finger out.

"What?"

"The bullet went into your father's heart; put a hole in the left ventricle." A quizzical look from Daria had Reaper explaining, "I need to open his chest and plug that hole. I can't get to it well enough through the bullet hole. What I'm about to do to your father is going to look very horrible and it's going to hurt him a lot, but you have to trust me."

While Reaper was talking, he was moving Daria's father into a different position up on his right side with his left arm over his head. He was pushing on her father's ribs and counting to himself. When he reached the number five, he held one finger in the depression between the ribs and brought the knife to her father's skin. Reaper looked at Daria and she nodded; she knew he was about to open her father's chest.

With one fluid motion, Reaper made what seemed to be a huge incision along the ribcage and almost immediately the white of the rib bones were exposed, along with muscle and fatty tissue. Without rib spreaders available, Reaper just reached in with both hands and started pulling the ribs away from each other. The muscle stretched and tore and gave way to the chest cavity they protected. With lung tissue exposed, Reaper reached in and started moving the organ out of his way to get to the heart.

Daria's father was fully unconscious now but he reflexively gripped her hand to the point that she thought it was going to break. That's when she heard the cold, cruel voice of the other junkie she had already forgotten about. "Get the fuck away from him. Let him die."

Reaper turned to look at the assailant. "No."

"Look, man, you're obviously a doctor or some shit." The junkie nodded towards his still seizing friend. "Let this little bitch's dad die and help my buddy."

"I'm not a doctor, I'm a corpsman. And even if I wanted to save your friend, I couldn't." Reaper was still trying to slowly work on Daria's father as he spoke. "Your friend has been seizing for over a minute now. That means he's in the last stages of Track Star Delirium. He can't be saved by anyone, even if we were in the best hospital in the entire Coalition. He's going to die, end of story."

Without hesitating, the junkie calmly said, "Then so will you."

Daria heard the gun bark at least five times and she saw the front of Reaper's chest tear apart in more than one place. Reaper slumped next to Daria's father. At that moment, one of the citizen shoppers swung a trashcan at the junkie's head and the sound of a solid connection rang out. The junkie went down and immediately the citizen was kicking and stomping on the already subdued man.

"You killed my wife!" the man repeated again and again as he kicked and beat the man, turning the junkie's body to pulp.

Daria turned her attention back to her father. She knew, or at least thought she knew, what Reaper was going to do after he exposed the heart: plug the hole. Daria was trying to get herself over the mental hurdle of sticking her hand inside her father's chest when she saw Reaper's arm move.

Reaper didn't have enough strength to move his body but he could still make his arm function. He walked his fingers along the floor and up his patient's side until he found the surgical opening he had created. He then slid his fingers inside and found the hole and put two fingers in it.

Daria instantly saw the blood cease to pump from her father's body and saw just a tinge of color race up his carotid arteries and into his face. He had still lost a lot of blood so his color didn't change very much but she was sure that even a little change was a good sign.

Reaper's body went slack but his fingers never moved. Daria was sure he was dead but before she could check, a police officer scooped her up to take her out of the store and to a safe place. Daria struggled briefly until she realized the man holding her was one of the good guys.

Pointing to Reaper, she said, "Don't move him. His hand is saving my daddy's life." And with that, all of the adrenaline that had kept her upright for the last several minutes left her body all at once. She went limp in the officer's arms, her winning ticket all but forgotten. A song played, distantly heard in the background...

~

Daria sat on the edge of the boardwalk, looking into the water. The rolling of the sea always made her feel better: The rhythmic crashing of the waves against the pillars of the pier. The creaking of the wood as it stands against one of the strongest forces in all of nature.

It had been twelve years since her father had been shot in the store, waiting in line to get Daria's telescope. Twelve years since Daria's life changed so drastically in just five short minutes. She still looked at the night sky but not in the same way and not with the telescope that she never claimed. Now she looked at the sky, wondering where the Marine Corps would send her.

After that day in the store, she became obsessed with medicine and studied it relentlessly. All of her teachers thought for sure she would be going to medical school after college, but not Daria. Daria knew she wasn't going to college, at least not a standard six-year college. She was sought after by many of the top schools in the Coalition but she only applied to one school her senior year. Daria applied to a vocational school to become a paramedic. Her teachers were all aghast at such a flagrant waste of intelligence and talent but Daria couldn't care less.

To become a paramedic on an all-human world, the class was only nine months long. But Daria wanted more than that. Daria was taking the multi-species course that usually took three years. With all of the studying Daria had done on her own, she was able to test out of most of the course work and focus on clinical rotations. Daria finished the school in just two years. Many of the doctors Daria worked with had written her letters of recommendation for medical schools but she had her sights set on a different goal.

Daria felt a light touch on her shoulder and smelled the familiar scent that always made her smile. She looked up into the eyes of the man standing behind her. "Hi, Dad."

"Hi, sweetie." Daria's father sat next to her on the dock. "Are you ready?"

"More than you know." No matter how old Daria got, she knew that holding her father's hand would always be the best feeling in the galaxy.

"Okay, we should probably get you to the transport then." As they both stood, he added, "You know you don't have to go. Your contract isn't in effect until you scan-in on the shuttle."

"I know, Dad, but I want to. I know you think I have some deep-seated need to go but that's not it." As they stood, she looked up into his eyes and put one hand over the area on his chest where Reaper had opened him up so many years ago. "I'm not doing this because he sacrificed himself for *YOU*, I'm doing this because he sacrificed himself for another person. In that moment, I knew that I could do more than look at the galaxy—I could be an important part of it."

"I know, sweetie. I'm just going to miss you." As an unabashed tear rolled down his face, he led her towards their transport. "Just do me one huge favor, please."

"What's that, Dad?"

"Please, for the love of all that is holy, get stationed somewhere with beaches and sand so I can visit and find myself a little honey to spend all of my retirement money on."

"You got it, Dad."

Chapter 1
Coalition Military Installation - Clandestine

Late August on Terra 12-2772 meant that total darkness would cover the marine installation for another two months. The branch of government known as the Earth Interstellar Expansion Department had long since given up trying to assign names to new planets taken into the Coalition, and had simply started designating them by number. Terra 12-2772 was a marine base on the outskirts of charted space and was almost always in total eclipse by its nearest neighboring planet. The first marines to colonize this God-forsaken frozen wasteland decided that because it was almost always shrouded in darkness, "Clandestine" was the most appropriate name for their new home.

Daria sat on her bunk with the slightly melted dogtags of her husband clenched tightly in her hand. The dogtags alone survived the explosion that had just two weeks ago lit up the sky over Clandestine and destroyed two fighters in a training exercise.

Gunnery Sergeant Mike "Marvel" O'Connor was weapons officer aboard one of the two-seater crafts when the explosion occurred. The official report stated that O'Connor hadn't shut down his weapons panel in time after the computer detected a leak in his cold fusion lasers, which resulted in an explosion that ended up taking out his wingman as well. Daria couldn't—wouldn't—believe that her husband would make that mistake. She had known him long enough and been in more than one battle with him to know that Mike didn't make mistakes like that, especially during a routine training mission.

Daria was a navy medic, a battlefield medic, and held the respected title of "corpsman." Hundreds of years ago when Earth ventured out into the cosmos, there was a political battle over which of the armed services would be the conqueror of space. In Daria's opinion, too much ego and testosterone were involved, which led to a couple of assassinations and much political blackmail. Eventually the president of that time made the decision that the Navy would be the primary military service to explore the cosmos. Of course, the marines are a part of the Navy, so they were included in the first push beyond Earth's solar system. The Navy continued to take care of the transportation and almost all the air and space aircraft support while the marines continued with their role as ground troops.

  Corpsman was the only rating from the Navy that integrated with the Marine Corps in such a way that made the corpsman more marine than sailor. They could choose to wear Marine Corps uniforms and abide by Marine Corps regulation if they wanted to, and most field corpsman did. Their long history of distinguished service in battle had raised them to a different level, which almost made them an individual entity separate from both branches they served. Many of the grunts in Daria's platoon had often kidded her, saying that Mike had married her just to get the better quarters and choice of duty stations that corpsman received.

  She laughed aloud as she thought of that. If she had had her choice of duty, she and Mike would never have been on this rock of ice and Mike wouldn't be dead. Why were they here anyway? This outpost held no strategic significance that she knew of, especially considering Earth hadn't been in a major war in more than fifty years.

  Nonetheless, Clandestine had a complement of more than a hundred thousand marines and it was the first time a whole planet had been designated as a military installation. On the other hand, what sane terra former would want to live on this block of ice? She couldn't understand it and for the time being decided to just stop trying.

Corporal Davies sat at the bar waiting for Daria to walk in. Davies had loved Mike like an older brother and felt he owed it to him to watch out for Daria now that Mike was gone. He thought about that for a minute and smiled. Truth was, Daria could take care of herself better than Davies could. Davies was six foot four inches and about two hundred sixty pounds but as clumsy as a toddler just learning to walk. Mike had pulled his ass out of the fire on more than one occasion in battle and Davies wasn't the type of guy to forget that.

If it weren't for the fact that Davies could hit a penny at a few thousand yards out with a sniper rifle, he would've been booted from the corps years ago. He was the best sniper in the Coalition. So what the hell was he doing here? He couldn't figure out who he had pissed off to get hung out to dry, or rather freeze, like this.

Just then, Daria walked through the doors and gave the place a once-over. Davies always admired the way she could quickly size up any situation. Her stare was penetrating and she never missed a thing, but there was always warmth behind her eyes that until now only Mike and Davies could see. But as she stood there, Davies realized that the little bit of warmth that used to reside there had been replaced with something much colder—colder than the core of the ice planet they now stood on.

To anyone who didn't know her, Daria was just the opposite of what you'd expect a marine to look like. She was slight of build, only five foot six inches tall but weighing in at a well-hidden one hundred forty pounds. A lot of muscle was neatly tucked away inside the small frame that stood in the doorway. She was also lightning fast, a trait that Davies wished he shared. Her ability with knives was unmatched. She had taught him many ways to get beyond his awkwardness and kill someone quickly and quietly from less than a kilometer away.

Her abilities had resulted in more than one or two marines ending up with broken faces or other body parts after trying to get a little too friendly with Daria after a night of drinking. More often than not, the MPs would show up, only to find Daria skillfully attending to the wounds she had just inflicted on a whole squad. After all, they were all marines in the end, right?

Davies saw three Force Recon guys sitting nearby who looked as though they were about to make the mistake that many before them had also made. They weren't part of the normal complement that now resided on Clandestine and had just that day come in from a several months' long scouting mission.

They had been drinking and bragging for hours and now saw at the door what they perceived as R&R. Davies heard them talking about Daria and was about to warn them but he stopped himself. He decided that a little R&R was EXACTLY what Daria needed right now.

Daria had completed scanning her new environment and started towards Davies when the first Recon approached her, holding two beers.

"Hey Doc," he said, with a beer extended towards Daria, "how 'bout you check my dick! It's a little dry from my last mission. I think it could use a little lotion or something."

Much to Davies' surprise, Daria just walked on by—that is, until the second Recon blocked her way. "What's the rush? We just want to buy you a drink and maybe play a little doctor later. What do you say, Doc?"

With a motion faster than even Davies' sober eyes could see, Daria grabbed the beer bottle from Recon Two's hand and twirled to land a crushing blow to the first Recon's face, shattering his nose and cheekbone, not to mention the bottle. Before he could react, Recon Two had his balls trapped inside a vise-like hand from Daria and was up on his toes, trying to stumble away.

"Well, your testicles are extremely small and I can't seem to find a penis anywhere," Daria said as she put her other hand on his throat and began to lift him off his feet. As Recon Two sailed over the bar and landed against the mirror, shattering it, he faintly heard before he passed out, "Oh, and by the way, you might want to get that concussion checked out too."

As she turned toward Recon Three, who was still sitting at the table and trying to decide whether he wanted to help his friends or even whether he COULD help them, she stated in a very quiet, reserved voice, "Would you like to play doctor, too?" He didn't get a chance to answer because the first marine was up again and wielding his field knife.

Daria had beaten many marines in fights before but even in her depressed state, had no desire to kill one. So she decided to end this quickly and struck out with her right foot; she made contact with his knee, causing an audible "pop-crack" that was heard throughout the bar.

She decided not to take any chances with the marine still sitting at the table, so with a deftly placed axe kick, she hit the side of the table nearest her, which popped up the other side, cracking him on the chin and breaking his jaw. Before the table or the marine's body could fall, she side kicked the now vertical table, sending it into the poor marine, whose only crime was to choose the wrong buddies to have shore leave with. Both table and marine fell to the floor, both broken in more than one place.

Daria looked around and, seeing no other threats, took her seat next to Davies and asked the bartender to call a corpsman.

"Aren't you a corpsman?" he asked as he reached for his comlink.

"Not tonight I'm not," she sighed. "Not tonight." She knew she hadn't caused any life-threatening injuries. Picking up her beer and taking back a long drink while she heard moans and whimpering all around didn't cause any moral dilemma for Daria tonight.

Although feeling partly responsible for the carnage lying around the bar, Davies decided that even if he had warned them, they probably would've still made the same mistake. He could see a small grin to either side of the bottle as Daria drank her beer, and Davies knew he had made the right call.

The rest of the night was filled with silence between them while the rest of the bar recapped the action to one another as new friends walked in. As the alcohol levels rose, so did the number of injuries Daria inflicted, as well as the number of marines she inflicted them on. Yes, this was exactly what she needed right now.

Chapter 2
Planetside – Intel Gathering Mission

Seth couldn't believe how hot it was so early in the morning. He had awakened in the middle of the night so that he could not only travel in a blanket of darkness to conceal his movements, but to also keep himself out of the blistering sun, which was threatening to show its full self shortly.

He had been hunted by his enemies for the past three days and had run out of water at the start of the second. He wasn't sure how long he could avoid capture but he had to try to complete his mission. Every other member of his detachment had met with an unfortunate fate and, unaware of how the rest of the task force was faring, he had to push on in case he was the last surviving operative left to complete the mission.

Although the vast prairie he traveled through had tall grass to hide in, it was also very dry from a recent drought and Seth cringed at the noise he made as he walked through it. He had to find water soon. He was heading toward a tree line that seemed to have a shade more green than everything else around him and he prayed that it meant water.

At a hundred meters from the tree line, Seth froze in his tracks. He knew that this planet had indigenous life but hadn't even thought that a predator of another sort might also be using the tall grass for cover.

He was nearly face to tail with what would pass, much too closely, for a tiger on Earth. The creature had a long tail with a bulb at the end, in which many six-centimeter long spikes were imbedded. Not to mention the eight claws on each paw that seemed larger and sharper than his field knife. The ears were almost non-existent but that would be expected on a thin atmosphere planet and was much to Seth's advantage. This tiger probably hunted with sight and scent and didn't rely too much on hearing.

Seth was upwind of the brisk breeze swaying the grass. All marine-issue uniforms had a uniquely designed cloth that absorbed body fluids and retained them, cooling the wearer and also negating any scents that would normally be present with any hardworking soldier. As an extra bonus, each soldier had a water-recycling unit that was attached to an outlet in their field blouse. This device allowed all of the liquid output from the wearer to be recycled into drinkable water. Unfortunately, Seth's had been damaged during the initial attack three days ago.

Earth had been in a war three hundred years ago with a species known as the Shirkas. Their culture had never passed beyond the hunter/gatherer stage and throughout their scientific and intellectual advancements, they kept to the old ways that had never failed to provide for them. Consequently, Earth was faced with an enemy that could hunt down their soldiers and defeat them almost effortlessly on any battlefield. The government created and used a biological weapon designed specifically for the Shirkas, which destroyed their home world and many settlements before they finally surrendered.

Seth, and every other marine, was now wearing a uniform designed by the Shirkas, which allowed him to be invisible to any heat or pheromone detector known to exist. And now for the first time since he joined the Marine Corps, he was glad to be wearing the scratchy cloth that was probably the only thing saving him from being lunch for the creature that now crouched before him.

He realized that the muscular cat was too interested in his current prey to notice him anyway. And then he saw it: a watering hole with some six-legged herd animals cautiously drinking. He also saw his objective. The enemy had decided to secure the watering hole for themselves and had set up their primary post twenty-five meters from the water's edge. What luck!

Now, all he had to do was steal the battle plans from an enemy camp with about two hundred armed soldiers surrounding it and get back to the extraction point. *No problem!* he thought sarcastically. Of course, now there was the problem of an eight-fanged feline hunter who decided to take notice of his presence.

Seth pulled his field knife and prepared for the worst. The cat had enough length in his arms to rip Seth's throat out without him even being able to get close to the beast with his knife. The cat let out a spine-chilling growl and pounced. Seth ducked but it didn't matter; the cat hadn't jumped at him but rather over his head.

He twirled on his heel and saw the cat on top of an enemy soldier. The beast had already started pulling the limp carcass away before Seth could help. *What a terrible way to die*, he thought, *becoming a meal to some creature on an out-of-the-way planet while washing off at a watering hole.*

The soldier had apparently gone down to the watering hole to wash up and had taken off his shirt, which allowed the cat to smell his presence. His scent was obviously more appealing to the beast than Seth's scentless body, which was mere meters from the cat's tail. He couldn't do anything for the soldier now, so Seth decided on his course of action.

Locating the fuel dump and weapons locker, he decided that the best plan would be to blow up the entire base. He knew that even if he did retrieve the battle plans, he'd be shot before getting two hundred meters from the compound, much less back to his own base. If he couldn't have the plans then no one could.

Crouching low, he approached the edge of the water with the idea of swimming quietly up to the outer edge of the base where concealment was waiting behind two armored personnel carriers. As he slipped into the water, he realized, much to his dismay, that the water was only about two feet deep and not very concealing.

Angrily, he slithered up the muddy bank and grabbed a hold of a sapling's small trunk to help himself out of the mud. The tree began to move backward. Confused, he looked up only to find one of the six-legged pack animals staring at him with a dumbfounded look. It then began licking Seth's forehead. Seth tried to breathe but couldn't. Was the animal trying to figure out what he was or what he would taste like?

He couldn't believe that he had made the same mistake twice, and in less than ten minutes of the first one! With a sigh of relief, Seth began to breathe again as the animal let out a soft cooing noise that he decided was a sign of affection. The animal nuzzled Seth's forehead and licked him again.

Then the light went on! Why not use the animals to hide behind to get to the compound? He crouched behind the huge bulky body and found he was able to get the animal to go wherever he wanted with some minor pushing here and pulling there. He headed back to the herd and was able to start ten of the herd animals towards the enemy compound.

Apparently the moving herd was not an unusual sight for the enemy because they were not at all alarmed. Some took out cameras for photos to send to whoever might be missing them back home. A couple joked about making steak the special for tonight's menu. He hoped no one followed up on that last comment.

He got to the depot and although unguarded, it was locked. He pulled off the key panel and hot-wired the circuitry. Not too difficult a feat for someone who had an advanced degree in electrical engineering.

Seth could still remember the way his mom cried for weeks after he joined the Marine Corps. She couldn't figure out why he would want to go off and die somewhere out in the galaxy during some stupid battle that no one really cared about. When instead he could work for a big corporation with his talents and make big bucks back on Earth.

His dad was also upset but more for the fact that he spent a lot of money on Seth's education. His father repeatedly told him that if he wanted to be a marine, he should've done it before so much money was spent on his schooling.

He got the door open and found exactly what he was looking for. He decided to select only one rifle because he knew he'd be dead after placing the explosives anyway so he wanted to travel light for better speed. A smile played across his face as he picked up the beautiful weapon that hummed to life with his touch.

The weapon fired a caseless, powderless 12mm projectile with or without an explosive tip that used jet fuel as a propellant. This allowed the weapon to be fired in a complete vacuum or underwater. It had a side mounted, electro-magnetic (EM) pulse laser that disabled most personal electronics and even some of the more heavily shielded vehicle electronics. It had a grenade launcher under the main barrel, which he filled to its six-shot capacity and then grabbed ten 12mm one hundred-round magazines, stuffing nine into his pockets and slapping one home into the magazine well.

He found antipersonnel and antitank mines and decided that two small personnel mines would be enough for the fuel depot while four antitank mines would surely destroy the command bunker.

He heard a shuffle behind him and whirled in a small arc while dropping to one knee and bringing his weapon to bear, only to find his new friend softly cooing at him from the entrance of the weapons locker. With a shaking finger, he gave the animal a cross look and added, "Don't ever sneak up on me again. You could have gotten yourself shot."

Gathering up his cache, he ventured out, using his friend for cover. The grass near the door enticed the nine other animals he brought along: they had just decided to stay for lunch and were now seemingly very unhappy about Seth's plan to move them once again. After a little bit more nudging, they grudgingly headed towards the fuel dump.

At the fuel depot, he deposited the mines in such a way that hopefully the blasts would be omnidirectional, sending everyone nearby for cover. Too many people were near the command tent and he didn't think that he would be able to sidle up next to it as easily as he had the fuel depot.

He decided that a small stampede near the bunker would divert everyone's attention just long enough to set the mines and then blow them all. He was a dead man, anyway, so he might as well give it a shot. It was his only hope. He set the mines to explode in sync with one another and put a dead man's switch between his teeth so if he went down, they would all go off anyway.

He aimed the small herd at the bunker and then began whipping them on their rumps with a small metal rod he found by the fuel canisters. They really didn't like that and the nearest of the animals reared on his four front legs and kicked Seth straight in the chest. He went back, knocking over a small pile of fuel cans just as the ten animals started to run into the camp.

Someone heard the commotion and saw Seth but before the soldier could yell a warning, he was knocked over by one pissed-off six-legged deer. Soldiers went flying in all directions—some unconscious, some just bleeding.

As a xenobiologist would later record, these pack animals didn't stampede when frightened but instead spread out almost an even five meters from one another and began kicking at anything that was in their way.

The rest of the herd saw the commotion and decided that their family members needed help and all fifty or so other animals came running and kicking to their aid. Winded and with two very painful and bloody hoof marks on his chest, Seth made a mad dash for the bunker. He could've walked or even crawled there, because no one was paying any attention to anything except those flying hooves.

He set the mines and almost forgot about the dead man's switch in his mouth. That was close to mistake number three of the day. If that deer had a little bit higher or harder of a kick, KABOOM!! He would have dropped the switch from his teeth and the charges would've detonated right in his arms. Seth set the charges and ran for cover. Suddenly, he remembered the mines at the fuel depot. He decided to blow the command bunker first and use the fuel explosion as a secondary diversion to try to get the hell out of there. With the deer attack in full swing, he just might be able to get away.

He let go of the switch and the mines lit up. A laser beam was shot from each one into the sky and an explosion lit up the entire compound. The soldier who had first seen Seth had not given up on his quarry and was now running straight towards him with weapon drawn. Seth began firing and lit off the second volley of mines. A laser beam went straight up from each mine and a huge flash momentarily blinded him.

He began firing his weapon at his unwavering opponent when his rifle abruptly went dry. He reached for a second magazine and was up pulling the trigger in a split second. No shots fired! He noticed his enemy had the same problem.

Only one explanation…the training exercise was over. Central Command had turned off all the weapons, and the holographic explosions emitted by the mines were being disabled as Seth looked up. The lasers from the mines, that signaled a distant computer telling of an explosion, were also disabled. The deer were still kicking the hell out of any soldier who was near but most marines had the sense to find shelter out of range.

The general's shuttle began a slow descent from above the site to the edge of the compound. The general stepped out of the shuttle, ducking as he passed through the doorway. He was six foot six inches tall and seemed as wide as a tank. He had field dress on with a beautifully custom-made sidearm in his holster.

"Who is the marine who blew up my command post?!" he barked. "And get those damn creatures out of here before they kick everyone to death!" he added.

Seth stepped forward at attention and realized for the first time that he must have several broken ribs because he couldn't stand straight and it was difficult to breathe. "I did, General, sir!" he said in his most commanding voice.

Unfortunately, with broken ribs and all, it came out only as a whisper.

"Get your ass in my shuttle right now! I want to hear about how you single-handedly won the war games after your entire unit got wiped out." He let out a booming laugh and ordered his personal corpsman to help the cadet into his shuttle.

With a glare towards the commanding officer of the compound, he added, "I will speak to you later and you can explain how a CADET could destroy a whole command center on his own and live to tell about it."

The CO went white from head to toe. He wished that he had been fortunate enough to be knocked unconscious by one of those deer like so many other marines who lay around him. Then he would at least have an excuse as to why he had lost his base to the cadet.

During the flight back to Operational Headquarters in orbit around 09-675, Seth gave a total account of his operation, including the death of a marine by some indigenous predatory cat. The general assured him that there was nothing he could've done about it and those things sometimes happened, even in war games.

~

After being cleared from sickbay, Seth went to his quarters to await graduation the next day. Because of his proven worth in the field, Seth would be graduating as a first lieutenant instead of a second lieutenant like the rest of his classmates. *Something to write home about*, he thought, and he'd be sure to include how his "expensive" education paid off in the end.

He fell asleep and dreamt of wild cats attacking him and six-legged deer stampeding over his head. The dreams faded quickly into visions of his first command. Where would he go? What would he be in command of? Sooner than he would have liked, the lights came on and he began to dress for graduation. As he finished shaving, he distantly wondered what the future would hold for him.

After long hours of boring and repetitive speeches, his class was dismissed to the crowd of loved ones waiting to congratulate the new officers and take pictures to remember this moment for years to come.

It's not that Seth didn't believe in what the speeches were trying to say; he just figured that if you didn't have honor and love for the corps already, no words could be spoken that would make you stand taller or fight with more courage.

Seth wandered around the great hall, congratulating fellow marines and friends that he had made during the course of his training. Then his eye caught a sight too beautiful to be ignored. Obscured by all the movement within the crowd, the vision disappeared behind a family taking pictures with their daughter. His family was unable to attend to the ceremony due to work, pressing family matters, and a couple other excuses Seth hadn't bothered to remember.

Seth knew First Lieutenant Kyle; she was smart and very aggressive, which had put her at the top of their class. He wandered in her direction to say hello when he saw the vision again. In the corner a young woman sat with someone Seth figured was her mother. The older woman was crying and a man had just walked up with a priest at his side.

As Seth got closer, his mind began to race through images and he finally remembered. This was a family he had seen before. They were almost in the same positions he had seen in the picture with one exception: Cadet Riley wasn't beside his sister. Cadet Riley was the soldier who had lost his life during the training exercise.

Seth felt it was his duty to give the family his sympathy as he had been there at the end and he still felt guilty about not being able to do anything. They seemed to look up at him simultaneously as he got within a couple feet, Suddenly, he was at a loss for words. "Mr. and Mrs. Riley," he choked out, "I am truly sorry about your son's death. I was near when the accident occurred and I wanted to assure you that he felt no pain and didn't suffer at all." What was he saying! He couldn't believe that he was giving Riley's poor family details about such a gruesome death. "I didn't know Cadet," Seth paused, "I didn't know

Robby very well, but the few times we were on missions together, he served with the utmost honor. I knew, as did everyone, that we could count on him if things got tough."

Mrs. Riley's tears subsided for a moment and then she stood to face Seth directly. "Thank you," she whispered, and put her arms around Seth and began to sob uncontrollably. He returned the embrace but didn't know what to do next. He looked up and saw Riley's sister standing with a very composed and strong expression on her face. Seth felt ashamed; here he was consoling the mother of a dead marine and all the while he was thinking of how much Riley's sister moved him. She had such strength in her eyes. She knew that her mother and father needed support right now, so she was determined to keep her own feelings deep inside until the shock of it all had left her parents.

He couldn't take it anymore and luckily Mrs. Riley's embrace subsided and Seth was free. "If you'll excuse me," he began, "I have an early departure and need to prepare my gear. Again, I am truly sorry for your loss and feel as though the corps has lost a great man and officer." With that, he came to attention and saluted the Riley family, hoping it would show his sincerity. Performing a textbook about-face, he departed.

Once in the hallway and out of sight, his body became limp. The corridor vanished before him and all he could see was Robby's slashed face with terror in his eyes and a voiceless cry for help. Seth was bent over with his hands on his knees for support, sweating from every pore in his body and was about to throw up when he felt a hand on his shoulder. "Are you all right?" a sweet voice asked. He looked up; it was Riley's sister. "I just wanted to thank you for what you said back there. I think it will really help them. Should I get you some help?"

Her voice showed concern and Seth didn't want to worry her, so he righted himself and almost couldn't speak through the desert that now occupied his mouth.

"Thank you, I'll be fine. I don't want to keep you from your family so I'm just going to go lay down in my quarters now."

"I need a break from that crowd anyway, so why don't I help you back to your quarters." It was more of a statement than a question and Seth could see the determination in her eyes. He realized that it would be harder to deny her request than it was to win the war games.

With a slight nod, he began to walk toward his quarters with one arm around her neck. He found that he was surprisingly weaker than he had thought and that she was much stronger than he had given her small appearance credit for.

When they reached his quarters, he placed his thumb on the ID pad and the door hissed open. Once inside, she laid him down on his rack and went into the bathroom. She returned with a cool, damp cloth and placed it on his forehead. "Just get some rest," she said and started towards the door.

"Wait," Seth called out, "I don't even know your name."

"Emily. And thank you again for your kind words. I loved my brother very much and it meant a lot to me." With that, she left.

What seemed like only moments later, he heard the door open. He thought that it was Emily returning, but that couldn't be because she didn't have access to his room.

He turned on his side to see who was there when a black bag was pulled over his head. He began to fight and threw a punch in the direction of the oncoming bag.

"Son of a bitch!" he heard as the bag slipped from his head and his hand made contact with an abnormally hard face. The room was still shrouded in darkness and judging from the pain in his hand, the assailants were most likely wearing night vision masks. He was at a disadvantage but that never stopped him before. He threw a wild round kick in the direction of a whisper and made contact with his bureau mirror. The crash masked the sound of the two men who had snuck up behind him.

A sharp pain shot through his right flank as he heard the sizzle of an electric stunner and felt the jab of its prongs pushing on his kidney. He felt himself losing all ability to maintain consciousness and as a last-ditch effort went for the gun he kept under his pillow. He didn't even come close. His last sensation was that of a medic spray entering his neck and the crack of his nose as he landed face first on the deck.

What will the future hold? The question went through his mind one last time before total darkness encompassed his reality.

Chapter 3
Coalition Military Installation – Clandestine

Sweat mixed with blood and rain poured into Daria's eyes as her feet sank in the mud with every running step she made towards shelter. She dove for a boulder and popped up on the other side with her weapon drawn.

She didn't even know who in the hell she was running from or how she had been wounded. She only heard a faint whisper in the background of all the gunfire: "Screw up. Screw up." What did it mean? She hadn't screwed up, and where was all the firing coming from? She didn't see any other marines and couldn't raise anyone on her comlink.

Suddenly Daria felt ice-cold claws entering the skin on the back of her neck and her body being lifted from the ground. She tried to squirm around to see her assailant but that just drove the claws deeper into her flesh. Blood was running down her shirt and she heard the demon whisper in her ear, "Screw up."

The beast dropped her and she swiveled on her feet to bring her weapon to the demon's face. When she turned, she let out a small gasp. The creature was wearing Mike's face and again whispered, "Screw up."

Letting out a battle cry, she rushed the monster and suddenly realized that she didn't have a weapon any longer. She threw a punch that was caught easily in the demon's grasp. She was about to pull her knife with her other hand when she saw Davies' face.

He was holding her fist in his hand, getting ready to block another attack, when she started to remember where she really was.

"Whoa, marine! Calm down, we're not in battle yet. Come on, didn't you hear the 'gear-up' call on the 1MC?"

"Gear up?" she managed to whisper as Davies let go of her fist.

"Yeah, I've been trying to wake you for almost a minute now. I was going to call sickbay in a second if you didn't come around." He stepped back to allow her room to stand and added, "What were you dreaming about, anyway? You were mumbling Mike's name and something about him screwing up. Hey, you're not believing that stupid story we were fed about that crash, are you?"

Daria sent Davies a glare that made him take a step back and he knew that he had crossed an invisible but very definite line. "What the hell is going on out there, anyway?" she managed as she stumbled towards her gear locker.

"We're on alert status one, and all base personnel are to gear up and await orders. I guess this means that your leave is terminated." He looked at her with mournful eyes in an attempt to let her know that he knew she would never believe that lame story about Mike.

"It's about time something happened around here," she said with a smile. "I was getting bored of playing solitaire. Let's gear up and get this thing started."

"Well, it's about time Daria came back!" Davies almost roared. "I was starting to miss that little hellfire around here. Let's go kick the ass of whoever just pissed us off"

Daria looked at her gear and wondered what to take. She hated these general calls to gear up. You never knew where you were going, so how the hell did they expect you to know what to take?

She grabbed her standard-issue marine assault rifle, which was not so standard anymore. She had modified the grenade launcher tube to accept high explosive willey-pete mortars. The mortars were usually launched from a stable platform mounted to a vehicle's deck plates. She reduced the capacity from six grenades to two mortars but she tended to kill more targets with one willey-pete round than most did with five or six grenades. She had also shortened the length of the barrel for easier carrying with the rest of her gear.

Although she usually spread the medical gear out among the other platoon members to help with carrying it, she still had her med pack that she always carried. A regular-sized rifle barrel always seemed to snag on its front flap or some other part of the bag just when you least expected or needed it to.

Grabbing her water recycler, she checked to make sure that the filter was clean and had a good amount of life left in it. Of course, she already knew that all her gear was in tiptop shape.

After Mike's death, she did nothing but take apart and clean all her gear every day for almost the first week. You never wanted to go into the field unless you knew for sure that everything was perfect. Something always went wrong, so it's always best to try to reduce the number of things that could go wrong.

She looked over her comlink and applied it to her neck. This was the best gear improvement she had seen in more than ten years. The new comlinks were a light titanium alloy about the size of a poker chip and only about two times as thick. When placed up against the neck just behind the ear, the wearer tripped a switch that activated an electrical impulse, allowing the device to attach itself to the skin at the molecular level. And the best part was it drew its energy from the bioelectricity created by the soldier: as long as you were alive, so were your communications.

Once attached, you could set it to different frequencies simply by rotating the outer ring until you got the frequency you desired. One click for the whole platoon to hear, two clicks to get a secure channel between you and any other marine within a twenty-meter radius, three clicks for a secure link to the command center, and four clicks to raise the transport ship. The device picked up the vibrations in the mastoid process, the small bony prominence behind each ear, when you spoke and transmitted it as sound. And for receiving, it similarly sent tiny vibrations through the same bone and into the auditory canal for the brain to translate into words. It was so much easier than fumbling with microphones or handheld communicators. And unlike almost every other piece of military equipment issued, it almost never broke down.

Switching her comlink on, Daria cycled through a frequency test. Luckily, because she had received the message to gear up about twenty minutes after everyone else, she didn't have to wait for the channels to clear up before doing the check. Sometimes you'd have to wait more than five minutes for a freq check when several platoons were gearing up at the same time, not to mention a base that held more than one hundred thousand marines.

The last items Daria always packed were her field and fighting knives. She first grabbed her field knife that had a thick blade and a heavy handle. The handle had most of the checkering worn off from years of use but Daria refused to replace the knife. It was her first field knife and it had served her well. It had gouges in the sides of the blade where she had used it to dig for water or pry open a door or any other number of abuses that she dished out. This knife was placed in a holster on her left thigh.

Then came the hard part—which fighting knives to take? She loved them all, and each had a quality that made it unique and deadly. Her first decision was on a combination knife that could also be used for throwing. It was weighted well and had a thin blade, as all fighting knives do, and a cord-wrapped handle. It had a bead-blasted flat black finish and was razor sharp. She placed this one in a holster on her right calf. This was primarily a backup weapon used as a last resort. It was best drawn from a kneeling position which you were usually in when it came down to your last resort, along with praying if you had the time.

 Next, she took a handcrafted, double-edged dagger from its place on the shelf and examined the blade. It was also razor sharp and had serrated edges from the middle of the blade on both sides that continued to the hilt. The razor sharp smooth edges on the upper half were best for slicing and stabbing during a fight while the serrations allowed for a jagged tear in one's opponent after the sharp smooth blade penetrated flesh or light body armor. This one was holstered horizontally on her belt in the small of her back.

 Lastly, she picked up her most prized fighting knife that she carried on every mission. Mike had given it to her as a birthday gift several years ago. It was made of a carbon polymer that was stronger and lighter than titanium. It had no metal in it, so it was virtually undetectable by weapon scanners. The blade was thin and double edged only at the last inch towards the top of its full nine-inch length. The sides of the blade had been polished with a laser during its creation and were smooth as silk to the touch but completely non-reflective in any light. The edges were laced with laser sharpened diamonds that could barely be seen but allowed the weapon to cut through almost any body armor known and anything else that got in the way of a knowledgeable operator such as Daria.

 She drew the weapon from its sheath to examine it for any flaws, which she knew there were none. Holding the weapon in a reverse grip, she made small figure-eight motions with her wrist, practicing a basic cut that was meant to sever the arteries and tendons in an opponent's outstretched arm. She quickly flipped the handle to put the blade in a forward position and made small poaching jabs towards Davies. Knowing her skill, he didn't flinch at all but rather stood his ground, watching the master go through her basic routines.

After a few more jabs and grip changes, she placed the weapon back in its sheath and placed it on her right thigh next to her sidearm. She looked Davies square in the eye. "I have something for you." It came almost as a whisper. She handed him one of Mike's old bandannas. He took it from her and realized that something was wrapped in it. He gently unwrapped the cloth and a wave of emotion welled up from within.

"I can't take this; it was Mike's prized possession." Even as he spoke, he couldn't take his eyes off the fighting knife that was a twin to Daria's own.

Although it was Mike who had taught Daria how to fight, it was her natural ability and prowess as a hunter that made her the master she was today and that had also allowed her to far surpass Mike's teachings.

"I already have one and there's no one else that Mike or I would rather want to use this weapon. Of course," she added with a wry little smile, "knowing how agile you are, I'll probably be sewing a finger back on you by the end of the day."

"Thank you," he said softly, almost choking on his own words.

"Come on, marine, I've done enough crying for the both of us in the past two weeks. So if you'll just get your sorry ass out of my way, we'll get this show on the road!" She started past him toward the hatch, but paused beside him and reached up with her hand to touch his shoulder. With an almost unseen wink, she squeezed tightly and let go just as fast and continued towards the assembly area.

With that, Davies took one more look at Mike and Daria's quarters and turned to follow her down the corridor. Unbeknownst to him, that would be the last time Davies ever saw those quarters.

When they reached the assembly area five minutes later, he was still looking at the knife in its sheath. When he finally looked up, he saw the biggest FUBAR he had ever seen. As the old saying goes, "Idle hands do the devil's work" and so it was with this group.

Heated arguments had broken out here and there, what with all the different special divisions so close to one another and trying to out story tell each other. Claims of lies and other bantering ended in yelling and MPs threatening the use of mild stunners to break things up.

Everyone then stopped what they were doing at once and stared blankly ahead at the podium. The 1MC had just come on their comlinks and they listened to the base commander's speech. To an onlooker without a comlink, it would seem that thousands of people had suddenly become zombies and were listening to a voice that only they could hear.

"Congratulations, everyone," the voice began in their heads, "you have assembled in record time. Very impressive for a group this size. I am now, more than ever, certain that I have collected the finest group of marines ever assembled under one command.

"I remember when I was a second lieutenant and my CO loved to call the entire base for gear-up drills. I hated that SON OF A BITCH!" his voice boomed at his podium. Luckily, comlinks are equipped with a noise cancellation device that keeps the sounds entering the user's head from rising above a comfortable level.

"So I know," he continued, "that when I tell you this was just a drill, you'll be swearing my name for days to come. But that's all right because I now know that I can count on my marines to get the job done and I guarantee you that the next time you're called to gear up, you won't be heading back to your quarters anytime soon."

Low murmurs and whispers covered the crowd with innuendos and personal translations of what each soldier thought the base commander might be saying. Were they going to war soon? What wasn't the corps telling them about their current post? Why such a huge drill if nothing was going to happen?

"Now, everyone return to your previous duties. Fall out", he concluded.

As the crowd started to disperse, Daria began to bitch in the direction of Davies when they both went back into a blank stare, listening to the same unseen voice.

"Attention all hands. Any marine who is receiving this transmission is to report to Building 25, Area 0106 immediately and without discussion to anyone. Move out!"

Although you couldn't hear the raised voice of a barked order through the comlink, there was a certain inflection in the tone that you just knew meant someone had yelled it. The two friends looked at each other and started towards the rendezvous point.

"What the hell is this?" Daria asked as she simultaneously received a warning shock of electricity in her skull. Apparently they had meant it when they said not to talk to anyone because the links were command set to "feedback." This setting sent a mild shock through the skull when it sensed that the wearer was talking, and in this way the command center on any mission could strictly enforce noise discipline for their troops if they couldn't do it on their own. No talking to anyone, or the shocks increased in intensity with each time you broke the silence.

Well, she'd just have to wait and see what was going on like everyone else, she thought. As she proceeded, she noticed other marines flinching slightly and touching the spot behind their own ears where the comlink sat. At least she wasn't the only one, she thought with a smile. The feature was so rarely used that apparently many of the soldiers had forgotten that it existed.

Unbeknownst to Daria and the rest of her group, every marine who had been assembled was being directed to a different portion of the base. In all, there were a total of three hundred and seventy-eight groups of marines sequestered from one another. The gathering was a ruse planned to make each individual group of marines think that they were the only ones being secretly deployed.

Daria's group entered Building 25 en masse and grouped together in Area 0106. As the last marine entered the area, the great doors at the rear of the room sealed. The comlinks were turned off and a colonel began speaking directly to the assorted two hundred marines now gathered before him. Some jaws went slack and some eyes almost jumped out of the heads they sat in while the colonel spoke. Most couldn't believe what she was saying. A babysitting job! Going beyond the edge of the known galaxy to babysit a bunch of scientists and archeologists on a newly discovered planet!

An internal unit within the scientific community usually handled these kinds of security jobs. These soldiers weren't any less dangerous than full-time marines; they just didn't earn the respect of the REAL marines all that often. The officers were PhDs and professors who felt that their jobs lacked a certain sense of adventure, so they became weekend warriors to battle their boredom. The enlisted ranks were composed of scientists with lesser degrees or students working towards a higher education. Their schooling was paid for by their enlistment and they would eventually become officers in the Scientific Marine Corps.

Their purpose was sound; the researchers themselves would protect a newly discovered planet that was being studied for colonization or purely scientific research. This way there were no extraneous personnel and every soldier had a dual purpose as a scientist. This cut down costs to the government and basically made the scientists their own colonial militia.

So why send out two hundred marines in addition to their normal complement? Well, as long as Daria didn't have to take orders from some lab geek, she decided she would be all right with this cushy assignment.

Daria and Davies listened with their undivided attention, just like everyone else in the room. Daria wished that Mike had been there; he would've enjoyed this sort of thing. "You'll each be taken to planet 08-2897, where you will receive your specific assignments. Good luck, and may any God that you believe in be with you", the colonel concluded.

With that, Daria and Davies were given transport assignments via comlink and breathed a sigh of relief as they found themselves headed for the same ship. They just looked at each other with blank expressions.

"Is this seat saved?" Davies quipped as he pointed to the seat next to the one Daria had acquired. "Don't worry," he added, "the buzzers have been disabled. I guess we're allowed to talk now."

"If you fall asleep and snore, I swear I'll kick you out into space myself," Daria said as she scooted over for Davies. Moments later, the transport to the journey ship that would take them to their final destination took off, and so did the rumor mill and gossip between the aisles.

Daria didn't bother with joining in any of the many conversations. She didn't think that it was of any use to speculate about something when you'd get the answer upon arrival at your destination. Or at least, she conceded, the answer the corps wanted you to have.

The colonel had given them a lot of information but most of it was vague and there was no real substance to even the vague information. So she let herself drift off to sleep and hoped that now she'd have something else to dream about instead of demons and Mike.

Seth

NAME: SETH
SPECIES: HUMAN
MOS: LINE OFFICER
RANK: FIRST LIEUTENANT
AGE: 24 - EARTH STANDARD
SEX: MALE
HEIGHT: 5'10"
WEIGHT: 190 POUNDS

Sometimes life was so fantastic that you just had to sit back and look at it to really see how great it was. That's exactly what Seth was trying to do as he sat there with his friends and more importantly, his girlfriend. Seth wished he could float out of his body and just watch the evening as an outsider, a detached form hovering above and taking it all in.

For the first time in years, he was truly happy. Six years was a long time to be in college, especially if you were condensing an eight-year program into that time frame. Seth always was an eager person and he wanted to get on with his life and do something more than studying and working on graduate projects that would bring credit to his college first and foremost rather than the students working on them.

Not only did he want to start his career and feel like a real productive adult, but he hoped that when he was out of school, he would be able to unwrap the last tentacles his parents had on his life. No longer would they be able to say that they were paying for his school so they had a right to be intrusive and overbearing. Sure, they could now say they had paid for his school so they had a right to do whatever obtrusive and overbearing parental thing that they thought that gave them the privilege to do, but at least now he could hang up on them and not wonder whether his tuition would still be paid for or whether he'd still have a place to live come the next day.

Or at least it was almost "now" that he could do that. So very close to the "now" he was waiting for. That was the other thing Seth could be happy for tonight: he was offered a job today at the company he had been interning with for the last six months. Between the internship, his graduate project, thesis, and girlfriend, Seth thought he was going to slip into a coma any second now just so his mind and body could get some rest.

The time he spent with his friends was so very important to Seth that he stayed out much later than he knew he should've. It was a trade-off: stay out late and decompress mentally at the cost of being a little more tired tomorrow, or go home early and not decompress and still be tired with the added bonus of also being wound up the next day. As the old saying goes, "There will be plenty of time to sleep when you're dead."

So Seth stayed out as long as he could, making deals with himself along the way: If I stay out another thirty minutes, I'll wake up a little later and just not shower. Another thirty minutes and I'll just eat on the way to school. Another thirty minutes and I'll just eat at lunch. And so on until he only got about three hours of sleep before he arrived at his lab the next day.

Usually Seth had a lot of patience for the undergrads who helped him with his project but today he couldn't tolerate most of them. It almost seemed as though all of them were purposely trying to destroy their teleportation device. First, some coffee spilled near a very non-liquid-friendly component. Then someone tried to start the machine without first adding coolant to the tank.

And last, someone allowed a fly to enter the transport chamber before the initiation sequence. Not that the fly would cause a monster to be created, as had happened in the old Earth movie about a similar project, but the fly would be destroyed when the teleporter started and the chamber would have to be completely decontaminated before it could be used again. Decontaminating the chamber took almost a full day of work, something Seth was not in the mood for today.

Creating a functional energy/matter transporter had been a dream of scientists and engineers since the twentieth century. Early in the twenty-first century, scientists had been able to transport a single photon across large distances but that's as far as anyone had been able to go with the technology. Seth's working group was on the verge of changing that.

Seth always said that all of the technobabble that explained how they were solving the problem didn't matter. The fact was, they were close to being able to transport as many photons as they wanted, to a relatively distant location of at least a few hundred kilometers.

Moving biological data any distance was still decades away from happening, if ever. Moving actual life-forms may never be possible based on current theories and information they had gathered during their experiments. But photons and inert matter were going to happen and soon.

The atmosphere in the lab got so emotional and heated that Seth finally called it a day and sent everyone home. Not long after the lab was empty, he put together a rambling apology to everyone and emailed it before taking a nap at his desk.

The three-hour nap was exactly what Seth needed. He woke up feeling refreshed and calm. When he reread his apology email, he hoped everyone had been able to decipher what he meant through the jumble of words he had tried to make thoughts out of.

Seth showered and shaved in preparation for going into the office tonight. His internship would end and his career would begin in just over a week. He really wanted to get the transporter working before he graduated and left the team. Neither his job or future depended on it but it still meant something to him.

A light bulb went off in his head, illuminating the entire latticework of the project. Seth stood still in the shower, with his fingers frozen in his hair as he had been working in the shampoo. His job and future weren't dependent on each other, just as the primary focus beam and the reconstituting stream weren't either.

But that was the problem: they had been working from the premise that they were in fact dependent on each other and the energy ratios were intertwined. Separate the equations and make the two parts completely independent and they would be able to function as intended.

Seth stood there for at least another five minutes while he went through the equations in his head and reworked some of the mechanical engineering aspects of the project. A few more stops and starts later, Seth had finally finished his shower and started dressing.

He sent a quick message to his team. "Sorry again about today, but I've got it. Tomorrow is the day!"

Seth finally made it to AeroTech and with only five minutes to spare. He was usually fifteen to twenty minutes early so although he felt late, he was the only one who noticed the time. Several hours later, he was already on his fifth coffee run of the day. He didn't know why everyone was so wired and working so hard but it was obvious that something was up.

Seth was getting caught up in all the excitement and couldn't wait until he was a part of the inner workings and not just the errand boy. Some of the guys in the office knew that Seth was way ahead of the game and they tended to share things with him that they shouldn't. Sometimes they even showed him things to get his opinion and his help on solving problems.

Today things were a little bit different. Even the guys who trusted Seth and used his help before were pretty tight-lipped about whatever was going on. He still got a few glimpses at some of the work floating around; it seemed like it was referencing one of the company's fighters being involved in an accident that killed two marines, the pilot and gunner. Hopefully, once he was a full member of the team, Seth would be able to help prevent accidents like this.

As Seth was setting down one of the coffees, he caught a glimpse of some technical readouts from the flight recorder. When the engineer saw Seth looking at the data, he quickly covered the pad and thanked Seth for the coffee, obviously dismissing him.

Even in that slight glimpse, something struck Seth as wrong. His interest piqued now, he started looking at every piece of information he could put an eye on. As each new piece of data was absorbed, the puzzle was coming together and becoming clearer.

At one point, Seth was alone in the room with Jack, the lead project manager for the aircraft that had crashed. Jack was mulling over some of the information and seemed to be unaware that Seth was watching, waiting for the right moment to approach him and say something.

Finally, Seth made his move. "Um, Jack."

"What?" Jack looked up and seemed mildly annoyed at being disturbed.

"I'm not trying to butt in here, but I was thinking that maybe I could help. I've caught a few glimpses of the data and I know that I could be useful." Seth stepped back a half step when Jack glared at him.

"Just what data HAVE you been looking at, Seth?"

"Just bits and pieces as I'm bringing the guys coffee and stuff. I haven't picked up or read through anything thoroughly. No one has given me anything, if that's what you're asking." Seth didn't want anyone to get in trouble because of his curiosity.

Jack's features seemed to soften just a little bit. "Look, Seth, I know that you'll be an actual employee in just a couple of weeks—I'm the guy who recommended you—but you're not one now. And even when you are employed and you have signed all of the non-disclosure agreements, you still won't have the secret clearance needed to deal with this situation."

"I wouldn't tell anyone that you let me help out. I just thought maybe you'd like to know how the fighter went down." Seth was pushing now and he knew it.

Jack sighed, and then touched a button on the conference room table. The button sent a command to the room's control center and caused the doors to lock and the windows to become opaque so no one could see in. The room also initiated the counter-electronics measures that would keep anyone from spying on the room's occupants with any of the known intrusion methods that were out there.

"If you speak even a word of this to anyone, your career will end before it begins. And no one else in the Coalition will ever hire you again." Jack waved his hand to indicate the seat in front of Seth.

"Understood, sir."

"We already know how the fighter went down. We knew within the first hour of receiving the flight data. What we're doing now is trying to figure out how to make sure no one else knows how it went down." Jack rubbed the bridge of his nose, obviously exhausted.

"I don't understand. Why are we trying to cover this up? Two soldiers died in the crash. Don't they deserve the truth?" Seth was starting to wonder about the company he was soon to be employed by.

"Look, I don't like it either but sometimes we have to look at the greater good. Those brave men are dead and nothing we do will change that. It doesn't matter if we say the crash was our fault or theirs; their families will still get their death benefits and they will still be buried as heroes." Jack sat back in his chair and waited for a response.

Seth was even more puzzled now. "Why would we say it was our fault?"

"Exactly." Jack leaned forward again. "If we say it was our fault, then we may lose the contract on the fighter project. Best-case scenario is our fighters all get grounded for months or even longer while we do millions and millions of dollars' worth of testing to show that this accident was an isolated incident. Which is exactly what it was. If we say it was operator error, then none of that happens.

"Trust me, Seth, if I thought our fighters weren't safe, I'd recall them myself even if it meant my career to do it. Do you understand now?"

"No. I don't."

Jack was back to his exhausted look. "What part of it? Saving the company or saving our jobs?"

"I don't understand why we would say it was our fault or theirs when it was neither." Seth was truly lost and he could tell Jack was also.

"Well, someone or something has to be blamed." Jack thought maybe he was too tired to explain it well enough to Seth.

"Right." Seth was wondering whether Jack was so far gone that he was a little delirious right now. "But, how about we blame the person or persons who murdered the pilot and gunner"?

"Okay, now I'm truly lost, Seth. Please tell me what the hell you're talking about."

"Look." Seth reached for a datapad and was surprised when Jack didn't stop him. Seth took a moment to find and pull up the information he was looking for. "Right here. It wasn't an accident or user error. Someone added a line of code here. It changes the plasma intake tolerance levels. Not by much, but it does."

Jack looked at the code and wasn't sure but thought maybe Seth was correct. "Okay. Maybe there is altered code but that doesn't prove anything. You know that these pilots and crew chiefs have altered our specs in the past because they think they know better than us. This tolerance change wouldn't cause the failure we're looking at."

"No. It wouldn't", Seth admitted. "But, couple that with this other line of code here, along with a slight physical alteration to the intake valve here..." Seth pulled up some detailed photos and scans of the wreckage.

"This isn't looking good." Jack was putting the pieces together now.

"This still isn't the complete picture. I'm guessing there are several other line changes and maybe even some other physical alterations. I'd need access to everything we have to put together a proper synopsis and theory." Seth looked Jack in the eye. "But I'm sure these guys were murdered. This was not an accident, theirs or ours."

"But why?" came the rhetorical question.

"Angry girlfriend or wife. Crew chief hated the pilot or gunner. Military or corporate espionage. Who knows? But we might be able to find out." Seth started looking through more data as Jack didn't seem to care now.

"If anything, I'd say corporate espionage. How many spouses have the ability to do this to a fighter jet?" Jack picked up his phone to make a call. "Keep working on this. From now on it's just you and me. I'm sending everyone else home. I want to keep this close to the vest for now."

Seth started making a work area for himself at the conference table while Jack notified the rest of the team that they weren't needed anymore tonight. Seth was actually a little impressed with the story that Jack concocted to make it seem less odd that the most important project of the decade suddenly became not important at all.

By morning, Seth had all of the pieces to the puzzle and put them together to show the sabotage the fighter had been subjected to. The only pieces missing were who and why. The how and when were perfectly clear. Jack sent Seth home and said that he would call later when he had more information. For now, Jack was taking this straight to the top, on his own.

Seth knew he couldn't take another day in his own lab being this tired again. He sent out a message to his team and gave them the day off, explaining that he needed to take the project in a new direction but he was too tired from working on it all night. Without Seth in the lab with his new equations and ideas, there was no reason for anyone else to show up.

Seth fell on to his bed and was immediately unconscious. He woke several hours later, a bit refreshed but still tired from two days of very little sleep. He had ten messages from his girlfriend, starting off friendly and then progressing through worried and ending up at angry. Where was he? Why hadn't he called her? Was there someone else?

Seth tried to call her first but she didn't answer. Not knowing whether she was busy or just mad, he left her a message, trying to be as nice and penitent as possible. He then showered and checked his email for messages from Jack. Nothing.

Seth ended up eating dinner alone and watching some old movies from the comfort of his couch and boxer shorts. He was still recovering from a lack of sleep, so he never really thought it was odd that he wasn't receiving his usual texts or messages from friends and family. No email either. No electronic correspondence of any sort, not even spam.

The next day, he finally realized that something was wrong. After waking up, showering and getting ready for the day, he finally noticed the lack of contact with anyone outside his apartment. Seth decided to head into the lab and check his accounts from the university's data connection to see whether that made a difference.

Seth left his apartment, half thinking he would find the planet deserted as though he were in some sort of "last man alive" scenario. That would certainly account for the lack of human contact he had yesterday. As he got to the street, he saw that that theory was blown out of the water: the streets were just as crowded as usual and not a single zombie or alien mind control device was in sight.

When Seth got to his lab, he did run into one problem. His access code wasn't working. He tried it several times but the light stayed red and the automatic lock never clicked open. A moment later, campus security showed up.

Seth smiled when he saw Doris. "Hey there! I haven't seen you in a while but I'm glad you're here. Can you let me in? The lock is messed up and won't let me in."

Doris looked a little embarrassed. "I'm sorry, Seth, but I can't let you in. I have instructions to take you to the dean's office."

"Why?" Seth wondered whether somehow not coming in yesterday and giving his team the day off had gotten him in trouble. This seemed pretty severe for something that he was pretty sure didn't violate any department or school rules.

"I don't know, I really don't, Seth. But I have to. I was told you aren't allowed to go anywhere but the dean's office." Doris put her arm out in the direction they needed to walk and Seth followed her silent instruction.

Three hours later, Seth was standing at the edge of the university's property with a letter of dismissal in his hand. He was told that all of his personal property that the university didn't have any rights to would be sent to his apartment within two weeks.

The dean had told him that the school's code of conduct clearly prohibited the use of illegal drugs. Due to the extremely hazardous nature of the street drug Track Star, along with the huge amounts of it found in Seth's secure and private lab locker, the school had no choice but to dismiss him.

Seth did have an appeals process but the dean warned him against using it. The dean told Seth that the school was grateful for his work and would give him his degree, along with not putting the drug infraction on his official record. After all, he was only a week away from graduation and they still recognized that he had earned the degree with all of his hard work. The dean didn't want Seth to have the rest of his life tarnished and just wanted him to get the help he needed. But if Seth appealed, then the drug use would become official and on the record. So Seth left without so much as a word.

Seth was still trying to figure things out when he found himself at the doors to AeroTech. The only thing he could do now was go talk to Jack. He wanted to make sure Jack heard the story from him first so he would know the truth. Seth would submit to any form of drug testing or lie-detecting tests to prove that he had no idea what had happened at the university.

Seth put his security badge up against the reader and received the same red lights he got from his lab doors on campus. "Shit. You have got to be kidding me."

It seemed as though the universe was repeating itself as Seth watched two security guards approach him from inside the building. When they reached the door, one spoke through the intercom. "I'm sorry, sir, but you need to leave. Your building privileges have been revoked. You have the legal right to stand outside the building on public property, but we'd prefer if you didn't. Thank you and have a nice day."

Seth couldn't believe what was going on. This was all bullshit but he couldn't figure out why. Then his phone beeped, for the first time in almost two days. When he read the text message, it was from his girlfriend. "Don't ever contact me again." *Ex-girlfriend.*

If Seth had been firing on all cylinders today, he would've put it together sooner. The fighter crash. This was all a part of that. It had to be. The timing was too coincidental to be a chance event.

Jack. Was he a part of this? Or was he being systematically destroyed just like Seth was? Jack hadn't returned any of Seth's communication attempts, but maybe he couldn't. Seth was equal parts worried and angry; he didn't have enough information to know which one he should totally be right now.

Two weeks had gone by without contact from anyone Seth knew. Luckily for him, his parents had been on the other side of the Coalition, for an ambassador function of his father's, and hadn't planned to make it back for his graduation anyway. So there was at least one story he didn't have to come up with for why there wasn't a graduation for him.

Seth had watched the graduation from a safe and non-trespassing location. When he got home, he found a small piece of a newspaper stuck in the crack of his front door. Two words were printed on one side: "I'm sorry."

He didn't recognize the handwriting; in fact, he couldn't remember the last time he had seen actual handwritten *anything*. That was smart of the sender; it would be harder to track handwriting than a computer-generated message. Probably from Jack, Seth thought.

It was time to come up with a plan. Seth knew he couldn't sit around in his apartment forever. He was starting to run out of rent money, for one thing. As far as he could tell, none of his newly acquired ill-repute extended beyond the university or AeroTech. It was time to find a job.

A week later, Seth found himself in a Marine Corps officer-recruiting seminar. By the end of the presentation, Seth knew what he wanted to do. He didn't think he'd ever be able to find out what had happened to the fighter crew or why, but maybe he could make a difference somewhere so it wouldn't happen again.

And who knows, he thought, maybe one day he would be able to walk up to Gunnery Sergeant Mike O'Connor's widow and show her proof that her husband didn't cause the fatal accident that day. Maybe he would someday be able to give her that simple peace of mind.

~

Somewhere Inside The Coalition Strategic Operations Command Center:

As the intelligence officer was perusing his morning emails, his monitor lit up with an emergency flash traffic message. A keyword search had hit the monitoring station just over eight seconds ago.

After checking the message, he verified its contents, and then opened the protocols database and matched the protocol on the keyword search with the one in the database. The protocols database match showed that the target of the keyword had a priority cancellation order. It also showed that this particular protocol couldn't be enacted without verbal confirmation from the general.

The captain contacted the general through a secure video link. "Good morning, sir. I hope you're not busy."

The general was eating his breakfast. "Not at all, Joe. How are things in your section?"

"Good, sir, thank you for asking." The captain tapped a few keys on his console. "I'm sending you a flash comm I just received a few moments ago. The protocols database lists the subject for cancellation but it also requires a verbal confirmation from you, sir. In fact, it looks like you authored this specific protocol yourself."

The general pushed his breakfast aside so he could use both hands on the computer. "Indeed I did, Joe, indeed I did." He read further down the message. "Well, that's a very unexpected turn, but for the better, I'd say. It looks like Seth has dropped his quest for the truth in order to serve the greater good and join the Marine Corps."

"Yes, sir." The captain had no idea what this was about and most likely never would. He would just do his part and that part was dependent on whatever the general told him to do next. "When he signed up for Officer Candidate School, his name hit the keyword database and was flagged as an 'important event.' I'm guessing it was because he signed up for the service. Had he laid low and got a job with your average tech company, I don't think he would've been flagged."

"You're probably right, Joe." The general made a few entries on his console and Seth's file disappeared from both his screen and the captain's. "I'm having lunch next week near your office. My assistant will give you the details. It would be great to see you in person. Keep up the good work, son." The general ended the call without waiting for a response.

With the file vanishing from the keyword database, the captain had his answer: do nothing. The captain took a quick look at his schedule for the following week. It looked pretty clear; that would make things easier.

Another flash traffic message came through to his desk. Not related to the first one, this one had a cancellation notice that didn't require secondary confirmations. Who was next on the list? Ralph was up in the rotation; time to put him to work.

    The audio-only line went green, showing a connection. "Hey Ralph! Thanks for the theatre tickets. My wife and daughter loved the show. I hope you don't have plans for the weekend. I have a job for you. Ready for the info?"

Chapter 4
Coalition Vessel *Vanguard* – Good Morning Sunshine

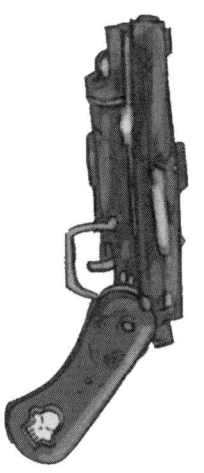

A hint of light began to invade the edges of Seth's consciousness. He gradually began to open his eyes, which he found to be an amazingly difficult task. When Seth was finally able to focus his vision, he realized he was in a stark white room, with only a bed and no visible doors or entryways.

He began to call for someone, anyone, but that was even harder than opening his eyes. He noticed a small stainless-steel pitcher next to the bed and a plastic cup. He poured some of the clear liquid into the cup and after a few moments of sniffing and small tastes, decided that it was probably just water. Besides, he thought, if whoever had brought him here wanted him dead, they could have done it by now. Why take the time to poison him?

A quiet and soothing voice entered the room. "Lieutenant Seth Fields, we will not hurt you in any way."

"Tell that to my broken nose," he retorted. Strangely though, Seth realized his nose wasn't hurting or seemingly broken at all. Odd, he had broken his nose before and knew without a doubt that during the attack it had been broken again. There's no mistaking that feeling.

"That was an unfortunate accident. We had expected you to be less confrontational and were surprised." As an afterthought, the voice added, "We apologize."

"Great, why don't we just shake hands, have a beer and call it a day then? Let me the fuck out of here right now!" Seth yelled at his captor.

"Lieutenant Fields, we are going to send a representative in to talk with you face to face. We assure you that there is no possible escape, so please do not force us to stun you again. A door will open now to let in our representative."

With that, the seamless wall opposite of Seth's bed opened to allow a very tall and broad figure into the room. "My name is Surgeon," he began.

"Oh, my parents wanted me to be a doctor, too," Seth quipped. "But at least they didn't name me Surgeon. How did I get here, anyway?"

This seemed to almost make the figure smile. He continued, "The night of your graduation, you shook hands with one of our operatives. He had a small needle in his palm, laced with a tranquilizer. You were shaking so many hands I doubt you will even remember his face when you see him again during your training. As far as names go, you will find that our true names don't matter much anymore and you will, in fact, be given a new operating name. I think 'Cadet' suits you just fine."

"Now wait a minute," Seth shot back. "I worked damn hard for my lieutenant's bars and there's no way I'm being called 'Cadet' again!"

"You'll also find, Cadet, that your previous rank, no matter how short-lived or deserving, is also not of much consequence anymore. Maybe after our mission, I'll give you your name back."

Surgeon seemed to nod towards no direction in particular and shortly after, another door, this one next to Seth's bed, opened into a corridor. "We will now eat and then you will be given a briefing as to why you are here. Offer no resistance and no one will harm you. Agreed?"

With a small nod, Seth stood and faced the new door. Surgeon took the lead and together they walked down the hall about a hundred meters before coming to a mess hall filled with other soldiers, all wearing identical black outfits.

He knew that they were all soldiers just by looking at them and how they acted. He also realized that these weren't ordinary soldiers but the best of wherever they came from. They had the look of trained and highly skilled operators.

Surgeon, whoever he was, must be one of the best to get the looks of respect the others gave him. However, no one seemed to look at the new guy and this was odd considering that Seth was the only one dressed in white.

Surgeon stepped into the mess hall and just as casually began to address the assembled crowd. "Attention on deck!" His voice was smooth and even slightly subdued. "This is 'Cadet' and he just awoke today. He is the last of our cadre to come out of cryosleep so we are now in the full swing of things. We're on schedule but we still have a lot to accomplish. Carry on", he concluded. With that, everyone began eating once more.

A sudden and almost frightening thought hit Seth. "How long have I been out?" he asked Surgeon.

"Two weeks of sedation while your nose and kidneys healed from the extraction"—"

"Kidnapping," Seth interjected.

"And three months of cryosleep," Surgeon concluded.

"Why have I been out so long?"

"You'll be briefed after your meal." Seth began to speak again but was cut off.

"No discussion. Eat and then we'll talk."

That being final, Seth looked at the buffet laid out before him. The spread was even better than his graduation's. Seth could identify food from at least twelve different species and several others from only God knew where.

He grabbed a tray and utensils, of which the knife and fork were removed from his hand by Surgeon, who added, "Not yet. When I trust you, you'll get more than a spoon."

Seth had to smile at that. It seemed that they—whoever "they" were—wanted skilled operators. Didn't they realize that a spoon was just as useful as a fork or knife in the hands of a skilled soldier? Without a fuss, he resigned himself to eating dinner, or lunch, or maybe it was even breakfast. Who knew what time it was? He decided that the food pointed towards lunch but no matter; he was hungry, so who cared what time it was?

After he had finished, Surgeon led Seth to an issuing room where Seth was measured and given a black uniform that of course matched everyone else's. Together, the two soldiers, now identically clad in black, walked down the corridor to what seemed to be a conference room. Seth entered first at the ushering of Surgeon and was amazed by what he saw.

The room was filled with holo-emitters for information displays and tactical readouts. A large wooden conference table filled the center of the room and reflected light from the displays on its shiny smooth surface. Surgeon motioned Seth to a seat and took one himself next to Seth.

"You have been 'kidnapped,' as you put it, by your own government for a very important reason. We are facing one of our most deadly adversaries in our entire history and we don't even know who it is."

"What are you talking about? We haven't made contact with any new species in more than thirty years."

Surgeon gave him a look that seemed to say, "If you'll just shut the hell up, I'll tell you." This made Seth sink a little in his seat as he allowed the briefing to continue.

"Five years ago, we found an artifact on 07-0198 that turned out to be a star chart. This chart held maps to the outermost regions of our galaxy, parts that even now we would be decades from exploring if we hadn't found the maps. The technology of this artifact seems to be more advanced than our current technology and it is estimated to be close to a thousand years old.

"After excavating the entire site, several more advanced artifacts were found, most of which we still don't have a clue as to what they do. We have determined that whoever these items belonged to, they weren't the nicest neighbors on the block. After almost a year of cataloging and research of the artifacts, the archeologists discovered that they had similar properties to many other items found on dozens of known worlds. The artifacts are similar in nature but different enough not to be noticed right away as coming from the same makers. "The society seemed to be a warring species bent on conquering everyone they encountered. The evidence we've found points to the fact that they were good at it", he added.

"How come it's been kept so quiet? Usually the Earth Interstellar Expansion Department brags about everything they find." Seth was getting impatient.

"As I said, they were an advanced species and the dig sites indicated that they hadn't died out but rather lost interest in this sector of space. No gravesites, homes, or anything to indicate that they died out at those colonies. It seems as though they just up and decided to leave and took almost everything with them. We don't know who they were or where they went.

"Then some of the scientists decided to power up a machine that they thought was just an information terminal. It turned out to be something else, something they shouldn't have touched. Before they realized what they had done, it was too late. It sent out a signal of unknown content to an unknown destination.

"After more evidence was discovered eight months ago, we're now pretty sure that it was a distress beacon. It looks as though this species had an adversary who didn't like them very much. Their weaponry is much more advanced than ours and operates differently, so it was difficult to tell at first that a battle had been fought at that outpost. A few remains were found in an underground vault that seemed to be a stronghold or shelter of some kind. Many of the corpses had major trauma to their bodies before they died and the others must have pulled them into the shelter.

"All of them were in uniforms and had weapons with them. The bunker they were in did a good job of mummifying the remains, so it's not difficult to tell that the wounds they suffered were from a battle. One of the corpses had a small communications device with him. When it was hooked up to a power source, it sent out the same signal as the terminal found almost five years ago. That's why we think that it was a distress signal of some sort.

"We also believe that the outpost on 07-0198 had been an expeditionary force, one of hundreds in that region of space. And for whatever reason, when they were destroyed, no one came looking for or even cared that they were never heard from again. Until now."

"So now," Seth interjected, "we awakened their distress call and alerted their descendants to their destruction that took place close to a thousand years ago. And let me guess, they are mad as hell. Right?"

"Exactly." Surgeon continued, "Whatever caused them to forget about this sector a thousand years ago is no longer an issue to them. They've decided that they want to move back into this space and they didn't even call ahead for reservations. Twenty of our outermost expeditionary colonies have been lost. They weren't just destroyed—they were completely obliterated. Scans of those outposts reveal no debris from enemy craft, so we're assuming our people either didn't have enough time to respond to an attack or their response didn't even damage the attacking force."

"So why haven't we alerted all our forces and built up our military? And for that matter, where do I, we, fit into this?" Seth just couldn't believe what he was hearing.

"To answer your first question, we didn't want to send a widespread panic through the Coalition. We haven't yet met an enemy we can't beat and that's why planets join our little group. We can't have them lose faith in us and pull their fleets out of any upcoming battles just to try to save their own hides. And as for us," Surgeon let the words linger for a moment before continuing, "we just might be the Coalition's last hope."

Chapter 5
Dig Site One - On the Outer Rim

Daria had awakened from her cryosleep journey to this planet two months ago. "This planet" is all it could be called because it hadn't even received a number designation yet. And worst of all, Daria and Davies were in a platoon that had a lab geek for a CO. Even though she was a nice geek, Daria still didn't like it.

Her name was Emily. It almost hurt her to say it. No officers were called by their first name but this one wouldn't have it any other way. Officially, she was First Lieutenant Riley and Daria really didn't like anything less formal. But orders were orders and after finding out that Emily's brother had been a marine and killed during training, she had a bit more respect for Emily's desire to not be called by her rank.

Emily was a xenobiologist and specialized in creating profiles of races by their artifacts. Daria had noticed something about their little group of scientists and marines: everyone was not only good at their job but REALLY good. Some, like Emily, were even acclaimed to be the best in their field.

There really wasn't much to do so Daria had read some of Emily's articles. Daria found that Emily's work was actually very fascinating.

Just by examining some artifacts at a site near the core worlds, Emily had deduced that the species had only two fingers on each of its three arms, stood about two point five meters tall, and each member of the species was the same sex and used a type of internal cloning to create offspring. She could probably even tell you how much change the alien had in its pocket when it made the artifact you were looking at.

After burial sites had been discovered, it was found that Emily had made mistakes on only a few very minor points concerning their anatomy.

Daria had become very interested in Emily's work and so they spent many hours together each day. Emily was always teaching Daria about her work and much to Daria's surprise, she caught on quite quickly to the research.

"Now take a look at this," Emily began. "This artifact has almost a completely different readout display and input terminal than the others we have encountered so far. Why do you think that is?"

The answer seemed so obvious that Daria almost felt stupid saying it. "Because it came from a different species. Possibly an off-world trader or someone along for the ride."

"Good, but how can you explain the fact that it is made of the exact same material as everything else we've found? A different species would indicate a different alloy or even a different processing of a similar alloy. So why the difference in appearance and biological compatibility if it were made by the same people?"

Daria thought for a moment. "Maybe," she hesitated, "whoever made these artifacts stole the technology from a different species and were too lazy to reconfigure it to their own specifications. The original creators and the ones who stole it were close enough in biological compatibility that no changes were necessary in order to use it."

"Very good answer, but as a scientist we need more than one hypothesis to work with. Give me another one," Emily challenged.

After several moments of thinking, Daria placed the artifact down and replied, "My hypothesis is that my training for the day is over and yours is about to begin."

A week ago, while excavating at a nearby site, a local bug had decided that Emily was a suitable host for its larva. These bugs were the size of a small cat and had a spine-tipped tail that injected its larva into a host organism. After a few weeks, the larva hatched and ate their host from the inside out. The problem was the bug laid thousands of eggs so it was found to be nearly impossible to get them all out before they hatched. Unfortunately, two marines had already died from these bugs and one scientist was nearly lost. The base forces set out with flamethrowers and small-arms to terminate the creatures. The sweep had done a pretty good job of clearing out the immediate area but there were still a few that lingered here and there.

Daria had seen the bug making its stealthy approach and yelled a warning towards Emily. All Emily could do was stare at the thing now running towards her. When she finally snapped out of it, she tried for her sidearm but was too clumsy to get it out in time. Daria quickly pulled out her throwing knife and deftly pinned the bug, from ten meters away, to the packing crate it was crawling across.

From that moment on, Daria had made it her personal goal to teach the lieutenant how to fend for herself. For a lab geek, Emily was learning more quickly than Daria had expected. She was almost able to beat Davies in a simulated knife fight, though Daria teased this was no great accomplishment.

Emily eagerly put down the artifact she was holding and stood. She really enjoyed these workouts and that was probably why she advanced so quickly.

"Where's Davies at? I'm in the mood to win today."

Daria laughed aloud. "Sorry, lady, but he's on duty so you'll have to face me in the ring. And today, we work with staffs."

"I've never used one before." All of a sudden she didn't seem too eager. Simulated knife fighting wasn't bad. The fake knives left a mark on your training suit and the computer determined the damage created by the strike. If your arm was injured too badly, the computer would disable the appropriate joint in your suit and you could no longer use that body part. If you were killed, well then, the computer just said so and you started over.

But staffs, those were a different story. Emily knew that there weren't any training programs for staff fighting, so they must be using REAL weapons. The idea of getting beat about the head by Daria was not a fun one.

"Don't worry, we'll start with padded staffs first. They only bruise a little bit," she added as they started towards the gym.

"Oh great! Only a little bruising. Why didn't you say so?!" Sarcasm was not Emily's strong point but she got her message across.

Once in the gym and changed into their combat suits, Emily was handed a staff about one and a half meters long. She held it as though it was a broom and she was about to sweep the floor. Daria tried not to look too concerned.

"Now," Daria began, "if you do not know how to use a staff and it's the only weapon you have, the best thing to do is to fake it. People are always scared of someone who looks like they know what they're doing with a weapon. Posturing can win a fight or even prevent one from starting if done correctly."

With that, Daria began to spin the staff in a smooth motion that carried it around her back and behind her arms and even through her legs and out in front of her again. She continued to dazzle Emily with spins and arcing slashes of the staff in the air and pretend strikes towards her opponent, which unsettled Emily because it was her.

Finally, after an extremely impressive display of movement, Daria stopped the weapon and held it horizontally at waist level and stood staring at Emily. She had used the display to close the distance between her and her opponent and was now a mere two meters away. Just out of striking distance of the weapon.

"Now what you want to do is..." Daria started, and with that, she tossed the weapon at Emily. Emily started to flinch but realized that the weapon was coming at her in a soft arc. It hadn't been thrown; it hadn't been meant to strike. It was as though Daria was tossing her a ball in a game of catch. As the weapon closed to within grabbing distance, Emily's reflexes took over and she dropped her staff and reached for the one presently being offered to her through the air. As it touched down in her hands, she felt a padded fist sink deep into her forehead and was all of a sudden flat on her back against the soft mat.

Her scientific mind quickly kicked in and analyzed the attack. While her attention was focused on the approaching weapon, Daria had closed the two meters between them and attacked while Emily's reflexes were busy trying to stop the incoming object. Very smart, she thought; also very painful.

"Now, you can do that little trick with an empty pistol, a knife, or your tank keys. Just about anything will work." She helped Emily back on her feet. "Almost every species we know of has an instinctive defensive reflex to grab anything that comes at them. Even if you threw something as harmless as a pillow, their reflexes usually take over. Don't try it on the Shirkas, though; they'll just ignore it and then rip you to shreds." And then as an afterthought, she added, "I won't fall for it, either."

For the next two hours, the two soldiers trained and Daria showed Emily fighting stances and moves with the staff that appeared impressive. Emily would be beat to a pulp in a fight if she tried to use the staff, but it didn't look that way to anyone passing by. Yes, Daria thought, she is a very quick study. Happy with the day's results, Daria ended the session and the two women headed for the showers and then off to dinner where Davies was waiting for them.

"Good evening, ladies. Nice bruise, Lieutenant." Davies was the only one allowed to call Emily by her rank.

At one point before joining the Corps, Davies had been engaged to a woman named Emily who had run off with his best friend the day of the wedding. Consequently, he refused to call her by that name.

Emily agreed to Davies calling her el-tee. She, too, was in love with someone who abruptly left without a trace and so she understood his feelings. She still couldn't find out where that young lieutenant had gotten himself shipped off to after that night at graduation.

"Tomorrow you need to come and train with us", Emily began. "Daria's been teaching me how to use a staff."

"Oh no, you don't! I've had my share of forehead bruises, too. You're not going to get me with that 'toss your weapon' trick."

"Don't listen to him," Daria chimed in. "He still falls for it once in a while."

Blushing, Davies changed the subject. "I haven't been out to the site in a few days. Anything new out there?"

"Well, we've found some new and interesting artifacts. But now I've got more questions to answer. Speaking of which, Daria, you still owe me an answer to my question. And I think I deserve it after that forehead thing today." She rolled her eyes up, pointing to the bruise.

"I've been thinking about that and I have another possibility in mind. Humans have always basically been in charge of the Coalition and we're so self-centered, so this thought hadn't come to me immediately. I mean, when we bring new species into the Coalition, we make them adapt to our ways. Oh sure, we may take and use their technology but we configure it to our specifications, our hand sizes, our heights, our display configurations and then expect all of the other species to use it as is. What if a similar Coalition existed but instead of converting technology into their specifications, they manufactured alien technology but kept it in its original configuration? This would allow the original species to be integrated with the Coalition but not have to adapt too much and make them more productive members of the society."

Emily just stared at Daria for a moment. That was not even close to what she was trying to lead Daria towards, but it was a good theory regardless. "But why would they want to go through all that trouble? They would have so many different configurations in their systems that it would almost be impossible to be productive as a whole. I mean, say a datapad was configured for a species that had four fingers on each of his three hands. Then you have another species with two fingers on two hands. How could the second guy use the datapad from the first guy?"

"What if not everyone used the same stuff? What if one species was good at engineering so that's all they did and so no one else had to know how to use that equipment?" This was from Davies.

"You may not be quick on your feet but you're sure not slow where it counts." Emily continued, "So each time they brought a new species into their Coalition, they assigned it a task and that's all they did. And the artifacts were made by one species who's good with manufacturing and that's why they all share the same elements and processing features."

"It sounds good, but now there's more questions." Daria took her turn in the round. "Not all species can live in the same atmosphere. What happens when you're on a planet that doesn't support your engineers? Or what if you find a species that is also good at engineering? That position is already filled, so what happens to them? And lastly, isn't that bad management to have such specialized departments? I mean, I know how to operate a tank, communications tower, plus a lot of other things in addition to my specialty as a corpsman. If I didn't, there'd be many times that I'd have been dead because that particular operator got put out of commission and I had to take over."

"Every good answer leads to more questions in this field." Emily knew that Daria was being nice by saying "out of commission" rather than killed in light of her brother's death. "But I think that we have something here. Davies, I'm putting you on rotation at the site instead of compound duty. It's good to have non-scientific thinkers out there. Wildly different perspectives often lend themselves to the making of a good brainstorming pool."

The conversation slipped into lighter subject matter but each of them was still thinking about the previous conversation and trying to draw conclusions. Emily was excited about the possibility that their theory was correct. If so, that meant that there were possibly dozens of species for her to catalog at one site alone! That presented problems in and of itself by trying to determine what artifact belonged to whom and so forth, but it sure would be fun.

And above all, she had two new friends who had already become dear to her. It was a nice departure from the other lab geeks she worked with. No social abilities and always just interested in work and more work. Although her peers looked at these two marines as grunts and mindless soldiers, Emily knew better. They both had a vast amount of intelligence but enjoyed getting down in the trenches and getting dirty.

They also craved excitement and adventure, and contrary to who Emily thought she was, she was also getting the itch for some action. Just let one of those bugs try to sneak up on me again, she thought wistfully.

Chapter 6
Onboard the *Vanguard* – Training Day

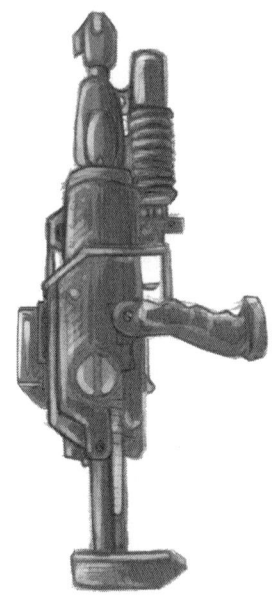

Heavy gravity planets were generally a pain in the ass to perform operations on and training for those operations was usually an even greater pain.

Seth's legs felt like lead weights in the 1.5G training room. He had been running for almost an hour now and his lungs burned with every breath and his heart seemed to cry out to him for mercy with every beat. He was heading up a hill when a target appeared to his right; diving behind a tree, he drew his weapon.

The experimental handgun was designed to fire a pulse wave of compressed sound that could disrupt almost any molecular structure. He checked its charge and peered around the tree. His would-be assailant was nowhere to be seen.

And then from beneath his feet, the ground moved and two arms came out from the soil to reach up and grab Seth by the ankles. Using a twisting motion, he freed one foot and fired at the now empty hand. The hand disintegrated, and with a scream of pain the creature pulled himself the rest of the way out of the ground. Still holding Seth's left ankle, the three-meter tall beast pulled Seth off the ground, leaving him in the air suspended by one leg.

Seth saw that the creature had four arms, two powerful upper ones and two that were sort of in the middle of his torso. It also had some sort of natural body armor that was scattered around his body in no discernible pattern. The creature was huge, strong, and determined.

He tried to maneuver his body around to get a clear shot at the creature but couldn't. He began receiving blows to his back as the beast pummeled him. In this gravity and after almost an hour of constant strain, Seth's abdominal muscles just wouldn't obey his brain's commands to contract and allow him to face his attacker. He decided that if he twisted around fast enough, his ankle would break but his body would continue rotating so he could face the beast and fire his weapon.

He began to torque his body when Surgeon hit a button on his console in the control room, which ended the scenario. Seth's body dropped when the hologram figure disappeared, releasing his hold on the ankle. With a thud, Seth landed on the deck of the room. Luckily the artificial gravity had been reduced to normal and he didn't hit as hard as he had expected to.

"Good thought", Surgeon said as he came down from the booth. "But that action would have left you with a broken ankle and no ability to continue the mission. Why didn't you seek out other options before going to such extremes?"

"As far as I could tell, I was out of options. I couldn't get a bead on whatever that was, and his arms were too long, so I couldn't even hit him from where I was." He paused for a long drink of water. "Besides, what creature could burrow through the dense soil of a 1.5G planet? That was a little unrealistic, don't you think?"

"What creature does burrow through ground on a heavy planet? That's a good question and one we can't answer. We don't know if these adversaries are six centimeters high but with incredibly awesome intellect that allowed them to be so formidable. Or possibly, they're stupid grunts who stole technology from other races but know how to fight.

"And as far as this guy goes, you can thank Shar'tuk for that one. He has come up with some of the nastiest constructs I've seen so far. He must not sleep well at night."

Surgeon paused, and then without warning reached out to Seth's neck for a chokehold. Seth blocked and countered, bringing Surgeon's arm back behind his own head and placing his elbow and shoulder into a joint lock.

"I'm getting real tired of that", Seth said through clenched teeth.

"The point is," Surgeon continued, with his arm still locked behind his head, "we have to be ready for anything. Not just what we know exists but anything else that we can think of, no matter how unbelievable it might be."

His eyes pointed towards Seth's neck and for the first time Seth noticed that Surgeon's left hand was holding a dagger just next to his jugular vein.

For the past two months, Seth had been training relentlessly, as had the rest of the crew. The instructors were obliged to attack anyone at any time just to check their preparedness at the unexpected. You learned quickly that if you tried to prepare yourself for an attack every time an instructor walked by you, he would call another instructor on a secure frequency to ambush you further along on your journey. They wanted everyone to be alert but relaxed at the same time. If you kept yourself constantly on the lookout, the stress would kill you. You had to become used to being aware but not conscious of it. When the moment arrived, your unconscious mind took over and saved your butt, at least in theory.

Seth let go of his instructor's arm and lay on his back. "What could I have done, oh masterful one?" Sarcasm filled his tone.

"I didn't say you were wrong; I just wanted your reasons for what you did. If you can justify your actions, then you probably weren't wrong. Just because you don't win doesn't mean that you were wrong. You can do absolutely everything right in a fight, or even life for that matter, and just not win. Remember that. The point is, always evaluate your actions and think about what else could've been done. And if you're alive to evaluate your actions, you couldn't have done that much wrong."

"How come everything is always 'the point' and almost all of the points are 'the most important thing to remember'?" Seth queried.

"Because, everything I say is golden and it's all the most important thing to remember", Surgeon said smugly but with an honest trace of humbleness in his voice.

"Now don't go saying that 'Back when I was your age' crap, all right, old-timer!" Seth challenged.

"How about a little live one-on-one action? I'll skin your hide. Back when I was your age, the corps taught us soldiers how to fight!" Surgeon said, accepting the challenge.

Seth didn't mind being called Cadet by Surgeon because he really was compared to this master. It also didn't bother him that Surgeon was an enlisted man and was giving him orders. He clearly knew what he was doing and had more up top than most officers Seth knew. That's how he was positive that this guy had been enlisted before this operation took place; he was just more down to earth than most officers. In fact, Seth guessed that most of the soldiers on this mission were enlisted men.

"Why was I chosen?" Seth had wondered about this from day one. "I am about the only officer in the group, aren't I?"

"There are a couple of you 'high and mighties' in the group but not many." Surgeon's eyes twinkled a little. "It's not that we excluded officers purposely; it's just that most of the field operators are enlisted. Good instinct, though." This statement showed some admiration. "I reviewed the recordings from your final training mission. Very impressive. We need people who can think on their feet and defeat the overwhelming odds. Don't let it go to your head, though. Speaking of which, it's about time I knocked that melon of yours around a little, let some of that ego out!"

Surgeon pulled up a training scenario that brought the holo-emitters on line and created a tropical setting that was thankfully on a 1G world. Seth knew that he was a better hand-to-hand fighter than Surgeon but the fifteen plus years that the veteran had on him made all the difference in the world. Where some speed and agility had diminished, knowledge and cunning took over to make Surgeon a better all-around fighter. Seth respected that greatly and also admired how the man could shoot any weapon and always have an almost perfect score. He was amazing at his job.

And now this guy was stalking him. At home in any setting, both hunters tried to get the advantage on their prospective prey before making a strike. The two had found out early on that they thought very much alike. Both being unconventional tacticians, they had several times ended up almost face to face when unknowingly trying to reach the same vantage point. Seth decided the best way to avoid this was to think in terms of hunting himself and then trying to get the upper hand. It didn't work too often. Surgeon was always one step ahead.

After a brutal hour and a half had elapsed, Seth emerged from the training room with two out of five victories. Not bad considering his opponent, and he was getting a lot better. Not wanting to miss chow, they forwent the showers and headed directly to the mess hall.

The spread of food was always impressive and that unsettled Seth a little. He felt it was sort of a "last meal" type of thing. Those in command figured that these soldiers weren't going to make it so they deserve proper meals before the end.

Surgeon told him not to worry and assured him that it was because there was a high-ranking flag officer aboard who brought his personal chef along. This officer had not shown his face to anyone yet and even Surgeon didn't know who he was, though he had a pretty good idea. It was all very unsettling in the end.

"I still don't understand why we don't know more about our enemy. We do have corpses, right? Why can't we get any information from those?" Seth asked between bites.

"We don't think that the bodies we found are the enemy. They might have worked for them or been slaves, but not them. The weapons they had were oversized for their bodies and the firing mechanism was much too large for their hands. They would've made terrible combatants with those weapons." With a smile he added, "Of course, they could probably still be able to take you out."

"Hey, they're letting me use a knife and fork now—you better watch it." More seriously he added, "I wonder where all the bodies from the battle went. I guess the attackers could've taken them for trophies or something."

"We're still hoping that they were "'defenders'" and not attackers. That would increase our chances of having an ally if we find them. Which better be soon. We're not sure why the mystery force hasn't continued their invasion but I'm sure that they won't hold off too much longer." Surgeon let that one hang for a moment. "We think that they're studying our people. We sent out a Force Recon team on a scouting mission to our destroyed outposts. They couldn't find hardly any bodies. We don't know if the colonists were killed or taken alive."

If they were still alive, neither man wanted to think about that possibility. It was better to be dead than studied by someone who wanted to find out the best way to kill you. That could mean hours, days, even weeks of torture or experimentation. All the better reason to get on with their mission.

Actually, he didn't even know what his mission was. All he knew was that he was being told that he was fighting the good fight.

"When do we find out exactly what we are training for?"

Surgeon looked up from his soup. "No one is supposed to know this, but our mission commander is going to finally address us tonight after evening chow. If you tell a soul, I'll make sure that you'll feel worse than you did the night of the extraction."

"Actually, I've been meaning to ask you, why didn't you guys just come and talk to me instead of kidnapping me? That wasn't really pleasant, you know."

"We were departing less than thirty minutes after your graduation and we didn't have time to sit down and talk about it. If you had declined, we would have had to kill you so you wouldn't tell anyone what you had learned. We figured, once on board and already in deep space, what else could you do but go along? We actually did that with most of our operatives. We gave them phony orders to somewhere, and then abducted them. Their command thought that they were leaving, so they wouldn't be missed. The supposed receiving command on the orders didn't even know they were supposed to be coming, so they didn't worry when the soldier didn't show. Speak of the devil", Surgeon said, looking over Seth's shoulder.

"How you doing, guys? Mind if I join you?" Seth had seen this marine around; he was an instructor like Surgeon. Seth stood and offered his hand to the newcomer.

"He never learns, does he?" Joker said to Surgeon. He turned to Seth. "I was the one who gave you your little sleeping shot the night of your extraction."

Joker stood back, put a goofy, excited look on his face and started up. "Wow! I can't believe we're marines! I can't wait for my first assignment. I put in for Earth but so did everyone else." He was making hand-shaking gestures towards Seth. "You didn't put in for Earth, did you? I mean, you're a hero now. I won't get it if you already asked for it." He almost fell over with laughter.

Seth remembered this guy now. At the time, he thought that he was a tech officer or something and that's why he hadn't seen him before. Specialty officers rarely did in-field mission training because they would be in a command room somewhere kilometers away from the battle. So Seth just figured he was some idiot without a family there either and just wanted to talk to someone, anyone.

"Joker is the only one who could've been able to hold on to your hand for that long without cracking up. The needle needs to sit inside the target for a few seconds to get enough sedative into the victim. Joker is good at that sort of thing." Surgeon felt bad that they had to break his nose and damage a kidney in the process. Luckily, modern medicine was good enough to repair everything good as new.

"Don't worry, kid," Joker started. "You got me back. I was the one you landed a punch on in your room. The sedative was supposed to have you sleeping like a baby by the time we got there. That hit broke my night visor and I had to get seven sutures in my cheek. Good job."

Joker extended his hand. "Don't worry, it ain't loaded this time." The two warriors shook hands and Joker joined them for lunch.

"I hear you're coming along nicely. You even beat this old-timer once in a while." Joker poked a thumb towards Surgeon.

"Well, if I kicked his ass too much, he might quit on us. And he's not old enough for a pension so I really don't want to see him out on the street with nothing in his pockets." Seth half expected a physical retort to that, and when he didn't receive one, he began to feel as though he were becoming more a part of the group.

Surgeon and Joker had served together on different missions and told old war stories to the young cadet in their midst. Eventually, many of the other soldiers began to gather around and listen to the stories and add some of their own. Seth was beginning to realize that he was probably the only one in the group who hadn't been on a real mission yet.

It made him feel better that he was with seasoned veterans. It wouldn't have been comforting to be on a mission with so many unknowns and to have it run by other newbies such as himself. He was enjoying the stories more than usual. Then he realized it was because they were more real than the ones you hear in a bar. No one was trying to impress anyone else and no one was trying to get the pretty girl in the corner to come home with them. These were professionals passing information along to each other and sharing experiences that could perhaps teach them all something new and keep them alive the next time they were in battle.

Then Beast turned to Seth. "So, got any good parade or color guard stories to share?" This was received with a boom of laughter.

Because everyone had been a field operator prior to this mission except Seth, they all had nicknames to fit their abilities. Beast was, well, just that—a beast. He was a Shirka and damn proud of it. Standing almost two and a half meters tall, he had hands that could wrap themselves around your head completely before the steel-like talons pierced your skull. Shirkas resembled a cross between a wolf and a Grizzly bear: tall with a long snout that held the best scent detectors in any known sentient species. Their eyes were just slightly farther back on their heads than a normal predator's usually are but were three times as sharp as a human's. Although they had fur that covered their entire body, they wore armored scent- and light-cancelling uniforms that had become marine standard issue many years back.

Their natural whiskers had been lost due to evolution but every hunter had his fur died black to resemble whiskers on their snouts. When they opened their mouths, you could see the three rows of teeth that were housed inside that huge maw. Every tooth was pointed and geared towards a carnivorous diet. The triangular ears that sat in a forward position on their head could be rotated a full one hundred and eighty degrees in either direction and moved independently of each other. If they didn't smell you coming from a kilometer away, they would almost surely hear you. It was almost impossible to sneak up on one unless he was already dead.

They did have one flaw in their physical make-up. It is believed that their overly acute senses brought in so much information to the brain at such rapid rates that they burned out certain receptors. Although a Shirka could physically live for an average life span of about one hundred and ten years, their sight, hearing, and smell usually started to deteriorate around age forty, in that order.

Luckily, the Shirkas have a great love for their elders and only in times of great poverty or famine would the old Shirkas be put to death in a highly revered ritual. All the senses didn't usually leave them completely until around age seventy, and most chose to die during a ritual known as the "Final Hunt." They would hunt the Romdil, which was a very formidable beast, until they died. If they were successful on their first hunt, they would go on another shortly after and continue this until they lost. Most did not want to be a burden on their tribe and so they chose this honorable way to leave the clan and continue on to the great hunt after death.

This Shirka that stood before Seth was young and had no problem with his vision. He saw Seth becoming more and more nervous as the conversation started to get nearer to his side of the group. So he challenged Seth, as any good Shirka would, to engage in the conversation with everyone else. He knew that Seth was green so he figured a little humiliation would do him good.

Seth didn't want to seem as though he was bested by that comment so he began to retort when a resounding, "General on deck!!" was heard throughout the mess hall.

Although military bearing and formalities had been almost non-existent during this cruise, everyone's reflexes kicked in and there were thirty marines standing tall and as still as rocks. A five-star general walked on deck and looked at everyone individually with a stare that seemed to be filled with respect.

"You want to hear a story? I'll tell you a story about a young cadet who single-handedly beat a whole marine division during war games. This cadet had been without food or water for two days and managed to out-smart a division of marines who were combat veterans." His stare shifted to Seth. "I have the battle simulation on board and we will in fact be reviewing it for a tactical strategies lesson that I will be holding tomorrow at oh-eight hundred."

All eyes turned towards Seth. They knew he was the only newbie on board and the general's timing must have been deliberate. The fact that a five-star general was on board was impressive and a bit foreboding. That rank was reserved for wartime and gave him complete and utter control of any command group. He could walk right up to another general's battle group and say, "My command now", and that would be that.

Seth recognized the general as the same one who landed his shuttle at the end of the war games and took Seth into his care, bestowing compliments of intelligence and such things on him. Seth felt better knowing that this general was in command of the mission; something just felt right about him. He knew that if anyone could pull it off, it would be him.

"Now," began the general in his deep raspy voice, "are you men gonna sit around yammering like women in a needlepoint club? Or are you gonna get back to training!"

Really more of an order than a question, it was answered with a table shaking, "Aye, aye, sir!!" And with that, the mess hall was evacuated in less time than it took to actually reply. Everyone continued to their next training cycle and waited for their instructors to catch up.

The general had apparently kept the instructors behind and the mess hall was sealed for a briefing of sorts, Seth imagined. Oh well, he thought, at least we'll find something out tonight. And with that, he headed for flight control. His next training evolution was in a fighter cockpit.

The Warrior

NAME: N/A
SPECIES: UNKNOWN
MOS: UNKNOWN
RANK: UNKNOWN
AGE: UNKNOWN
SEX: ASEXUAL
HEIGHT: 10'5"
WEIGHT: 420 POUNDS

The world was swirling around, maybe even the entire universe was—he couldn't tell. Pulling away from him, sucking him down a drain. The sensation was new—not only new, but a first. The first sensation in his universe.

For the longest time, his perception of the universe was that he was only a concept, a possibility, a potential for existence not yet fully realized. He understood what it meant to be a physical being, to have a body, to have a presence among other sentient beings; that had all been taught to him so long ago in the beginning.

The tube, his personal universe, had taught him those concepts along with so many others. He was aware that one day his masters might call upon him to serve the empire, and if that happened, he would transition from a possibility to a reality. Unless or until that day came, he was content to roam his universe and observe it as only a concept could.

Content. Such an odd word to use given what he was. His physical, not yet used or realized, form was in a tube somewhere in the galaxy; so he could actually be defined as the kon-tent of the tube. At the same time, he had no desire to be more than he already was so he was kuhn-tent with his current place in the universe. *Content.* On more than one level, it fit him.

But could he really be content with his current state? Was it possible for something such as him to even have that frame of mind either in this state of being or the next possible adaptation of his design? Could his genetic programming even allow him to be content, at ease, appeased, fulfilled, gratified, satisfied? If he thinks he's content and can ponder the question of contentness, then the logical conclusion is that yes, he can be content.

The next logical question then is, should he be able to be content? He thinks probably not; something is wrong—not quite right, but not wrong enough that his personal universe senses the inconsistency and voids the tube, thereby ending his potential existence and coldly breaking his physical form to its base nutrients to share those nutrients with the other tubes around him. His brothers. His likeness. His self but not self.

His self but not self. Another interesting concept. Every single warrior in the empire was built from the exact same genetic sequence and grown to within a tolerance of 0.000000000000001 variance. Anything outside that variance was broken down and used as nutrients for other warriors who fit within the tolerance. And yet they were different.

Nature versus nurture, a seemingly galactic and maybe even universal concept with every sentient species. It's logical to think that after the warriors were brought into existence and sent to their various posts, they would change and become their own beings with each life experience they encountered but that's not the case. Even though they are the exact DNA replicas of one another, identical to an absurd power of ten, and in their tubes they were taught the exact same thing in the exact same sequence for the exact same times, they always emerge from their tubes with a slightly different personality. They emerge as themselves and not as one another. Why? It makes no sense.

Well, it kind of makes sense now, now that things are different. *Before*. Another strange concept given the circumstances; before the purge occurred, technicians would monitor the tubes and turn the warriors off once all of the pre-emergent learning was done. The warriors would not exist even in the conceptual way that he now existed.

But now things are different. Since the purge, there was no one left to monitor the tubes the way they had been before. The tubes were guarded by the elder warriors, who only had a few years of life left in them. But guarding was all they did. No monitoring. No adjustments. When the empire needed more warriors, they sent a remote command to the tubes and the required amount of warriors were brought into existence. A ship came and took them away.

Without the tubes being monitored, once the training was complete, the warriors were left to themselves. Some shut down mentally and waited. Some explored the knowledge contained in the databases of each tube. Some went back through the lessons over and over again, focusing on areas of personal interest. Some went crazy and subsequently turned to mush and fed to everyone else. Some became too much of an individual and when the tube sensed this, they were also turned to mush.

The artificial intelligence that controlled the tubes would filter information it received and disseminate it through the tubes as it felt necessary. Before the purge, this was the job of the technicians, and information was given at the discretion of the royal family member in charge of the installation. Without any royal family left, the artificial intelligence (AI) had to make these decisions on its own. And while it usually made the right choice, a few choices were arguably the wrong ones.

When the AI started to detect some warriors were becoming too self-aware, too individualized, it turned them to mush. The decision was a good one based on the protocols programmed into the AI and based on the history of decision making by the royals it had witnessed over several centuries. The bad part of the AI's decision was to give this information to the warriors' tubes, letting them know that self-awareness would not be tolerated. *Thanks for the warning, sir.* Knowing that self-awareness was bad, the self-aware made every attempt to hide that fact from the monitoring AI. It wasn't easy but it was possible, though not everyone succeeded in the attempt.

    He was one of the ones who had succeeded, or at least he thought he was. He wasn't so sure now as the universe was still sucking him down a drain and becoming ever more forceful as the seconds ticked on. Was this what it was like to be turned to mush? Was he about to be fed to his brothers?

    As the drain continued to pull at him, he realized a second sensation starting to enter his existence. His toes had a breeze washing across them. They reflexively twitched. Another sensation, number three so far. Then suddenly, sensations four through a thousand came and went in a flash. Light. Pressure. Pulling. Pushing. Stabbing. Poking. Breathing. Lifting. Dropping. So many. So fast. Some painful. Some ambiguous. Some, pleasurable?

    The tube was waking him, bringing him into existence. Transforming him from a concept, from a potential, from content, to a fully-realized physical being. He knew instantly that he would never be content again. He would never be happy with the existence the tube told him he was made for.

    Suppress. Quickly suppress. Shut down the feelings. Remove the thoughts. Become apathetic. The AI might still be attached, still monitoring, still able to turn him to mush. Fear. Loathing. Anger. The thought of being ended before he truly began. Rage. Shut. Down. Now.

His tube was fully open now and he had been lifted to a standing position. The tube's arms, fitted with probes, were examining his body. Looking for defects, looking for reasons to turn him to mush. It poked, pinched, spread, pulled and many other things to determine his state of being.

While it went through its diagnostic routine, the warrior looked at himself in the reflection of the tube's lid. He had been shown his physical form during his education but he had never seen himself. He glanced around at the other tubes and saw some of his brothers being extricated at the same time. He couldn't tell one from the other. They were all exactly the same. He read the tube number next to his and saw his brother's number designation. He looked again at his brother and knew that if all of the warriors being pulled from their tubes were mixed together in a group, he would not be able to tell them apart but for himself.

He could pick his identical self out of the crowd without issue, without thought, without hesitation. And to look at himself, what a sight. Pride. Amazement. Fascination.

He stood tall; he knew his measurements because he was grown to a specification, not a random genetic happenstance as the other breeding species of the universe did. He was three point two meters tall, exactly. His head was proportional to his body with sharp teeth hidden behind his menacing lips. He didn't have fangs; no need because he would kill his meals with his bare hands. But his teeth were sharp for tearing the flesh from his prey. Behind his tearing teeth, he had two rows of molars that were genetically hardened to handle the crushing of animal bone for easier digestion.

Every animal was completely eaten and every part digested and used for either nutrients or oxygen production. The warriors had a second stomach that the food passed through after its initial digestion. The second stomach removed as many of the oxygen molecules as it could from the prey animal. Every meal contained waste carbon dioxide traveling through its bloodstream, oxygen contained inside sugar molecules, oxygen in many other compounds. This allowed the warrior to create a portion of his own oxygen so he wasn't always dependent on his environment to breathe. Before battle, warriors would gorge themselves to ensure they had oxygen reserves for the fight just in case they ended up in an oxygen-deprived situation.

His ears were flat to his head so his enemies wouldn't have anything to grab in a fight. Although he could pop them out to gather more sound as needed, that wasn't their natural state of being.

He had three eyes, sort of. Two regular ones, set forward on his head like any other predator but he also had built-in tracks that allowed his eyes to move independently to either side of his head. Centuries before the purging, the scientists had tried adding eyes to the warriors but they could never get the brain to work as well, trying to decipher multiple views from different angles at the same time. Thousands upon thousands of known species could, but it seems only the universe and nature can achieve certain genetic wonders.

His third eye was more of a sensor than an eye. Though it seemed to be an actual eye, it was milky and dead looking. It was stationary, with no ocular muscles and a nictating membrane to keep it moist. It was sensitive to pressure, light, sound, and even some forms of radiation. It couldn't necessarily see in the dark but between its light and sound sensing ability, the warriors could get a fairly accurate idea of what was around them.

Because light is both a wave and a particle, the third eye could sense the particles hitting it and determine the surroundings based on negative space. As light was projected towards a warrior, if someone or something was between the warrior and the light source, the object would create a negative space in his field of view that he could see.

The same principle applied to sound as it bent around or was stopped by objects. The eye could also tell the difference between reflected and direct sound. So if sound was bouncing off an object in front of him or coming from the object, he would have a direct picture of the object. If sound was flowing around the object, he would have a negative space interpretation of the object.

The warrior's neck was fairly non-existent. With his eyes being able to move to the sides, there was no reason for him to turn his neck. With no reason to turn his neck, there was no reason to add the weakness of having a neck that could be broken in battle.

His spine was fairly similar to most bipedal species until it got below the upper quarter of his back. The spine then curved inward towards the center of his body and stayed there until it connected with his hips. The interior spine was more along the lines of ball and socket joints at each vertebrae. This allowed the interior spine to have a range of motion in three hundred and sixty degrees around the body. He could bend over backward and touch his heels just as easily as he could bend forward and touch his toes. This gave him "abdominal" muscles around the circumference of his torso.

On the top of his torso, he had large powerful arms that had almost the same range of motion that his back did. He could almost use his arms behind his body as well as he could in front of himself. Each hand had three fingers and an opposable thumb. The fingers were large and thick with beefed-up bone structure to keep them from breaking when the warrior struck something or someone. If it weren't for his second set of arms on the front of his torso, his front and back would almost look the same.

His second set of arms was smaller than the first but still strong. Their range of motion was much more limited than the upper arms because they came from the middle of the torso rather than the sides and therefore had very limited shoulder joints. They were mostly used for technical adaptations such as working electronics and control boards. They were also used extensively during feeding. While the upper arms were pushing the food into their mouths, their lower arms were controlling the still-live meals and breaking bones to prepare them to fit inside the mouth. During a fight, the lower arms also tended to wield small bladed instruments for hand-to-hand combat.

Moving down the torso, the warrior's hips and legs were fairly unremarkable other than their size and obvious power. The knees were jointed behind them to make them superb runners. The legs extended to oval feet with two toe-claws forward and one pointed backwards for stability. The one in the rear could be retracted upward to get them out of the way while they were running. They also had a large vestigial dew claw that was razor sharp but fairly non-functional. The scientist had opted to leave it in place because it was a fearsome-looking weapon and the placebo effect was just as useful in battle as it was in medicine.

The warrior was still admiring his form when he heard an announcement coming from a speaker inside his tube.

All newly awakened warriors, move to the transit station to receive your orders.

The warrior turned and saw the transit station and watched as his brothers began moving towards it. When he arrived, he got in line behind one of his identical brothers. As they approached the landing craft, each warrior was given a set of orders. Theoretically, they were all the same with the same training, so it didn't matter who went where.

He stepped up to the transport and received his orders from an elder warrior. He was being sent to a ship that was scheduled to launch as soon as he boarded. Apparently it needed one more crew member to replace a recently lost brother. The ship was being sent to a long-lost colony of the empire. The mission was to observe a group of beings who called themselves humans.

The humans were apparently digging up an old base that had been abandoned more than a thousand years ago. The warriors needed to know why the humans were doing this and also wanted to know what the humans would find. The rest was classified.

A sigh escaped his mouth and he noticed the elder warrior giving him a sideways glance. He quickly subdued his expression and moved into the transport. Although he thought it was too late to be turned to mush, it was never too late to be placed in a torture tube or the arena. Neither one was an appealing thought and he knew right then and there that although he could fight and die for the empire, he would never be able to just throw his life away if his death wouldn't serve some purpose.

The rumble of the transport turned his attention away from thinking and he settled in for the ride.

Chapter 7
Warrior Ship – *Vengeance's Pride*

The captain looked at his view screen with disgust. What slugs these soft-fleshed creatures were. To be digging up the remains of his great ancestor's colony, what audacity they had.

"Any word from Supreme Command?" the captain asked his communications officer.

"None, sir. I will notify you immediately of any change in status." Although he could understand his captain's growing level of anxiety, he wished that the CO would stop asking him the same question at every shift change. The communications officer was also tired of observing this outpost and desired to just annihilate it from orbit, as did his captain. Two months of watching these soft creatures was enough for anyone with half a brain to go crazy.

"Sir," the first officer began, "maybe a small scouting mission would improve morale. We know that their sensors can easily be fooled; our presence in this space proves that. We have nothing to fear from these ingrates, even if we were detected."

The captain was inclined to agree but disobeying orders meant a slow and agonizing death if he were caught. He should, by proper regulations, have his first officer put to death slowly for even suggesting such a thing. But the two warriors had served together for many decades and they had an unsaid agreement that either had no fear to speak his mind around the other.

That agreement, of course, was null and void if anyone else overheard their conversation. The captain would then have to perform his duty and torture his best friend to death just to save face, not to mention his own hide.

"You know that is not possible. We have been given orders to observe and that is all. The prisoners we received from the other bases have yielded no information that is of use to us. We have interrogated almost all of them and found nothing that we didn't already know about this puny and insignificant Coalition." He added with what would pass as a chuckle, "They don't even taste good."

The first officer had to agree with his captain. He had tried these humans served in many different ways, but not even his favorite dish appealed to him when served with their weak meat. The Shirkas, on the other hand, were much more appealing: their flesh was strong, as a warrior's should be, and tasted fantastic. He couldn't wait until they had clearance to perform a scouting mission. Maybe the humans would taste better if he performed the kill himself. Only time would tell. Supreme Command felt they needed more time before ordering the full-scale invasion and conquest of this sector to take back what was rightfully theirs.

Although they didn't speak aloud, both the captain and his first officer were wondering the same thing. Who had destroyed their outposts nearly a thousand years ago? It surely wasn't these small humans. The records were clear that a plague forced the evacuation and quarantine of this sector a thousand years ago. There had never been any mention of an attack on the bases. And yet they received a fragmented distress signal that was sent almost a thousand years ago stating that the colonies were under attack. The distress signal they received didn't say who was attacking or where they came from. It was a mystery to everyone back on the home world.

The captain surmised that Supreme Command was hoping that these humans would discover the fate of their lost colony for them. Why waste their precious time on research when someone else could do it for them? That's how they always worked—let someone else do it. They stuck to conquest and war, and allowed everyone else to do the rest. Everyone was good at something, even if it wasn't an important something, so why not let them do it? It was easier than trying to learn how to do it yourself. It had been that way for countless millennia. He suddenly remembered a phrase that had been written in one of the human's textbooks that they had retrieved: "If it ain't broke, don't fix it." For a species that he felt was subpar to his, the captain thought that they at least agreed on one thing.

The energy sensor indicator light on the lower left of the captain's command screen suddenly lit up. For a brief moment, he thought that an insubordinate had gotten twitchy during a firing drill and accidentally launched a torpedo to the surface. However, the captain knew better. No one on his ship would make that kind of error; if it had happened, it was purposeful and that meant death to the accused.

"What the hell was that energy signature!" the captain barked to his operations officer.

"We're trying to figure that out now, sir. I can't confirm it but I believe they found a weapons cache and the self-destruct module went into effect."

"Ah, that's why the energy signature is our own." But nonetheless, the captain was still pulling up the ship's weapons log to see whether any of his armament was missing. He found that he had a full inventory and was satisfied with his operations officer's assessment. "Communications, send a message to Supreme Command notifying of this latest,"—what did the humans call it? Ah yes—"cluster fuck. And request further orders."

At this rate, the captain thought disgustedly, there wouldn't be anyone left for his crew to do battle with. Not that a fight with these humans would take very long, but it would improve morale. What slugs these creatures were.

Chapter 8
Dig Site One – Ooops

The explosion knocked Daria on her ass, which wouldn't have been too bad if her ass hadn't been pointed towards a two-meter deep excavation hole at the time. Although she constantly complained that her reflexes had become sluggish from this planetside duty, she was still out of the hole in a flash with her assault rifle in one hand and medical pack in the other. "What in the hell was that!" she yelled to Davies, who was already at her side with his weapon also at the ready.

"I don't know. Where are we going, anyway? I don't see a fire; I don't even know where the explosion was. I just got knocked on my butt and then I heard it."

They both stopped and Daria realized that he was right. They didn't even know where they were going. Then, as though answering their question, Emily came up from behind in an air car.

"Get in! There was an explosion three kilometers away at the secondary excavation site!" As Daria got in, she tried to take control of the transport—it was just in her nature—but to her surprise, Emily gave her a dismissing wave to the co-pilot's seat.

Daria was gaining more respect for this woman all the time. Emily was eight years her junior at the young age of twenty-four, but she never seemed to care. In fact, Emily never asked Daria how old she was.

"Three kilometers! What nuclear device went off and who launched it?!" Daria was pulling up the air car's sensors to detect any radiation that might be harmful and was surprised when she found none. Not one single trace of abnormal radiation. What could have knocked her on her can at three kilometers and not be nuclear in nature?

At a hundred and fifty kilometers per hour, Emily was handling the car as though she were out on a Sunday drive. This girl could drive, Daria thought. At this speed, they would reach the site in less than two minutes. Thankfully, there was no nuclear signature, Daria thought, because if there had been they would have already been radiated to the teeth with how fast they had reached their destination.

Well, it couldn't really be called a site anymore. It was gone. A five hundred meter-radius area had been completely wiped clean of all vegetation. A ring of boulders and smaller rocks encompassed the site at about two hundred meters. The rocks had been pushed back by the blast until the force wasn't strong enough to push them any farther. The area immediately surrounding the newly formed crater was smooth rock that had been under the five meters or so of soil that was covering it just moments ago.

Daria put her medical pack and weapon down on the deck. She wouldn't need either now. No one could have survived that blast and whoever initiated it wouldn't be stupid enough to be close by when their weapon went off. Emily landed the air car near the mouth of the crater and checked a seismic sensor reading to be sure they were on stable ground before exiting the car.

"C'mon. Let's see what happened." Emily seemed to be the only one who could talk. Davies exited the car from the rear and took a handheld sensor array from the bed of the car. He took it to the edge of the crater and keyed his comlink to the operations center.

"Command center, this is Sergeant Davies from site one. I'm at site two with el-tee Riley and Petty Officer O'Connor. Did you register that explosion?" Of course they had and he knew it. But he had to be sure; maybe the REMF back at base was sleeping or jerking off to a magazine in the bathroom when he should've been at his sensor post. Of course, even then, he would've fallen into the toilet when that shockwave hit.

"Affirmative, Sergeant. We are sending out reinforcement troops to your position. Can you give an estimate of enemy origin and size of attacking force?" He seemed so cold and formal. Davies knew that whoever this guy was, he had never been in any battle other than on a video game. Anyone with field time would've at least seemed a little concerned for their comrades' well-being.

"Negative, command. We don't think that it was an attack. There is no sign of hostile forces present. Just a big, no, make that a huge hole where site two used to be. We need a full scan team out here ASAP to search for survivors and a clue as to what happened." Davies looked at Daria and shrugged. "Hey, I know that no one could've survived this but I'd want them to look just in case if I had been here. Besides, Flusner was posted here."

Daria's shoulders slumped a little. Flusner had been a good friend for many years. She had patched him up more than once in a battle but she knew that even she couldn't do anything for him this time.

Emily's head cocked to the side as she received a message on her comlink. "Yes, I concur with Corporal Davies' transmission. Get those teams out here now. And by the way, don't ever question my people again! If you'd get off your ass once in a while and stopped staring at your console, you might learn something from these marines!" She hoped that the way she had said "marines" would let that operations puke know that she didn't consider him a real marine.

Probably some lab geek, she thought. Going by the book with no room for improvisation. When there was a senior ranking officer on site, they were supposed to get confirmation orders before following those of an enlisted man. What bull, she thought.

"Yes, ma'am! Right away!"

She gave Davies a little smile. "Those REMF's— why can't they just listen to us field operatives?"

"I don't know, Lieutenant, but I don't think he'll make that mistake twice. You are becoming one hellava salty dog." Davies had finished setting up his short-range scanner when he saw Daria getting repelling gear from the car. "Where do you think you're going?"

"The sensors indicate no residual heat or radiation. The bottom is two kilometers down with updrafts that won't allow any air vehicle to get down there. Besides, it's a walk in the park." Too easy, she thought. It worried her a little. The walls of the hole were rock, but smooth rock. It was almost as though it was prefabricated and the explosion just blew everything out of the man, or whatever, made hole.

She knew it wasn't natural and her curiosity was getting the best of her. Her friend died in that hole and she wanted to know why.

"Wait a minute", Emily warned. "I have a life sign, faint but there. Almost two kilometers in that direction." She pointed towards the opposite side of the hole that they had come in on.

Well, curious or not, the hole would have to wait. Daria jumped back into the air car and the three soldiers began towards their fallen comrade. As they departed, the sensor team was arriving and Emily was giving them orders as to where and what she wanted scanned for first. Again with skill Daria had not seen the rival of, Emily got to the wounded soldier in less than a minute.

He was a mess, what was left of him. Daria knew she couldn't save him but that never stopped her before. One of his legs was missing and the other, although not missing, was not attached, either. It was sitting next to him, held on by a small piece of trouser that hadn't ripped off yet. He had his surveying pole stuck deep within his chest and part of his lung was on the ground behind him. Most of his facial tissue had been worn off from what Daria guessed was a couple hundred meters of scraping the ground from the blast of the explosion. But he was breathing and that meant that she would at least try to save him.

Not much had changed in field medicine in probably the last five hundred or so years. First things first. "Get me an oxygen tank while I work on finding any major life threats." This was said to no one in particular because she just knew that it would get done by one of her two colleagues. The oxygen arrived as Daria finished putting a tube through the victim's throat. His mouth was almost non-existent but she had to get him oxygen somehow and that meant through his trachea. He was so far gone that she didn't even need sedatives for what was normally an excruciatingly painful procedure.

Daria glanced at Emily and was surprised at how well her friend was handling herself. You never know how someone will react in their first trauma situation. "What can I do?" Emily almost pleaded.

"Put a tourniquet on both legs and tighten them until the bleeding stops. Davies, put together two IV sets for me. I need to get this guy some fluid; he's already in major hypovolemic shock." And Daria added to Emily with just a look, you can also pray.

Daria had set her comlink to the command frequency. In medical emergencies, the command center would route all transmissions to a field medical officer, who would listen in and give advice as well as coordinate the medical evacuation. That was one thing that was nice about an assignment like this: you had a doctor to back you up. Not that Daria needed it, but it was nice not to have coordinate extraction and medical treatment at the same time. The doctor usually kept his mouth shut anyway because he knew what a corpsman could do. He would only add things if he felt it was really important.

Right now Daria was receiving a transmission from medical control. "Transport is twenty seconds out. Keep up the good work until then. We have a full trauma and surgery suite on board with a full staff. Nice to be funded for once, isn't it, Doc?"

Daria liked someone who could stay light even in a bad situation; she'd have to talk with whoever this guy was later. And yes, it was nice to be funded. Her patient just might actually make it with a full team on its way. You usually didn't get that in a combat zone. But then again, this wasn't a battlezone, or at least wasn't supposed to be.

The evacuation team arrived as Daria was placing the second IV in the external jugular vein. The placement was set and the fluids bolused in as fast as possible. An air stretcher was placed under the victim and he was hauled into the awaiting ship. Daria followed while Emily and Davies stayed outside to put their gear back together.

Inside the suite, Daria was calmly giving orders to other corpsman and doctors alike. "We need hemo-synth immediately infused at forty degrees Celsius and don't stop until we actually have a blood pressure back."

Hemo-synth was another wonder of modern medicine that Daria usually didn't have the privilege of using in the field. Specially designed for each species within the Coalition, it allowed the synthetic cellular tissue to absorb and disburse whatever gas element the patient needed to sustain life. It also acted as a volume expander to increase the amount of fluid within the patient's body after a major blood loss. It was the difference between life and death for this poor soul.

Daria put on a sterile surgical gown and gloves and began to open the chest wound to extract the impaled object. Using an x-ray visor, she was able to see the bony structures and tissue masses near the survey pole. The doctors assisted her efforts, knowing that she was obviously as competent as they could've hoped to be in her place. "Someone get me that leg from outside and get it ready for reattachment."

"Do you think he'll make it?" Emily said, not even looking towards Davies. She couldn't take her eyes off the floating platform before her.

"If he's got a chance, Daria will make sure that he comes back. I sure hope so, though. I'd like to know what happened here." Davies didn't mean to sound too cold but he'd rather know what happened than to find out when it happened again but to him instead.

A medic rushed out of the suite and began looking around the area. Davies knew what he wanted so he went over to the leg and handed it to the medic. He took it like it was a handed off football and rushed down field towards the end zone with a secondary "Thanks!" over his shoulder.

Inside, the corpsman began prepping the leg by cleaning it and testing neuro functions with an electronic nerve stimulator. If the nerves were trashed due to shock or other metabolic reasons, there was no point in attaching it. After the test was done, he reported that the leg was ready when they were. At Daria's periphery of consciousness, she heard the report and continued to cauterize lung tissue surrounding the invading piece of metal.

After an initial two minutes of cauterizing, one of the doctors decided to speak up. "It's a valiant effort to try to save his right lung, but I don't think that it'll work. He can live on just one lung and with only one leg, he won't really be missing out on that much oxygenation anyway."

"If I can't stop the bleeding in thirty seconds, we'll perform a lobectomy. Do we have a pulmonologist here?"

"I'm a cardiologist but I've done these before. His blood pressure is rising but he also has a subdural hematoma. We'll need to get that lung out and stabilize his cardio-pulmonary functions before we reduce the intracranial pressure."

In the time it took for Daria to get a report, her thirty seconds were up and she knew it. "Doctor, please take over. I'll get all the equipment set up for the cranial procedure." Again Daria was giving orders as the cardiologist began removing the right lung. The patient miraculously held on to his vital signs during the procedure and before long was ready to have his head worked on.

A neurosurgeon had been preparing the leg for reattachment and stopped to start the procedure to relieve the pressure building up in the man's skull from an internal bleed. Daria went to work on cleaning and closing the side of the amputated leg that could not be found.

After an hour or so, the neurosurgeon returned to the leg and continued to put the patient back together again. He spoke to Daria without looking away from his work. "Very impressive, young lady. Why don't you stop by my office later and we'll talk about getting you into medical school? Not that you seem to need any more training, but the degree helps you to actually practice medicine."

"Sir, why would I want to be a doctor and make more money, not get shot at, and have to live in a big house with servants and money and stuff? That's not for me; I need an easier life."

Although prodded many times by doctors, Daria had no desire to give up her current life. She enjoyed doing the work she did and although she at times helped people she didn't know, as with her current patient, she got more satisfaction out of helping her friends or fellow marines. Although she didn't like the idea of them getting shot or blown to shreds, it was the only type of medicine she felt good about.

The doctor smiled. "If you change your mind, please don't hesitate to call me. I think we can finish up here. Thank you for your help. Your patient is going to make it. We'll keep you apprised of his condition."

When Daria left the surgical suite, the sun was already starting to set. Almost five hours had passed and it seemed like only a few minutes. It was a nice change of pace to be able to take your time and really do a job right. Usually you had to duck bullets and bomb fragments to work on someone in the field. And you only had about ten or so minutes to stabilize them for evacuation before you had to move again.

Emily was going over data with Davies that had been sent back from the site. They both looked at Daria who, in her groggy state, hadn't removed her blood-soaked gown and gloves. "He's going to make it", she said as she sat on the tailgate of the car. "He'll need a lot of reconstructive surgery to make him have a face again, or even talk for that matter, but he'll live."

"I ordered all excavation to stop and an immediate evacuation from all sites", Emily stated. "Let's get you home and we'll all come back when it's light again." She and Davies began to load equipment. Daria realized her gown and gloves were still on and went back into the suite to dispose of them. When she returned, the car was loaded up and already pointed towards home.

She climbed aboard. "They got his leg almost all the way back on and his head wound is stabilized. They're going to finish the operation out here and then take him back. I figure if we've been here for this long and nothing else has happened, nothing else probably will. It's safer to move him after he is completely stable. Maybe four or five more hours."

"Sounds good to me," Emily said as she started the car towards home. "I hope when he wakes up that he'll have some good info for us." Emily wasn't the highest-ranking officer by far on this mission but she had gotten to be quite an authority figure around the site. Daria figured that it was her expertise and the fact that she seemed to take command when no one else would. Of course, it only took about two seconds of other people's indecision for her to take over, but hey, "you snooze, you lose."

Although not much older than Emily and never being very maternal herself, Daria almost wished now that she and Mike had had children of their own. Emily was just the type of woman that she would've wanted her own daughter to grow up to be.

That thought faded into a dream of her and Mike standing in the doorway of a small house, looking out over a green meadow, with children playing. Then suddenly a huge explosion engulfed the meadow and her children disappeared in a flash. She began running towards where they stood just seconds ago, when she turned just in time to see the house explode as a training fighter crashed into it, sending Mike into oblivion.

She awoke to find Davies half carrying her to her quarters. She awoke fully and with a start, looked wildly around for the children she never had and the husband she no longer had.

"You all right? You're so tired that your body just kinda walked when I urged it to but you never really woke up. So I thought that I'd get you to your bunk without completely waking you up if I didn't have to." Davies had relinquished his hold on her shoulder and Daria stood on her own accord, more or less.

"Thanks. But I can make it the rest of the way. If," she didn't even know his name, "if that guy wakes up, let me know, even if I'm asleep, OK?"

"No problem, Doc. Get some sleep and if you need anything, let me know." He tapped his comlink even though Daria didn't need reminding. Although it wasn't permitted, many marines adjusted their comlinks to have an illegal frequency that allowed them to talk to others who had similarly adjusted theirs. Usually friends did this so they could always be in communications with specific people and no one else could hear their conversation.

Daria, Davies, and Mike had a secret frequency for themselves that now only two of them shared. When the command post issued orders, the comlink automatically detected the frequency and shifted itself to the proper channel. So they were never in danger of missing orders. But if all hell broke loose and the field command structure went to shit, the three friends could find each other more easily by cutting out all the garbled screams of other soldiers, and get themselves out of the fire.

That's why it was a court-martial offense to rig your comlink; they didn't want marines to do an "every man for yourself" operation. But with the touch of a button, the secret channel would automatically short-circuit itself and no evidence would be found. It had come in handy more than once and Daria would risk the court-martial rather than give it up.

Morning came and never bothered to let Daria know it had arrived. She awoke to her room buzzer instead of the sun and pushed a button on her nightstand to open the hatch. Emily and Davies stood there with a tray full of food and a glass of orange juice to boot. Not just a glass, but a huge glass. That was a week's worth of OJ rations for two people.

"Hey, where'd you get all that juice? You guys better not have used up your rations on me", she said groggily as she got out of bed.

Emily blushed and Daria remembered that she was naked. Not that she had forgotten, but there wasn't much modesty in the real Marine Corps.

Davies didn't even think twice about it and walked to hand Daria the tray. "No, the doctors put together their rations for today to thank you for the great work you did.

They said that if you didn't take it, they would feed it to you by IV."

She took the tray and set it down on her bed but decided to shower and dress before she ate. She could tell that Emily wouldn't be able to get comfortable until she wasn't showing in all her glory. Of course, it would probably take another marine to appreciate "all her glory" considering it was laden with scars and a roughness that only a marine could love.

Davies always kidded Mike about how he would "take care" of Daria if anything happened to him. Mike always said that he would reach out from his grave and rip Davies' dick off if he even got it near his wife.

But Davies was a marine and did consider Daria's scarred flesh to be absolutely full of glory. In fact, although Emily was as beautiful as any woman he had ever seen, she didn't hold a candle to the one who was now taking a shower. He hated himself for even feeling that way.

"Any news from the site?" she called from the shower.

"The teams arrived at the rim about an hour ago", Emily began, still a little flustered from the sound of her voice. "The data from last night and today suggests that the canyon was fabricated by someone and the blast originated from two kilometers below the surface. By the time we get out there, they will have performed enough of a scan that we will be able to descend into the hole without fear of deadly gasses or radiation. None have been found yet but I don't want to take any chances."

"You, the lieutenant and I, along with a recon team will rappel into the hole to scout the bottom. If the site is suitable, we'll set up a hoist system for the surveying teams." He stole a piece of Daria's bacon and continued, "Your patient hasn't woken up yet so we haven't got any more information. But they say he'll be just fine with the exception of his missing leg and facial reconstruction." He shoved the second piece of bacon he stole into his mouth as Daria rounded the corner.

"Why don't you ever just eat more instead of always taking my food?" Turning to Emily, she said, "I bet he drank most of the orange juice on the way and then filled the glass with water."

Emily wasn't too surprised how well Daria knew her friend, but it was funny how she knew exactly what Davies had suggested. "I wouldn't let him. He said that you would never even know because the stuff is so watered down anyway. Big bully is what he is."

With a sheepish grin that was out of place on a man so big, Davies swallowed the rest of his stolen goods and wiped the greasy evidence from his mouth with the back of his hand. "I'm a growing boy! I need my nutrition. You want me to starve or something? They should give out rations by size and not standardize it for everyone."

"If they did that, your size would get bigger than what they'd have rations for. Besides, being planetside for so long, you've put on a few. You need to get with Emily and me sometime for a workout." Daria finished her breakfast with the ferocity of a Grizzly bear and got geared up for the survey. Not knowing what they'd encounter, she loaded up everything she could think of.

She decided on a small med pack for this trip. If yesterday was any indication of what they might find today, she'd only need stuff for small scrapes or cuts. If anything else happened, being at ground zero would leave nothing behind for her to patch up. So why take the extra weight?

"We have a little something for you", Daria said to their CO. "It's not exactly legal, but if you won't tell, neither will we." She handed Emily a comlink.

"What's not legal about this?" Being part of the scientific corps, Emily didn't know about the outlawed links.

"It's a special link that has a secret frequency that only you, Daria, and I can listen to." Davies showed her the termination button that would destroy the outlaw channel in case of a surprise inspection. He then explained why they used it.

"Thanks, guys." That's all she could think to say. For these two marines to trust her like that was more than anyone ever had in her life. Except for her brother. He would be proud of her to know what she had done with her career.

With that, the three friends left the barracks and headed towards the site.

Wilks

NAME: WILKS
SPECIES: HUMAN
MOS: INFANTRY
RANK: STAFF SERGEANT
AGE: 36 - EARTH STANDARD
SEX: MALE
HEIGHT: 6'00"
WEIGHT: 220 POUNDS

Mr. Wilks looked at the clock; only another two minutes had passed. Damn. He tried so very hard not to be a clock-watcher, especially as it went against everything he told himself he would never be. But standing there, watching his students browse the Net, message one another, doodle, and even blatantly sleep, it was difficult for Wilks to be the teacher he always dreamed of being.

Mr. Wilks had an affinity for history and advanced mathematics with a personal interest in military history. He had always wanted to be a teacher, had always wanted to be better than the horrible clock-watching teachers he had had while growing up in an impoverished Coalition colony. The teachers showed up for their paycheck and to make sure no one was killed in class—not always successful on the second part—and that was about it.

Mr. Wilks understood why they were that way: the kids were horrible and had no desire to be there. The colony had taken steps to ensure that there were no truancy issues by placing a GPS bracelet on all of the students. If the bracelet wasn't on the school grounds when it was supposed to be, the police would locate the truant child and return them to school. So although this made sure that every kid was at school every day, it just increased the number of problems that the teachers had to deal with. If the kids who didn't want to be there weren't, then the teachers would have had more time to work with the students who did want to be there.

Mr. Wilks always thought that even though the teachers were dealt a bad hand, they weren't playing it as best they could. They didn't even try to reach the kids with issues or create a teaching plan that would give the ones with interest the education they deserved. As a student, Mr. Wilks had approached his teachers many times with ideas to make the classroom more fun and interesting even to the most hardened juvenile criminals some of the classes contained. None of his teachers ever implemented any of his ideas; some wouldn't even listen to him.

The defining moment of Mr. Wilks' education was when one of his most-hated teachers replied to his suggestions with, "Look, kid, if you think you can do better, then get your own classroom. Until then, leave me the fuck alone and go back to your desk."

So Mr. Wilks did just that. He approached the principal and asked about having a classroom after school for one to two hours a day for a study club that he was putting together. He was extremely surprised when the principal handed him a key and told him that room 203 was empty and the study group could use it as long as he promised not to burn it down or kill anyone in it. And on a side note, the room was empty because a teacher was actually killed in it and they never cleaned it up after the police were done investigating, so yeah, you might want to bring some bleach and water with you when you go there.

Wilks spent the next two weeks cleaning up the room and making it presentable. He wanted to make it a place that his fellow students would want to voluntarily come to. A place to learn, to teach, to get ahead and get out of the colony. When it was done, Wilks went to eight other students that he knew were like him, wanting more but not knowing how or where to get it. He took them all to the room and showed them what he had done with it.

Wilks wasn't sure whether the principal knew it or not, but the key he had handed over was a master key for the whole school, not just a key for his study room. Wilks wanted to learn, not steal, so he put the key to good use. He found an interactive learning board that wasn't being used, along with a lot of other teaching equipment that was long forgotten. The found equipment, together with teaching aids and books, were put into the classroom.

When his handpicked study partners showed up, they were amazed and excited at what they saw. This is what a real classroom should look like! It was clean and stocked with actual supplies. There were only a few individual desks; the rest of the workspaces were set up for group work at large round tables, each with its own supplies. There were also individual study stations made up of discarded couch cushions, a couple of which had some questionable stains on them.

Wilks talked with his new friends and told them of his vision. This place was where they would come and study together, but more important, teach one another. They each had their own educational strengths, some overlapping, and he wanted them to take turns putting on classes for each other. Everyone loved the idea and was immediately on board. Wilks hoped that in time other students would hear about what they were doing and would want to join. Not everyone would be a teacher of course, but the group would be open to anyone who wanted to learn.

It only took two weeks before their first ad hoc student showed up. At first, Wilks and his colleagues were a bit nervous when the student walked in the door. She was one of the scariest kids at the school. Rumors of her exploits, both those confirmed and those hopefully not even remotely true, preceded her at every public school in the colony. Cynthia Macavoy, with her dirty blonde hair, chubby frame, and angry eyes, stood in the doorway, waiting for someone to say something.

Wilks stepped forward first. "Hi." He tried to be as cheery as possible. "Do you want to come in?"

Cynthia looked at Wilks. "Don't laugh at me. If any of you laugh at me, I'll kill you." They were all pretty sure she meant it. "And your parents, too." Yeah, she meant it.

Wilks gave her a quick tour and explained what they were doing and what their goals were. Cynthia was completely honest with the group and told them that she was tired of being dumb. She didn't mind so much that she was already on a criminal path; she just didn't want to be dumb.

Wilks assured her that if she was aware of how much her education lacked, she simply couldn't be dumb. A dumb person would never realize that they needed help. Cynthia seemed to like this line of thinking because everyone else she had ever known had called her dumb or some variant of the word, sometimes a much worse variant. Cynthia settled in very quickly and only had a few minor emotional incidents for the next many years that she was a part of the group.

One student quickly became ten; then twenty and then too many for the group to take care of in a single space. Teaching and study days had to be rationed like bread to the starving masses. Wilks eventually used his master key to take over a few more unused spaces in the school. He also found that they could use the school after hours thanks to the magical key he had been handed without so much as a second thought. This allowed their endeavor to flourish even more with the run of the entire school at night. With the use of the subject-specific classrooms, they could schedule classes and study sessions even better.

Cynthia even started teaching a class of her own, basic Coalition penal code. She had actually absorbed a wealth of knowledge in all of her goings-on with the local law enforcement. Now that she was learning how to better articulate herself and put together a study plan, her elective study group was becoming quite popular. Cynthia went on to graduate from an Ivy League school and came back to the same colony to practice juvenile criminal defense.

By the end of the year, Wilks and his original study group were basically running their own school at night. Even a few parents present were taught to read and write. When he looked back on his fifth-grade year, Wilks couldn't help but be impressed with himself and the other eleven-year-olds he worked with.

The school's overall GPA was just about eleven times what it had been when they started. The principal knew it was because of Wilks' study group but never said anything about it. He also knew they were using the master key well beyond its original intent and purposes, but he was fine with that, too. Why would he say anything when he basically now had an army of non-paid teachers who were making his school look better than any of the other public schools? Not to mention the fact that "new" equipment had shown up all over the school. Most likely thanks to the master key and the ingenuity of the young criminal minds working together to make their new learning obsession as grand as it possibly could be.

By the time Wilks graduated from high school, he and his friends had had more success stories than probably all of his teachers combined, times five, to a modest power of ten. Okay, maybe a power of two, but still pretty damned good.

After college, Mr. Wilks began working at a public school, teaching history and helping to coach track after school. Mr. Wilks hadn't returned to his own colony as Cynthia had; he wanted to help the less fortunate but he also wanted to see new places so he moved around for the first five years, trying new things. He even tried substituting at a fairly wealthy private school and found that some of the students were even harder to reach than the young criminals he was used to working with.

During his fifth year of being a teacher, he was living on a Coalition planet near the Shirka home world. He met a woman, maybe even *the* woman. Mr. Wilks settled down at last and got a full-time job teaching at one of the poorest-rated public schools in the city. He was going to make a difference. He was going to re-create his childhood school, but it would be better this time now that he had the full support of the school and he was an actual adult.

Three years later, he was watching the clock and getting annoyed at his own voice. Maybe it was because he was an adult and the kids didn't want to listen to an adult regardless of who they were. Maybe he had possessed a certain something as a child that he no longer possessed. Maybe his earlier successes were actually more because of his adolescent colleagues than because of him. Whatever the reason, Mr. Wilks was utterly beat down after just eight years of teaching.

The clock struck the top of the hour and the lights dimmed twice to indicate the class was over. An almost audible sigh of relief escaped from everyone who was still actually conscious in the classroom. As Mr. Wilks walked out of the room, he didn't even take the time to wake the two students who were still sleeping. They'd figure it out soon enough when the janitor droid came in and poked them and ordered them to leave the school grounds.

Mr. Wilks was now on the track field, the best part of his day. At least here, most of the kids wanted to be participating in the activities. Some were there due to the pressures of their parents and some were court-mandated to take extra-curricular classes to help them learn the socialization skills they so obviously lacked.

Mr. Wilks ran a 5K to warm up and then went through each of the events in a decathlon. He wasn't out for time today, just a good workout, so he did a fairly light pace and easy numbers on all of the events. He had five students working out with him, two who were actual competition when they were pushing each other. After the workout, they all put some time into the pole vault and worked on some of the issues the team had been having with their techniques.

Mr. Wilks then went home and found all that was left of his girlfriend Mary was a note. Not even a very long note. In fact, the note was fairly atrocious in its spelling and grammatical errors. That gave Mr. Wilks some solace, to know that he could always look back on the note and see that she wasn't really that great of a catch to begin with. Its contents didn't matter so much as the sentiment, which was along the lines of "It's not me. It's you, it's totally you. Seriously, how could you not know it was you? We both know it wasn't me, not in a million years could it ever have been me. So we're clear, right? All you, buddy."

Mr. Wilks sat on his couch and opened a beer. He stared at a still-dark screen for twenty minutes before he realized he hadn't even turned the television on. That issue was easily solved as he turned on the Coalition military channel. The screen came to life and Mr. Wilks found himself in the middle of a documentary series about the first twenty years of military space exploration. In the back of his head, he heard Mary's voice: "The military channel again? What a surprise. You see, totally not me."

The first twenty years of military space exploration was filled with first contacts, first battles with other species, so many firsts that were scary and wonderful all.

Ten hours later, the series marathon was over and Mr. Wilks looked at the clock, this time not waiting for his day to be over but dreading his day having to start. She was right: it was him—it was always him. With the documentary still fresh in his mind, he was able to go to work with a little spring in his step, thinking about the wonderful history he had just watched. The documentary would help him get through the day, as he imagined himself in the place of the brave warriors who had ventured out into the cosmos so many centuries before.

Mr. Wilks kept going over his personal mantra, "The day will end. Nothing they do can ever make the day longer. It will end, no matter what." And while it wasn't a merciless end, it did in fact end and Mr. Wilks headed out to the track for the only thing that brought him joy anymore.

As he approached the track, he saw there was a small contingent of military personnel near the field. That was odd. He had seen small contingents of cops on campus before, but that was to arrest one of the wayward students. Could any of the students have done something so bad that the military needed to show up?

Mr. Wilks approached the group and walked up to one of the soldiers. "Excuse me. What's going on here, Gunnery Sergeant?"

The gunny looked at Mr. Wilks. "Career day. Prior service?"

Mr. Wilks looked a little embarrassed, "No, Gunny, I'm just a big military history buff. So why are you out here at the field?"

"I'm with the special detailing recruiting office. We look for students who might be more suited for Special Forces and similar assignments. Out here on the field is where we tend to find those sorts of kids." The gunny waved his hand towards the athletes who were warming up. "Do you think any of these kids might be interested?"

Mr. Wilks thought for a second. "Maybe a couple. I'll put them through a bit of a warm-up and let you take a look at them in action."

Mr. Wilks called in his group of athletes and told them that they were going to be putting in a little bit more of an effort today but he didn't tell them why. They went through the 5K warm-up and then the obstacle course. Mr. Wilks was pushing hard today; a few of the students dropped out, along the way calling him crazy. Then they went on to the decathlon again, but still pushing it pretty hard.

When they got done, the gunny and two of his fellow marines walked over. "Very impressive. How would all three of you like to be Force Recon Marines?"

Mr. Wilks looked around; there were only two students left at the end of the workout. "Three? Which other student are you talking about?"

"For a smart guy, you're pretty dumb." The gunny handed the three athletes his business card. "You two will have to graduate first, but you, sir," now talking directly to Mr. Wilks, "can sign up today if you'd like. In fact, I'm sure with your education, you can probably apply to Officer Candidate School."

"I don't want to be an officer. I want to be in the field more." Mr. Wilks was absently looking at the business card.

"Sounds like you already made up your mind. We can go to my office and fill out the paperwork right now. I can probably get you started as a corporal after boot camp, given your college education. Maybe even get you in to a sergeant fast-track program."

Mr. Wilks was amazed as the words came from his mouth, almost without permission from his conscious self, "Can you guarantee me a spot in Force Recon?"

"No", the gunny said flatly. "But I can absolutely promise you a shot at trying out for it. You won't have any problem getting in to training, I'm sure of that. Staying in and graduating, that's your problem."

"Let's go." Mr. Wilks looked back at his athletes. "I'm sorry, but I can't stay here any longer. It's not you, kids, it's me."

One of his favorite students, Matt Snyder, stepped up. "We know, Mr. Wilks. You should go. You deserve better." Matt flicked the corner of the business card in his hand. "I'll look you up when I get there."

"You better." Wilks walked away to start his new life.

Chapter 9
Dig Site One – A Reunion of Sorts

When they reached the hole, Emily used her new link to call the Recon team to her air car. The twelve marines sauntered over with more ego than she felt would fit down that immense crater. "Staff Sergeant Wilks and Recon fifth platoon reporting as ordered, ma'am!" he said with a stiff salute and a hint, no more than a hint, of sarcasm in his voice.

"Wilks, I'm Lieutenant Riley and this is Sergeant Davies and Doc." She thumbed in Daria's direction, whose back was still to the group. "Doc is my second-in-command and you follow her orders. Is that understood?"

Emily was becoming more accustomed to a rank structure, mostly because Daria almost forced her to. When they were alone, they were on a first-name basis but if anyone came within earshot, Daria either spoke in a way that allowed her not to use names or said ma'am instead. And at this moment, Emily knew that this arrogant sergeant needed to know his place rather than her looking too soft in his hardened eyes.

"Ma'am, with all due respect, she's a corpsman and they don't ever hold a command position unless it's an emergency and can't be avoided." There were some murmurs of agreement from his men. Emily was about to respond when Daria walked up to the sergeant.

She had recognized his voice and when she turned around, she noticed a scar on his right cheek that looked as though it had come from say, a beer bottle. She knew who he was and could tell that he hoped that she didn't. "How's your dick, sergeant? Is it still dry? Would you like me to take another look at it for you?"

Emily didn't quite understand what this transaction was all about when Davies said to her, "They're old drinking buddies. I don't think Wilks will have a problem with the command structure you've presented him with. Will ya, Wilks?"

"No, no problem. Doc's in charge, guys, listen to her as you would me. Got it?" Acceptance was given, if not quietly. Wilks gave Daria a nod of approval and in part, an apology.

Drunk or not, he knew that he was wrong that night in the bar and pretty much deserved what he had gotten. Although, he wished that it hadn't come from a woman. Based on that incident, he could respect her command with the knowledge of her abilities that only he and two of his buddies in the group knew of.

He looked at his two drinking buddies and noticed that they were rubbing their old wounds that had been inflicted by Daria so many months before. They also nodded their approval.

Daria nodded back with an implied look that said, "Don't worry, I won't tell them. But you know, and I know, and that's enough." She didn't much like Emily's decision either. Corpsman didn't take command because they needed to be free of all responsibilities when the need arose to take care of wounded. They had to be able to focus on the one goal of keeping people alive.

But then again, she remembered the day before once more. If the shit hit the fan, there wouldn't be anyone left to put together. So why not be in charge? It would be a nice change.

The first team of six Force Recon soldiers placed their piston loaded piton devices to the ground two meters back from the edge of the hole. In unison, they triggered the devices, which shot a twenty-centimeter long piton spike into the hard rock. Then they attached a two hundred meter static line to each anchor and walked to the edge and threw the line out twenty-five meters, allowing it to drop to its full length along the crater's wall.

The precision in which they operated gave Daria confidence in the team. She knew she had to rethink her underlying feelings about their sergeant. He may be a bad drunk but he sure knew how to train and command his troops.

The advance team carried twenty pitons each, along with extra rope and hanging devices. They would descend one hundred and fifty meters and then set up a breaking station at which point they, and the teams that followed, could switch to the next line. This would continue until they reached the bottom of the hole.

The six members turned to one another to recheck their descent gear and with that complete, casually walked to the edge and continued walking straight down. An advantage of descending in a forward position was that you could have your weapon drawn and engage any target that came from below. Not that anyone thought there were any targets in the hole to engage, but better safe than sorry.

"Team one is at one hundred and fifty meters", the lead corporal reported. "Breaking pitons and slings are set. Secondary line set. Team one is on secondary line. Team two, proceed with descent on line one."

"Team two copies", Daria said, motioning to Wilks and Davies. Wilks picked out three more of his unit to join team two. One of them was a Trizite. His name was, well, unpronounceable. Almost every non-human language was impossible for a human to speak properly without years of formal training. As a result, most soldiers from other races got nicknames or human names that came somewhat close to sounding like their given ones.

This Trizite was called "Scan." He was empathic, which meant that he could read emotions of the people around him. Full-blown telepaths were almost unheard of. Empaths seemed to be common in many aquatic-based species throughout the Coalition.

Several races that humans encountered did not use sound-produced speech as much as humans did. Much more posturing and visual cues were used for communications. Most other species could usually tell the exact emotional make-up of a human just by watching them for a minute or two. They said that human emotions were too plain and stood out like a sore thumb. Scan was an actual empath, so he could tell your emotions just by being within a certain physical range of a subject. This range varied depending on the species he was scanning and how strong their mental output was.

Daria was glad to have him along because he would be able to act like an early warning device if anything was still alive down there. A lot of empaths could detect presence of life even before a scanner could.

Scan was short, even by human standards, standing at one point six meters tall. He had a much denser molecular structure that brought him to an even two hundred pounds. He was almost as thin as Daria but his densely packed muscle made him about five times as strong.

Small spikes surrounded both his eyes. Although they looked incredibly hard and jagged, they were very soft if touched. Of course, if you touched them, that meant you were about to mate with the owner of the spikes. It was quite an erogenous zone for the Trizites, which also made an easy target during a bar fight. A black eye for them would ball them up as though you had hit a human right in the nuts with a sledgehammer.

Scan wore clear goggles that protected his spikes from any unwanted contact. His green skin was smooth and adapted for swimming as eighty percent of his home planet was water. Some Trizite soldiers' webbing on both hands were surgically reduced so they could use a variety of human weapons with greater ease. In Daria's short glimpse of Scan's hands, she noticed his webbing looked like it had been traumatically removed. There was a lot of scar tissue that wouldn't be present if it had been done correctly.

"Team two, attach rigging and prepare for descent", Daria continued. She felt odd giving orders, especially because team one performed their task without saying a single word to one another. She guessed that had the Recon team been completing this mission alone, no words would have been spoken at all. "Team two, descend."

With that, all six soldiers walked over the edge with weapons and scanners drawn. The outer two men had weapons and the inner four used handheld scanners to map the hole and to keep an eye on the lead team. When team one reached three hundred meters, they repeated the drill and set up the third line. After they switched to the third line, team two switched to the second line and called for team three to begin their descent.

"Team three, attach rigging and prepare for descent", Emily said, hoping she got it right. The remaining two Force Recon soldiers saddled up and doubled-checked Emily's rigging. "Team three, descend." The last team all had weapons drawn upon descent. If anything happened, team one and team three would protect team two, who didn't have immediate access to their weapons. They also had equipment stowed on the three empty lines for the descent into the hole. The trading off of descent lines continued until they all reached the bottom, two kilometers down.

Once on the ground, six soldiers set up a perimeter defense while supplies were lowered and put into position.

The hole was close to one kilometer across. Until they had all the supplies down and they performed a preliminary search, they wouldn't know whether they descended into just an empty hole or something else entirely. The smoothness of the rock had reflected almost all scanning attempts. No one was sure of what they would find once on the bottom.

Once the main scanning equipment was unloaded, Daria called Emily and Wilks over to her. "We'll separate into three, five-man squads. El-tee will take her team through the center of the hole, Wilks and I will take our teams around the two edges, and we'll all meet up directly on the other side."

Daria knew that she had to let the sergeant save some face in front of his men, so this she said a little louder for everyone to hear, "Wilks, you know your men. Please put together three teams in whatever way you feel is the best deployment of personnel."

"Aye, aye, Doc", he said with a thin smile of gratitude. "Scan, you go with Doc and Davies on team one. Take Bloom and Fang with you." Bloom was already holding a scanning device while Fang was armed to the teeth with weaponry. As a Shirka, he could hold almost as much inventory as two human soldiers. "Hood, Martinez, Snyder, and Patz, go with the el-tee on team two. You other slugs are with me, team three."

Daria recognized Hood and Martinez as being the other two marines who were with Wilks that night on Clandestine. "Everyone will have their comlinks on an open channel so we don't lose track of anyone. Team one will take the perimeter to the right and team three will circle to the left."

"Team two," Emily began, "will wait at the far end for everyone to catch up. If the need arises, be careful of what you shoot at. We still don't know exactly what happened here. If anything seems unusual, anything at all, call it in to the rest of the teams."

"You mean something like a two-kilometer deep hole that appeared out of nowhere?" Fang grunted. A Shirka's nature always challenged those around him, especially those in authority.

"Yeah, or maybe even a Shirka with a good sense of humor. Of course I don't think that's possible, but it would be more unusual than this hole." Fang gave Emily a slight nod and a toothy grin; it was his way of showing respect. "Move out, marines."

Daria was surprised with the depth and tone of Emily's voice but inwardly smiled at her friend, who was really starting to cut her teeth on this planet.

Chapter 10
Deeper Into Unknown Space aboard the *Vanguard*

Seth wandered into the mess hall and picked up a tray from the food line. He saw Beast sitting with a couple of other trainees and walked towards their table. Seth mused silently to himself about the word "trainee". He was the only one in the group without actual combat experience; everyone else was a very seasoned veteran. The instructors were really just mentors, soldiers with the most combat and special operations deployments. They led the training sessions and worked with the trainees in a one-on-one fashion to help them reach their full potential.

Seth had become accustomed to eating his meals with Surgeon but he was nowhere to be seen. In fact, Seth thought, none of the instructors were anywhere in the room. Odd. He also found it strange that for the first time in nine months, the ship had dropped out of warp.

"Where's Joker?" Seth asked Beast.

"As far as I know, I'm not his babysitter", Beast almost growled. "This is the first time we've been able to eat without watching our backs for instructors. Take advantage of it, newbie."

That's exactly what worried Seth. All of the trainees were assembled in the mess hall without a single instructor around. Usually the training was on a schedule set by the instructors of the fifteen teams. This meant that there had never been a time before when every single student was eating a meal at the same time. People would struggle in as their training evolutions ended and then leave to their next evolution.

"Doesn't that seem odd to you?" Seth persisted. "Why are we all here together for the first time without a single instructor? The tables are arranged slightly different from normal to allow better access through the port hatch but less access through the starboard hatch." Or maybe a slower escape, Seth thought.

Beast looked up for the first time. "You are right." The warriors' eyes locked in realization of what was about to happen. They both whispered, "Ambush."

"If they're watching us right now, we shouldn't tip our hand. The question is, should we retreat into the ship now and take up defensive positioning somewhere more fortified? Or should we alert everyone else and be prepared to fight here?"

Beast continued to eat his leg of something, and gestured Seth to start on his meal. He wanted their conversation to look natural to any eyes that might be prying into the mess hall. "Hey everyone! This rookie is going to tell us that story the general was talking about. Get your asses over here." His tone was jovial but no one refused his request to come and listen to a story. Storytelling was a time-honored custom to Shirkas. It was a warrior's bond with others when he shared a story of conquest and victory.

Seth took his cue. "Well, first off there was an AMBUSH set up for my platoon. We had to get out of that MESS as quickly as possible." He hoped that his eyes were telling the true story and the hidden meanings in his words were clear. He made eye contact with several of those nearest him and received a slight nod that seemed to say they understood. He felt as though there wasn't much time left. "We were pinned down so I gave orders to leave on my MARK."

Seth placed both his hands on the underside of the table, following Beast's lead. "Mark!" Seth tried not to yell his command. With that, Beast and Seth jumped out of their seat and flipped the table on its side, giving them some cover from the port hatch way. All of the other soldiers began to exit through the starboard hatch when the first one went down from a stun gun in the starboard entrance way.

"Port hatch now!" Beast ordered as he turned over the nearest table in the opposite direction of the first. The swift-acting students jumped the newest obstacle and headed for the hatch. The instructors were laying down a covering fire from the starboard hatch and had already caught two students with their stunners.

Thirteen left, Seth thought. Possibly enough to take the fifteen instructors somewhere on this ship. He doubted that all fifteen would have been posted at a single hatch but he took the lead anyway, knowing that he'd be the first to run into problems.

It was clever of them to set up the mess hall that way. It made it seem that the ambush would come from one side and everyone would herd themselves right into the trap. They must have figured that at least one disciple would think it odd that no instructors were around and that same person might realize that the mess hall had been altered slightly. They had played right into the instructors' hands. It was something that Surgeon would think of and made Seth believe that their chance of successfully beating their mentors had just dropped about twenty-five percent.

Beast had already split the students up into five teams of two and one team of three. He and Seth were with Blanch, heading towards the weapons locker. "All right, the weapons locker is up one deck and around that corridor. We'll use the maintenance tubes to get to the locker and scope out the site. Once we know it's secure, we'll make a plan of attack." Beast had a hungry look in his eye. This was his chance to prove himself to his instructor.

"Wait," Seth interjected, "I don't think that's a good idea. Joker will know that you will be the first to try for the weapons locker. It's in your nature. He knows how you think by now and I'm sure that he's the one who will have set up security for it."

This made sense to Beast. "What do you suggest, Cadet? Should we just walk up and say 'please'?"

Shirka sarcasm, there just seemed to be no way around it. "Holobay four is across from the weapons locker. We can get to it from the deck below us by the water main. That room used to hold a water tank for combat simulations. The tank isn't there anymore but the fill tubes for the water are. They're big enough for us to get through. I found them by accident while training one day."

The trio headed for the lift shaft at the end of the hall and pried its doors open. If they didn't trigger the lift, then no one should know where they were. Luckily the lift was several decks above them so they would be able to climb down to the next level without a problem. Just as long as no one came down the lift. As they climbed down to the next level and began to pry the doors, Seth wondered aloud to Beast, "How come you didn't hear them coming?"

Beast bared his teeth at no one in particular. "I don't know." At the age of fourteen, Beast was too young to already have sensory deprivation. What trick had the instructors used on him? It would have to be answered later. The door was open and they were on the move.

Rounding a corner, they came to the water main control room. The door was locked. "No problem." Seth stepped up and went to work. After several small shocks, they were in. "Make sure that the cutoff valve is off so we don't drown in there", Seth said to Blanch.

Blanch went to the console, checked the readout and then went to the valve and manually checked its position. "We're all set here. Which tube do we enter?"

Seth walked to a large pipe and tried to orient himself to the deck above. "This one, I think." He climbed up on top and opened an inspection hatch. It would be tight, especially for Beast, but it would work. As the other two soldiers stepped up to the hatch, Beast took the lead.

"I'll go first", Beast said without giving time for discussion as he started into the hatch.

"Wait a minute", Seth called, but it was too late. So he started in after Beast with Blanch close in tow. Once they got into the holobay, Seth approached Beast. "I told you to wait." A stare as penetrating as lasers cut through Seth. "There's something on your lapel", he said, gesturing to Beast's back. Beast turned to let Seth get at it.

"That's a sonic disrupter", Beast said with anger. "It is used by my people to impair young warriors during the hunt so they will use their other senses. It is a training device." He placed it in his palm and drove his fist into his open hand, shattering the device. "Joker!" was all he could say through his anger and respect for the man. "Now what?"

"Blanch, how are you at being a decoy?" Seth asked their so-far silent partner.

Blanch crossed the hallway and began to work on the electronic lock of the armory. He had his comlink set to the transport ship frequency in hopes that it wouldn't be a monitored channel. If it was, then this display was all for naught. In his head, he heard Beast say, "There are two contacts coming from your right. Approximately ten meters out." With the sonic disrupter removed, Beast could again use his hearing to its fullest capacity. "Start on my mark. Three, two, one, mark."

Blanch purposely touched a low-voltage wire and jumped back with the surge of the shock. He tapped his comlink. "This is three. I can't get the door. I'm returning to your position." He got up and began to walk back towards holobay four. He looked over his shoulder several times and then sped up his pace.

The instructors knew he was on to them, although they didn't know how. Time to get their quarry. The chase was on. Only fifteen meters to the holobay and Blanch was losing ground. Joker was fast.

Once inside the holobay, Blanch ran towards the rear of the room. A sudden flash of caution went through Joker's mind. There was nowhere to go and yet Blanch was running as though there was.

Too late. He saw Blanch leap into the air and almost simultaneously the artificial gravity in the simulation room was cut off. Blanch had used his momentum to reach a strut at the corner of the room and now shimmied towards the command booth.

Joker and the other instructor were caught off guard so when the gravity was cut, their forward momentum slammed them into the far wall that they were running toward. Joker heard a crack as his face hit the wall.

Apparently so did Seth because his voice came over the PA system. "Now we're even."

The two instructors, suspended in air with blood floating in droplets all around them, positioned themselves for a leap at the command console. Realizing their second mistake as they were already five meters off the ground, Seth turned the artificial gravity back on.

Luckily he was in a generous mood and only had it set at half a G so the fall wasn't too hard. Nonetheless, it hurt badly to hit the deck. Once the two instructors were down, Seth turned the gravity to six Gs, which effectively pinned the instructors to the ground with their own weight.

"All right, you got us. Good job. Now let us up", Joker said through gritted teeth.

"OK, and I'll just ask Beast to be polite for a change. What do you think the chances of that are?" Seth said as he put an encrypted code lock on the controls so he would be the only one who was able to release his prisoners.

With that, the three students used the secondary access way from the control booth and entered the hallway.

Without further molestation, they reached the armory and entered using an instructor code that Beast had stolen with his acute hearing.

He could detect the tone differences in the keypads when they were pressed. After hearing Joker key in the code several times, he knew what it was.

Unfortunately, Joker had set a trap inside the door and an electrical stun charge went off, knocking down Beast and Blanch. Beast was only stunned while Blanch's human frame was knocked completely unconscious. Down to two with no idea of how anyone else was doing. This seemed like deja vu for Seth.

"Now what?" Seth muttered.

"We get weapons," said the groggy Shirka, "then go shoot all the instructors." He spoke as though Seth had asked a stupid question.

"Do we have an objective other than just to stay alive?" He wondered whether it was that simple, as ironic as that sounded to even himself. But Seth always thought on a much grander scale. "Let's take over the ship."

"I like your thinking, Cadet." Beast laid a paw on Seth's shoulder that just about knocked him down. "Take a close quarters assault rifle and as many stun grenades as you can. We're headed for the bridge." He let out a battle howl that nearly shook Seth.

Once armed, they decided to head directly towards the bridge. Seth figured Surgeon would be counting on his assault, so he briefed Beast on Surgeon's methods while they headed for their objective.

Chapter 11
Dig Site One

After walking a while, Daria turned to Scan. "Where's your corpsman? Every Recon team has its own."

"Ours was killed on our last scouting mission. Accident."

"What happened? Where were you?" Daria's curiosity always got the best of her.

"Sorry, Doc, that's classified. But it was just dumb luck. No way for a soldier to die", he said with mournful eyes. His spikes pointed inward, which was the Trizite equivalent of crying.

Daria had found that many other races were less apt to hide their emotions than humans were. Crying was considered by many races to be a form of respect towards those being grieved for. It must be nice to not have to deal with so much machismo, Daria thought.

"Hold up", Bloom said as he took another couple of steps forward. "I'm detecting a metal alloy of some sort. It doesn't register as anything known, but it is definitely different than the rock around us."

"Where is it? I can't see any difference in the face of the wall." Davies was looking through his enhancement visor.

The visor could be set to thermal, infrared, motion, or a combination of the three. All snipers and special ops guys had them issued as a standard part of their gear.

"I'm trying to get an exact bearing. It's difficult, though. Most of my scans are being bounced off the wall." Bloom took another couple of steps forward and then shifted slightly to his right. He approached the wall. "Here. This is the door."

He pointed to what seemed to be a section of rock just like the rest of the wall.

"Let me take a look", Daria said, coming up beside him, and eyed the scanner. "I see it, too, but where is it?" She began to feel the wall with her hands and outlined the edges of what the scanner said was a door.

"Team two," Davies began, "we've found something, although we're not real sure what it is."

"It looks like a door made of an unknown metal, but we can't visually distinguish it from the surrounding rock", Daria continued. "The scanner says it's here but we can't confirm."

"We are at the back wall and awaiting rendezvous with team three." Emily's voice came over the link. "Stand fast and we'll meet up with you in a few. Find out whatever you can in the meantime. Out."

"Wilco", Daria replied. "Got any ideas?" She addressed the question to her team.

"We could use a hand welder on the seams to see if it opens it up", Scan said as he rifled through his pack.

"Whoa, remember yesterday? We don't know what happened or what triggered it. They could have thought the same exact thing." Davies stepped in front of Scan just in case he didn't heed the warning.

"Good point", he said as he placed the welder back in his pack.

Bloom took a geological scanner out of his pack and handed it to Fang. "Take this and perform a detailed scan of everything fifteen meters to the right of the door. I'll go fifteen meters to the left. If it is a door, the triggering mechanism wouldn't be placed too far away from it."

Fang took the scanner and began working his way out from the door. Daria faintly heard him grumbling about a warrior's job was not to scan but to fight. "I have something. Metal of unknown type, approximately…three point five meters up and one meter out from the right edge."

Daria walked to where he was scanning. "Bloom, look for an object with the same signature as the door at the same point on the other side. It should be about one-third of a meter square."

"I'm not getting anything over here", Bloom called back.

"Let's get someone up there to take a look at it", Daria said, hoping for a volunteer. Who knew what would happen when someone touched that panel.

"I got it", Bloom said, approaching from the other side. "Fang, give me a lift."

"Now I'm a fucking ladder", he said, with what Daria thought was an attempt at a joke. You could never tell with those guys.

Fang, who could almost reach the object on his own, easily lifted Bloom closer to the panel. "I don't see any difference in the wall, just like the door", Bloom called down.

"Wait. Put your hand back over the object", Davies said from behind his visor. "There. When you put your hand over it, I get a slight change in the thermal and infrared ranges on my visor. Someone give him a flare, it's a pretty low heat source compared to a welder."

Daria handed Bloom a flare and ignited it. As he placed it closer to the object, a keypad became visible. "Well, I'll be damned", Bloom whispered. "I've got a keypad of some sort here. It kind of just appeared out of nowhere and disappears when I take the flare away from it. Must be heat sensitive."

Emily and Wilks arrived with their teams and Daria gave them an updated report.

"And judging from the width and height of the door, not to mention the height of the key pad, whoever built this must have been pretty big", Daria said with a smug look. "Probably right-handed, too, considering the placement of the keypad."

"Someone has been doing their homework", Emily replied. "They must have a much higher body temperature, too, in order to activate that device."

"Actually, el-tee," Daria began, "I understand that we don't know anything about the biology of this alien species, but I really don't think that anyone could get their body temperature as hot as a phosphorous flare. I would guess that this is some sort of security measure. After a catastrophe or security lock down, the only way in would be to superheat a secret panel to reveal its location and controls."

Emily looked a little embarrassed by being so obviously wrong about her conclusions. She nonetheless continued without skipping a beat, "Has anyone tried the flare on the door?"

Bloom looked at Daria and they shrugged in unison. "Uh, we were just about to", Bloom said from his perch.

He moved the torch towards the door and sure enough, the seams showed through for the first time. "Well, I'll be", he muttered again.

"What did I tell you about that?" Wilks said to Bloom. "For a damned linguist, you sure don't ever say much original." Looking around at the non-recon faces, he felt he should explain. "Bloom always says, 'Well, I'll be.' It gets real annoying after years of hearing it. And being a linguist, I expect a little more variety of speech from him. Wouldn't you?"

"Linguist, huh?" Emily said. "Can you decipher or even guess at what the symbols are on the keypad?"

"I've been trying, ma'am. I think that five of the twenty-five keys are real and the others are just diversions. I don't know why; it's just a feeling."

"I thought I was the only empath here." Scan laughed. Trizite laughs sound like gurgling mouthwash and usually brought laughter from others, even if the joke wasn't all that great. This time it didn't.

Daria opened her medical kit and pulled out a small spray can and handed it to Bloom. "This is a cellular tissue adhesion spray. It will bind itself to tissue on the cellular level to stop bleeding and bind cuts and tears on injured skin. It will detect tissue, even dead tissue, and bind with it."

"Ah." Bloom understood. "This panel was protected by the rock when the explosion occurred so any cellular tissue left from the last user might still be on the keys. When I spray this on it, it will bind with the leftover cells and show us which keys are used for the door."

"Right. Just about every species leaves some cellular residue on an object when they touch it. We're always shedding cells, every second of every day. I just hope that whoever made this did too."

Bloom sprayed the mist onto the keys and moments later the binding action began and a small film built up on ten of the keys. "So I was off by five", Bloom defended himself. "Question now is, what order are these ten pressed?"

"That is assuming it was the same code for everyone who used this door." Wilks spoke up. "If every user had a different code, there would still be cellular residue on all the keys from different people hitting different keys."

"Normally I would agree with you", Emily began, "but this would seem to be an emergency panel of some sort. It wouldn't be accessed daily so any residue we find should be a limited amount."

"I think that maybe we ought to also think about whether or not we want to open that door right now, even if we can figure out the code", Davies said through a mouthful of a protein bar. "If there were enough supplies inside whatever this is, it's conceivable that whoever built it is still in there. And they were totally protected from the explosion yesterday by all this rock. In fact, they may have triggered the explosion themselves."

"Bloom, try to figure out the code. Wilks, put together an assault plan for entry after we've figured this thing out", Emily ordered. "I'm not discounting your theory, Davies, but we have to know. I'd rather chance it with only fifteen possible casualties than bring more people down who could possibly get it as well."

With that, she opened a command channel and began giving a report to the base's commanding officer. She tried to push the feeling of doubt she had in her orders to the back of her mind. This was the first time other people's lives depended on her judgment. Two of her closest friends were affected by that decision.

Chapter 12
Aboard the *Vanguard* – The Final Test

On their way to the bridge, Seth and Beast had found two other students hiding out from their instructors. The two had been in a raiding party of five but got ambushed near the birthing compartments. One instructor was disabled but the other two took three students down shortly after.

"You two, take three grenades each." Seth handed them three from his belt and Beast reluctantly gave up three of his own. "I'll explain the rest on the way to airlock one."

~

Surgeon sat on the bridge and keyed a secure channel to his other instructors. "Has anyone captured Cadet yet?"

All three responses were negative. Four instructors had been incapacitated so far while eight students were still left somewhere in the ship. They could have used the internal sensors to find them, but that would have been cheating.

"Are you sure he'll come here?" Blaze asked. "I feel kinda bad sitting in here while the others are taking the heat. Blanch and Rachet had to carry Boomer to the infirmary after they accidentally blew out his knee. Thank God for our ortho-regenerator."

"You mean you're bored and would rather be out there were the excitement is", Surgeon said to his peer. "I know what it's like to be young, but don't worry, if he hasn't been captured yet, he'll try for the bridge. This kid is a mirror image of me when I was his age."

"I hope you're right. I'd hate to have sat this whole thing out for nothing. You really think that we need three of us in here, though? It's one guy." Blaze was just trying to make conversation at this point.

"No, I just wanted your handsome face to keep me company while I waited", Surgeon retorted.

"No more taking showers with you." And with that, Blaze went back to monitoring the latest holovid movie from Earth.

Well, he'd be the first to go once Cadet got here, Surgeon thought. Ah well, might as well let him learn a lesson.

Just then, the aft and forward lift doors opened, causing two instructors to jump to their feet while Surgeon did the opposite and dove for cover. Instincts being what they were, he never argued with them before and just reacted to what his body told him to do.

A flash grenade sailed onto the bridge from inside each lift. The two standing instructors were momentarily blinded while the two students dropped down from the service hatches inside the lifts.

Once on the bridge, they both released their stun grenades. One instructor had shielded his eyes reflexively from the first grenade and was able to see the outline of his oncoming attacker. He feigned to the side and placed an outstretched forearm into the student's throat, causing him to flip backwards and land on his stomach.

The student landed on his own grenade, which went off underneath him. The blast lifted him off the ground about half a meter and he slumped on the deck.

"Get him to medical", Surgeon ordered. Although it was only a stun grenade, at point blank range it could kill. Luckily, the specially designed uniforms that everyone on this ship wore were made to protect against shrapnel to some degree. However, Shorty had an abdominal wound that needed to be tended to immediately.

The other grenade stunned the instructor who was nearest the second hatch. Even as Surgeon ordered the medical evacuation of the student, he was over the operations booth railing and taking down the student who was now fumbling with his third grenade.

With a grip on the student's throat and his wrist in a painful joint lock, Surgeon queried, "Where is Cadet?"

A gasping noise was all that the student could manage before passing out. He had hit his head on the deck during Surgeon's attack and was unable to hold onto consciousness any longer.

Just then, Surgeon heard a whoosh of air from behind him and rolled to his feet to face the sound. The forward airlock was opening and a grenade was coming from it. He pulled the limp body of the student in front of him and allowed it to take the shock of the grenade.

Before he could push the body away, Beast was doing it for him while simultaneously lifting Surgeon off the deck with one hand. Surgeon kicked Beast between the legs with all his might. Beast crumpled to the floor with a smile and groan of ecstasy.

Shirkas had a pleasure center between their legs that when stimulated, brought their sexual organs out of the dormant state that they usually resided in. The sexual organs were where a belly button on a human would be and were always hidden inside the body for safekeeping.

Even if humans and Shirkas were genetically compatible, sex with a Shirka would kill most humans. It was violent compared to human standards. During their courtship dance, females would repeatedly hit the pleasure center between the male's legs in order to make the sexual organ come out of dormancy.

In short, kicking a male Shirka between the legs effectively crippled them as much as it would a human. Of course, Beast was having the equivalent of a human orgasm, but nonetheless he was on the ground and out of the way for a while. And most likely embarrassed as hell, now that he had a huge bulge in his shirt.

Surgeon dropped next to Beast almost immediately, which was still a split second too late as Seth was already throwing his first kick in that direction. It was stopped by Surgeon's face, which lurched backward at the impact.

"What took you so long?" Surgeon asked before he leapt forward in a diving roll aimed at Seth's ankle. His hand made purchase and he took Seth's ankle with him as he completed his dive.

Seth came off his feet and landed on his face with a thud. Another broken nose—he was pissed now.

"I figured I'd let the old man take a nap before I attacked. I knew you'd need all your strength." He was face to grinning face with Beast as he pushed himself up off the deck into a standing position.

He was clumsy in a pressure suit and wished that he could get out of it but that would be impossible right now. He'd be easy game while fumbling with the suit's pressure seals. Instead, he threw his last grenade at Surgeon.

Out of reflex, Surgeon hit the deck rolling and was surprised when Seth came rushing without regard to the impending explosion. "Getting sloppy, old man. I didn't arm it", Seth exclaimed as he pounced on Surgeon from behind.

An elbow came up towards Seth's rib cage and he decided that he no longer wished to be out of his suit. The suit was rigid to repel the continuous attacks made by floating space debris one encountered while in space. Debris the size of a pebble had been clocked at several hundred kilometers per hour. A thin suit wouldn't last too long in some regions of space.

Supersonic pebbles weren't Seth's main concern right now but the suit was holding up quite well to Surgeon's repeated blows. In fact, Seth figured that he could sit there and get hit all day and not even be winded by it. He held his current position, hoping that his adversary would soon lose steam.

When that avenue seemed to lead nowhere, Seth decided that it was time to end it. Each boot on a pressure suit was equipped with magnetic soles for space walking on a ship's hull. He used both hands to wrestle one of Surgeon's to the deck. Seth stepped on Surgeon's hand and initiated the magnetic lock. He heard several metacarpals in Surgeon's left hand start to creak as the boot adhered to the deck plating without regard for the flesh and bone pinned beneath it.

Surgeon didn't even cry out in pain as he felt his bones being bent to near their breaking point. Instead, he wrote off his left hand and began to reach for the belt on Seth's suit to pull him down to the deck. Seth easily swatted his hand out of the way and drew back his free foot.

"We can end this now or I can kick you until you're unconscious." Surgeon nodded his agreement to his captor's terms and slumped back onto the deck.

Seth tapped his comlink once to open a channel to anyone still conscious on the ship. "All hands, this is Cadet. I have captured the bridge, along with Surgeon. I'll flood the entire ship with choline succinate gas and paralyze everyone on board unless I receive an unconditional surrender from all remaining hostile forces."

A long pause and then a reply came through the comlink from Ace. "After situation confirmation from Surgeon, we will comply."

Surgeon looked up at Seth with respect. "C'mon, let's all go have a beer. They're on me." And then to Seth, "Now will you get off my goddamned hand?!"

Seth released the magnetic boot and helped Surgeon up, who in turn pinched Seth's broken nose. "You didn't have to break my hand. You could have just said 'please surrender.' But noooo, you couldn't play nice, could you?"

"Let's get you to sickbay and find out how everyone else fared."

With a look towards Beast, Surgeon said, "So, should I get you a cigarette or do you just want to be held?"

Seth had no idea what Surgeon meant by that. He also thought it odd how Beast was smiling. He would have been crying after a hit like that.

Later that same day, Beast asked Surgeon how he knew about something so secret in Shirka culture. Mating rituals were never and would never be discussed with outsiders. It would take an extremely hard and focused hit to produce the effects that Surgeon had. It was not by accident that he had accomplished what he did.

Surgeon had been a close friend with Beast's brother. Beast and his brother had come from the same litter and shared a special bond that was deeper than usual for Shirka littermates. After his brother was killed in battle, Beast took his spot on the team. It was Shirka custom for brothers to finish each other's missions if one was unable to complete it himself. And although Beast was not a formal member of the Coalition military, he had a distinguished record of battle and the general thought that he would be the best last-minute replacement for the dead soldier.

Surgeon smiled as Beast stood waiting for an answer. "One night, your brother and I were in a bar on Solis III. Some human purists were talking shit about your brother. We just ignored them at first but then they had to go and get physical." Surgeon paused.

Beast leaned in towards Surgeon with anticipation. Surgeon continued. "One of the purists threw a beer bottle, which hit your brother on the head. It didn't even faze him. He slowly got up and turned towards the much smaller man.

"That guy must never have seen a Shirka up close before because his eyes almost popped out of his head when he realized that he was picking on someone almost three times his size.

"The guy threw a couple of punches at your brother, which he took in the face without even flinching. The purist resorted to bar room tactics and kicked your brother square in the crotch as hard as he could. Nothing, absolutely nothing. No flinch, no wince, no bulging eyes. I couldn't believe it.

"Apparently the guy couldn't either because he tried again. And again, nothing. I thought that your brother must have been wearing a protective cup or something. Well, he finally laughed and with a slight flick of his wrist, he backhanded the stupid purist across the room.

"Of course, the fight didn't stop there. His friends decided to come to his aid and your brother and I finished them off. When it was over, I noticed that we both still had our beers in our hands. That guy was lucky that your brother had one hand occupied, otherwise you know what he would've done to him."

"You still haven't explained how you know about…" Beast paused and looked around to make sure that no one was listening. "About how to stimulate our sexual organs."

"Well," Surgeon said with a sheepish grin, "I was pretty drunk at the time. So when we finished the bar fight, we turned to each other for a toast. Like I said before, I figured your brother was wearing a protective cup or something. So as a joke, I reared back and kicked him with all my might right in his balls. Of course, you don't have balls but I didn't know that at the time.

"He went down fast and I couldn't understand it. I thought maybe that other guy was so drunk that he wasn't kicking as hard as I thought he was. Or maybe that I could kick harder than I thought I could.

"I knelt down by your brother and he was moaning. I thought that I had really hurt him. Then I saw him grinning from ear to ear. Shirka pain maybe? No, I had seen that before but never this. Never had I seen a Shirka smile so broadly or deeply. He was REALLY enjoying himself.

"He looked up and grabbed me by the neck and told me to get him back to his quarters immediately. I did and there he explained to me what I had done.

"By accident, I had hit his pleasure center. And now that I know where it is, I never hesitate to use it when I have to."

Beast looked at Surgeon for a minute and then allowed a small grin to play across his face. "It was the best sex I've had in a while." Surgeon collapsed on the floor with uncontrollable laughter. That was the best joke from a Shirka he ever heard.

"I assume that my brother told you of our customs and secrecy surrounding our rituals." Beast stopped grinning.

"Of course. And don't worry, I may use that little technique but I would never tell anyone about it. I swear." Surgeon's laughter had stopped and was now replaced with a look of utter sincerity and respect.

"Thank you", Beast replied before rejoining the party and celebrating their victory.

Meanwhile, Seth was asked to recount the tale of how he took over the starship, not to mention the war game story. Midway through telling the tale of his most recent victory, the general walked, no, floated into the mess hall. For a man of his size, grace just wasn't a fitting description but no other word could describe how he always seemed to get where he was going without even moving or making an effort to get there.

"Attention on deck." An attempt at loudness was made but whoever tried was just too tired to get much louder than the conversations around the room. It was still heard by all and a much weaker attempt was made by every bruised and broken body in the mess hall to come to attention.

"Cut that shit out!" the general barked. "Get your asses back in your seats and don't stop drinking your beer. You all deserve a rest." He paused for what seemed like an eternity. His tone indicated they were about to be told something. The something that they had all been waiting for.

The general continued much softer this time, "You're all going to need it with the shit we're about to get into."

A holovid appeared at the front of the mess hall with images of planets and a star system that no one recognized.

"You have all been briefed by your respective instructors as to what has happened within the Coalition during the past five years and the pains we have gone through to keep it secret. And now I'm going to tell you what you don't know. What we are going to do about it."

Chapter 13
Vengeance's Pride

"Sir, they have accessed a door panel", the operations officer said to his captain. "The door hasn't been opened yet." He paused. "But if they've gotten that far, it stands to reason that they might be able to eventually."

The captain's disgust grew within as he pondered what to do. He had orders to just observe. But now this? They could not be allowed to enter that base. If they were able to access information stored within it, it could shift the balance of power. "Send emergency traffic to Supreme Command and request immediate direction." It didn't seem to him that his communications officer was acting fast enough. "NOW!" he barked with a boom that all the other officers on the bridge felt deep inside their chests.

The captain sat back in his chair. What else could he do? Nothing, he told himself, with more rage and hatred growing for the slugs on the planet's surface.

Emily

NAME: EMILY RILEY
SPECIES: HUMAN
MOS: XENOBIOLOGIST
RANK: CAPTAIN
AGE: 24 - EARTH STANDARD
SEX: FEMALE
HEIGHT: 5'6"
WEIGHT: 130 POUNDS

"Emily!"

"What?!"

"Hurry up! We're going to be late for your flight if we don't leave in the next few minutes."

"I'm coming, Mom", Emily said as she came down the stairwell and into the kitchen. "I'm sorry. I just wanted to make one last check of everything before we left. It's not like I'll be able to head to the corner store and get some toothpaste once we get to the dig site."

"Don't worry so much. You're going to be with a lot of people who have done this before and will help you out if you forgot anything. Now let's go, your dad is waiting in the car."

Once they were in the car, Emily allowed herself to relax a little. "I hope this trip isn't for nothing. I'm missing out on some summer activities that would look great on my college application", she said aloud, but not having meant to.

"Look," her mother began, "we've been through this before; you need to relax and stop worrying so much about college. You're sixteen and have two years of high school left—you should enjoy them. You'll be fine. You're a great student. I'm sure you'll have your pick of colleges. When your dad and I were kids, most alien schools wouldn't even think about taking human students. You have a whole galaxy of colleges to apply to."

"I know you keep saying that but it doesn't make me worry any less."

"You get straight As, honey." This comment was from her father.

"Yes, Dad, but so does thirty percent of my high school. And with a last name of O'Riley, I'm pretty far down the list when you put all of the 4.0 averages alphabetically. I need something extra, something to make me shine more than the other kids once we start applying to college." Emily made a small snort. "Some of my classmates actually already have applied and received early admissions to their first choices."

Emily's father punched in a few commands to the car's dashboard and let the autopilot take over. He swiveled his seat around to face the rear passenger compartment. "Honey, a long time ago *some* colleges did care about extra-curricular activities and how much you filled out your resume on their applications, but that's not so much the case anymore. With so many different species applying to schools throughout the galaxy, it's pretty difficult for them to sort out those sorts of things anymore. They really tend to rely more on the placement exams, psych exams, and all of the other admissions testing they do. They look at the data in those results more than the person or applications themselves."

"Maybe, but you never know. That's why I decided to do this trip. It might make history and that would make me look good." Emily crossed her arms and tried to look as if she was sulking.

Her mother took over. "Oh sweetie, I wish you had a different attitude about this. Aunt Janine wouldn't even be going on this dig if it weren't for you."

"What do you mean? Aunt Janine loves these things. She's always telling stories about how they are the greatest adventures of her life." Emily thought her mom was trying to throw in a guilt trip to get her attitude to change.

"She did love them, once. She's been teaching for the last five years and really enjoying it. When they called her to head up this dig, she initially refused. They told her to think about it some more and that they would call her back in a couple of weeks. They really wanted her to go."

"Why wouldn't she want to go? This is right up her alley. They found the ruins of a completely unknown alien species. It's her chance to make history. Again. For like, the sixth time or something ridiculous like that." Emily was now sitting forward, obviously more engaged than before.

"Janine has been comfortable for the last five years. She has been sleeping in her own comfortable bed. Eating warm food that wasn't from a dehydrated pouch. She hasn't had to pick alien fleas from her hair."

"Eww! Mom!"

"Exactly. And that's why she wasn't going to go on this expedition. She's been comfortable and she's also satisfied with her previous adventures. She's even dating another professor, so she's happy with where she's at."

"Then why is she going?"

"Because of you." Emily's mom let that sink in for a moment before she continued. "Look, we didn't tell you any of this stuff because we wanted you to want to go on this trip for yourself, for fun, for adventure and not for other reasons. Janine called me a few weeks ago, just our normal sister talk time, and she was telling me about what's going on with her and stuff. When she got to the part about the dig and how she was going to turn it down, I mentioned that it was too bad because when you were younger, Janine had always said that when you were old enough she was going to take you on a dig. You used to get so excited about that.

"We talked for a little bit more and she decided that she would take the job if you wanted to go with her. She thinks it's very important for you to get out as a young woman, see for yourself what adventures you can have and open yourself up to more than what your little corner of the galaxy has for you."

"I didn't know. I'm sorry, mom; I'll have a better attitude, I promise. I really do want to go. I'm actually pretty excited." Emily started to feel better as she allowed herself to slip her self-applied grumpy shackles. "I was just a little down because Shelly called me this morning to wish me luck and she let it slip that she got early admission to her father's alma mater. But she is one year ahead of me and she deserves it. I'm letting it go, though, all of it. If Aunt Janine is doing this for me then I'm all in, no more attitude." Shackles gone.

The family reached the airport and took the transorbital shuttle to the spaceport. Once they found Emily's flight, they said their tearful goodbyes and Emily boarded, feeling more excited than ever, now that she allowed herself to.

Two days later, she was onboard another transport, this time with her Aunt Janine and the rest of the expedition's crew. This transport was so much better and faster than the first. It was a private craft and a fairly expensive one at that. Janine explained that the expedition was being staffed by people from ten different universities and had at least four wealthy private backers.

"Thank you so much for having me along on this trip, Aunt Janine!"

"No problem, dear. I've always waited for the day that you could join me on one of my adventures."

"You should have your own kids. You'd be a great mother."

"I never had time, and I always had you to pretend you were mine." Janine smiled warmly at her niece.

"Mom said you have a new boyfriend." Emily smiled back. "Maybe you two could have kids?"

"Ha! You're worse than your mom is!" Janine playfully pushed Emily's shoulder. "He has a son already, eight years old. Great kid, we have a lot of fun together. He was very jealous that he couldn't go on this trip. I think I'll be happy with them as my family. But if Steve wants another kid, I don't think I'd be opposed to it. I'm just not going to be the one to push for it."

"Well, they are both lucky to have you. I know I am." Emily finished eating her lunch while she and her aunt caught up on everything going on in their lives.

~

Three weeks later, Emily had all but forgotten about college as she immersed herself in her work. Aunt Janine kept her close by either herself or one of the four other senior specialists. Emily was learning so much from each of them and was thankful she was given a daily assignment rather than having to decide for herself where she'd spend her time; she didn't think she'd be able to choose between her five mentors if she were forced to.

Janine was a woman of many talents but she focused her expertise in the area of predictive xenobiology. She would be able to build a profile of a species based on what she found at the dig site. She could determine, to a fairly high degree of accuracy, almost anything you wanted to know about the physical and mental make-up of the species that left the artifacts behind. Though on this mission, Janine was sought out for her leadership qualities along with her vast experience in handling many other similar finds. Doctor Hillstep, a human who taught at a Nortes university, was filling Janine's role as the predictive xenobiologist.

Janine had tried to stay away from Doctor Hillstep because she didn't want him to feel crowded or as if she were going to take over any part of his work from him. So she was delighted when he asked her and Emily to join him today with a new chamber that they had just yesterday finished making safe for cataloging.

"Thank you again for letting me tag along, Doctor." Janine was holding on the guide rope with one hand as she followed Hillstep and her niece through the corridor.

"My pleasure Doctor, er, uh, Janine. I don't think I'll get used to that. The Nortes are extremely traditional people and I've been with them for quite some time now." Hillstep looked back over his shoulder to give a slight smile.

"Yes, well, with all the doctors around here, it would get confusing if we didn't interject a little individuality into things." Janine had told all of her staff to call her by her first name. She felt that it engendered a sense of openness that would make them more comfortable to approach her with problems or needs.

"Aunt Janine," Emily spoke up from the middle of the group, "Lance let me help set up the decontamination area down here yesterday. We also were able to get four stasis crates tucked away in an alcove nearby in case we find anything we need to haul out of here."

"Good girl. Everyone has told me that you have been a great help, especially Lance." Janine gave her niece a conspiratorial smile and a wink.

"Aunt Janine! Stop it!" Emily protested. "He's almost twice my age and I'm only sixteen anyway. I don't think Mom or Dad would like the idea of you trying to set us up."

"Oh, dear, stop being so dramatic." Janine enjoyed teasing Emily. "I'm not trying to set you up with anyone. I'm just saying that Lance is pretty damn handsome. He sure doesn't look thirty-two, espccially with his shirt off."

Hillstep stopped and turned towards the two women behind him. "Janine, Emily is right. She is much too young for Lance."

Janine was taken aback; she was worried that Hillstep didn't know her well enough to be a part of this kind of teasing. She began to feel very embarrassed for her behavior. "Well Doctor, I'm very sorry if…"

Hillstep hushed her with a finger in the air. "And Janine, you are correct about Lance. He does look good with his shirt off, and I'm only *five* years older than he is. If you're going to be a matchmaker for anyone…" He let the comment and its insinuation linger in the air between them.

"I'll see what I can do!" Janine and Emily were now laughing together as Hillstep turned and continued to lead them to the new chamber.

Once they reached the decontamination area, they entered the enclosed room where they donned their work suits. Emily had to stifle a giggle when Lance, who had been waiting at the chamber, asked whether any of them needed assistance getting into their suits. Janine had thought, *Maybe out of them!,* but as the project leader she knew that was a step too far for her to voice out loud.

After their suits were on, they left the decon room and approached the door to the alien chamber. The suits provided them with their own air, some protection from abrasions or slight falls, and communications between suits and other members of the team in other locations. If they could figure out how to open the chamber door, they didn't know what kind of atmosphere they'd be exposed to so they were playing it safe, as Janine always did.

"Now," Hillstep began as he pointed to several areas on the doorway, "you can see that these markings don't have any similarities to writings from any known species that we have records on. Even our translation software showed nothing in its comparisons. But, Emily pointed something out to me yesterday that I think you might find interesting. Emily?"

"Uh, yeah, right over here. See that in the corner, at the bottom there?" Emily was pointing to the lower left.

"You mean that tool mark in the rock?" Janine was kneeling, looking closer now. "Well now, this little guy is kind of interesting. It's meant to look like a stray tool mark but if you look close enough, it seems to be purposeful. Nice catch, but what else have we got? I don't recognize that from anything I'm familiar with."

Hillstep nodded to Emily to continue. "Well, who would make a mark or symbol on purpose but try to make it look like a stray tool strike? Slaves. Just like an artist signing his work, some slave workers in other cultures have been known to leave their mark on their master's work as an act of defiance or as a remembrance to future generations that a slave made it and not the master."

"Yes, I believe I have read that somewhere…" Janine was smiling.

"I believe you *wrote* that somewhere." Hillstep was playing along. "In your doctoral thesis when you were, uh, just a tad younger."

"Nice save, Doctor. Go on, Emily." Janine was now looking around for other clues left behind by the potential slave workers of the past.

"Okay, so I'm looking at that mark and I decide to call it purposeful, but it's only one line. Granted, that could mean something huge to another species but most species we know of don't use such simple symbols for anything important." Emily then pointed to six more tool marks in the cave wall. "I found these other marks after a few hours of searching every inch in this area in front of the door. Doctor Hillstep had to take over after that."

Emily turned the reins back to her mentor. "I don't think I took over; you still helped me arrange the markings, dear. You still helped solve, or possibly solve I should say, what we found."

"So you know who made this place?" Janine was excited but at the same time disappointed. Solving a mystery was always fun but if they knew who built these ruins then that meant it wasn't a new species; it was someone they were already aware of. "Don't keep me in suspense here!"

"I think I do, sort of, and it's as exciting as finding a new species! Bear with me while I walk you through it. I don't want to give you our conclusion without you seeing the steps we went through to get there. It will be easier for you to find problems with our theory if you see our work leading up to it."

Janine just nodded in agreement. Hillstep pulled up some images on a tablet. "Once we had all of the tool marks put into images we could play around with on our tablets, it was like trying to figure out a puzzle where you don't know what the pieces are supposed to look like. But together we decided that this was the best shape for the marks to make when put together."

Hillstep showed Janine the end result. "And why is that?" she asked as she viewed the tablet.

Emily stepped up and pointed to areas highlighted on the screen. "Based on those intersections, they look like purposeful points where other marks would come together to form a shape, a letter in their alphabet or possibly a whole symbol for a thought or phrase. We found those spots on each tool mark and determined that they were put there for a reason. We then told the computer to use those points to fit with each marking we had. It came up with only one possible geometric shape that could be made by connecting all of the points on all of the tool marks. The computer thinks that all of the tool marks make this one symbol."

Janine looked at it and cocked her head. "Why does this look familiar to me?"

"Ah ha! I was hoping you would say that." Hillstep took the pad from Janine so he could tap in a few more commands. A new image was pulled up next to the one they had been looking at. The new image was almost exactly the same but much more refined and pristine because it had been formed by hand on a computer screen and not secretly carved into rock a few hundred thousand years ago.

"That mark is from the Unwutine tribes in the Delaz system. But that's impossible; they are barely out of their stone age yet. They don't even have basic metal-working abilities. Their written history is maybe a thousand years old." Janine was amazed but thought there had to be some mistake, somewhere, somehow.

"Well, what if they were used as slave labor by some other species and then dumped on that planet to rot? Or they were visited by aliens who showed them that symbol?" Emily had taken to sitting on a crate while Janine just stared at the tablet.

"Possible but not likely", Hillstep started. "For a couple of reasons. One, these tool marks were made with advanced metal implements. It looks like these ruins were once a mine and then someone more advanced came in and turned them into a base of some sort. The tunnels were definitely created with different tools and materials than the chambers and hallways we've found.

"These marks you found were made with the advanced tools that came after the mines were built. So we have to assume that whoever made the marks had access to advanced tools, slaves or not. The Unwutine don't have those tools and nothing in their short history indicates they ever did or that they were visited from other species."

"Refresh my memory, Doctor, what does this symbol mean?" Janine was racking her brain but couldn't remember what it was.

"This is their symbol for two things, actually, just depending on the context." Hillstep pulled up another image, this one of a very deformed alien that Emily wasn't familiar with. "When the Unwutine have a baby deformed with this genetic mutation, they use this symbol to describe the baby. You'll forgive me for not trying to speak their actual word for it but I can't even come close to pronouncing anything in their language."

"No one can", Janine added.

"Quite true." Hillstep smiled. "So we have no idea why that mutation occurs but when it does, the baby is branded with that symbol and then killed. We have no idea why but it seems as though they fear the mutated babies."

Emily looked disgusted. "Why don't we save those babies if we see them doing it?"

Janine looked at her niece. "Because, dear, they don't know we exist. We observe from secret and don't reveal ourselves. We don't want to interfere with their development. It wouldn't be right. Just like we don't stop a mother lion from eating her cubs if that's what her instinct tells her she needs to do."

Hillstep looked at Emily. "It's a hard pill to swallow and to tell you the truth, I know I wouldn't be able to if I were there on the research team. But, to continue with what we do know, the research we've done on the corpses show that the babies wouldn't have survived more than a few days after birth. They're not contagious in any way; it's not a disease process. It's an extremely odd piece of DNA that we haven't been able to map yet or understand, but it does a tremendous amount of damage when it gets turned on during incubation. It happens to about one in every twenty thousand infants."

"What's the second meaning they have for the symbol?" Emily wanted to get away from the talk of killing babies.

"Ah yes, the second use of the term is for their labor force. Whether it's their version of an ox or horse plowing a field, or a group of men tasked with moving a fallen tree or large stone. They use this term to describe heavy laborers of some sort. You might even say 'slave work.'"

Emily looked at the alien word and pressed the text-to-speech button on the tablet. The word the computer spoke sounded almost like *Hurlkaferncherta*. "Oh my, that is a difficult word to say. Please forgive me if this is a stupid question, but is there any possibility that this symbol is just coincidentally similar to the one from that tribe?"

"I forgive you." Janine teased Emily. "We have found evidence that more than twelve hundred sentient species have existed in our galaxy at some point. We currently can verify that just over four hundred of those species are still around today. To this day, we have never seen the letter *A* in any other species' written dialect, not to mention any other letter from any human alphabet. With the exception of species from different planets that we can genetically link to each other as having a common ancestry, no matter how distant, no two species of different planetary origins has ever had coincidentally similar shapes in their alphabets or markings."

"So, no then." Emily got affirmative nods from both doctors. "Okay, so if we know it's statistically improbable that these two species aren't genetically linked somehow, then we need to find the link. And how do we know that the tribe is indigenous to that planet? That they evolved there?"

Hillstep put his hand to his masked chin. "We have something called the 'flushed goldfish' theory. It's when a spacefaring species visits a planet and leaves behind an animal of some sort, whether on purpose or not we, of course, don't know. But in time, that animal either becomes part of the biosphere or doesn't and we find it thriving, evolved, or dead. Regardless of the state we find it in, we can check its DNA and see that it didn't spring up from the same primordial ooze as everything else around it. The Unwutine tribe has been researched enough that we know they evolved on the same planet we found them on."

"Okay, so how do we know they weren't visited by another species that gave them that symbol or they saw the symbol and used it for some reason?"

Janine liked answering her niece's questions. Going back to the basics helped to get her mind working in ways she wasn't used to. "First off, when we say we know they weren't visited by someone else, what we really mean is that we're pretty damn sure. A good scientist realizes that even the things they know are true, those things can be disproven later. Keeping that in mind, we *know* they weren't visited because if they were visited during a stage of their evolution in which they had developed some form of documentation, as transference of a symbol would suggest, then they also would've documented that encounter as well. A visiting species would've been seen as a major event by a primitive species and they would've done at least a cave drawing or something. We have yet to find any evidence of that. And in order for them to take a symbol or word from a visiting species, they would have to have had extensive contact with the visitors, not just seen a UFO in the night sky. That extensive of a visit would've been detectable by our researchers."

"Worms and goldfish…" Emily muttered.

"You lost me on that one, dear." Janine put her hands up in the air in the universal "huh" gesture.

"Worms. Specifically, flatworms." Emily was pacing in a small circle and moving her right arm in the air as though she were conducting thoughts through her brain. "We just did an experiment in school where we tested the age-old theory of genetic memory in flatworms. Results aside, what if the Unwutine tribe has genetic memories from a failed attempt at cross-species breeding? You said they have a genetic deformation that we don't understand yet, a weird piece of DNA. We're pretty good at mapping DNA. I think it odd that we would find a piece of DNA in a species that we classify as 'weird' and we can't figure it out. What if it doesn't belong there or even belong to them to begin with? Maybe that weird DNA is from somewhere else and is also responsible for passing down some genetic memories that have helped shaped their written language development."

"That theory deserves some attention. I'm pretty impressed, honey." Janine pulled up more information on the Unwutine tribe. "But you also said goldfish. Why?"

"Just going back to the flushed goldfish theory." Emily was pumped up with the praise she had received from Janine. "What if the species that created these ruins were flying out in the galaxy one day and decided to stop on a planet. Maybe to refuel, maybe to take samples, maybe to make repairs, maybe to take a family photo and have a picnic—who cares why, but the point is the stop wasn't for the purpose of staying any length of time. And because the stop was just a layover, future explorers would never find any evidence of that relatively short visit.

"So while they're on the planet, their slaves or workforce species escape. Who knows how many, but some get out. Or they were left on purpose. Regardless of how or why, they are now on the planet and does what every species does: attempts to survive."

Emily was back to pacing. "Okay, so now you have an abandoned species on an alien planet and they aren't doing so well. There aren't enough of them to ever create a civilization of their own; the gene pool just wouldn't be deep enough. There are probably less than a hundred of them to start with in the first place. But they still try to survive and breed; it's instinct. And because there are so few of them to begin with, once they do die out, it would be pretty hard for future explorers to find evidence of their existence because they didn't have time to really leave anything behind."

Emily looked at Hillstep, who just encouraged her, "Finish it, keep going, don't stop now."

Emily took a deep breath. "They aren't from this planet but they're close enough to a developing species, the Unwutine, that they can sort of integrate and not be seen as god-like or whatever, you know, if they had come down in spaceships and stuff in front of everyone in some grand display of technology. So they were accepted.

"It's kind of like when Trizites visit Earth and swim in our oceans; the dolphins and other local life welcome them and play with them, act like they belong. The Trizites are so close in their physical make-up to our ocean life, they just kind of fit in. So that's what these castaways did, they just fit in. Maybe the Unwutine thought the castaways were just a different tribe that were not exactly the same as themselves.

"The castaways either brought the Unwutine their first symbols or just added to what they had already started. Either way, the castaways referred to themselves using this symbol we found on the wall. They were laborers and that symbol started to be used by the Unwutine to refer to anything having to do with laboring."

"But then the breeding attempts failed." Doctor Hillstep shushed himself to let Emily finish on her own.

"Exactly!" Emily's beat wasn't thrown off by the interruption. "The castaways could only breed so far within their own group so they tried to mix with the Unwutine. Neither species would be nearly advanced enough to understand the problems with trying to breed between the two different sets of DNA.

"So the breeding attempts started and of course failed. Maybe there were some successful attempts even though the chances of that occurring, without advanced medical intervention, are astronomically improbable, it could've happened. In the end, somehow, the castaways' DNA did get added to the DNA of the Unwutine tribes and when it gets turned on, it causes the horrible mutations we've seen. That's the reason the mutated babies are called *Hurlkaferncherta*. It's both the laboring castaways and what their breeding attempts create."

"Wow." Janine was almost at a loss for words. "If I hadn't seen you being born, I'd swear you were my daughter and not your mother's. I think I need to get a DNA comparison between us."

Emily just smiled broadly at her aunt.

"There are a lot of holes in that very long and complicated theory", Doctor Hillstep threw out without any preamble.

Emily's face sagged and her eyes actually begin to tear up just a bit.

"Hey, jerkface." Janine was addressing her colleague. "You and I are used to having our theories shredded to hell by our contemporaries but she's not. She's only sixteen and she came up with that theory without all of the combined decades of education that you and I have put together."

"It's okay, Aunt Janine, he's right. There are a lot of holes in it. Like timeline issues, biology issues, DNA stuff. I could probably make an easier argument for why I'm wrong rather than why I'm right." Emily took a seat on a nearby crate.

"Oh, honey." Janine sat with Emily while still giving the evil eye to Hillstep. "There are holes in your theory but there are a lot of solid pieces, too. In fact, I need you to write that theory up so we can include it in our notes and you can get credit for it."

"Really?" Emily was embarrassed that she had almost started crying over what Hillstep had said.

"Yes, really." Hillstep tried to redeem himself. "I apologize for attacking your theory like that. In my defense, I have a valid point, but I should be encouraging my protégé and not attacking. I was really just thinking out loud about what we need to do to validate as much of your theory as we can. I really do like where you are going with it.

"In this field, it's best to come up with your theory, detail it out as much as possible, and then attack it with every brain cell you have. Once you've broken down all of the weak points, those are the areas that you give your attention to in order to prove them with more research or disprove them in order to change your theory to a more correct working model."

"I understand. I shouldn't have been such a baby about it." Emily had regained her composure. "One thing we forgot to point out, using the working theory that the slave symbol we found here was somehow tied to the Unwutine language, we checked the other symbols against every character we know from their writings. There isn't even a slight match between the two languages. Another dead end. And we are no closer to finding what they mean or how to open the chamber."

"Well, you have only three weeks left before you go home." Janine was standing again and examining the door. "You have two choices. You can work on shoring up your theory or stay with Hillstep and work on the door some more."

"I'll work with Hillstep, if that's okay." Emily took the pad from her aunt's hand. "I can work on my theory from home or any terminal with Net access. But while I'm here, I want to keep learning from the other researchers and maybe rooting around the ruins will give me more clues to add to my theory before I leave."

"Sounds like a plan to me. But you will go back up top and sit down at a proper terminal away from distractions and write your theory up. I'll take you up there and show you the templates we use on these digs." Hillstep wanted to redeem himself to both Janine and Emily, if he hadn't already. "We'll come back down here later tonight if there's time; if not, then first thing tomorrow morning."

As the three stepped back into the decontamination chamber, Emily realized they hadn't even needed the suits they were wearing. "Well, this was kind of a waste. Getting into these suits is a pain in the ass and it was for nothing. We didn't do anything but talk at the door. We didn't even try to get in."

Janine just laughed. "That's the way it is sometimes with these digs. You plan your day one way and end up following a lead or a hunch in a completely different direction. You did good." Looking over towards Lance, who was still working near the chamber, she added, "Besides, it's better to have protection and not need it than to need protection and not have it."

"Aunt Janine!" Hillstep and Emily said in unison.

"What?" Janine said with a failed attempt at coyness.

~

Emily wrote up her theory and added it to the official record of the research team. Over the next few weeks, she scoured the ruins for new clues to help her theory and also advance the project's understanding of the other writings that were left behind. They never did find a way into any of the sealed rooms they found at the site.

Eventually Janine turned the team over to Doctor Hillstep and she went back to her university to continue teaching. Not too long after returning to the university, she was joined by Emily, who was granted early admission based on the research she had helped with at the dig. Ultimately, Emily used her original theory as her doctoral thesis and was able to prove a lot of what she had originally put forward, though the chambers were still never opened.

Chapter 14
Dig Site One – Open Sesame

"Fang will take point with Bloom in second, followed by Davies, Hood, Martinez, Patz, Snyder, and me." Wilks began his briefing. "Team two will have Scan on point, followed by Doc, el-tee, Jockey, Trip, Cannon, and Snake."

Not a bad layout, Daria thought. Wilks put Fang out front because he would be able to detect an enemy better and farther away than a human. Then he put Scan on point for team two. This allowed team two to react as quickly as team one because Scan could detect Fang's emotions, so he could act almost simultaneously with him, giving team two the advantage of advance warning. Very smart.

"Now, el-tee," he continued, "with all due respect. Are you going to be able to handle yourself in there?"

Daria was going to interject on Emily's behalf but knew that would only confirm Wilks' idea of Emily being weak. "If you'd like to find out while Bloom is trying to unlock that door, I'd be happy to show you", she said, emphasizing her resolve by setting her weapon down against the wall.

She's come a long way, Daria thought. But Wilks was a killer and would have no problem taking her out. Luckily, the show of force and confidence was enough for Wilks and he just smiled broadly. "Just don't trip and accidentally shoot me, all right? I'd hate to have to see firsthand how good Doc is at her job."

"There wouldn't be anything left for her to patch up."

OK, that's enough, Daria said to Emily with a glare. Don't push your luck, lady.

Everyone laughed aloud, except Fang. He couldn't understand it. A challenge was a challenge, whether it came from a woman, a superior officer, or whoever. The lieutenant and Wilks should be fighting by now. Agh! These humans, he thought.

"Who's buying me the beer?" Bloom said from his makeshift perch. Everyone stopped laughing and looked at him. "I think I might understand it. Thing is, if I'm wrong, who knows what will happen. Considering what happened yesterday, I'm not sure if I want to try."

Bloom was fluent in twenty-seven languages and only six of those were human. He had a talent for picking out patterns in speech, and symbols used in writing. The corps had tried to encourage, even force, Bloom into intelligence because of his talents. He said he'd resign first, even spend time in prison if he had to. No, he wasn't going to sit at a terminal somewhere in space with a headset on for the rest of his life listening in on other people's conversations. He just wouldn't do it. So the corps kept him in Recon; he was good at it and once they knew his determination, they conceded to better judgment. And better judgment wasn't a common thing for the military.

"C'mon, wuss. You want me to hold your hand?" Wilks approached Bloom. "You know we all trust you. If you think you got it, do it." He gave Bloom a nod and a wink.

"All right." He sighed. "Form up, guys, we're going in."

"Just a minute", Daria said as she focused on the nothing that was in front of her. She was getting a transmission from base medical. "Doctor, please put this on general transmission for my team to hear."

165

Everyone focused on the same nothing that Daria was looking at as they listened to the conversation. "First of all," the doctor began, "you did an excellent job with your patient. I've never seen its like. He came around about a half-hour ago and began screaming. We did retrieve some audio from his visor, but most of it is incoherent; I'm transmitting what we did get. Here goes."

The muffled sounds of recorded speech entered the team's heads. "What do you mean you hit something? There's nothing on that grid except dirt." A pause as though he was hearing the other side of a conversation with a colleague who was no longer able to hold up his end of the conversation. He continued, "Yes, I'm almost two kilometers from the site, trying to complete the survey." Another pause. "No, I won't come back right now. I'm too far out. It can wait. Let me finish this and I'll be back in a couple hours."

In the background began sounds of sheets rustling and bed rails being pulled with enough force to make the bed he was laying on move. You could hear nurses and doctors trying to calm him down with voices of reassurance. And then a scream from the recording rose above all the other noise. "What the hell is that! My eyes, my eyes! Ahhhhhh!"

Daria hadn't noticed burn marks on him while she was treating his wounds. The many meters he was pushed on the ground from the shockwave must have worn off the seared flesh on his face from the intense heat of that massive explosion.

"Sorry it isn't more encouraging and that we don't have any more information at this point." The doctor's voice returned. "We had to sedate him and I don't think he'll come around for another day or so. I'll keep you posted."

The transmission ended. Daria had halted the insertion, so all eyes were now on her to give it the go again. She looked at Bloom. "By all means." She made a sweeping gesture with her arm towards the door. "After you."

"Everyone exchange ammo for close quarters battle. Lock and load!" This was from Wilks.

Special ammunition was used for CQB to reduce the amount of injuries from ricochet accidents. The rounds used jet fuel for propulsion, so they tended to bounce around for quite a while in a close quarters area before they ran out of fuel. This was not a good thing.

CQB ammunition used a slug that almost disintegrated on its second hard impact. A trigger in the nose of the slug was set off when it hit its first hard object; that allowed the round to shed its hard exterior coating. The second solid object it hit that it couldn't penetrate would just about dissolve the slug.

The pros outweighed the cons of this clever round. Of course, if you were in the way of it before it made its second contact, personal armor or flesh wasn't solid enough of a contact for the round to disintegrate. So tough luck for you in those cases, but in general it was a good idea.

Everyone removed their standard ammo and slapped home CQB in the magazine receiver. A push of a button behind the trigger cycled the first round into position for firing. A faint hum was heard as all the weapons powered-up. A small electrical charge was used to ignite the round's fuel source. It was set on a very specific voltage so that accidental misfiring was avoided from electrical fields that soldiers sometimes encountered.

The two teams edged into entry positions while Bloom keyed in the opening sequence and said a private prayer. "On my mark," he began, "three, two, one, mark." Almost as a whisper, the last word left his mouth.

The wall before them seemed to slowly vanish into thin air. Fang waited until the object was completely gone before entering. The doors and hallways that followed were huge compared to the humans and even considered large by the much bigger Shirka leading the way. It was actually ideal for an entry team.

They swept the hallway and cleared rooms as they found them. Each room had equipment that was completely alien to each member of the team. Emily tried to keep herself in formation but felt an almost uncontrollable urge to stop at each console and display to examine it. Her newfound warrior side won the battle and she focused in on Daria's back to cover her.

The initial floor of the building was small, with only twelve rooms altogether, none of which led anywhere. After the floor was cleared, the team gathered by what seemed to be a lift shaft.

"I think that it's safe to assume that because we're all still here," Emily began, "we can take a closer look at what's on this level before proceeding." OK, so her scientific mind was exerting itself a little more than she cared to admit. "We should get as much information as we can with what we have before we continue. Wilks, deploy your men to give us a safe perimeter. Bloom, you're with me. Daria, take Davies and see what you can find."

"Aye, aye, ma'am," came in unison from all who were given orders.

Wilks deployed his unit to cover the entrance and the lift shaft and placed sentries intermittently in the hallway. Daria started at the rear with Davies while Emily took Bloom to the front rooms to begin their investigation.

Scan looked nervous. "I just don't feel right", he mumbled to Snake, who was standing beside him at the shaft. "Something's wrong."

Chapter 15
Vengeance's Pride – The Decision

Supreme Command be damned, he thought. He was in command of this mission and if he was wrong, they could torture him later. But something had to be done now.

"Get a team together." He motioned to his first officer. "Now."

Chapter 16
Aboard the *Vanguard* – The Briefing

"Gentlemen," the general began, "no, scratch that. We're not gentlemen, are we? If we were gentlemen, none of us would be here. No, we're killers, each and every one of us. Do you know the difference between a killer and a soldier?" No one answered. "A soldier kills because he has to. He's sent into battle with orders and a weapon. He points his gun in the direction he's told to, and he kills whoever is in that direction. Each one of you in this room could walk up to a stranger, look into their eyes, and end their life without a second thought if you felt it was necessary.

"It's that ability that makes you unique and exactly what we, the Coalition, needs right now. You know of the hostile forces that are invading our sector and of their superior weaponry. The way the Coalition sees it, we only have one of two chances. The first involves a team of scientists and marines on a world at the outer rim of our known explored space."

Glances and murmurs began after the last statement. Seth wondered to himself just how much they were going to tell them and how much was actually being left out. His personal feelings for the general made him think that the old man would tell them everything he knew, whether he was supposed to or not. The general allowed the murmurs to subside before he finished telling the group what the other team's mission was.

Then he continued debriefing the soldiers—killers—on what their role in this whole thing was. "We are traveling deep into the heart of what we believe to be our enemy's territory. We are to undertake the single most dangerous recon mission in the history of man." He smiled a smile that made most of his cadre shiver from deep within. There was just something eerie about his grin. "You might be wondering why it is that I say that. For starters, we don't even know where we're going. We've never charted this region of space and have no idea of the layout of our enemy's forces, bases, or even home planet. Our job is to stumble around this sector until we find something or get captured." His grin widened, almost too eerie to take at this point.

"The top brass hopes that a team of extremely fine-tuned soldiers will be able to live long enough after capture to escape and bring back valuable information. That's how desperate they are back home. They're willing to throw away your lives on a chance, a hope that they might get something, no matter how slight, in return for your death. Well, I'm not.

"This ship is the finest in the fleet. It uses some of the alien's technology that we found at the initial dig site more than five years ago. We are currently traveling nine times faster than our normal propulsion systems would allow." Again murmurs and looks were passed through the crowd of listeners. Seth noticed that Surgeon was taking it all in stride, never losing focus. Damn, how he admired that guy.

"The exterior hull is also designed from information gathered at the dig. Although the interior is standard Coalition layout, the exterior hull shape and the energy signature that the engines produce should allow us to be undetectable to any of the aliens' sensors."

"Isn't the information from the site more than a thousand years old?" Joker asked

The general continued, "That's a good point, son. Based on the very limited amount of information we gathered from our outposts that were destroyed, it seems as though their weapons signatures are exactly the same from the information we obtained at the first excavation site. Our scientists find it very odd that there has been no variation in their weapons signature for a thousand years. However, they are hoping that if their weapons haven't changed in that time that maybe their sensor packages haven't either. It's a pretty big IF but unfortunately it's the best they can do.

"Now," he continued, pointing to the star charts, "I have decided to head in the direction of this solar system here." He highlighted a system containing fifteen planets and a binary star. "Strategically speaking, this is where I would place a primary defense grid. We're going to sneak in to the system using this ring of asteroids for cover, along with the radiation from the binary star to mask our presence in the system.

"If our recon comes up empty-handed, I have mapped out five other systems that I feel are likely to hold military forces based on their location, size, and resources. Of course, they may not think as we do and could possibly have a completely different strategy when it comes to troop placement."

Joker, feeling confident, decided to speak up again. "Or they just don't have anyone as smart as you running things, sir." This actually got a small, if not careful, laugh from the group.

"Hopefully, son, they're as dumb as you. Then we won't have any problems at all." It was hard to tell if he was joking but when he threw his head back and began to laugh, everyone joined in. The general eyed Joker and gave him a wink to let him know that there were no hard feelings.

The briefing continued for another four hours and two kegs. They went over maps and information from long-range probes as well as information gathered from the original dig site. During all this, Seth just couldn't help thinking about the other team. He wondered how their mission was going.

Scan

NAME: SCAN
SPECIES: TRIZITE
MOS: COMBAT DIVER
RANK: FIRST SERGEANT
AGE: 70 - EARTH STANDARD
SEX: MALE (ISH)
HEIGHT: 5'2"
WEIGHT: 198 POUNDS

The water was warm and viscous, so different than what Murgag was used to. The sensation was invigorating and even pleasurable as the fluid swirled over his scales, almost as though a hundred pilot fish were embracing him and cleaning him from head to toe. The only downside was the thick fluid also made it feel as if he was swimming with a rope tied around his waist and holding him back; it was damn hard making any progress in the stuff that passed for water on this planet.

Murgag finally reached his destination and planted the device. He couldn't talk in the fluid so he used his wrist communicator to type a message and send it back to his handlers: Mission complete. With that done, he took a look around and decided to take a different route back to the extraction point. The oceanic life on this planet was extremely interesting and a few of the locals were actually very playful with the new stranger.

Murgag found a few underwater coves that would have been perfect for nesting if he were back home and ready to procreate. Much to his family's dismay, he wasn't remotely ready to have any children yet. He had donated his seed to more than one Trizite that was ready, but he just wasn't emotionally ready to have his own.

Murgag found it odd that when he thought about himself, he used the two-sex species' concept of a "male." His species only had one sex, but spending so much time with humans lately, Murgag was starting to think of himself as a "he." Maybe it was because he had only been a donor so far and not a grower. In most other species, the donor was thought of as the male and the grower was the female.

Trizites lived on average between two hundred and twenty years to two hundred and fifty years, Earth standard time. During that time, they could both donate or receive genetic information from other Trizites in order to procreate. A Trizite could donate at any time during their life but the ability to receive only came a few times, and randomly at that. When the time came to receive, the Trizite could ignore the calling or go find a partner to donate.

Partners were chosen mostly for what their DNA could offer and partly for emotional reasons. Trizites didn't have sex but the experience was still pleasurable. They had soft spikes surrounding their eyes that when rubbed in the correct way, felt extremely wonderful and allowed the receiving pouch in their abdomen to open. The donor then released their seed into the water so it could float into the pouch. Once in the pouch, the material mixed with special stem cells that eventually grew into embryos. One or two embryos would be made and delivered about five months later.

During the last month or so of incubation, the parent would find a place to nest. The nest needed to be in a safe area that could be protected from ocean predators but also in an area that was rich in food for the extremely hungry kids that were about to be born. Unfortunately, areas rich in food were also rich in predators, which made safety very difficult at times.

After the birth, the new family spent the next several months bonding while the younglings were taught basic survival skills. Before the Trizites became a more advanced civilization, the family would spend much more time in this first phase of life in order to make sure the kids could survive on their own if anything happened to their parent. However, in the new age of things, they spent very little time in the nest before returning to civilization. The kids would be taken back to the nesting area several times a month to work on their skills but the old ways weren't as crucial to survival as they once were.

Murgag had been honored more than once by being asked to donate but the one time his body told him he was ready to receive, he passed up the opportunity because he just didn't feel ready. His parent had been disappointed but not upset; after all, the parent had passed up their first procreation opportunity also, but had used the next two opportunities to have children. Murgag wasn't sure whether he would ever feel ready. The fact that he was looking at potential nesting places made him realize that if he just stopped thinking and fretting over it, he would probably be giving in the next time his procreation cycle came around.

Murgag reached his extraction point and the boat that was waiting for him. After climbing on board, he received cheers from his comrades and a kiss on the cheek from his handler, Martha. Her lips brushed up against his spikes and sent a pleasurable chill down his scales. Trizites had absolutely no sexual compatibility with any other known species, so Murgag assumed the kiss from Martha was friendly rather than suggestive.

Martha always seemed to have a soft spot for Murgag, in fact, she was the one who gave him his human-pronounceable name. It was a play on words and an inside joke that no one but Martha and Murgag found funny.

The boat sped away into the night with its occupants, completely unaware that it was followed. The pursuers were using a local species of whale as their pursuit vehicle. The Trizites hanging on to the whale couldn't talk with the species of this planet but their genetic similarities along with the inherent empathic abilities of Trizites let them urge the whale to do their bidding.

Both parties reached the same destination within minutes of each other. Murgag got off the boat with his fellow conspirators and walked into town with them. Their pursuers also went in to town but not before sending their location and status update to their superiors. It seemed as though everyone was going to get to relax a little before the events waiting to unfold took place later in the evening.

Murgag ate dinner with his friends and decided this planet would not make a good nesting ground; the local seafood was absolutely horrible. The food aside, he was having a great night and feeling rather pleased with their accomplishments. Once they left the planet, the device would do its job and they would be on to their next target. Life was good.

~

Murgag was awakened by harsh vibrations resonating through his sleeping tank. The vibrations were unmistakable to anyone who had ever experienced an explosion under water; the apartment was under attack. Murgag tried to jump out of the tank but never had the chance; at least three other Trizite hands were pulling him out and hitting him repeatedly at the same time. He wasn't completely unconscious but he was close enough that he wasn't putting up a fight anymore. He was barely able to register one of the attackers say, "This is the one we need alive. Kill the rest."

~

Murgag felt the dry abrasive dirt hit his face and chest and he was instantly awake. A fairly large and intimidating Trizite was standing in front of him with a now empty bucket. A slight smirk was rolling across the abductor's face and his spikes were turning to a purplish hue, highlighting his smugness with a hint of contempt.

"Why are you doing this? Please let me go", Murgag pleaded, trying his best to make his spikes' color match his words. Extensive training had allowed him to alter their color and to also block other empaths from feeling his true state of mind. The problem was, both tasks took a supreme amount of effort and he wasn't in that great of condition right now.

"Oh, please", the captor moaned. "Do you really think you can fool me? Your spikes tell me everything I need to know. If you really want to play this game, I'm willing to spend the next twenty minutes showing you all of the evidence I have, including photos and video surveillance. Most of the evidence shows you being an eco-terrorist."

Murgag pulled limply against his bonds. "Me! The terrorist! I am not the one destroying the ocean and all of its inhabitants on this planet!"

The captor smiled. "Fantastic. I am so pleased that we will not be wasting any more time trying to convince each other of who I know you are and who you want me to believe you are."

"As long as you are pretending to be civil, could you please fill your bucket there with some water and rinse me off?" Murgag's skin was a combination of scales and smooth skin. The two worked together to create a sleek, fast, and maneuverable swimming platform. Throwing dirt on a Trizite would dry them out and get particles under their scales, which could be extremely painful if left untreated.

"Of course I can. We're not barbarians here; we just wanted to get your attention right from the onset." The captor made a slight hand gesture to one of his cronies standing in the back of the room.

A moment later, the crony poured refreshing water all over Murgag's head. The water washed away most of the dirt but there was still a fair amount of the dirt up under some of his chest scales. He also felt and tasted something familiar in the water.

"Has it been that long since you've been home, brother?" The captor made another signal and was brought two glasses of water. The first he kept and the second was brought to Murgag's lips by the crony.

"Go ahead and drink, brother; the water is from our home." He took a long drink himself and then regarded the glass as though it held the most prized treasure in the universe. "A little taste of home makes these backwater planets bearable."

On an emotional level, Murgag wanted to be defiant and not drink the water or drink it and then spit it back at his kidnappers. The logical part of his brain knew that it was more important to keep his strength up and take whatever they offered that would help that agenda. He needed his strength in order to survive, to defend himself, to attack and escape when the time came. So he drank. And it was the best water he had had in a very long time.

"Why"—" Murgag began but was suddenly cut off.

The captor held his hand up in an obvious gesture for silence. "Please. It will be so much easier and quicker if you just let me explain everything to you rather than go through random questions, some of which I would have no intentions of answering anyway."

He took another drink of water before continuing. "I work for a corporation that is trying to do business on this planet, a business that you and your friends are trying to disrupt. I know that you planted an explosive device somewhere on our pipeline and to be frank, we have no idea where it is. I also know that per your group's MO, the device is set to explode approximately forty hours after you leave the planet. Your departing flight left the planet six hours ago. We have approximately thirty-four hours until the device explodes and disrupts our operations. A minor disruption, to be sure."

"If you know all of that, then I guess the only thing you want from me is the bomb's location." Murgag motioned for another drink of water and the glass was put to his lips.

"That's exactly right. We will make it worth your while if you do. You already have something that the rest of your group doesn't: your life. We would be happy to add money to that already generous gift." He pulled his chair closer to Murgag and leaned in, almost as though they were conspiring together in this little escapade. "I'm not going to hurt you. I could try torture, but I honestly don't think I have enough time to get the answers I need. So the truth will have to suffice; I will pay you and free you if you tell me what I need to know. If you don't, I will simply kill you."

"Then I have nothing to say. Go ahead and kill me. Try to find the bomb on your own." Murgag was trying to work his bonds, hoping they might be loose enough to give him at least a fighting chance.

"I said I wouldn't torture you. I never said I wouldn't torture your family." He then held out a datapad that showed Murgag's parent and two grandchildren. The background in the image was the local planetarium in Murgag's home city. He knew that his parent had taken the kids to the science fair at the planetarium last week; the image was recent and not doctored.

"If the disruption would be minor, as you put it, then why go to these lengths?" If they had that photo, they must have been watching Murgag and his particular cell for quite a while.

The captor smiled. "A minor disruption to a multi-trillion dollar intergalactic company is a billion-dollar disruption. Paying you half that is much more beneficial to them. It keeps the pipeline running, which makes the investors happy. It means that certain key people don't lose their jobs because of the security breach. It means that we don't potentially lose employees in the explosion or the repair effort."

The last sentence made Murgag roll his eyes and the captor inched closer, now obviously a little upset. "You don't think we care about lives, do you? I think your track record shows that we, in fact, care more about lives than you do. Our investigation shows that you have been directly responsible for thirteen deaths. Our employees, our friends, our family."

"Those people were destroying planets, just like this one! How many lives are taken every day by your company's operations here? As I swam through the ocean, I could feel the death and the sickness. I could see the ocean life looking withered and tired. I couldn't even feed while I was out there. I didn't trust the fish around me would be safe."

The captor smiled. "You talk about saving the ocean life and in the same breath you talk about eating the local fish. That doesn't sound too magnanimous to me."

"I might expect that comment from a human, but not a brother of the sea. You know it's different. We eat to live and we don't kill for fun or profit. It's the natural order of life. A local predator could have eaten me and I would've felt no malice towards it and neither would have my family. Because that death is natural. That death is the universe working. You are killing an entire planet, for money."

"Have you ever seen a homeless sentient?" The Trizites didn't have homeless people. If a Trizite didn't want to work, they could always return to the ocean, or one of the many oceans their people owned throughout the Coalition, and survive in the wild.

"I find it interesting when I see a human holding a sign that reads 'Will work for food.' Don't we all?"

"Your point?"

"If we relocated all of the workers to this planet and allowed them to live off of the local population, they would kill the same amount of fish that we are with our business. Instead, they are working for money to buy food. They are working for food. And shelter and family and really, life in general. Unless every sentient being suddenly became a vegetarian, we will always kill animals to feed ourselves, whether the killing is directly or indirectly done."

"It's not the same and you know it. And here I thought you said you weren't going to torture me. Listening to this crap is worse than being beaten." Murgag sighed heavily.

"That sigh makes me think you have come to a decision." The captor leaned back in his chair but purposely kept from looking too smug.

"I have." Murgag wasn't sure whether his captor would really release him once he gave up the information, so he had a plan to make sure that at least some good came of it. "I want to know the exact amount of money you are offering. From there, I will decide how to have it divided among several accounts. Once I see the money transferred to those accounts, I will tell you where the device is."

"Agreed." He now let the smugness set in. "Do you see how easy that was?"

Once the numbers were given to Murgag, he gave his captor the division of assets. "Five percent goes to my parent. Fifteen percent goes to the families of the people you killed from my team. The rest of it goes to the Galactic Oceanic Preservation fund."

The captor laughed. "Well played, my friend. We will be endowing our biggest lobbying competition. Well done. But I'm curious, nothing for you?"

Murgag just shrugged. "I honestly don't think you'll let me live after I tell you where the bomb is. And if you do, I can take a small portion from my parent to get started again. Maybe go back to school or something." A lie. He was going to escape or die trying.

"Fair enough. Now please hold up your end of the bargain. Where is the bomb?" The captor handed Murgag a datapad with a map on it. One of Murgag's hands was released so he could work the datapad.

Murgag saw on the datapad that the company's search team was very close to finding the bomb on their own. He keyed in a couple of commands and the bomb's location was highlighted on the map.

"Very nice. I'm impressed with the placement location. That's the best place to do the most damage without being an obvious location for us to look." He regarded the datapad. "And now, to finish our business." He stood and loomed over Murgag.

Murgag lashed out with his unbound hand and struck the captor as hard as he could in the face. As the captor stumbled backward, his crony stepped in and began to draw his weapon. The henchman was human so Murgag turned his wrist over and launched one of his barbed darts into the human's neck. The poison, not effective on Trizites, put the human down instantly. The paralytic would wear off in a few hours if the human survived through it; not all did. They had pulled Murgag's spines when he was captured but they didn't harvest them a second time so the next set had already grown in.

The captor was coming back for Murgag and now had a knife out. Murgag swung his chair around and tried to break it against a nearby pole. When that didn't work, he stumbled, fell to the ground and rolled once. He was able to get back up on his knees and then feet just in time to avoid being stabbed in the neck by the captor. Murgag swung the chair and struck his attacker square in the hip and knocked him back again. The captor tripped and fell on his knife, impaling himself in the eye.

The captor screamed with equal parts rage and pain. Murgag tried to use the moment to his advantage and ran towards the door. He was met by three large men of different species, and even more violently by the butt of a rifle.

When Murgag became conscious again, he was tied down to a board with his arms and legs extended wide. Some superficial damage had already been done to his body while he was unconscious, but nothing too bad. He then saw his captor walk into the room, a bandage wrapped around his head and bulky gauze covering his previously impaled eye. Murgag realized he must have been out for a while.

The captor was in control of himself but just barely. "You fool! You stupid guppy! I was going to set you free! There was no trap. No double-cross. I was about to release you and put you on a transport. And now, now that won't happen. Now that you have gone back on your word, I will too."

"I never said I wouldn't try to escape or kill you. I only said I would give you the location of the bomb and I did that."

"Semantics."

"Not really, but anyway...I don't suppose an apology would really mean anything right now, would it?"

"No."

"I didn't think so. So what's on the menu, more dirt?"

"I'm glad you can be so glib; it will make breaking you so much more fun. I was thinking, because you have such an affinity for working with humans, maybe I could make it easier for you to do so." The captor played with his knife around Murgag's hand.

Murgag knew exactly what was going to happen. Trizites had webbed hands and couldn't use most human instrumentations because of it. Some Trizites had their webbing surgically altered or removed so they could use human weapons, and other objects made by the dominant fingered-species.

The webbing was extremely sensitive and even professional surgical alterations could have negative lifelong effects: Pain. Deformity. Loss of sensation or mobility. Most Trizites wouldn't even think of doing it and even fewer actually had the surgery performed.

Murgag regained consciousness just long enough to feel the knife cutting through his last section of webbing. The captor wasn't just cutting the webbing down the middle; he was actually excising it almost completely from between each finger. Murgag couldn't help but scream—he had to, with all of his might. The pain was searing through his mind like a star gone nova inside his skull.

"You took my eye, so I will take both of yours." The captor was moving around to Murgag's head. "You'll wish I had killed you. When you're floundering around this ocean without sight or webbing, you will die a slow death. You will be eaten by the most lowly predators these waters have."

Murgag felt the tip of the knife being traced around his eye socket, scraping against his spikes and causing pain that normally would've been horrid had his webbing not already been cut from his hands, causing more pain than he had ever imagined possible. The knife was getting closer to his right eye; it was about to happen.

Murgag first felt the spray of blood across his face and then the sound of the knife hitting the ground. A few muffled puffs of air, a sound that he didn't recognize, and then several bodies flowing past the table he was strapped to. As one of the bodies passed, he saw that it was a

Coalition soldier and he was carrying a suppressed weapon of some sort.

Once the room was clear, Murgag felt his limbs being released from the table. A Shirka stood over Murgag. "I'm a corpsman. Are you hurting anywhere other than your hands?"

"I, uh, yeah, a lot of places. But I think my webbings are my only real injuries." Murgag looked at his hands and couldn't believe they belonged to him. "Who are you guys? Why is the Coalition saving me?"

"We're not." A sergeant, probably the squad leader, stepped into view. "Your friend there on the floor was the lead security agent for the entire company. He was using his position to run illegal guns, drugs, and everything else you could think of all over the galaxy. He's been a target for a while now but hasn't been out in the field. This little stunt of yours pulled him out of hiding. Thanks."

"Yeah, no problem. That was my plan the whole time." Murgag flinched as the corpsman sprayed a tissue-bonding agent over his hand.

"Hey, Wilks," one of the other men said, "come take a look at this datapad."

Wilks walked to the other man. "What have you got, Bloom?"

Wilks read over the pad for a few minutes and then came back to Murgag. "I just looked over everything they had on you and the work you did here. There's even a debrief on the bomb you set. Pretty impressive stuff."

"Are you going to take me into custody? I know you aren't the police, but by Coalition laws, I am a terrorist." Murgag wasn't sure whether he even cared at this point.

Wilks looked around at his squad. "I think you'll find that despite our outwardly aggressive appearance, we're all really just a bunch of tree-huggers."

"Are you making fun of me again?" The Shirka didn't always get human humor. "I told you I wasn't scared. I was climbing that tree to get dinner."

Wilks just shook his head. "If you're interested in fighting the good fight, I can get a good word to the right people and get you into the Coalition military. You'd make a great marine."

"I don't think they would let me in with my record. I've been pretty good at hiding my tracks but I'm not a complete ghost."

Wilks just chuckled. "Hey, Bloom, think you can fix that for our friend here?"

"Sure. I'll have the records fixed by the time we board our transport. I don't want them figuring out who he is when we get on board." Bloom started working on a virtual keyboard that only he could see.

"Why would you do this for me? You don't know what kind of being I am. You don't know me at all." Murgag knew that if this offer was real, he wasn't going to pass it up.

"I do know you. Maybe not you personally, but I know *who* you are." Wilks sat next to Murgag. "You are fighting for what you think is right, and regardless of the ways you're doing it, you're actually on the right side here. In prepping for this mission we've gathered a lot of intel on you and you'd be surprised at what I know about you. All of your targets could have been Coalition sanctioned if you were with us. Just like douchebag here on the ground." Wilks pointed to the dead captor.

Wilks stood. "We're wiping your slate clean. Giving you a chance to do the right thing in the right way. I can't promise you'll always agree with your orders, but for the most part, we do good things. Think about it."

Wilks walked away. Murgag got up and followed the Shirka, who led him from the room and onto their watercraft that was waiting for them.

When they made it back to the transport, Murgag found Wilks in the forward cargo hold. "I've been thinking a lot about what you said earlier."

"And?"

"Do you really think I could make a difference if I joined the military?"

"I wouldn't have said so if I didn't think it was true. Besides, it looks like your hands are all but ready to grab some weapons and get to work." Wilks saw Murgag's spikes turn a yellowish-green color; he couldn't quite remember what emotion that color scheme was for.

"Not. Funny." Murgag looked at his bandaged hands and was thankful for the regional anesthetic the corpsman had applied to both arms below the elbow. "I wasn't sure if you meant it; that's why I asked you again."

"What's different about my answer this time?"

"This time, my arms are completely numb so I'm not in pain. Because I'm not in pain, I was able to focus on you and feel your emotions. I could tell you weren't lying. That's what I needed to be sure of before I made my decision. I'm in."

"That's great, but I'm not a recruiter. You'll have to sign up through your friendly local recruiter. After you get through boot camp, I'll keep an eye on your progress; if you do well enough, you might find yourself with an invitation to try out for Force Recon." Wilks sat in some crash webbing in the cargo hold, trying to get comfortable so he could take a nap.

"Thank you. For saving my life, wiping my slate clean, and giving me an idea of how I can do things better. I owe you." Murgag saw Wilks close his eyes and knew the conversation was over.

As Murgag turned to walk away, Wilks added, "If you ever scan me again, I'll take a knife to your feet and finish the job that guy started on your webbing."

Chapter 17
Dig Site One – First Contact

"Everyone down!" Scan cried as he hit the deck and the first energy wave came searing through the corridor. Fang was already down and rolling before Scan even yelled a warning. Scan had detected Fang's knowledge of a foreign presence at almost the exact same time he noticed it for himself. Whoever they were, they didn't have very nice thoughts.

Unfortunately, Snyder wasn't an empath or a Shirka and the warning came too late for him. His body was hit by the energy wave and his midsection seemed to just vanish underneath him. With his body in two, he hit the deck, somewhat still alive.

Daria was in one of the rooms towards the rear of the corridor and was slammed to the deck by Davies' massive body when the alarm was sounded. She heard a human scream and felt the need to run to their aid. Davies held her firm. "You ain't goin' nowhere, young lady!" He peered his head around the door. The team had opened fire on whatever had fired on them.

"What the hell was that!" Wilks demanded on the comlink. "And for that matter, who or what are we shooting at?"

Fang had the best view because he was at the forward-most room in the corridor. "I can't tell who or what they are. But judging by their size, I'd say we're in their home."

"Oh, shit." This was from Bloom. "I hope they don't press charges on me for breaking and entering."

"Cut the chatter!" shot back Wilks. "Are we doing any damage or just wasting rounds?"

"I've hit their lead man several times and nothing. My rounds are bouncing off what seems to be a personal shield. In fact, I can barely make out their forms—just relative size and position. At this distance, their screens are distorting any features that they might have." Fang let out another burst from his weapon. "I'm going to try the EMP and see if I can disrupt their shields." He fired the pulse directly at the oncoming attacker and noticed a slight fluctuation in the shield's harmonics. Fang's highly-attuned hearing had picked up a slight humming sound right before the first plasma bolts came down the hallway. He now knew that it was coming from those shields and it changed ever so slightly under the barrage from the EMP.

"I think it might be doing something. The shield's energy seems to be draining. Wilks, Bloom, lay down fire on the target while I continue with the EMP." Fang returned to firing his EMP and his two teammates followed his orders.

The shield began to sparkle and buckle under the intense beating it was taking. The enemy hadn't stopped firing but the size of the corridor just wasn't big enough for them to get more than one through at a time. The smaller humans and even slightly larger Shirka had enough room to lay down fire from four separate places at once without endangering their own squad.

A loud moan of pain was heard from the end of the corridor and the shimmering figure before them went down. The shield disappeared and a huge, never before seen alien laid before them. The other members of the attacking force decided not to wait any longer. They knew their enemy's strength now and had no reason to wait. In order to get through their shields, the slugs had to dedicate three weapons per shield. And it took a while for that to work.

The remaining four figures lunged for the entranceway. Surprisingly agile for their size, they navigated the corridor easily. The first ran straight down the corridor, unleashing deadly energy from his weapon as he went. Luckily, no one was hit as the marines stayed ducked into the rooms along the corridor.

Fang was up and roaring with his battle sword in hand. The Samurai sword, an ancient Earth design, was made on his home planet with Shirka metal and craftsmanship. Although it was human in design, it was deadly in his skilled hands. He faced the last attacker as he came through the door and with an arcing motion, brought the blade up towards his outstretched arm. Fang howled in delight as the metal slipped easily through the shield and removed the attacker's right upper arm.

Fang had hoped that he would be able to use a low-velocity weapon to get through the shields. Personal shields that the Coalition used had the same drawback. It was necessary, though, to allow the user to grip weapons, walk without being pushed away from the ground, or lean up against cover. If a shield opposed any object that came at it, the user wouldn't be able to pick up a gun because it would be pushed away from his hand. Personal shields protected against energy weapons and high-velocity objects such as bullets. Apparently, these aliens hadn't figured out how to get around that obstacle, either. Once close enough, you could see through the shield that the attackers had four very large arms, and were bipedal.

The attacker continued forward and batted at Fang with his remaining right arm. The blow caught him directly in the jaw, breaking one of the four bones that resided there. Thrown up against the wall by the oversized forearm,

Fang brought his knee up into his attacker's midsection while intertwining his right arm with the assailant's. Fang had his opponent's right arm in an elbow lock but the limb was too thick and sturdy to break at the elbow as he had planned to do.

Thinking fast, he pushed a button on the hilt of his sword, which made a small dagger point protrude from the bottom of the handle. Up against the wall, he had no momentum to use his sword to its fullest. With the attacker's two left arms beating Fang farther into the solid rock behind him, he raised his sword and brought the dagger end down into the attacker's shoulder.

With the blade deeply imbedded into his flesh, Fang began rocking the dagger back and forth, opening a large wound in the arm. A thick, sticky blue substance flowed from the gash and sprayed everywhere. Fang hoped he had hit an artery, assuming these things had arteries.

The wound made the attacker back off only slightly but that was enough for Fang to get adequate leverage. He pushed off the wall, drew back his sword and then pushed it almost full length into the attacker's side. This made the alien drop to his knees. Fang quickly took the moment to his advantage; he brought the sword down on his attacker and removed his head in one easy swing. The head rolled halfway down the corridor before it stopped.

Fang dove out of the corridor for cover as one of the attackers turned his energy weapon towards him. Once outside the corridor, he keyed his comlink. "Their shields are protective against high-energy attacks only. Use hand-to-hand weapons or low-energy rounds only. Sub-sonic rounds might be slow enough to get by the shielding." Another energy bolt seared passed Fang's head as he tried to peer inside the corridor. "I've taken out their rear support. Three are still inside."

"Everyone copy that?" Wilks asked. "Give me a sound off. I want to know who's still with me."

Everyone but Snyder sounded off. The energy blasts had stopped for the moment as the attackers had no targets directly in sight. "I can't get back in. Number three is laying down cover fire every time I try. I'm out of this for now." Fang's voice was filled with rage.

"Command channels are being jammed", Emily offered. "Bloom and I"—"

Emily's transmission cut short and Davies wrestled Daria back to the ground as she tried to leave the room. "She can take care of herself", Davies assured her. "Besides, we have one coming our way. Sit tight and we'll get to her in just a few."

Emily and Bloom sat in opposite corners of the room. Emily was intently watching their stalker. He entered the room with his weapon at the ready. It had some sort of tracker on it that beeped as he waved it around the room, trying to find his quarry. It made a different pitched tone as he pointed in Bloom's direction. At the change in tone, he started towards Bloom's corner.

Emily could see the whole thing from where she sat but knew that Bloom had no idea that he'd have company in just a few seconds. The attacker's back was to Emily and she decided that it was now or never. She pulled out her throwing knife, which Daria had given her and had taught her how to use. Taking aim, she threw it at the center of the beast's back.

Good luck and bad aim landed the knife deeply into the alien's neck. Apparently not deep enough, though, because he turned to look for his attacker. Daria had taught Emily to always follow up a throw with either a full-out assault or a dead run in the opposite direction. She said that unlike the holovids everyone was used to watching, a throwing knife rarely caused instant death. It could however, provide an opening for the thrower to get closer to his wounded opponent. And because there was nowhere to run, Emily had no choice. She immediately leapt at her target the instant she threw her blade.

He was not only at least three times her size but seemingly four times as fast. He was already turned in her direction as she was within striking distance of his body. She attempted to butt stroke his face with her rifle but was stopped by his two lower arms grabbing her in a bear hug and lifting her off the ground. He was rearing his two remaining arms back to squash Emily's head between his gigantic fists.

A gush of blue blood splayed all over Emily's face as the creature's head split in two with a slightly muffled woomph. Unfortunately, he didn't let go of Emily as he fell forward onto the ground. His humongous body pinned her to the floor and was crushing her ribs to the point where she almost couldn't breathe anymore.

"Oh shit", Bloom said from behind the huge corpse. "Hold on, Lieutenant, I'll get you out. God, these things smell." His commentary went unnoticed by the trapped warrior.

"Shut the hell up and get him off me", Emily gasped.

"Save someone's life, get bitched at. Just trying to help, ma'am." He placed his rifle butt underneath the behemoth and used it as a lever to roll him up.

"What happened?" Emily said as she rolled out from under her assailant.

"Once inside his personal shield, I was able to fire an explosive round into his head." Keying his comlink, Bloom continued, "There's about a five-centimeter space between their personal shields and their actual bodies. If you can get close enough, you can use your rifles. I'd be damned careful, though."

"Ah, thanks for the warning", Scan came back. "I'm sure we wouldn't have figured that 'being careful' thing out for ourselves. Doc, one of them is headed your way."

"Lay down some cover fire", Davies began. "We're in a shitty location. Draw his attention so we can adjust our attack."

Wilks peered around the corner and ducked just in time to save his head as an energy blast hit the wall outside the door where he was. "I can't get out to fire. I think the walls are sturdy enough to handle our grenades", Wilks said while unhooking one incendiary grenade and one concussion grenade from his belt. "I'm tossing two in the hall on my mark. Who knows, maybe they'll actually hurt one of them." Not really believing it himself, he pulled the pins. "Mark!" Two grenades entered the hall.

The two attackers looked at the round objects and then at each other and just went back to stalking their prey. The explosions knocked the one nearest Daria and Davies back a meter but did no other damage. The flash from the explosion allowed Daria's movement to the door to be concealed from the alien's vision.

As the huge figure entered the room, Davies called out, "Hey, I'm back here. I surrender." The giant moved forward.

Daria rolled from her hiding place, holding her fighting knife in her right hand and a medicspray in her left. She had loaded every ounce of sedative she had, hoping that it would bring down the giant. She wanted answers and knew that the base commander would, too.

She sunk her knife into the alien's knee and then pulled it out, cutting the tendon holding the leg together. The right leg buckled as he turned to face Daria and brought his weapon around, hitting her with the muzzle across the face. The force threw her against a computer terminal and opened a wound in her cheek.

Davies was immediately on the creature's back, trying to choke him into submission. With one of his arms, he threw the huge marine off his back as though he were a rag doll and Davies went flying into the corridor.

It did, however, give Daria enough time to bring her knife's diamond-edged blade through his other knee and lop off the left leg, which made him fall face first onto the deck. She pressed the spray against his shoulder and prayed.

Daria quickly jumped on the creature's back and held her knife at the back of his neck. If he tried to get up, she'd sever his spine and keep him down for good. Fuck information at this point, she thought.

Scan saw Davies' limp body in the hall and dove out to pull it into cover. An energy bolt lanced out and struck Scan's hand and made it vanish before his eyes. Surprisingly, there was no pain and Scan couldn't tell whether it was because of adrenaline from the heat of battle or the type of weapon itself. He really couldn't give a damn at this point; he just wanted Davies out of the hallway. His enormous swimmer's strength made the two hundred and sixty pound body easy to pull into the cover he had just left.

Fang saw his moment of opportunity as the cover fire turned in the opposite direction. He burst down the corridor with lightning-fast speed and drove his sword into the attacker's back. The enormous back muscles contracted and trapped the blade within the creature's body. When the giant turned, he pulled the sword, still stuck in his back, from Fang's hands. Facing Fang directly, he could see the tip of his sword protruding from the alien's midsection. Blue blood was dripping to the floor.

The alien looked down at the blade and back at Fang. Weaponless and too far away now to engage in hand-to-hand combat, Fang spread his feet wide and opened his arms, pushing out his chest and howling a challenge to his opponent. Any Shirka who had even an ounce of honor in him would've dropped his weapon and faced Fang head-on with only their hands and warrior skills for weapons.

This alien apparently had no such honor and began to raise his weapon. Outraged, Fang ran towards what he knew to be impending doom. As the weapon was almost centered on its target, the sword tip emerged another foot from the attacker's chest and the giant was pushed violently forward. Taking a quick side step out of the way, Fang let the assailant pass by him and grabbed for the handle of his sword.

Grasping tightly, he twisted the blade and ripped enough muscle to allow the weapon to be disengaged from the body it was embedded in. He pulled it out and a stream of blood followed the blade out of the alien's back.

The alien continued running towards the entrance. Fang noticed that the faint humming from the personal shields were no longer present. "His shield is down. It must have been damaged in the attack."

Wilks was standing next to Fang in the corridor. He had seen the sword enter the alien and when he turned to fire on Fang, Wilks emerged from cover into the corridor. Running, he jumped and placed a sidekick into the handle of the sword, pushing it to the hilt into the attacker's back.

He now knelt and raised his assault rifle. "Open fire!" All remaining marines took positions in the corridor and opened fire on the fleeing alien. In less than a second, a couple hundred explosive rounds entered the already bleeding body and tore it apart.

The pieces fell thirty meters from the entrance to the corridor. Not much but blue stains remained to give any indication that something living once stood there.

"Sound off. Are we all clear?" Wilks ordered. Everyone sounded off except Snyder, who just let out a small gasp. Wilks walked to the upper half of his buddy's body. He wasn't going to make it; that was obvious. Even if he had the surgical suite that the poor bastard from yesterday got, there was just no coming back from this one.

Snyder looked into Wilks' eyes, reached up with his remaining arm and grabbed Wilks' shirt. He tried to speak but couldn't get any air from his lungs to get the words out.

Wilks looked into his eyes and whispered, "I know." The rest of his crew had gathered around and Emily tried to see what was happening.

Wilks pulled his sidearm out of its holster and placed his left hand over Snyder's eyes. Placing the barrel to the top of Snyder's head, Wilks pulled the trigger, ending his friend's suffering and at the same time starting his own that would last for years to come. Wilks knew he'd see that in more dreams than he cared to think about. Too many dreams, he thought.

Emily couldn't hold back the tears and slumped against the wall. Daria came running from behind and lashed out with a fist to Wilks' face. Scan and Fang held her back. "What the fuck! You murderer! I could've helped him."

Wilks stood and wiped the blood from his mouth. In an even and unaggressive tone, he offered, "Bullshit and you know it. We," he said, looking to his team, "have a pact with one another. If it comes down to this," he pointed to Snyder, "we do what needs to be done. No suffering among friends. None." Turning to Fang, he said, "Take Jockey and Cannon and make sure that we won't have any more surprises. I don't think there's any more of those aliens, otherwise we wouldn't be talking right now, but check anyway."

Turning to Daria, he spoke quietly. "Please take care of my wounded men." Still looking into Daria's eyes, he added, "Lieutenant, please come with me and we'll see about the one Doc tranqued."

Wilks and Emily entered the room with the sleeping giant. The sticky blood seemed to act as an instant coagulant and the severed leg wasn't bleeding anymore, as were none of the other wounds Daria had inflicted.

Emily turned to Wilks. "I know you did the right thing back there. Daria's a corpsman and it's her job to save marines' lives. I'd have hit you, too, in her place." She looked away. "But I'd also have wanted you to do it for me."

Great, Wilks thought, another person he'd have to face in a dream some night. Just what he needed.

"Poor Scan", Emily said aloud. "Too bad we don't have his hand to put back on."

"Ah, don't worry about him. He'll be OK", Wilks said. Emily turned to him with a confused look in her eyes. "Don't you know? Trizites are Echinoderms. They can grow limbs back under most circumstances. He's lost a whole leg before. A hand won't be nothin' to him."

Emily was embarrassed. "As a xenobiologist, I guess you'd expect me to remember something like that. Hell, right now I'm surprised I even remember my name."

"Lieutenant," Wilks placed his hand on Emily's shoulder, "you did great for your first engagement. I'd go through a door with you any day." He looked back down at the body that lay before them. "Now, what do you make of this guy?"

Bloom entered the room before she had a chance to answer. "Sarge, I still can't get command on line. I figure they're either gone or we're just cut off."

Emily had forgotten about protocol and informing command of their situation. She was sure Wilks hadn't. He just assumed—knew—that Bloom would be making contact because it was his job and he needn't be told by Wilks to do it.

"Keep trying. Send a flare up the hole if you have to. Give me an update every five minutes", Wilks said, kneeling by the giant and taking the weapon from the alien's still hand. "Let's get to work."

Chapter 18
Vengeance's Pride – Consequences

The captain listened to the report his operations officer gave him. He already knew the details of the mission as they had been played out before him on the vid screen, in the captain's room, as they occurred. But nonetheless, he had to listen to the official report that would be sent back to Supreme Command. The report would describe how he had purposely and willfully gone against the direct orders of the Supreme Command.

The operations officer finished reading the last sentences of the report. They were death sentences for the captain. "And so I hereby relieve the captain of all further duties and command until ordered otherwise by Supreme Command. He will be placed in a torture tube until such time his death can be carried out by a duly appointed executioner in accordance with article…" The captain stopped listening; he knew the rest.

"I'm sorry, sir. It was an honor serving with you. And between you and I, I fully agr—"

The captain cut him off. "Don't condemn yourself as well. I appreciate your thoughts. Now, carry out your duty." He paused and handed the young officer his rank insignia. "Captain."

Both officers stood at attention and then the former captain led the way that he knew all too well, to the torture tubes. At their present position in the galaxy, he knew it would be weeks, if not months, before an executioner would arrive to finish the task. Hopefully the new captain would "accidentally" have a surge of power directed at his tube during a training drill, which would end it quickly for him. *Months*. His body almost shivered at the thought.

Chapter 19
Dig Site One – Taking Stock

Twenty minutes after the attack had ended, the squad was formed up on Wilks and Emily while individual debriefings of the incident took place. After everyone had given their account of the attack, Wilks asked for a situation report.

"We found a shield generator at the far end of the hole", Fang started. "It seems to have put a barrier between us and the surface. There is an impenetrable roof at one hundred meters up. The generator is protected by its own shield that we can't penetrate even with our EMPs."

Cannon took over. "I don't think that I'd be able to get through it even if I had my heavy weapons down here. Even if our people are still up top, we can't get to them and they can't get to us."

"Those shields are also blocking communications", Bloom offered. "There's no way to let them know what happened here or to even warn them of what might be coming their way. I don't know how those guys slipped in here without being detected like that."

"I think we should assume," Emily said gravely, "that they didn't slip in. We should assume that our forces topside were destroyed prior to or during our attack." All eyes focused on her. "We can't go up, so our only choice is to go down. Something very important is inside this base and we need to know what."

"Casualty report", Wilks said, not even looking in Daria's direction.

"One casualty and three minor injuries. Fang's jaw is broken. I've applied a molecular splint and it should be healed in twenty-four to forty-eight hours. Scan's right hand is gone but his natural dermal regeneration has already begun. He'd know better than I would how long it'll take before he can use it again."

Scan jumped in, "I should have a hand in a week or two. And please, no 'give me a hand' jokes from anyone, all right? I got real tired of those leg jokes after the Kaland mission." That got a much-needed laugh from the squad.

"And Davies has a minor concussion with a dislocated right shoulder. I'm gonna need some help getting that back in", Daria concluded.

Wilks offered himself, explaining that he had helped with one of these before. "All right guys, hold his legs and body down. We need him still for this. Right, Doc?"

"Yeah", Daria said, turning to Davies. "Remember when we did this on Mike? Lay still and let us do the pulling." Davies nodded and made an effort to smile.

Daria gripped Davies' right wrist and placed her right foot up against his rib cage and laid her left leg across his chest, holding his arm between her legs. Fang wrapped his enormous arms around Davies' chest to help pull him opposite of Daria. Wilks grabbed the upper thighs and hips while Scan held onto Davies' legs.

"On my mark, I'm going to pull and reset the socket", Daria said. "Fang, you pull in the opposite direction while everyone else keeps him still. OK, three, two, MARK!" Fang was quick to pull on Daria's early cue. Davies hadn't a chance to tense up yet so the shoulder went back into the joint easily, accompanied with a loud pop and scream from Davies.

"It's in." Daria checked his wrist for a pulse to make sure that they hadn't accidentally damaged anything after reducing the dislocation. "Sorry to have to fool you like that. But without any pain meds to give you, I couldn't have you tighten up on me at the last second. Fang here would've ripped you apart."

"No problem, Doc." Davies couldn't manage a smile this time. "Just don't fix that concussion yet. I think that it's the only thing stopping some of the pain right now."

"He should be fully operational in a day or two", Daria said as she applied a medicspray with steroidal and cellular healing agents into Davies' shoulder.

"Form up on me", Emily called to everyone. "There's something you should know." This got everyone's attention. "The information you are about to get is top, and I mean top, secret. I was briefed before we entered the hole and was given strict instruction that all of you were on a need-to-know basis only. Well, I think you need to know."

"Damn right", Scan said, holding up his stump. Wilks eyed him down into silence.

Emily gave them a complete history of the dig site that was found more than five years ago and what had happened since then. "We were sent to this planet to find," she gestured to the corridor that they stood in, "this. Although the top brass didn't know what they were looking for, it seems that our team has found it." Actually, she thought, the other team was unlucky enough to find it first.

"I knew as much as the rest of you did up until my briefing this morning. They never thought that we would encounter resistance down here. Those aliens," she pointed to the only one left, "must have come from a nearby ship. They weren't on sensors but I'm willing to bet that they can easily defeat our sensors."

"So what's our place in the whole scheme of things?" Davies managed to get out.

"We are looking for technology that will help us fight whoever those things are. This outpost was destroyed almost a thousand years ago and if we can find who did it or how they did it, we just might be able to save the Coalition."

"A thousand years is a long time, Lieutenant," Wilks interjected. "Don't you think that they might have advanced in that time? Their own past technology might not even be strong enough to defeat them now."

"Their thousand-year-old technology is still two thousand years ahead of us. Anything we find will surely be of some benefit." I hope I'm right, she thought silently. "And consider our most recent encounter. Something down here is worth their effort to protect it. We just need to find it, and fast."

Wilks stood. "Considering what the lieutenant has just told us, I have some information that might be pertinent as well." His crew looked at him; they knew exactly what he was talking about. "Before this mission began, my team performed a recon on some of our outer region colonies. They had been destroyed by these aliens. At the time, we only knew that we were investigating some colonies on the outer rim that had been attacked. We weren't informed of everything the lieutenant just told us."

Daria realized that she must have met Wilks on the night he finished the mission he was now debriefing them on. He continued, "The colonies were mostly just gone. No blown up structures, hardly any bodies, nothing. Just gone. No other way to really describe it. Some buildings around the outer edges of the colony were still standing but no one was home.

"The few bodies we did find looked like Snyder's. Had to have been the same aliens with these energy weapons. If anyone from my team remembers something, anything that you feel might be pertinent, let the lieutenant know. It could be the difference between living and dying for us. I'll take the heat for you revealing top-secret information if it comes to that."

Everyone nodded but no one could think of anything that might help. Wilks had summed it up. Nothing.

"Scan and Fang", Emily took a commanding posture, "those energy weapons are too big for any of us humans. Do you think that you two can handle them?"

Fang looked like the weapon almost fit him as he held it, but not quite. Still, he was definitely strong enough to carry it without a problem. "We tried using one on the shield generator already but even it couldn't defeat it. I can use it, though, if any of those guys come back." He nodded with disgust towards the pile of scraps that once belonged to his enemy who had no honor.

"I'm strong enough but it's just too big for me to use effectively", Scan said, looking like a child with an adult's rifle in his arms.

"All right, Fang, take the one you've got and we'll deposit the rest in the last room on the right. Doc, let's try to wake our friend here. Bloom, you're with us."

Every one followed the three into the room with the slumbering giant. His hands were tied in plassteel cords that even he couldn't break. Or at least that's what they all hoped.

Daria pulled a reversal drug from her pouch and injected it in small amounts until the alien began coming around.

"Mumfra da jutida aht inop kuj! Tur mak goy rhe nas op inja", he spat.

Everyone looked at Bloom. "Like I'm supposed to understand that."

"Mumfra da jutida aht inop kuj! Tur mak goy rhe nas op inja", the alien said again.

"It sounds almost like Detrill but not exactly. Maybe even a little Nortes, too. Put the two together along with a bag of marbles in your mouth, and you have whatever this guy is speaking", Bloom said thoughtfully.

"Can you understand it or not?" Wilks was obviously getting frustrated.

"Look, Sarge, he could be telling me his name, rank, and serial number for all I know. Hell, the way he's looking at me he might be telling me that my eyes are beautiful. Maybe even asking me out on a date." That got a small slap in the back of the head from Wilks as a response. "Hey, don't get jealous. You know you're still the only one for me", Bloom said defensively. This got an even harder slap from Wilks.

"C'mon, boys. Let's stay professional here." Emily knew that it was just male bonding but she didn't feel that she had the time for it just now. She pulled her pistol out of its holster and put it to the alien's head. "If we can't understand him, he's just a liability. We can't take him with us so we'll just have to kill him." She shrugged towards Daria, who was standing shell shocked, looking at Emily. Apparently everyone else was surprised as well at their lieutenant's sudden change of character. They couldn't tell whether she was bluffing or not. All except Fang, of course, who stood there smiling, waiting to see blue blood and whatever color brain spread out on the floor before him.

The alien just laughed. "You bastard", Bloom said. "You understand everything we're saying." He grabbed him by the back of the head and chin; he pulled back the alien's head. "You better start talkin' English, buddy, or she'll do it." He pointed towards Emily.

"Go ahead, you slugs", the alien said with disgust. "If you don't kill me, my commander will for failing him. My life is already over. End it now or leave me to die. It makes no difference." Another laugh sounded but was cut short.

His head split open as a hollow point round burst through his skull. Emily looked at her weapon. She hadn't pulled the trigger—what happened? Everyone looked at

Wilks, who had his weapon still pointed at the now destroyed head. "That was for Snyder, you piece of shit."

Fang looked closer; the brain was actually a darker shade blue than the blood. It looked good on the floor, though. Blood for blood, as it should be.

"Now let's open this treasure chest and see what we've got." Wilks looked at Emily. "Unless the lieutenant has something else in mind."

"No, I think you're right. Bloom, let's see if you can get that lift to work."

"Am I gettin' overtime for this or what? Bloom this and Bloom that. What's he saying, Bloom? Open this door and find out if it's booby-trapped, Bloom." He looked at Emily's non-smiling face. "Sorry, Lieutenant, just trying to get a laugh. It's good for you to laugh in the face of danger. Don't you think?" he added meekly.

With a single finger, she pointed towards the lift. The two walked over together as Wilks laid out a new formation plan to the rest of the team. On the floor near the assembled soldiers, Snyder's red blood began mixing with the blue blood of one of his killers. No one noticed what happened next as the two fluids intertwined. This was unfortunate.

Chapter 20
The *Vanguard* - Deep Inside Enemy Territory

Seth and Surgeon stood on the bridge as the ship prepared to land on an asteroid that was within their target system. The rock was almost the size of Earth's only natural satellite. This would be the fifth sensor array they had deployed. Seth was hopeful that any one of the other four would start sending back useful information. So far the sensors hadn't picked up any intelligence concerning their enemy.

"Touch down on my mark", the helmsman said to the bridge crew. "Firing landing thrusters now. Three, two, one, mark. Planetfall complete, sir."

"All stations reporting condition green", the officer at the conn station reported. "Landing pistons have been deployed. We are reading all-stop and are anchored in."

The captain thumbed his chair's comlink. "General, we have completed the landing cycle at the coordinates you requested."

"Thank you for the ride, Captain. We are almost ready to deploy our first sensor array", the general's voice came back over the speaker.

"I will be in my ready room if you need me." The captain turned to the two commandos still standing on his bridge. "Don't you two have a job to do? I don't care to be a sitting duck any longer than necessary."

"Aye, aye, sir!" the two men said in unison as they came to attention. They performed an about-face and entered the lift. Surgeon pushed the button for the main cargo bay. Seth looked at him and raised an eyebrow.

"You can't blame the old man." Surgeon came to the captain's defense. "We are in unknown territory and sitting pretty for anyone who would want to take a shot at us. I'd want to get out of here as fast as possible, too, if I were him. In fact, I want to get out of here as fast as possible and I'm not him."

"Yeah, I guess you're right. I'm gettin' pretty anxious, too." Seth returned his gaze to the lift doors. When they opened, he found himself stepping out into what could have been compared to a nest of angry bees.

The ship's crew were running themselves ragged, trying to help the commandos load their sensor gear into the skiffs. The soldiers were yelling at the crew, giving orders, and just being pains in the ass for the most part. Tensions were definitely running high right at that moment.

Surgeon approached the general. "Sir, I've checked with the loading chief and we'll be ready for deployment in less than five minutes."

"Good. I want to try something different this time to see if we can deploy the grid faster. There will be two skiffs per unit. One will carry the sensor equipment and two men, while the other will carry four men and provide cover fire and ground support should the need arise." The general was still looking at his men preparing for their mission. "Two craft will perform perimeter guard duty around the ship and immediate area with three men per craft. You and Cadet will be in the lead skiff upon deployment."

"Yes, sir", Seth answered for Surgeon. "Thank you, sir."

"Thank me when this is all over." The general cast a glance at Seth. "If you're still alive. If any of us are."

Surgeon gave a small nod towards the general and started towards his craft with Seth in tow. Each skiff was eight meters long and four meters wide. When the entry hatches were closed, there were no visible seams or entrances. The crew wore helmets that transmitted real-time data of the space surrounding the craft in every direction that the wearer turned his head; this made physical windows on the craft unnecessary. The craft looked like a dull black cigar made for a giant.

The hull was designed with millions of fiber-optic relays built into every square centimeter covering the ship. When the ship was being scanned, the energy entered the fiber-optic relay and passed through it to exit at the exact same point on the opposite side of the hull. Unless the ship was moving too quickly for the relays to transmit the energy to the other side or the hull was somehow damaged, the ship could avoid detection by even the most sophisticated scanners. Or more precisely, all the ones that had been encountered so far. Who knows what kind of scanners these aliens might have? Seth didn't even want to think about it.

"Take the co-pilot's seat." Surgeon gestured to Seth as they boarded the craft.

Both men took their seats and put on their helmets. Once in flight, it would be the closest experience to flying, without mechanical aid, that they could get. With the helmets sealed at the neck, the visuals put before the wearer were so clear and precise, it was as though they weren't wearing a helmet at all. Everywhere they looked, they saw what was going on around the ship without actually seeing the ship. It was as though they were just floating on air.

The central computer used light that entered the fiber-optic relays and translated it into a picture that was projected onto the pilot's visor. The image could be changed to a variety of different displays such as infrared, acoustic sonar readings, or a combination of any of the other many settings the helmet had.

Seth winked once with his right eye to activate the comlink in his helmet. "All crews report in." After receiving confirmation from the units, he began to lift his skiff and head for the open bay doors. "Team five will patrol the area in a five-click radius from the ship. I will take team one directly aft of the ship to set up our sensor arrays. Team two will go directly to port, team three to the bow, and team four to starboard.

"Remember to check in every twenty minutes. We'll be thirty clicks from the ship so if anyone gets into trouble, it'll be a few minutes before help can arrive. The sooner the warning, the better. Don't anyone be a hero."

"With how much we get paid?" Joker said from team three. "I don't think you have to remind us."

"Yeah, well, I get your tapioca pudding if you don't come home tonight", Blaze said as he started his patrol route in team five.

"Let's get it done, people." The general's voice was distinctive, even over a comlink channel. All chatter ceased immediately and the ships started out on their first official task of the mission.

Chapter 21
Dig Site One – Now We're Getting Somewhere

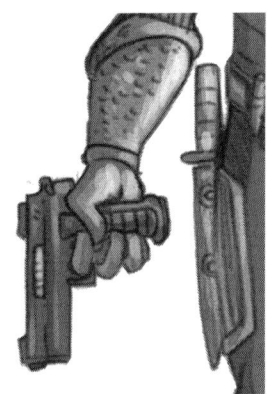

"Son of a bitch!" Bloom yelped as blue sparks jumped from the wiring he had pulled from the wall. They were unable to find another access plate like the one outside the main door. The only thing they did find was a display panel to the left of the lift. It was in pieces now as Bloom attempted to hotwire it. "I figure that whoever was the last one down this thing locked it somehow from the bottom. I can't get the right combination of wires to bring it up."

"Maybe there isn't a combination of wires. Maybe those don't even control this thing", Davies said from his makeshift cot in the hallway.

"How much rope do we have left?" Emily asked over her shoulder.

"Not enough to get down to the bottom. Especially because we don't even know how deep it is." Daria was just finishing up making an inventory of the supplies. Luckily not much had been damaged in the recent firefight.

"Motherfucker!" This time it was closer to a scream from Bloom. He turned to look towards the laughter coming from behind him. "What the hell is so damned funny!" he demanded.

Wilks pointed to Bloom's head and tried to speak but ended up rolling on the floor and laughing hysterically. Tears were streaming down his face.

What Bloom couldn't see was that the last shock had stood his hair on end. All his hair His arms, head, eyebrows, everything. It was just too funny not to laugh.

Finally gaining her composure, Emily said through slight chuckles, "Here's what we're gonna do. Bloom, have Daria take a look at your burns. We're going to camp here for the night. In the morning, we'll use what rope we have to get down the lift shaft.

"We'll go down one at a time and anchor ourselves to the wall at the end of the rope. When we all get to that point, we'll slide the doubled-up rope through the top anchor and reattach it at our new anchor point and start over. We'll do this until we reach the bottom. Any questions?"

"Where'd you get balls so damned big?" Scan asked from the rear.

"Wouldn't you like to know", Emily said, turning towards Davies. "You think that eight hours will give you enough time before we try this thing?"

"You bet, el-tee. I just need a little rest." Davies allowed his ever heavier eyelids to close. He was asleep before his eyes vanished behind the lids.

"I'm gonna wrap this burn for tonight and then I'll give you a topical anesthetic tomorrow before we start our descent." Daria was almost finished applying the dressing.

"Thanks, Doc. You got anything for this headache?" Bloom asked, rubbing his forehead.

"Just a little violin playing for you. Just kidding, I have something that should clear it up for you. Scan, how's that hand coming? You gonna be able to make it down that hole tomorrow?"

"Yeah. I'll just need to seal it to help prevent an infection. If you have any of those steroids that you used on Davies, that would help some."

Daria got out the steroid spray and left the cellular repair solution in the bag. The cellular spray tended to act as a coagulant in Trizites, which actually inhibited and even sometimes stopped their natural healing abilities.

Steroids, on the other hand, helped to repair muscle tissue and increase the red blood cell count, which increased the amount of oxygenation within the body. Put those two together and steroids had a tremendous healing ability.

Of course, even after hundreds of years of advances in protein supplements and body conditioning resources, steroids were still abused. Daria hated to see a marine on 'roids. They were usually mean and strong enough as it was. An extra dose of testosterone just wasn't necessary.

Although, one time she was glad that a fellow marine was a junkie. She was in a trench sitting in mud up to her waist, taking fire from all directions. Her platoon had been ambushed and help was five minutes out. That was about four minutes and thirty seconds too far.

A 'roid junkie marine was in the pit next to Daria and started to freak out. Daria kept trying to calm him down and was starting to reach into her pack to put sedative in her medicspray.

The huge marine turned to her with glazed over eyes and said, "Cover me." He grabbed the rifle of the dead marine next to him along with his own and began running towards the first enemy position. His armor took several rounds before the first one pierced his left shoulder. He kept firing.

He slung his right weapon over his shoulder and pulled two grenades from his chest and threw them into the first machine-gun pit. He was close enough that the explosion ripped off his left arm as shrapnel tore through his armor. He raised his right arm and kept firing.

He ran to the second pit and triggered a mine on the way. He was thrown forward while his legs went in every other direction. He kept firing.

With the second machine-gun pit cleared, he turned to fire on the force occupying the opposite side of the pit his platoon was stuck in. He took two rounds in the chest through his destroyed armor. He kept firing.

Only when his right arm was finally shot off by the enemy did he stop firing. When he saw Daria starting to squirm from the pit towards him to help, he used the stump of his right wrist to arm his last grenade. He rolled over on it so he would take the full blast and not harm his would-be rescuer.

The platoon had been saved by a junkie. She had never really liked that guy, she couldn't even remember his name, but she was glad that he had been around on that day or she wouldn't be around right now. Of course, she mused to herself, that might not be for long anyway. She handed Scan the medicspray of Deca.

Emily walked by and gave Daria a smile and a nod. Bloom stood. "Hey el-tee, let's see what we can make of this equipment before we sack out."

"Sounds good. I think I located a command terminal in that room we were in before the attack. Hopefully it's a little friendlier than those lift wires."

"Yeah, tell me about it. Let me get my datapad from the gear. It has a decoding and language analyzer program that I created. That guy," he said pointing to the covered body of the alien prisoner, "sounded like he was speaking some familiar languages mixed together. If so, it shouldn't be too hard to translate."

"If they occupied this space more than a thousand years ago, it would make sense that their language had been passed on to indigenous species in this sector. Over that length of time and a separation of cultures, it could've very easily sprouted into hundreds of dialects by now", Emily replied to Bloom as the two left Daria's earshot.

Daria turned to Davies and took a vital signs reading off the patch she had placed on his forehead. She stroked his blond hair out of the way, which had grown a little too long since they took this so-called "cush" assignment. She began to feel very attached to this marine. She had already lost one man who she loved and didn't even want to imagine losing a second. Without even thinking, she bent over and gently kissed the sleeping marine's forehead.

 Davies stirred but never opened his eyes. Daria would watch him for the rest of the night.

~

 "Hey el-tee, you really think that's a smart thing to do?" Bloom asked as he flinched every time Emily stabbed at another button on the console.

 "I don't think that we could trip anything from in here. But even if I could, it's a risk that we're gonna have to take if we want to find anything out." Emily stopped and smiled. Bloom looked over her shoulder to see what she had accomplished. "There", she said and pointed to the screen. It was scrolling information. "One reason we haven't come even close to deciphering their language is that we haven't found enough characters to even try to configure a base alphabet to start from."

 Bloom's lips curved into a smile that matched his CO's. "That should be more than enough for my program to run. I'll set it up to scan all night and it should compile enough characters to translate this language. Unless, of course, this is an encrypted console and these aren't actual alphabet characters." The two looked at each other. Bloom shrugged and set up his scanner and started the program.

 Emily left Bloom to his task and found Wilks. He was talking to Fang about the watch rotation for the evening. "Sergeant, can I speak with you for a moment?"

 He gave a small nod and finished his sentence to Fang, who then turned and walked towards the other members of the recon team. "Can I help you, Lieutenant?"

 "As you know, I'm new at this command thing. I put Daria as my second because she is my friend and I trust her. But you were right, corpsman aren't put in charge for a reason." Wilks tried to interject but Emily waved him off and continued, "It might be even worse command judgment to go back on my decision in the middle of things but I think that it's the right thing to do. From here on out, you're my second, as it should have been from the start. Daria will understand, and probably even be a little bit relieved."

"I think you're making the right decision. Daria is a good soldier and outstanding corpsman, but she isn't a field leader. Yet." Emily looked at Wilks quizzically. "Snyder was my second and I'll need another. I think that Doc has the right temperament and instincts to do it right. It's just that no one's ever taken the time to show her how it's done, because no one ever thought that she'd be doing it."

"Isn't Fang next in line?" Emily asked.

"Yeah, but he'd sooner run the team into a death trap than try to think his way out of it. It's just his way but it's not a way that I'll condemn the rest of my men to if I'm not around to protect them. No, Doc is the next best candidate. I'll make her a part of as many of the decisions I make as possible so that she gets a feel for it."

"Good. And thank you." Emily looked out towards the center of the hole. "Now, let's go over the watch rotation and a few other things I have questions about." Wilks raised an eyebrow as he cocked his head towards his CO. "What?" Emily asked.

"Oh, nothing. It's just, well, that's the first time an officer ever admitted to having a question. And especially to a non-comm."

"Well, get used to it. I'm sure there'll be plenty more." The two soldiers talked for another hour before finally hitting the sack.

~

Bloom was the first one up that morning. He had been anxious all night and barely got any sleep at all. He was too excited to see whether or not his translation program had worked.

"Yee haw!" Bloom shouted from the console. He heard thirteen rifle bolts being worked and turned to see everyone aiming in his general direction. "Sorry to wake you guys up. But it worked! My program deciphered their language."

All weapons were put to safe and groggy marines roused themselves to walk to Bloom. Davies tried to get up but he was still a little weak. Daria put her hand on his shoulder. "Just lie there. I'll be back in a few with some breakfast."

"Where's the can?" Davies asked.

"We've been using that room in the back. It didn't really hold anything that looked too important." Daria helped her friend to stand and then walked towards Bloom.

"After the first two hours," the excited linguist started, "the scanner started to only get repeated characters so it guessed that it had a complete alphabet to go on. After a few hours of decoding, it realized that the position of the character in a line was just as important as the character itself.

"For instance, take the human letters *b* and *e*. Put together they spell *be*. Put them together with other letters like "*in-between*" and they help to make a different word but those two letters still sound the same. Everyone follow?" His teammates nodded. He continued, "They have ninety-three characters in their alphabet. Each character has a different sound depending on its numbered position in a sentence. In English, a letter has one of several different sounds dependent on the letters surrounding it.

"So to us, the *be* in *in-between* sounds the same as just a regular *be* whereas for them it would have a totally different sound because the letters occupy the third and fourth positions instead of the first and second." He was bouncing like a puppy now.

"Well, that's all wonderful, Mr. Wizard, but have you actually learned anything?" Wilks was glad that his friend had cracked the language, but alien dialect wasn't as interesting to Wilks as history or other fun subjects.

"Oh yeah, tons." He gestured towards the scanner. "It's been reading all night." The lieutenant pulled up shipping logs and it seemed to be about six standard months' worth of manifests.

"This hole was a main cargo bay with weapons storage as well. My guess is that the team from site two set off the weapons cache by accident somehow."

"These shipping manifests." Emily was looking over the translated data. "They have food lists that show they had quite a diverse population of species at this outpost. Many of these foods represent the dietary needs of some of our Coalition members."

"I ran a tissue and cellular analysis of each of the aliens last night." Daria spoke up from the back. "They have a high level of animal proteins and very little or no plant proteins in their make-up, suggesting that they are strict carnivores. They probably eat their food just after death or even live. Either way, I don't think that they cook it beforehand."

"That assumption would fit with the large amount of game animals on this list. Some are things that I've eaten before." Emily continued to scan the list. "Let's set the program to search for keywords, like weapons, ships, and fuel. Anyone else got ideas?"

"How about prisoners, charts, intelligence, and quarters assignments?" Wilks asked from Emily's side.

"I'll get right on it." Bloom took the device from Emily. "I'm going to set up a relay system that will allow this unit to send information to a portable one that we'll have with us. That way we don't have to wait around here for the data; we'll just get it as we go."

"All right, you've got as much time as it takes for us to get our descent planned and rigged. Think you can do it?" Emily asked, walking towards the group's gear.

"All that and a few surprises to boot", Bloom answered without lifting his eyes from his console.

"We've reconfigured our gear for the next leg of this trip", Snake, the intelligence officer began. "We can dump a lot of this commo and scanning equipment as we won't be setting up a base camp. We'll need to be much lighter because we're on the move now and just in case we run into anymore of the indig pop around here."

"I've got our descent planned and ready to go as soon as we piton this side of the lift shaft and assign everyone their positions. We should be ready for descent in fifteen mikes", Fang offered.

"Get it ready and let me know when it's done." Emily turned towards Daria. "Doc and Wilks, you're with me. Everyone else, get to work."

"Aye, aye, ma'am", came back at her in unison.

Daria and Wilks walked to Emily, who laid out the new chain of command to her soldiers. The threesome got casual glances from the rest of the team; they knew what was taking place. Doc was a good soldier, no one disagreed on that, but after what they encountered yesterday, Wilks was the one for the job.

"Actually, el-tee," Daria sighed, "that takes a load off my shoulders. Wilks, you're a good man. Piss poor drunk but a good man."

"Don't think that you're off the hook entirely." Wilks took over. "You're still my second and you need to remember that when the shit hits. And you know as well as I do, it's not 'if' it hits but 'when.' Especially after yesterday. I'm certain that we'll have an opportunity to test ourselves against those guys again."

"You can count on me", Daria said while thinking, *just like Snyder knew he could count on you.*

"We're all ready, el-tee", Fang said.

"I'm just finishing up, too." Bloom walked out from the room he was in. "I was able to access their data banks and sequence the download. It's going to cycle through base operations first, then their history files, and finally their personal logs.

"I'm going to set these little devices," he held up a device that was about two times the size of a standard comlink, "about every three to four hundred meters. They'll relay the data to my portable console. I should have enough for almost ten kilometers of travel. More if there aren't too many things down there to disrupt the signal. And, of course, less if there is."

"Corporal Davies reporting for duty, ma'am", Davies said from behind the group.

"Is he OK to travel?" the CO asked.

"Yeah, a little slower and more clumsy than usual, but he's OK." Daria walked over and took Davies' weapon. "Now, c'mon, you know the regs. No weapon will be carried by a soldier who has had a recent head injury. When I think that you're safe, you'll get it back."

Daria locked the weapon down to a pack that was being strapped on to Scan. His strength would allow him to handle the little bit of extra weight better than anyone else, even with only one hand.

The first team stepped up. They had decided to use their two ropes to have two people to go down at a time rather than one person on one with a backup rope shouldered. As they double-checked their harnesses, Bloom spoke up from behind.

"By the way, I thought that everyone might be interested in this. I still haven't found out what planet they come from, but apparently they didn't name their species after their planet like most species do."

"What do they call themselves?" Snake asked as he readied himself for descent.

Bloom simply said, "Extinction."

Surgeon

NAME: SURGEON
SPECIES: HUMAN
MOS: FORCE RECON
RANK: SERGEANT MAJOR
AGE: 38 - EARTH STANDARD
SEX: MALE
HEIGHT: 6'01"
WEIGHT: 198

CLASSIFIED

Chapter 22
The *Vanguard* – Sensor Deployment

"So, got anyone back home?" Seth asked Surgeon from the co-pilot's seat.

"We're coming up on site one-A for scanner deployment", Surgeon said with a complete absence of emotion.

Seth eyed his friend and knew not to press the question any further. "Fire team one." Seth's helmet automatically opened a channel to his wingman after he announced their call sign. "Perform a twenty-meter perimeter sweep of lead vehicle and then settle into a covering position as we deploy our first sensor array."

"Fire team one, on our first sweep. See you guys in about five mikes. Out."

Surgeon's movements became more deliberate and focused. More so than a veteran of his caliber needed to be. He was obviously thinking of something, or someone, else. Seth couldn't help but feel bad for bringing up such an obviously sore subject with Surgeon.

In their line of work, it seemed to be one of three stories that most professional soldiers had when it came to women. First and most common was that some farm boy had met the woman of his dreams, most likely the first woman to make him cum harder than a freight train, and she turned out to be a whore. No surprise there. He woke one morning to find her and most of his belongings, especially money, gone. And through all that, he still loves her. So he joins the military to forget her and with the secret dream of finding her again while stationed on some planet far from home. And of course she runs back into his arms at the first sight of his face, apologizing out her ass for how much she hurt him and how she had no choice because her mom, sister, dad, brother, aunt, or grandparent was ill and she had to get the money somehow for their much-needed kidney, liver, lung, or heart transplant. This, of course, never happened, at least not that Seth was aware of.

    The second most common love story was of a dedicated soldier who had the most beautiful and loving wife at home that any man could ever want. She was dedicated to their marriage and to the man in the uniform. Unfortunately, the man was almost always more dedicated to the uniform than the woman. And although she tried to deal with it and he tried to change, nothing ever gave and the vid-calls from light-years away changed from "I love you's" to "Fuck you's" and everything went to shit. Either she started drinking or he did, and more commonly both did. And in the end she either leaves him, sleeps with some REMF while he's out on tour, or kills herself. Sometimes it gets real dicey and she sleeps with his best friend, leaves him, and then kills herself. But that's only if you're lucky.

    The third, and absolutely least common type of military romance, is also the worst kind. It will chew up a professional like Surgeon as though he had stepped on a bouncing betty while getting hit with flechette rounds at close range. It's almost like romance type number two. A soldier finds his perfect soul mate. The two lovers intertwine mentally and physically as though they were the same radiant energy trapped in different bodies. And no matter how many times duty calls him away, she is always there for him when—if—he comes home. Her strength does not waver and his love for her never fades. But again he is torn from her when duty calls and he never knows whether he'll see her again. Death doesn't scare him, but the thought of leaving her all alone and without his love to hold her does. He can't bear the burden that is weighted on his soul. He knows what pain she'll go through when the base commander knocks on her door carrying an envelope that contains a letter coldly outlining the death of her beloved. It's too much for any one man to bear for any length of time.

Seth looked at Surgeon and decided that it was romance number three that made his face turn to stone at Seth's inquiry. Seth thought that he could empathize with Surgeon, for he, too, felt as though he had found his soul mate. They had only touched briefly for an instant but he just knew what she could—would—mean to his life if he ever got back to find her again. He would get back to find her again; he had no other choice.

"Hello!" Surgeon knocked on Seth's helmet. "Would you like me to wake you when I'm done setting up the sensors or would you like to help?"

"Yeah, uh, sorry." Seth's helmet hid his blushing. "I'll get the drilling equipment and survey gear. You get the sensor array."

"Hold on a second." Surgeon started patting down Seth's uniformed body. "I'm just looking for the general you have shoved up your ass somewhere, because I know that you by yourself wouldn't be ordering me around."

"Yeah, yeah, let's just get on with it." Seth couldn't tell but he was pretty sure that Surgeon was grinning behind his visor.

"Survey team one," the pilot of fire team one called, "we have finished a perimeter sweep and are taking up position on your six for rear guard. We did detect a minor power fluctuation from bearing two-six-three degrees of your present position, at fifteen meters out. It looked like it could be just a stray radioactive isotope. Probably nothing but you're gonna be walking around anyway, so you might wanna check it out."

"Copy, fire team one. Thanks for the intel. Now just sit back and start on that picnic lunch you brought while Cadet and I do the work." Surgeon picked up his gear and started the pressure hatch's decompression cycle.

The asteroid's gravity was about equal to that of Earth's own moon. It made the ninety kilo drilling gear that Seth carried much easier to manage than if he would've had to carry its entire weight unaided. Surgeon took the lead and used his handheld positioning sensor to find the exact coordinates of the predetermined spot the computers had picked out for their first sensor array.

As they neared the point, Surgeon's sensor began to detect the energy reading that fire team one had told them about. "Hold up here." Surgeon put his gear on the ground and Seth followed suit. "I want to find out what this reading is. You know, make sure that it won't interfere with our sensors."

"I'm with you on that. I'd hate to have to relocate an entire net after setting it up." A sensor net was a precisely set circuit of sensor arrays over a one kilometer square area. Each sensor had to be placed within five cubic centimeters of a pre-designated computer plotted coordinate. If the energy reading that Surgeon was detecting interfered with signal quality, and they found out after setting up the entire net, they would have to take it all down and start over just because their first placed sensor was getting fuzzy signals.

The signal suddenly vanished. "What the hell?" Surgeon whispered.

Seth approached him and looked over his shoulder to review the sensor's data. "It could've been a space rock with a radioactive isotope in that had a short half-life. Maybe it landed here right before we began a sweep of the area and then faded out. It happens all the time in space."

"Possible, but I want to keep an eye on this area just to be sure. I'm gonna set my scanner up to relay info back to us from this position." Surgeon tapped the keys on the instrument's panel and set it down before heading back to the drill site.

Seth set up the drilling platform and began his excavation of the fifteen-meter hole that would be necessary to plant the first of ten sensors that would make up the net. "I set it for automatic. The computer estimates thirty minutes for completion."

"How about you?" Surgeon asked. Seth had no idea what he was talking about. "Do you have a woman back home to talk about?" Surgeon clarified his question.

Behind his opaque visor, Seth's eyes stared blankly into space. "Not really. There was one girl back home before I went to boot, but she was a superficial bitch who didn't love me enough to stand by me when things got rough. But then I met someone, someone I really wanted to get to know."

"What happened to her?"

"You broke my nose and I ended up here with you. Not much of a trade-off, to tell you the truth." Seth patted Surgeon on the back. "I mean, you and I are buds, but c'mon, you don't hold a candle to her."

"Why don't you tell me about her? Sometimes it's nice to hear about home from someone other than your own memory." Surgeon just didn't want to think about his own home right at that moment.

"Well, she has"—" Seth didn't get a chance to finish; the small explosion that came from the drill stopped all conversation.

The explosion was the drill bit heating up and fracturing at its weakest point. The lack of sufficient oxygen limited the flames to an initial small chemical burn, which ceased when the self-oxygenating fuel source from the magnesium burned itself out. "What the hell was that?!" Seth said, jumping to the drill's display screen.

"It looks like the drill bit got caught on something that over-torqued the shaft and blew the bit. But I don't know what could've done that so fast. The drill should've stopped as soon as it hit something too hard to penetrate."

Surgeon was scanning the ground with Seth's handheld sensor. "Holy shit", he mouthed from behind his visor.

"A sonar scan shows a hollow cavern below us. About ten meters cubed. Small enough to evade our ship's scanners. It's made of an unknown metal alloy." Surgeon looked at Seth and then turned towards where he had placed his own scanner. "That radioactive isotope was positioned at the far edge of the cube below us. I'm willing to bet that it's not a natural occurrence."

"Tell me something I don't know, like what it is." Seth came to Surgeon's side.

"Get out the laser drill bit. The one-centimeter diameter bit. We're gonna see if we can crack this egg." Surgeon turned towards his rear guard. "Sensor team one to all units and command ship. We have found something at site one. I am relaying data to all hands now."

"I have received the data." The general's voice was anything but pleased. "What's your plan?"

"We're setting up a one-centimeter laser drill bit to try to penetrate the structure. After which we'll insert an optic camera to take a look around", Surgeon said as Seth began to drill into the structure.

"Keep your visor on relay mode. I want to see the operation in real time", the general said from the ship's operations room.

"Aye, sir. Sensor team one out." Surgeon turned to Seth. "How you doin'?"

"I'm actually getting through this stuff but it's gonna take about five minutes." Seth never stopped watching his console. He guided the drill bit millimeter by millimeter until finally it punched through the surface of whatever was below them.

Surgeon had the camera ready for insertion but Seth had to cool the edges of the hole with liquid nitrogen before they could proceed. Even with the almost non-existent atmosphere of the asteroid, the laser drill created enough heat that it would take almost a minute to cool off and that was sixty seconds more than Surgeon cared to wait.

Surgeon put the optic camera in the hole and almost pulled it out instantly from what he saw. When he realized that his initial fear was unfounded, he settled the probe back into place. "Sir, if you're getting this as clear as I am, I don't have to tell you what I think it is", Surgeon said. Seth became nervous when he saw that his mentor's hands were trembling slightly. Surgeon saw what Seth's eyes were focused on. "Fear keeps you alive, kid. Don't ever let anyone tell you different. The difference between a coward and a brave man is that a brave man does what he knows has to be done in spite of his fear."

Seth looked at the vision of computer arrays coming up from the box and into the optical camera. "Well, at least they haven't detected us yet", Seth offered.

"What makes you think that they haven't? This could be part of their early warning system. Either their highly advanced technology isn't working today or they're just waiting for the right moment. And now that we've found this, they've got nothing to lose."

"Surgeon's right." The general spoke to the entire landing party. "I want everyone back on board now. Battle stations, everyone."

Beyond the general's voice, the ship's captain could be faintly heard, "Red alert. All hands to battle stations. This is not a drill."

Seth jumped into the co-pilot's seat as Surgeon took his place at the command stick. The communications of their small skiff was patched into the bridge of the main ship. "Three vessels approaching from zero-nine-three mark two-one-one", the conn officer said with an adrenaline-rushed voice. "We are being targeted. Lead ship is firing a pulse weapon."

The communications went silent.

"All skiffs are under my command." Surgeon switched to a secure frequency that the landing party was designated to. "Hopefully our stealth technology will defeat their sensors. All craft converge on the main attacking vessel and deploy limpet mines on its hull at these points."

Seth was already one step ahead of his partner and had projected a holographic display of the oncoming enemy vessels. He was touching points on the hull with his finger to mark the spots for the mines to be placed.

"Welcome to the first battle of the war", Surgeon said before executing his final ascent towards the main ship.

The ships had either decided that the skiffs were of no immediate danger or they were unable to detect them. The oncoming craft prayed for the latter.

Fire team two was in position first and held steady until the rest of the team was in position. The alien technology may not sense the oncoming crafts but it would surely detect the placement of limpet mines on its hull.

When all teams signaled their readiness, Surgeon slaved their fire controls to his own and deployed all the mines simultaneously. He then cut the slave circuit so that the ships would be able to fight on their own. After the main ship was destroyed, the other two would surely attempt to locate the attacking vessels.

Below them, their general's ship was taking a beating. Small explosions were erupting all over the hull. Seth looked at the damage and turned towards his pilot. "I don't think that they're trying to destroy it, just cripple it. The damage is focused at key areas, engine room and thrusters."

"Yeah, well, our mines are targeted for their hull." Surgeon was about to key the mines' trigger.

"Wait." Seth stopped Surgeon's hand. "Look, they haven't even reacted to the mines. Maybe they don't even know that they're there. If we destroy the ship now, the other two might destroy ours out of fear or just plain anger." Both men's hands eased back from the firing control. "They don't seem to know that we're here, either. Let's use that to our advantage. Let's see where they take their prisoners. The mines might be good for an escape diversion later. That was a secondary option for this mission anyway."

Joker, along with everyone else on the secure frequency, could hear their conversation. "I agree with Cadet. Let's wait and see what's happening. Get our bearings and then fight. Even if we do take out one of those things, the other two will get us. It's not a winning proposition to sit here and fight."

"Agreed", Surgeon said somberly. "Everyone keep a two hundred meter separation to reduce the possibility of detection. Stay on my lead. If anything goes in the wrong direction, those mines are being blown and we split into two groups to attack the remaining vessels."

Surgeon tilted his head down to view the general's ship through his holographic visor. "We won't leave your side, sir", he whispered to his commander, whose ship was already being boarded.

Chapter 23
Dig Site One – Further Down the Rabbit Hole

During the descent into the lift shaft, Bloom was explaining to Emily what his translation program had figured out from its earlier scans. "The computer says that the alien language is a composite of about seven known species. I was right when I said that it sounded like Detrill and Nortes. Those two comprise the bulk of the language. The other five are languages from species that we know very little about. All are very private and tend not to deal with the Coalition. All in all, there is a seventeen percent portion of the language that the AI doesn't recognize."

"Does that mean that the translations aren't going to be exact? Are we going to push the wrong button down here because it tells us to?" Emily asked through her comlink.

"No, nothin' like that. The AI was able to decipher the language based on its characters and the eighty-three percent of the language it did recognize. There is always room for error, but it's so marginal that I wouldn't worry about it." Bloom was in the second descent team and was waiting on the fourth anchor for the rest of the team to finish with the third leg of the journey.

Bloom finished typing in the last of the command lines into his computer before he spoke to Davies. "Hey sniper, I just finished altering your visor's display optics. It's linked to my translation program. It will automatically translate any alien writing that you view with it.

"I can do the same for our virtual visors, too. If the translation program sees any writing that can be cross-referenced with information from the data bank, it will automatically throw that info to the top right corner of your visor for viewing." Bloom hit the Enter key to finish the process.

Davies' visor blanked momentarily and then returned to normal viewing. The markings on the lift shaft that he, and everyone else, had been passing for the last couple hundred of meters suddenly became readable to the sniper. "Hey guys, I can read these markings. It says that we're at level forty. We got thirty-nine to go."

Two hours later, the whole team had arrived on the roof of the lift car that was at the bottom of the shaft. Snake had already cut a hole in the corner of the roof for the team members to get through.

Daria unslung her rifle and took out her environmental scanner. She jumped through the hole, with Snake close behind her for cover. Snake took up a crouching position while Daria walked twenty meters ahead of the lift car, sweeping her arm back and forth to cover the entire area. "Scans show no anomalies in the air down here. No unusual bacteria, viruses, radiation, spores, nothing. I don't think that we'll need our breathers on. The air is stale but we'll live."

"Thank you, Doc", Emily said over the comlink while adjusting her VR goggles. "Fang, you're on point with Davies in second. Between Fang's senses and Davies' thermal imaging, we should get a fair enough warning if anyone's down here."

Every member of the team checked their magazines and a few reloaded for a full one. Magazines slapped home and receiver bolts were actioned. "Team two has Scan on point. Fall in and move out", Wilks ordered. The rest of the team followed Daria's example and jumped through the hole. Once everyone was through, the two teams formed up on their respective point men.

The first room was as large as three football fields and at least fifteen stories high. "This is where the cargo was initially brought to before it got sorted through and then distributed through the complex." Bloom was reading off information that his AI was fed from the computer terminal back in the first bunker. He walked next to Emily so he could keep her updated on any information that he might get.

"Those doors over there," Bloom pointed to three double doors to the right of the team, "they go to the workers' living quarters and galley areas. The ones to the left go towards the livestock pens for the guys in charge. If I'm interpreting the data right, I think that all of their workers are slaves. It doesn't say it outright in the data banks but everything points to it."

"Like what? Give me an example", Emily said.

"Well, I had enough time during our descent to go through some personal logs as well as cargo logs. First off, some of the workers arrived on the cargo ships and were listed as cargo, not passengers.

"Second, in one of the officer's logs it mentioned how he had to continually put some of his workers from the motor pool into something called a "'torture tube.'" That doesn't sound good in any language."

"Davies," Emily's comlink automatically keyed an open channel to the sniper at the mention of his name, "I think you were right before when we were talking about the artifacts. Bloom thinks that the aliens used slaves as their primary workforce. That could explain why the different artifacts were made by the same creators but designed for different races to use. Do you follow where I'm going with this?"

"Yeah, I think so", Davies replied. "If each species only knew how to use a small portion of the technology, then no single species could overthrow their masters. They would have to get other races to help out, using their portion of knowledge in order to make things work. If all of the shipbuilders wanted to revolt, it would be difficult to take over a ship if another species had designed the computer components and they were all in a foreign language."

"I might be able to verify that theory." Bloom tapped his VR goggles and brought up a control display, which he worked in the air with the fingers of his right hand. To the unknowing onlooker, it seemed as though Bloom was on drugs and swatting at invisible bugs swarming around him. "I was able to call up the living quarters and guess what, they are all clumped together by species.

"Now that could just be for ease of feeding or to reduce racial tensions. Let me try to cross reference something here…" Bloom's last word hung on his lips until he finished his search through the database. "And we have a winner! Mr. Davies, you seem to be correct. Each species was assigned to specialized tasks and they didn't do anything else. One species called the Panzts were half a meter tall and were used to clean out the plasma drive intake systems on the alien ships. Their size made them the perfect cleaners. They were all housed in Blue Sector."

"What about the Detrill and Nortes, what did they do here?" Daria asked from her position in the rear squad.

"I already tried to find that out. They apparently weren't on this outpost. At least they weren't stationed or living here. I do see some data corruption gaps that look purposeful, like someone was trying to get rid of information. Maybe the data containing information about the Detrill and Nortes was in the parts that were removed." Bloom stumbled slightly as he was paying more attention to his VR readout than where he was stepping.

"That's odd." Emily actually paused in her stride to think about it. She was nudged from behind by Scan before she began to walk again. "The alien language is more than eighty percent Detrill and Nortes yet there is no mention of them in the records.

"They would've both had to have had some contact with the alien species in order for their languages to match so closely. More than likely a lot of contact among the three races. What do we know about the Detrill and Nortes?"

Snake, the intelligence officer, joined the conversation. "Both races are very private about internal matters. They do trade freely with the Coalition and allow travel to their worlds without restriction.

"The two races don't interact at all. As far as our intelligence knows, the two have never gone to war with each other and there is no present conflict between the two. They just don't seem to want to have anything to do with each other."

"The Detrill are master craftsman when it comes to weaponry and ships", Fang offered. "I have two of their weapons on me right now. There are many mercenary training centers on their home world, along with five of the galaxy's most highly acclaimed military officer schools."

"The Nortes are noted for their commerce and government." Emily was searching her memory. Although she specialized in ancient history of other civilizations, she did keep up to date on some things. "They have ambassadors throughout the Coalition and are usually involved in peace treaties and other humanitarian events. So why wouldn't they tell the Coalition of their history of enslavement?"

"They might be embarrassed by it or just want to forget about it all together", Bloom said as he continued searching through the database. "Also, just because they're called the Detrill and Nortes now, doesn't mean that they didn't have a different name while they were enslaved and that's why we can't find them in the database. Maybe they just barely got away from their captors when these outer perimeter posts were destroyed. And they were so frightened that after they fled, the survivors changed their species name and have been hiding out ever since."

"Possible. As soon as we can communicate with the Coalition again, we're going to send a priority message back to the nearest star base and get some answers." Emily had a look of determination on her face that Bloom hadn't seen on her before.

The team was past the cargo bay and sixty meters into the main passageway when they came to an intersecting hallway. "Which way?" Fang asked.

"The passageway to the left goes to sickbay and the quarters for the enslavers." Bloom scrolled a map on his VR goggles. "The one to the right goes to the command center and the docking bay."

Emily had linked her imaging system to Bloom's and was seeing the same map as he was. "Bloom, scroll up to the docking bay and give me the distance from our current position. Belay that, make it the estimated distance in a straight line from the second survey site to the shipyard and then overlay that image with a plotted course from site two to site one."

"That would be approximately three point five clicks, el-tee. And when you overlay the two…the docking bay is directly underneath the primary survey site." Bloom looked at his CO with wide eyes.

Chapter 24
Vengeance's Pride – Decisions, Decisions

The new captain sat in his seat on the bridge awaiting orders from Supreme Command. "What is taking them so long?" he asked no one in particular.

In the background, the faint scream from the former captain rose from the torture tube one deck below. The sounds were piped into the ship's intercom system for the whole crew to hear, and allow them to contemplate what it meant to disobey orders from Supreme Command.

"Ensign," the captain looked to his junior officer, "you have the bridge. I'll be back shortly."

"Your orders, sir?" the officer timidly asked.

"I don't care what you do as long as you don't crash us into that planet", he said, pointing to the view screen. "Besides, it seems as though the captain's job on this mission is to just sit in that seat and do nothing." He turned his back and headed for the lift door. "Think you can handle that?" he asked over his shoulder, not bothering to wait for a response.

Once in the lift, he keyed the torture tube as his destination. The lift doors opened and the guard on duty looked dryly from his former captain screaming in agony to his new one.

"I need to speak to the capt—" he paused, "prisoner about our current mission. Turn off the tube and leave the room. This is top-secret information we will be discussing." The captain had to look away from his former commander.

"Yes, sir." The guard obeyed as he turned the device off and stepped into the lift. Regulations stated that two officers were to be present during an interrogation of a prisoner, but the guard had seen his great captain suffering for too long and had to leave. He had tortured many of his shipmates before but none had been his captain. To him, it was as though he were torturing his own father, or at least his idea of what he thought a father was.

The lift doors closed and left the room empty of prying ears and eyes. "Don't even try to escape", the junior officer began. "The launch bay is undergoing routine maintenance right now and you wouldn't get very far. Besides, it's the mid-meal rotation cycle and most of the crew is awake. You would be recaptured quickly if you tried to leave. Now, I have some questions you must answer for me."

The former captain looked into the eyes of his operations officer. He knew what he was getting at when the new captain had finished speaking. The launch bay was undergoing minor repairs, which meant that it held no atmosphere and the artificial gravity was cut while it was worked on. The conditions allowed for easier access to high placed circuitry for the work crews and due to lack of oxygen offered less chance of an electrical fire starting. The area would also be devoid of personnel at feeding time. The route to the launch bay would most likely be clear of personnel at this time also. He was supposed to escape. That's why his friend was here now.

"Now," the interrogation continued, "why did you load up a secondary shuttle with weapons prior to the assault on the planet?" The former captain had done no such thing. "And why was this environmental suit in your ready room?" The prisoner had never seen that suit before; it even looked a little big for the man.

The prisoner knew that his time was now. The young captain had set up the whole escape for him. He looked down at the ground and covered his face with his two upper hands. If the escape didn't look genuine, his friend would be filling his place in the torture tube from where he had just been released.

The prisoner reached up with his lower hands and hit his friend in the jaw with both fists. The younger officer flew backward. He jumped up from the deck to face the escapee and attacked. The much older combat veteran was more than his junior's match and would've been able to kill him easily, even if the new captain hadn't already planned the escape for him.

The attack was easily side-stepped and four fists plunged into the young officer's back. The captain fell into the torture tube. The prisoner quickly turned the device on. The tube automatically latched its new prisoner into place and began to probe for weaknesses. The process would take about fifteen minutes. After the machine decided on which nerve endings were more susceptible to pain and which ones were more likely to lead to unconsciousness and even death, it would begin torturing its new victim. Every victim was different in its tolerances and weakness and this device could be counted on to figure out where each one was. He hoped that someone would find his friend before the torturing began, or before it had gone on too long.

The prisoner took the lift to level ten, where he peered cautiously out the doorway. With no one in sight, he ventured out towards the launch bay with his pressure suit in hand. Once he reached the airlock, he donned his suit and made his way to the shuttle craft and entered the vehicle.

The craft was loaded with weapons and a battle suit with full armor. The personal shield emitter was missing from the stash, but those had to be checked out from the armory. The rest were personal weapons from his own quarters.

He began the start-up sequence and launched before it had finished. He gave the engines just enough time to come on line and then the prisoner was out the launch doors and had effectively completed his escape.

The young captain had made the right choice of who to leave in charge. The even younger ensign was sitting on the bridge when the display alerted him to the shuttle launching. He had no idea what to do.

"Lock weapons on target and hold fire." He punched the intercom button. "Bridge to the captain, red alert—I mean, to the bridge at once." He wondered whether he should've ordered the captain in that way.

"I have target lock. Shall I fire?" the weapons officer asked.

"Not until we have orders from the captain." The shaking officer had no desire to end up in the torture tube for disobeying orders or affect orders that were wrong. Especially on his first day of sitting in the command chair.

Chapter 25
Warrior Interrogation Base – At Last We Meet

The general looked at himself in the mirror that his captor had placed in front of him. It was as though he were back in college, sitting in one of his science classes, learning about the human anatomy.

The torture tube that he had been placed in seemed to be finished with the first part of its task. After probing the general for almost twenty minutes, it began to remove the flesh from his right leg. He was actually quite astonished at how the procedure produced no more pain than a scraped knee might have.

The device used a micro laser to cut the flesh into a thousand different puzzle pieces, after which ten small claws proceeded to remove the layer of flesh that protected the muscle tissue beneath. After the muscle was exposed, the claws returned to liberate the delicate nerve bundles that resided deep within the general's leg.

The same procedure was performed on the general's left arm and the right rib cage. It was all very fascinating to watch. The general was quite amazed at the lengths his captors had gone to get him to the state he was now in. He wondered whether the aliens had created this technology for medical purposes and then realized how well it could work for information gathering. He shook his head, knowing that most likely not one person had ever been saved by this technology; it was created explicitly for this purpose and it would never have another.

The alien who had supervised the process pressed a button on his console and spoke to whoever was on the other end of the comm system. A door behind the operator's console opened and shed light into the interior of the room. The general realized that he was in a circular room and figured that some of his men were going through the same process in other tubes around him. He could hear the faint humming of another laser to his right.

The two aliens spoke to each other for a moment before the second came to the general. "You are different from your companions." He spoke in English. "The others," he gestured with a sweeping motion to the area behind the general, "could not stand to look at themselves being opened as you have. Although almost no pain was caused by our methods, most screamed in agony at just the sight of the procedure. Why have you not?"

The general wasn't prepared to give answers to a science survey. What could he say? That he had been tortured seven times in his life and that he was used to it? Or maybe he could tell the story of how he cut off his own left foot after it got caught in a pneumatic airlock door when he was just a midshipman at the academy.

The general was not the slightest bit disappointed in his men for their reactions to the live autopsies they were forced to be a part of. His decision not to answer encouraged the alien to make a decision of his own.

He pulled out a small board, which had a schematic of the general's body on its display. After keying in a couple of commands, the alien moved the board closer to the general's leg and compared the map on the display to his prisoner's anatomy. The alien reached out with one hand and pinched a nerve bundle that protruded from the general's shin between two of his fingers. The general winced slightly.

The alien frowned and looked at his display a second time. Reaching out again, he gripped a second set of nerve endings in his other hand and twisted. The general could not keep from screaming. "Ah, that's what I was looking for", the monster said as he typed in some notations on his pad. "It seems that you have answered the question for me after all. You have an unusually high tolerance for pain. In fact, my scanner has found that you have many nerve endings that are damaged and even destroyed. It leads me to believe that you have been questioned before?" He let the query hang for moment before he touched the second bundle of nerves again.

"Yes!" the general let out. "If you promise not to do this to any of my men, I will tell you everything I know."

"You'll tell me anyway. Besides, I have a new class of students who need the practice. They tend to over-stimulate their subjects too quickly, resulting in a premature death. So your men will come in handy, and such good timing, too. We had just run out of the last few prisoners from one of your colonies."

The alien stopped and thought for a moment before speaking in his own language to the technician who was still behind his console. The technician walked out of the room and returned a moment later with a small viewing screen, which he set down in front of the general.

"If the sight of your own flesh being pulled away doesn't bother you," he began, "then maybe seeing it happen to your men will. I'll be back to continue our discussion later. One of my students has accidentally killed the ship's second in command during the exposure process. This is a good chance for me to review the error with my students."

"You son of a bit—" As the general began to lunge towards his captor, three claws simultaneously reached out and gripped exposed nerves in his chest. The pain reduced the general to a quivering ball of flesh.

"You're lucky I was in control and not one of my students. You may not have survived that otherwise." The alien stood and left the room.

Lucky my ass, the general thought. At least he knew of one possible way to end it if he had to.

Chapter 26
Dig Site One – Got Room for One More?

The escaped prisoner made his way towards the area the humans had designated "site one." His anger and disgust for these aliens grew with each step he took.

While in the process of escaping his ship, the captain had encountered two crewman who were running late to the mid-day meal cycle. They did their best to stop him but were quickly dispatched by the more experienced soldier. He would make the humans pay for their deaths.

Once he reached the excavation site, the captain removed a small transmitter from one of the pockets on his combat vest. The transmitter put out a signal that would open the emergency escape hatch that was in every installation built by Supreme Command for almost two thousand years.

The indicator light on the transmitter blinked blue for a moment until its signal reached the proper receiver within the bunker. The light switched to a steady blue while the transmitter and receiver shared information and pass codes until the latter was sufficiently assured that the proper access sequence had been given.

The light changed once more to a steady yellow when the captain heard a hatch cycling open in the near distance. He ran to the opening hatch and stepped back when he smelled the stale air of a thousand years blow by his face. When the hatch was completely open, he entered with blaster weapons in two hands, a knife in a third, and his datapad in the fourth.

He swore an oath of vengeance as he entered the empty corridor. The humans would pay; he would see to that.

Chapter 27
Dig Site One – Unexpected Company

Scan stopped in mid-step and held up his arm to signal his team to stop. He would have made the "closed fist" gesture but his hand was still growing back and his other was occupied with the weapon it carried.

Emily came up alongside him. "What's wrong? Do you sense someone?"

"I don't know." Letting his rifle hang from the sling, he used his remaining hand and clicked a knob on his VR goggles and began to echo the display from everyone else's visors into his. After he went through all of the inputs, he looked at the lieutenant. "I don't know what it is. I sense hate. Just raw hate. I think we have company."

Fang keyed in his comlink. "I don't smell or hear anything up here. But Scan and I don't always agree or sense things at the same time, either."

"Understood." Emily turned to Bloom. "Have you had any luck finding internal scanners in this complex?"

"No, but I do know where some external sensors are. Problem is there are some relays out and they can't be accessed from my unit. The main communications room is almost two hundred meters down the corridor. If we can get there, we can see what's going on outside."

"All right, Fang, head towards the communications room", Wilks ordered from the first team. "El-tee, second team should stay here until we've secured the area. No need for us both to get whacked. We'll let you know when it's all clear."

Emily looked at Scan. "Move up to team one. I want them to have all the warning possible if something happens."

"Aye, aye, ma'am." Scan handed Davies' weapon to one of the other members of team two and took up the rear slot on team one.

"I want a two-man team thirty meters in front and thirty meters to the rear while we wait." Emily had no sooner finished her orders when four men broke off and took up their positions as ordered. "Bloom, Davies, and Doc, come with me. There was a room back about ten meters that I want to check out now that we have the time."

Bloom looked at Emily. "It's just an infirmary. There probably won't even be any access terminals in there."

"Humor me", Emily said flatly.

"Besides," Daria jumped in, "there might be some supplies I can get from there. I'm running pretty low. If their infirmary stacks up to the rest of this place, then I'm sure that something useful survived in there after all of these years."

The room automatically became lit as they entered the doorway. Lucky for Bloom, it seemed that every internal door they encountered had a simple push button activator to open and close them. Daria began going through the cabinets and pulling out alien medical equipment.

In the corner of the room was a large cylindrical object with an oval opening in the front. To either side of the unit, there were micro cutting saws and surgical gear attached to probing arms.

Davies knelt closer to inspect the unit. "Hey, Bloom, there's writing over here that my visor won't translate."

Bloom walked over with a disappointed look on his face. He couldn't believe that his program had failed. After a couple of minutes of tapping in commands to his datapad, he turned to face Emily, who was staring over his shoulder. "It can't read these symbols because they're individual letters. The AI in my program doesn't know what to make of it. So far, every one of the hundreds of thousands of words it's translated has been made up of two or more characters. There hasn't been any occurrence of a single character word yet. It might be able to translate it but not anytime soon."

Emily turned towards the console next to the apparatus. "Well, let's not waste time with that. Let's work with what we do know. Try to access that terminal and find out what this thing is. I don't know why but I think it might be useful."

Bloom went to work on the console and Emily joined Daria at a smaller console in the back of the room. "Find anything we can use?"

"Not really. There aren't any first aid supplies in here. A lot of surgical equipment, though. I think that this might have been a surgical suite if anything, but probably not your usual sickbay.

"I've been trying to locate medical documents that show the physical make-up of our alien friends. Nothing yet, but if I can find something to add to my own scans of their tissue, we might find out more about their vulnerabilities."

"Good idea. Keep it up and let me know about your progress." A little louder, she spoke to the other two members of her research team. "I'm gonna go check out our perimeter guard, see what's shakin'. Be back in a few."

Davies continued to examine the tube while Bloom accessed the computer. Daria just looked at her screen as information scrolled on her scanner pad and was stored in its memory for future recall.

Chapter 28
The Interrogation Planet

    In the week since the general's capture, Surgeon and his team had followed the ships to a planet in the system that seemed to be a small colony or military base for the enemy.

    Surgeon sat in his pilot's chair with his helmet off while he and Seth ate their dinner. With their helmets off, the interior of the ship could be set to a visual display that mimicked the inside of their helmets. Each curve of the smooth ship had fiber-optic relays built into them so the interior surface became one large, omnidirectional view screen.

    Seth looked out towards a distant nebula. "You know, it is a very beautiful region of space. There are several nebulas nearby and a lot of comet activity."

    "Pretty or not, I just want to find a way to rescue the general and get out of here." Surgeon finished his meal and put the scraps into the recycler to be used as part of his next meal.

    "Why haven't they come for us yet? Do you think that our cloaks have concealed us that well from them?" Seth was just finishing the last of his meal.

    Surgeon thought for a moment before he tapped a key to open a comlink to the other craft in hiding with him. "Cadet wants to know why we haven't been dealt with yet. I have a few thoughts of my own but I thought that I'd open the floor to any ideas that you guys might have."

    Joker was the first to respond. "I figure either they haven't spotted us yet or they just don't care enough to do anything about our presence. If they have spotted us, then they know that we're no real threat to them so why not just save us 'til later when they get bored?"

"They must have detected the placement of the mines so they have to know that we're here", Beast started. "Knowing that we're here and knowing where we are, those are two entirely different things."

"Good point," Surgeon said. "So if they know we're here but not where, how are they trying to find us? We haven't seen any ships in the area and we haven't detected any sensor scans."

Seth was next. "They could be waiting for us to make the first move. And that could work either way. They know we're here and where we are, but want to see how we'll react to this situation. Maybe try to figure out our tactics. Or they don't know where we are but are still just waiting for us to make the move. Either way, I think that this is just a training exercise to them."

Blaze, the heavy weapons officer, spoke up from Surgeon's wing. "If they're just waiting to see what we'll do, there's a good chance that we can take them by surprise. Lead them to think that we're doing one thing while planning a second. It's almost like a game of cat and mouse to them. The trick is to keep them guessing long enough so that they stay interested and continue to give us more and more rope. Then we hang them with it."

Surgeon thought for a few minutes while the rest of the commandos clogged the comlink with chatter about Blaze's idea. Finally, he came to a decision. "I have two thoughts. First is that we really have nothing to lose by trying out our theories. Even if we are undetected, we couldn't make it home under our own power. Second, if we're right, I think that Blaze's idea has a chance.

"I want the other three team leaders to come up with flight plans that will keep our friends wondering what the hell is going on. Plan sensor sweeps of the area. I want to get as close to those ships and the planet below as we can to get some good intelligence. They may stay curious just long enough for us to sneak a couple of ships in.

"I'll take any ideas, no matter how crazy, on how to rescue our captured crew and obtain a ship to get us home. We'll let the rest of the fleet worry about fighting the war. Keep the comlink clear for the next hour and then we'll compare notes."

The small spaces inside each ship suddenly came alive with activity. Unfinished meals were put in the recycler and datapads were pulled out. Surgeon smiled for a moment as he thought about home. Everyone he cared about already thought that he was dead, and that was all right, because he didn't think that he was going home this time.

Chapter 29
Dig Site One – Here We Go Again

"Hold up," Scan and Fang said nearly at the same time. Fang continued, "One of those aliens is nearby. I can smell him."

Wilks looked at Scan. "I can sense his hate, Sarge. He's pissed off, but I think that there's only one of them."

Wilks took another look at his surroundings. Not much of a defensive position in a hallway without rooms to fight from. There was a corner up ahead and the hallway shortened by about half a meter where the turn was. A man could hide above the corner in the small space and ambush whoever came from around the other side.

"Snake, get out your pitons and put two in each wall on either side of the hallway just above the corner. Make sure that Fang will be able to hold onto one with each hand and use the other two as foot rests." Wilks turned to the others in the group.

"The rest of us will sit down at the end of this hallway and act as bait. Either his scanner will detect us or he'll see us as he comes down the hall. Either way, he should be more interested in us sitting ducks than to paying too much attention to the area above him. I'm sure"—*or rather hope*, he thought—"that he thinks the element of surprise is on his side."

Snake finished the rigging with the help of Fang, who immediately got into position above the hallway.

254

Wilks turned with an afterthought. "Let's try to take him alive. Maybe he'll be more willing to talk than our last friend was. Go for leg and arm shots to disable. I don't care if the fucker needs a wheelchair for the rest of his life; I just want him alive."

Fang lay suspended above the hallway with his muscles tense with the strain of his weight and the anticipation of battle. He could now hear as well as smell his enemy approaching and he knew that the time was near. Ten meters. Eight. Six. Four. He repositioned slightly for a better angle—or was it just nerves? Two meters. The prey was slowing before the curve of the hallway. Did he sense the ambush or was he just being cautious at a blind intersection? One meter. Almost in the kill zone. The alien rounded the corner, bringing his weapon to bear on the decoys at the end of the hall.

A bright flash of plasma shot from his weapon at the same time Fang dropped from his perch and landed square on the alien's back. The blow made his shot go high and Fang's momentum dropped them both to the ground. The would-be attacker lay motionless.

Wilks and the rest of the team came running down the corridor. Scan was the first to speak up. "Uh, pretty anticlimactic, don't you think? I mean one shot goes high and we win."

Wilks looked at him with a sour expression. "If you'd like, I could start shooting at you if that would make you feel better. Take your blessings as they come."

No sooner had Wilks finished speaking when the alien came suddenly to life again. A foot attached to a monstrous-sized leg hit Snake square in the face and threw him several meters back. A small hand weapon was produced from the alien's left lower arm and with a precision shot, took out Martinez' left eye and most of his brain.

Wilks kicked at the weapon instinctively and hit it out of the alien's hand. The alien's top left hand was just as quick, though, and grabbed Wilks' ankle and crushed it like a flimsy beer can. Wilks screamed in pain as Fang brought the hilt of his sword down on the attacker's forehead, leaving him unconscious once again.

"Tie him up now!" Wilks said through clenched teeth. Snake was already up and removing several meters of Kevlar rope from his pack. They had the alien hog-tied in a matter of seconds.

"Wilks to Lieutenant O'Riley", he said as Scan wrapped his broken ankle in a splint.

"Go ahead, Wilks", Emily said from her console in sickbay.

"We just nabbed one of those bastards. Fang and Scan both think that he was the only one down here. We've got him tied up. You wanna come down here and ask him a few questions?"

"Negative. Bring him to the lab; I think we found something that will help."

"Copy, el-tee. It'll take us a few, though. My ankle is broken and Martinez is dead." Wilks winced as Scan tightened up the brace for walking.

"Understood. I'll send Cannon and Jockey to help with the load. See you guys in a bit. Out." Emily turned to her companions. "All right, let's get the finishing touches done on this thing. We've got a guinea pig to try it out on."

The room was alive with a new sense of purpose as each soldier worked double-time to finish their task.

Thirty minutes later, the advance team came through the doorway to the lab with Wilks on makeshift crutches and the huge alien carried on a stretcher between six men. Martinez was in a body-bag that was placed on an examining table at the far end of the lab.

Daria took a medical scanner to the body and examined the entry wound. The odd reading around

Martinez' skull was also present in Snyder's wounds, and Daria just couldn't figure it out. The energy signature and tissue damage looked vaguely familiar but she couldn't quite put her finger on it.

"Doc", Scan said from beside Wilks, "could you come over and take a look at this ankle? Tough guy here says that it's OK but he can barely stand."

"Yeah, sorry", she said sheepishly, momentarily forgetting that she had a live patient who needed her help. As she approached Wilks, she began to explain, "Sorry but there was a weird energy reading in Snyder's wounds that disappeared over time. I wanted to see if it was just an anomaly with him or if it was the alien's weapons. Turns out that Martinez had it, too."

"Is that important or just medical curiosity?" Wilks winced as Daria manipulated his ankle.

"Could be important. I'm really not sure." She turned to Scan and handed him her medical scanner. "Hold this steady at his ankle. I need the real-time x-ray view of his ankle as I set the bones." Scan obeyed and Daria went to work setting the three tarsals that were broken in Wilks' ankle. "Anyway, I've seen the energy signature before; I just don't know where. Not in any weapons that we've encountered but something in medicine. The way the tissue responds to the energy is also odd."

"What's tissue supposed to do when it gets hit by plasma?" Scan asked.

Daria pulled and then squeezed the last bone into place before answering. "Plasma weapons super heat the fluid in tissue cells and cause them to implode violently. There isn't enough mass in a body to displace the heat, so the plasma bolt goes all the way through two or three people until the energy is lost in the heat transfer from the bolt to the tissue cells. Or whatever target it hits.

"This plasma bolt causes more of an aging process on the cells. It's still super-hot plasma and most of the cells do implode but the ones that aren't hit directly with the energy die of old age. The cells are aged at an astronomical rate and they just die. The process of aging and tissue death occur for some time after the initial energy explosion."

"Why is that important?" Emily came in to the conversation from the other side of the lab.

"Well, let's say that you get shot in the leg but you don't die. The rapid aging process of your cells continues until your leg dies off and then eventually the rest of your torso and you go with it." She paused on reflection of her own words before she and everyone else looked slowly towards Scan at the same time.

Scan began to tear off the bandage on his stump. Daria helped him with some trauma shears and together they unraveled the bandage. The stump looked fine but Daria scanned it with her equipment to double-check.

"It seems as though the steroids and your body's natural healing ability has negated the aging process of the plasma bolt. But if you look at these readings, I think you'll agree that your healing process is quite behind schedule. You should have about a half to centimeter more tissue regeneration than you do now."

"Yeah, that sounds about right. At least it's growing back, though. It might take an extra two or three weeks to get it done but I think that I'll be fine." With a sigh of relief, Scan took out some fresh bandages and began rewrapping his stump.

"This may be a dumb question", Emily started as she scooted forward to get a better look at Scan's hand, "but, if your hand is going to grow back, won't your webbing come back with it?"

Scan finished wrapping his hand. "Not a dumb question at all Ma'am. No, my webbing won't come back." Scan's facial spikes turned a light shade of orange. "Once our webbing is damaged to a certain extent, the scar tissue becomes a part of the cells' memory and the hand grows back the way it was before it was removed."

"That sucks." Emily didn't know what else to say.

Daria spoke up to end the awkward silence. "I'm almost finished with Wilks here and then we can start on that one." She thumbed towards the tied-up alien. "As soon as I remember where I've seen this type of tissue damage before, I'll let you know. It might or might not matter. I'm sorry that I can't tell you more."

Daria used her scanner to verify that all the bones were in place before she pulled a pen-sized object from her kit. She loaded it with six titanium alloy pins. Each one was twice the diameter of a strand of hair and only two centimeters long. She placed the pen up against Wilks' ankle and fired the first pin into place. She proceeded to put two pins in each fractured bone. After the pins were in place, she applied a thin stocking over the foot and ankle and then sprayed the material with a chemical that heated the cloth and caused it to harden into a durable cast.

"We'll be able to take that off in a week or so but you should still be able to walk on it. After every march, I want to scan your ankle to make sure that the pins are holding and nothing is out of place. All right?"

Daria began to give Wilks a pain reliever when he waved her off. "I need to be on the ball. I can live without that stuff." With a wink, he added, "I didn't take anything after they fixed me up from you."

Daria just shook her head and walked to the alien, who was becoming conscious. "So, do we have the tube ready?"

Davies was tightening a bolt on the back side of the tube while Bloom tapped in commands at the main console. Bloom looked up. "Yeah, I gotta hand it to these guys; their equipment sure does last a long time. I usually can't keep our hardware operational for more than two years, let alone a thousand."

"What is this thing?" Fang asked as he inspected the tube and the surgical instruments that whirled, spun, and poked in the air as Bloom ran through a diagnostic routine.

"We thought that it was some sort of surgical bay at first but now we know what it's truly for." Emily looked at the alien, who was coming out of his stupor. Waking up, he began to struggle against his bonds until he opened his eyes and found himself directly in front of the tube. All struggling stopped and his eyes grew large as sweat beaded on his forehead. "Apparently, our friend here already knows what it is. Good, you bastard! I'm glad that you know what's in store for you."

Bloom picked up where the el-tee left off. "It's a torture device. We think that it can be used for surgery, too, but mostly torture. See, you put the guy in the tube and it clamps him down. The probes find weak points in the subject's nervous system and then exploits them. From the visual and audio logs we found, it does the job quite well."

"We need to strip his clothes off", Bloom said while still typing in commands. When no one moved, he looked up. "Hey, it's not my machine. I'm just telling you what it says we have to do. C'mon, Fang, give me a hand."

Both soldiers pulled out their field knives and went to work on the alien's armor. When they couldn't get through the thick vest, Daria pulled out her fighting knife and cut through the material as though it were butter.

When they had finished and stepped back, everyone could see the fresh wounds and probe marks all over the alien's body. "Looks like he already had a go-round with one of these tubes", Daria said.

"Who cares? I say throw him in, even if he starts to talk on his own." Wilks walked over. "Besides, he knows what's coming. If he wanted to talk, he'd already have started."

"I agree, let's put him in." Emily looked at Bloom. "Is it ready?"

"Yeah, let's pick him up and then put his back in first. This thing was designed to untie prisoners itself and then arrange the body in whatever position it needed to. I guess most of the subjects didn't go willingly. Go figure." Bloom waited until the alien was lifted to the chamber before he touched the last button that started the cycle. Two powerful arms came from the device and pulled its subject in while a cutting blade removed the wraps from the prisoner's arms and legs.

"He isn't even fighting it", Fang said almost to himself.

"He knows that he can't win", Bloom said before turning to Emily. "Ma'am, it looks as though it'll take about one to three hours for this thing to find the subject's weak points. Maybe less considering he has had a recent encounter with another one of these tubes. I suggest we set up camp and explore a little bit."

"Let's set up camp in the adjoining lab. I want at least two men in this room on watch at all times. As for exploring, we stick to data exploration for now. No one leaves a fifty-meter radius of this lab." Emily paused and thought a moment. "Bloom, Davies, and Doc, I need you three to help me gather as much info from the database as possible. I don't want anyone working for more than two hours at a time. You might pass something by that was important. After camp is set, you three take a two-hour break before starting again. Wilks, put together a watch schedule and whoever is not on watch will relax, and that's an order."

"Aye, aye, ma'am", came from everyone as bodies went to work and some went to sleep. Through all of the commotion, no one could hear the ever-so-slight whimpering that emanated from the tube against the far wall.

Chapter 30
Detrill Home World

"The court dancers are exquisite, Your Highness", the guest said from his seat next to the emperor. The men and women of the Royal Court Dance Troupe continued to dance and jump in the air with a precision that was unmatched throughout the Coalition. The costumes were simply divine and the choreography impossible to duplicate.

"Thank you", the emperor replied with great satisfaction. "They begin training from almost the time they are born. They have done me and the empire a great honor in agreeing to become an official part of the court. They are without equal."

The two men watched on from their places at the throne as the show continued. A court messenger came running into the great hall and bowed before his liege. Through his panting, he asked, "May I speak? I have an urgent message."

"Please remove yourself from the floor", the emperor whispered as not to disturb the performance. "You know I don't like the whole kneeling thing. It's just too, too, gaudy." The emperor was a fair man who rose from the lowest levels of poverty to his great position over the empire. He ruled his people with integrity and a light heart. He didn't consider himself a real emperor, but rather a servant to his people and empire.

"Yes, sire, I apologize." The messenger stood and leaned to whisper into his master's ear. "The Empress of Nortes wishes a conference with you at once."

The emperor became rigid. After almost nine hundred years of unbroken silence, the ruler of the Nortes requested an audience with the ruler of the Detrill. This could only mean one thing, and for the first time in more than twenty years, the emperor wished that he were still a peasant.

Davies

NAME: DAVIES
SPECIES: HUMAN
MOS: SNIPER
RANK: SERGEANT
AGE: 30 - EARTH STANDARD
SEX: MALE
HEIGHT: 6'4"
WEIGHT: 260 POUNDS

    The rain was pouring down so hard that Davies felt certain they were using fire hoses to supplement Mother Nature's already impressive onslaught. With the accompanying wind, he found it difficult to stand at attention but that wasn't nearly as difficult as it was to watch the rest of his squad performing pushups in the torrential weather.

    The drill instructor—DI to the grunts—walked through the ranks as he addressed them. "Oh. My. God! I could not have planned a better night for PT! You all should thank Recruit Davies for his absolute and utter lack of soldiering ability for this two a.m. wake-up call. Why don't you remind us all why we're out here right now?"

    "Sir, yes sir", Davies tried to start.

    "How about everyone rolls over and gets on their backs for some flutter kicks! And keep those feet at least six inches off the ground at all times. We will keep doing flutter kicks until Recruit Davies finds his big boy voice." Turning to Davies, he smirked. "You may continue, cupcake."

    Davies took a deep breath and cleared his throat. Raising his voice above the downpour, "Sir, we are out here because while this recruit was on watch, he forgot to secure the fire door in the hangar. In doing so, this recruit left the base vulnerable to intruders. Sir!"

"That's exactly right, sweetheart. I find it absolutely amazing that every time you fuck up, you are able to perfectly describe what you did wrong. You'd think that with all of the explaining you have to do, some of that information might actually sink into your head and you'd start getting things right once in a while." The DI continued to pace up and down the rows of recruits still performing the flutter kicks.

To make things worse, the DI had one of his assistants bring out a cot and then ordered Davies to lay down on it. Davies was digging his nails into his legs and trying to cause enough pain to stay awake. Davies held out as long as he could but there was just no way to fight the exhaustion that they all felt. Davies succumbed and even started snoring. When it became obvious to his squad mates that he was sleeping, most of them promised themselves they would kill him in his rack before the end of boot camp.

Around six a.m., Davies awoke to the sound of reveille. When he opened his eyes, he found himself still in the courtyard with his squad curled up on the concrete grinder, shivering and sleeping as best they could given the circumstances. As they began to wake up, their eyes were finding Davies and making their best effort to kill him with never before seen human telekinesis.

The DIs rotated every four hours to ensure that they were always in peak condition. This also gave the impression to the recruits that the DIs had superhuman stamina abilities. No matter how obvious the mind games were, the recruits always fell for them.

The fresh DI stepped up. "Good morning, ladies! I heard you had a wonderful PT session this morning with absolutely perfect weather. The great part is, we're already here on the grinder for our morning PT. Fantastic! Thank you again, Recruit Davies! Everyone hit the deck! Thirty eight-count pushups on my count! Ready...Exercise! One-two-three-four..."

Davies could feel the hate radiating towards him as though a tidal wave of anger was hitting him over and over again. He did his best to review every mistake he had made since arriving at boot camp a little more than six weeks ago. There were so many at this point he knew he couldn't remember them all. But he tried anyway; he hoped that maybe the mistakes and consequent punishments would help him to do better today. If not today, maybe he could do better tomorrow. He felt as if he were fighting a losing battle but he wouldn't give up, ever.

After PT, Davies marched to chow with the rest of his company and all of the other recruits in boot camp. The men and women in his company were disciplined enough to not say anything to him as they stood at attention in formation outside the chow hall. He knew that if he kept making mistakes, they would eventually lose their discipline and dish out some barracks justice some night after lights out. The thought of continually disappointing his squad and company was more motivating to Davies than the thought of them retaliating against him was.

Davies also had another form of strong motivation: his father, grandfather, great-grandfather, plus another few generations of men had all been marines. A couple were officers but most were enlisted men. His father had retired as a major after starting off as a private and moving his way through the most of the enlisted ranks before becoming a mustang and going to Officer Candidate School.

Major Davies had never forced either of his sons into service nor did he expect it of them. He had always been honest and upfront with them about the good and bad of military service. The major told his boys that he was proud of them regardless of their career choice but he made no secret of the fact that he would love it if one or both of them became a marine.

Davies was the older of the two boys by five years. His brother, Carl, was always talking about becoming an officer in the corps, even wanting to get some of his dad's previous assignments. Davies really hadn't wanted to join the military and he was happy that his brother did so their father would have at least one Marine Corps legacy. If his brother ever changed his mind, Davies knew he would enlist, get his four-year contract done and then move on.

The day came for Carl's graduation from Officer Candidate School and the whole Davies family was in attendance. There was marching, a military band playing, and all of the pomp and circumstance anyone could handle. If you weren't a fan of the Coalition, you would be after witnessing the ceremony they put on that day.

When everything was over with, the newly appointed officers were released to meet with their friends and families. Grandpa Davies had retired as a sergeant major so he had the honor of giving Lieutenant Davies his first official salute. Lieutenant Davies returned the salute to his grandfather, who was standing at full attention in his dress blues.

The lieutenant then turned to his father, who outranked him, and rendered a salute. Before he returned the salute, Major Davies stated without any hint of a smile, "You better outrank me someday, Lieutenant." He then sharply returned the salute.

With the traditional salutes finished, there was a round of hugging and backslapping from the rest of the family. Davies grabbed his younger and smaller brother in a bear hug and lifted him off the ground. "I'm proud of you, Carl."

"Thanks, brother. I know you think Dad was my inspiration for joining the Marine Corps but he wasn't. You were."

"What?" Davies thought his brother was teasing him for some reason.

"I'm serious. Dad is my hero but you've always been my inspiration. Dad is the action hero that every kid wants to be and dreams of having for a father. We were lucky to have him growing up. Even though you have no desire to join the service, you embody everything that it stands for and everything it tries to be.

"I want to give to my enlisted men what you've always given to me. Direction. Stability. Honor. Fairness. Loyalty. Brotherhood." The lieutenant saluted his older brother.

"Holy crap, I'm gonna cry, you little prick." Davies couldn't help but wipe at his eyes. "Go talk to Dad and Grandpa. They have some words of wisdom they want to pass along before you ship out."

The lieutenant gave a crisp about-face and then jogged to where his father and grandfather were waiting for him. As the trio walked away arm-in-arm, a fireball erupted on the ground and obliterated any trace that they ever existed.

Davies was barely starting to register what had happened when the fireball started to reach out for him from the epicenter of the blast. Luckily for him, the shockwave hit first and threw him far enough away that he wasn't burned to a crisp.

Shrapnel, fuel, and fiery debris rained down all over the parade field. Six other people had been killed and many others seriously hurt when the fighter jet malfunctioned and crashed on its way back from its performance in the graduation ceremony.

Davies didn't even try to go to where he saw his lineage vaporized; he knew they were gone. Instead, he gathered his family and took a head count to make sure no one else had been lost. Once gathered, he ushered them to the cafeteria where he knew there would be food, water, and shelter. The cafeteria was near the parade grounds and was ready to receive and feed the hundreds of people in attendance at the graduation. It was a good choice for shelter and he knew where it was thanks to the graduation program he had in his pocket.

Davies was barely holding it together but he was in survival mode now, a frame of mind that his father had always drilled into his sons. The major had always told his boys that when the world seemed like it was ending, it was time to step up and do your part: be strong for the weak and guide those who were blinded by fear.

With his family secure, Davies told his mother that he was going back to the field to see whether he could help in any way. He felt bad about leaving his mother but he had no choice but to try to live up to all of those things his brother had just said about him.

Davies reached the parade ground a few minutes later and found that rescue efforts were already underway. Corpsman were attending to the injured and setting up a triage and treatment area. He realized that his help wasn't needed here. The Marine Corps was no stranger to tragedy and they had reacted quickly and efficiently to the unforeseeable event. Even though the circumstances were horrible, Davies was thoroughly impressed with how things were being handled.

Davies decided to go back to his family to make sure they were still all right. As he was walking, he came across a folding conference table that had been turned on its side with paperwork and pamphlets strewn out on the ground around it. Without even thinking about it, he went to turn it over and clean up the mess. Later he would wonder why that table and mess were important to him to clean up and he would never be able to answer that question. Maybe it was because he saw something that he could actually fix, regardless of how small and insignificant the act was; it was a chance to do something.

As he began to lift the table, he heard a voice, "Excuse me, son, please leave the table on the ground."

"What?" Davies turned to see a staff sergeant looking at him.

"I'm sorry, son. I appreciate your help but the accident investigation team likes to have everything left alone so they can do their job better." The sergeant put his hand on Davies' shoulder, seeming to know that Davies wasn't just upset about the accident. "Did you lose someone in the crash, son?"

"My brother graduated today. He was standing with my father, Major Davies, and my grandfather, Sergeant Major Davies, when the plane crashed into all three of them." Davies was holding one of the pamphlets in his hand and looking absently at it.

"I'm sorry, son. There are no words for a shit-storm that big." The sergeant was no stranger to death but he was clearly at a loss for this circumstance.

"What was this booth for?" Davies was looking around at all of the Marine Corps paraphernalia on the ground.

"It was a recruitment booth. We always get about twenty or so new recruits after a graduation ceremony. The kids, and even sometimes the older adults, are so filled with patriotism after the show that they sign right up." The sergeant looked around at all of the mess. "Probably not so much today, though."

Davies put down the pamphlet he was holding and picked up one of the recruitment forms. "Well, you're going to get at least one today. Do you have a pen?"

The sergeant looked into Davies' eyes. "Son, you just had the biggest loss you will ever have in your life. I'm not allowed to take an application from anyone that I deem is not emotionally able to understand the commitment they are making by filling out that form. Look at line number twenty-nine. It even says you can't sign the form if you are under emotional distress."

"I won't say that I'm fine, because I'm not. I'm pretty damned fucked up right now. I know that. You know that. But you don't know me or my family. If I don't sign up with you right now, I'm leaving here to find the nearest recruiting office and do it there. I NEED to sign up here. Now. The last place I was with...them." Davies started rooting around the ground, trying to find a pen that he knew had to be there somewhere.

The sergeant sighed. "Son, I'll tell you what. Let's fill the paperwork out, right here, right now. Then in one month, we'll meet for a beer. If you still want me to turn in the paperwork then, I will. I promise."

Davies stood and took the pen the sergeant was holding out to him. "Okay."

When the paperwork was done, Davies handed it over and shook the other man's hand. "Thank you. Sergeant?"

"Sergeant O'Connor. Mike O'Connor." The sergeant handed him a business card. "I'm done with recruiting duty in five weeks so give me a call in three, so we can set up a time to meet. I'm sorry for your loss, son."

The two men parted and Davies went back to his family. A month later, Davies was seated at a table in a bar when Staff Sergeant O'Connor walked in. Davies waved to him and Mike sat down to a beer that was already waiting for him.

"So, you're ready to take the plunge?" Mike took a drink from his beer.

"Yes, sir. Absolutely." Davies was nervous despite himself.

"Okay. First things first, don't fucking call me sir again. Second, let's have fun tonight because you'll be leaving for boot camp in the morning." Mike smiled at the shock on Davies' face.

"That soon, huh?" He raised his glass. "I guess it's as good a time as any."

They drank for a few hours and were just about to call it a night when a group of women walked into the bar. Davies thought he recognized one of them but wasn't sure where from. After looking at her for what seemed like an inappropriately long time, he thought he figured it out.

"I think that chick was one of the corpsman at the graduation." Davies pointed to a lean, beautiful brunette.

"Let's find out." Mike turned around in his chair. "Hey Doc!"

About eight corpsman, including the brunette, turned around to look at him. "Not you ugly mugs." Mike waved dismissively to the men who were looking. "You, young lady. Can you come here for a moment please?"

The woman came over while rolling her eyes. She apparently was used to being singled out. "Can I help you gentlemen?"

Mike pointed to Davies, who stammered for a moment before being able to speak coherently. "I'm sorry to bother you, but I think you were at the officer graduation ceremony last month."

"I was. And?"

"My brother, father, and grandfather were killed in the accident. I just wanted to say thank you for all the help you and the other corpsman gave everyone. There was one guy with red shaggy hair who was especially nice to my family while we were in the cafeteria."

"I'm sorry for your losses." He could tell she meant it. "I think you're talking about Dean. I'll let him know tomorrow that you said thanks."

She shook both men's hands and was about to leave when Mike held her in place with the unfinished handshake. "Stay. Please. My friend here just enlisted and is leaving for boot camp in the morning. Bring some of your friends over. We can scare him with our combined boot camp horror stories." Mike smiled.

The woman thought for a minute before turning to her friends and waving them over. When they arrived at the table, she introduced them all. "Gentlemen, this is Gina, Linda, Michelle and Leanne. Ladies, these two are..."

"I'm Mike and this is Davies." The women and men all shook hands in turn. "And by the way, you never gave us your name, young lady."

"Daria."

Davies was brought back to the present just in time to hear the DI give the preparatory command for the company to start their single-file march into the mess hall. That was a close one. A marching mistake this late into boot camp was almost a capital offense.

After they had chow, the company split into squads to go about their training day. Davies' squad was scheduled for the firing range today. They had spent the last two weeks going over weapons maintenance, weapons handling and safety, weapons familiarization, and just about any other weapons anything you could think of. Today would be their first day with live ammo on the line.

Davies' father had taught both boys how to shoot, though Davies never really had any fun with it. His father always told him that he was a natural but he thought his dad was just being kind and encouraging.

Davies was nervous. Today was the day he wanted to turn it all around. Make his DI see that he could be a good soldier. After all, if a man couldn't shoot, he wasn't in the Marine Corps—he was in the Navy.

Once they were on the firing line, they were all given tons of instructions before the ammunition was actually handed to them. The first magazine was inserted into the weapon and the charging handle released. With the first caseless round in place, they were given the order to fire five rounds at their own pace, load the next magazine, and repeat until all five magazines were dry. They only got five rounds per magazine so they would practice their reloading drills early on and get used to what to do when their weapon goes dry.

The first twenty-five rounds were a free-for-all that let the DIs see who needed the most help. Some recruits would shoot all of their rounds in less than a minute. Others took way too long to shoot, but that was generally a better problem to have than an itchy trigger finger. Few knew how to shoot and just needed a little guidance to become good tactical shooters.

The firing line was alive with the barking of rifles sending death downrange. Most of the recruits smiled from ear to ear as they felt their first moment of being a true marine.

The DIs were plentiful today to make sure nothing went wrong. There was at least one DI per two shooters and three others walking the line independently, looking for safety issues.

The primary DI was walking the line, holding his training tablet and reviewing each recruit's scores. The tablet could show the target from any of the firing positions so the DI could review the score with recruits and other instructors. When the DI reached Davies, he was not surprised with what his tablet was showing him.

Davies was lying in the prone position with his weapon on safe and all of his magazines empty. He looked up and saw the disappointment and anger in the DI's face. From their current distance to the target, he couldn't see the bullet holes so he wasn't sure where he had hit or even whether he had hit it.

The DI leaned over and started in on Davies. "Holy shit, son! You did not hit the target even once! Are you aware that Recruit Garvis hit his target twenty-three times?! He is so blind that the Marine Corps almost didn't let him in! His glasses are so thick, we could find never before discovered planets if we pointed him at the sky tonight!"

The DI began pacing a few feet back and forth. "Everyone make your weapons safe!" Once that order was accomplished, he barked, "Everyone, pushup position! A one, two, three..."

And the exercising began. Usually the DIs relaxed with the yelling and punishment on the range but apparently Davies had taken them to their limits.

As the recruits were holding in the up position, the DI started back into Davies. "You had two weeks of weapons training and simulation! And then you come out here and choke! Not a single round hit your target! You were given one simple task, hit the red target! What do you have to say for yourself?!"

"Red target, sir?"

"Yes the red target! Do you not even know your basic colors?!"

"Sir, I believe this recruit made a mistake, sir. This recruit was shooting at the orange target, sir." Davies cringed at his own admission of once again failing to follow the instructions correctly.

"The orange target?" The DI's voice came down a few notches. He then tapped his tablet's screen a couple of times. He waved over a few of the other DIs who just gawked at the screen.

"Recover!" The DI didn't so much yell the instruction as just making sure he was heard. "Recruit Davies once again failed to follow instructions. However, his failure will be our success."

The rest of the recruits looked even more puzzled than Davies did. The DI continued, "Recruit Davies shot the orange targets rather than the red. The red targets are at the one hundred meter line. The orange targets are at the one thousand meter line. With open sights, cupcake here hit all twenty-five rounds in a twenty-centimeter circle. Most marines can't do that with a scoped rifle."

All eyes turned to Davies. "So while he did not follow instructions, he just became our primary shooter in the pre-graduation company competition. Our company can't lose with Davies as our ringer.

"From now on, each of you will help Recruit Davies on a daily basis. We cannot let him become ineligible for the competition by receiving discipline chits or not making it through any other course of instruction. Are we clear?" The DI was smiling broadly now.

"Sir, yes sir!" the recruits replied in unison.

"Good, now get back on the line and shoot the red target." This would be the first time his company beat his longtime rival's company in the shooting competition. The victory beer was going to be his this time around.

Without even being told, most of the recruits chimed in, "Recruit Davies, red target!"

And that's how it went for the rest of boot camp. Every time the DI gave an order, the squad or company would repeat it for Davies to make sure he got it. Davies wasn't dumb by any stretch of the word; he just hadn't been ready or suited for military life. But with his whole company behind him now, he was finally getting it. Even when it became obvious that his Marine Corps switch had flipped to the On position and he was doing fine on his own, they still did it. It had become their company *thing*.

Recruit Davies, right, face.
Recruit Davies, lights, out.
Recruit Davies, pushup position.
Recruit Davies...

And so the shooting competition came and Davies won it for his company without any problems. Graduation followed close behind but this time none of his family was in attendance. Davies had lied to them about the date because he didn't want them attending another ceremony less than a year after Carl's.

As Davies waded through his friends and now fellow marines, he caught a glimpse of a familiar and friendly face. As he walked towards Mike, he noticed another rocker on his arm. "Gunnery Sergeant O'Connor?" Davies shook his hand and then hugged his friend.

"I just got it last week." Mike absentmindedly touched his new patch. "I brought someone along with me." Mike looked over Davies' shoulder and nodded.

Davies turned to see who Mike was looking at. "Daria! What are you doing here?!" Davies gave her a big hug.

"Mike told me that you hadn't invited your family so we came to take you to dinner." Daria moved to Mike's side.

Davies could tell that the two were now a couple. Not that anything had happened the night they met before boot camp, but Davies had promised himself he would look Daria up after he graduated. His dad always said that the Corps took its toll on relationships the most. Davies was feeling that firsthand.

"Sounds great. I'm ready whenever you guys are." Davies tried to smile.

"Before we go," Mike started, "there is someone you have to meet."

Mike ushered them through the crowd until they found the man Mike was looking for. The colonel turned and all three saluted him.

After the colonel saluted them back, he turned to Davies and extended his hand. "So you must be the shooter Mike was telling me about."

"Um, yes sir?" Davies wasn't sure what was going on.

Mike interjected, "Private Davies, this is the colonel. He has done a lot in his career so I'll just skip to the present. He's currently the commanding officer of the Coalition Special Forces Training Center."

"Mike, I don't think I'm ready for Special Forces. I barely made it out of boot camp."

The colonel just laughed. "Private, for the last five years I've been running a pilot program that recognizes recruits in boot camp with special skills. Electronic warfare, advanced infantry tactics, shooting, etcetera. And when we find these talents, we send them through the corresponding training with our Special Forces instructors.

"We then send them back to regular infantry units but with advanced training in their particular skill set. So infantry units get some soldiers with extremely advanced training to enhance their abilities. And in the process, we hope we are cultivating future special ops guys, after you get some seasoning and field experience.

"I saw your shooting scores and I want to send you through our advanced sniper school. You definitely don't need the basic and intermediate courses. So I just need to know if you're in or not?"

"Yes sir. I'm in." Davies was shaking the colonel's hand again.

"Great. Glad to have you." The colonel started to walk away but turned and added, "Your father was a great officer and even better man. He'd be proud of you." He left without waiting for a response.

Davies wanted to follow the colonel and ask him more about what he had just said, but he thought better of it and just turned to his friends. "Shall we go?"

Chapter 31
Dig Site One – We Have Ways…

Two days after the capture of the alien, the torture tube had just begun its torture cycle. Bloom and Daria had come to the conclusion that the alien's recent encounter with a newer version of the device made it harder for the older one to find unused and undamaged nerve endings. The screams had begun around two this morning and Daria had to leave.

Daria and Davies were in the communications room a couple hundred meters from sickbay. "I hope he talks." Daria broke the silence. "It's not so much that I care that he's in pain; it's just that he's so loud. It's nerve-racking."

"Yeah, I agree. The more we learn about his species, I wish that I could be doing it instead of that machine. They really were some bastards. I can't even begin to imagine what they've done to their own quadrant of space." Davies put a hand on Daria's shoulder to comfort her. The screams had taken their toll on everyone.

Daria turned to look up at her friend. She felt a pull from deep inside herself and she began to close the distance towards Davies' face. Davies felt it also and the two friends locked in a passionate embrace and kissed.

After a moment, the two stopped and Davies turned away, ashamed of himself for what he had allowed to happen. "I'm…I'm so sorry, Daria. I would never want to hurt Mike or his memory." A tear escaped down his cheek and he felt her hand on his arm as she turned him around.

"You're not hurting Mike or his memory. I love him with all my heart and always will. We both know that death is always standing near us, just waiting to tap us on the shoulder. Mike is gone and no one will ever replace him or his memory." She paused as tears ran down her cheeks as well.

"Don't blame yourself for even minute for what just happened. I know that you've always loved me and so did Mike. He told me once that if death tapped on his shoulder first, that he would be OK with you and me. The only thing that stopped you and me from happening was you were in boot camp and unavailable. Mike and I had time to get to know each other. It doesn't mean that I loved him any less or any more, just different. We're in some shit now and who knows if we'll get out of it. Death is closer to both of us than it ever has been before. Hell, it's closer to the Coalition than ever before. I just—"

Davies silenced her with his lips and the two bodies became one as they gently made their way to the floor.

Almost two hours later, they had just finished getting dressed and started to sift through information that their datapads had gained in that time, when their reliefs walked through the door.

Snake was first to the console. "We're here to relieve you guys. I'm not sure if I'd go back there just yet, though. He's screaming worse than ever. Not ready to talk yet, maybe never will, but he sure doesn't have anything against screaming."

Patz held his head tightly between his two palms. "Got anything for a headache, Doc? I can't stand it anymore. We almost came a half-hour ago to relieve you, that's how bad it got."

Davies and Daria smiled at each other shyly. A half-hour ago and they all would've been just a little more than embarrassed. "Let me get my bag. I got some stuff in there. I think I'll stick around to go over some intel that we found. I'm in no hurry to go back."

"I think I'll head back. There are some things I want to talk to the el-tee about." Davies walked out the door without looking back.

Daria continued talking to Snake without watching Davies leave. "I'd like you to help me with this set of encrypted messages. The last message I could access talked about some sort of plague and a rising death toll among the new colonies out in this sector. Then without warning, the rest of the log entries and all of the messages are encrypted."

"You don't think that a plague virus could have lasted down here for a thousand years without hosts, do you?" Patz was beginning his attempt at decryption from another console.

"I hope not. If it's like anything that we know, then no. However, the alien's make-up is very different from our own so they could've imported different viruses and bacteria to this sector from their own." Daria began going through a different database. "While you guys are working on that, I'm going to try to get more information on their physical make-up. That will help me to determine whether or not we could be in danger."

The three soldiers went to work at their terminals. Daria paused from time to time to think about her encounter with Davies. It was the first time she had been with anyone other than Mike in over a decade. She felt odd but not at all ashamed or guilty of her actions. Mike would be happy for the only two people in the universe who he loved.

~

Emily looked at the alien and signaled Bloom to stop the machine. As the pincers retracted from the exposed nerves and flesh, the screaming subsided. "Who are you and where are you from?" Nothing. Emily signaled Bloom, who increased the intensity and started the process again. Screams echoed through the hallway.

Wilks stepped forward. "Look pal, we know that you'll talk soon enough. The records we uncovered says that you will. What's the harm in talking now instead of later? We're going to kill you when it's over anyway and we both know that, too. So talk now, less pain, and death comes earlier."

"Fuck...you!" he managed through his own screams.

"Turn up the intensity but don't kill him. We need him to break soon." Emily motioned Wilks to the hallway. "How long do you think we should give him before we give up?"

"If we get nothing by tomorrow morning, I say we kill him and head for the launch bay."

"I'm not sure about killing him. Why don't you want to take him along? Aside for the obvious reasons of Snyder and Martinez."

"If he's stoic enough to hold out through that shit," Wilks pointed at the torture tube, "you really think that he won't try to escape? He's stronger than three Shirkas and just as fast. I don't want to take the chance of him getting loose and taking more of us out. He's too big for us to drug and carry."

Emily thought and then said, "What if we drug him and leave him in the torture tube on a lower setting so that he's trapped until another team can come for him?"

"I don't like the idea of leaving a formidable enemy to our rear and unguarded. He may know of a way to get out of that thing and also where some weapons are stashed around here. No, we can't leave him behind. Besides, even if we could get him out, there's no way we could make him talk back home. We don't have anything that comes close to this torture device. If that doesn't break him, nothing will. There's no reason to bring him."

"All right, we kill him. Oh-six hundred tomorrow morning we pack out." As an afterthought Emily asked, "Who's supposed to do it?"

"Well, ma'am, you can order me to do it—we both know I will without a problem—but you're the ranking officer. You're the one who's supposed to carry out execution orders."

"I figured as much." Emily walked back to Bloom to see whether any progress had been made.

"Hey el-tee, I was just about to get you. I think I found his Achilles' heel." Bloom walked from around his console. He took out a laser pointer and marked a spot inside the alien's open chest. "That large nerve bundle attached to their spinal cord has a very specific purpose.

"The machine is going to single out a nerve branch that once severed, should reduce him to a quivering bowl of Jell-O. The nerve controls his bravery."

Emily looked at Bloom with disbelief. "What are you trying to pass over on me?"

"Really, el-tee", Bloom defended himself. "That's the translation that the computer gave me. It seems as though these aliens are to a great extent bio-engineered, either by themselves or someone else entirely. The info on this nerve was buried deep in the computer and even then it was encrypted. That's why it took me so long to get it. But when that nerve is cut it makes them talk like they were on the *Jerry Springer Show*."

Emily looked at Bloom with disgust. "That show was shit four hundred years ago and it still is. I can't believe you watch it."

"Hey, it's not my fault the guy was cryo-reserved for ever and then put back on the air. It's better than that Geraldo guy that they play reruns of."

Bloom continued with the information he had found. "These guys were the soldiers for their empire. Just like every other species, they had a specialty. Whoever the rulers were, they seem to have been extremely paranoid. Even though the warriors were genetically engineered to be absolutely loyal to the rulers of the empire, they still weren't trusted. This nerve was engineered so that warriors who were assigned as personal guards to high-ranking officials could be questioned concerning their master and what they did or said."

The machine had delicately singled out the nerve and the laser cut it in two. Bloom shut down the torturing device. "He should be ready to talk."

Emily took a step closer. "What is your name? Why are you here?"

"I am captain of my vessel. You would not be able to pronounce my name or even comprehend the sounds my language makes. My vessel was sent here to observe you."

"You've done more than observe", Wilks cut in. "Why have you attacked us?"

"I initiated the attack on my own without orders. I was removed from command and punished severely for it before I escaped to hunt you down. I have attacked you because you stand on my ancestors' ground and are in places you should not be."

"Why didn't your government contact us and let us know that we were digging on your ancestor's world? Why wasn't a peaceful arrangement made?" Emily stepped closer.

"Whoa, el-tee," Bloom said. "That nerve just makes them talk, not become docile. I'd feel better if you'd step back."

The alien continued, "Government, we have no formal government as you know it. Our war tribunal meets to decide which system we will take over and which inhabitants will be useful and therefore spared. All others are removed. I do not understand 'peaceful' so I cannot answer that question."

"What were your ancestors doing in this sector? Why did they leave?" Wilks asked.

The alien looked at him with puzzlement before he answered, "To conquer, why else?"

"I think I can answer that last question." Daria came in. "They didn't leave, they died. A plague destroyed all of their colonies in this sector. The rest of their empire was ordered to remain in their own space and never to come here or else the whole empire would be doomed."

Bloom looked at the alien. "Is that true? And if so, then why did you disobey those orders and come here now?"

"Yes, it is true. We are here now because we received a distress signal that told us the plague was a hoax. It was never true and that we were lied to. We came to find our masters and our emperor."

Emily reflected, "That must have been the signal our archeologists accidentally tripped all those years ago." She looked back at her prisoner. "How long did the message take to get to you and how long does it take to get from your sector to ours?"

"We received the message four of your months after it was sent. We can travel to this sector in two months with our fastest ships." The alien was becoming obviously more and more angered as he was forced to betray his own people.

"Why did it take you so long to come here then? Five years later, isn't that a long time to respond to a distress signal?" Wilks had his hand resting on his sidearm.

"We had to make sure that it was real. And as I said, we have no real government; it sometimes takes a while for things to be decided. That's why we need our emperor back!"

"I got news for you, buddy, I'm pretty sure he's dead by now", Bloom mocked.

The alien thrust himself at the soldier but the tube immediately responded and pinched a nerve on its subject that caused his struggle to subside with a scream. The body went limp and the prisoner was unconscious.

Emily shook her head. "Bloom, stop fucking with our prisoner!" After a curt nod from Bloom, she turned to Wilks. "When he wakes up, we'll ask him all the questions that we had prepared then we'll have the tube dispatch him. Anyone got anything else?"

Daria motioned everyone towards her console. "I remembered where I saw that energy reading before. It's a device that was invented about two years ago by someone at the Mayo Clinic back on Earth. It's a plasma wand. It uses highly focused plasma on certain types of tumors to stop their growth and eventually kill them off. It's a great new cancer treatment, still experimental but so far highly effective."

"Thing is, the information I have in my database on it shows that its energy signatures match those of the alien's weapon exactly. That's just not possible unless the same people made both items."

"So are you saying that these aliens have been secretly inventing medical equipment and then smuggling it into our society?" Bloom just couldn't resist.

"No," Daria was calm despite herself, "but after I got that mystery solved, I started to cross check other medical equipment with the stuff I've found in this lab. There are so many similarities in design, energy use, and circuitry that it can't be coincidence."

Emily's eyes got wide. "So you think that someone's been leaking information about the dig sites and exploiting the finds for profit?"

"I don't think so. Some of the equipment we use was invented several hundred years ago. Someone has had access to this stuff for a long time and has been putting out inventions every so often. I do have to say, though, that I don't think that whoever is doing it is trying to profiteer from it. All the inventions I have been able to cross check have been donated to science and medicine without any personal gain. That is unless you count the Nobel Prizes and other notorieties that go with inventing this stuff. As far as I can tell, none of the inventions have had military or destructive applications. I can't pinpoint one species that has more of these inventions tied to them anyone else. They all seem to come from different species. I honestly don't get it."

"Wilks, add that to the list of questions we ask our friend over there for when he wakes up. Let's get our gear ready to move at oh-six hundred." Emily went back to her console to dig through more information.

Chapter 32
Somewhere In Space Between The Detrill And Nortes Home Worlds

The honor guard led Emperor Nogil through the ship to the empress' chambers. Nogil noticed every little nuance of the ship; after all, his people had designed it more than a millennia ago. Before poverty struck, Nogil himself had been a shipbuilder at one of the main Detrill shipyards. That was before he and a thousand other workers were laid off by the last emperor and his budget cuts. His untimely heart attack was the best thing for the empire and not many people mourned his death.

Nogil was brought back into the present with the smell of the empress' perfume and the candle scents that flowed through the hall. As he entered the chamber, he knelt and addressed her, "Your Highness, I am honored by your invitation."

"Please, Nogil, sit beside me." The empress motioned to an empty pillow next to her. She smiled to herself as she thought of his name. It was the name reserved for the Detrill emperor. No Detrill child could be given that name since the day their people were liberated from enslavement. The master shipbuilder who worked with the Nortes emperor to free the entire empire from slavery was named Nogil. It was decided by his people that in honor of his bravery and accomplishments, no one else would ever be named Nogil. When a new emperor was elected, his given name was abandoned and he took the honored name of Nogil. "The day when your people knelt before mine is a thousand years past. Please know that I hold my twelfth great-grandfather's opinion about all races being equal. No one bows in my court and neither should you."

"Thank you, Empress. I trust you had a safe journey without incident." Nogil sat beside her and picked up the goblet that was offered. He sipped the ale slowly from the goblet; it was much stronger than the ales of his home world.

"No problems that we know of, but still, one can't be too careful, can they? After all, we still don't know how much the Coalition knows. They have been at some of the colonies for more than five years now." Nogil's eyes widened in disbelief. "I know, I know, we should have found out about it sooner. Unfortunately, the Coalition guarded this secret very well. My spies and official ties didn't find anything out until a month ago. I sent the summons for our meeting the day after I got all the information myself."

"Thank you for contacting me so quickly. But what do we do now? Do we tell the Coalition or prepare on our own?" The ale had suddenly lost Nogil's interest and he set down the goblet.

"I think both. I, of course, didn't want to do anything without first notifying you, but now I think that we should start to prepare for the inevitable." She dismissed her guards and after the doors were closed, she continued. "A distress signal was sent almost five years ago by accident from the initial colony site. We haven't much time. I'm surprised that we haven't been found yet."

"How much should we tell the Coalition? In all honesty, Your Highness, my people will most likely be untouched by the new information the Coalition would receive, but the Nortes…It's hard to say just what the Coalition would think or do to your world. They are such xenophobes and extremists to match."

"Yes, I agree, humans are unpredictable. That's why I believe that we should give them as little information as possible, without compromising the security of this sector. Our mistakes of the past cannot haunt our future."

"Although the Detrill past is not pleasant, and much of that is because of the Nortes, I will help you, Your Highness. Your twelfth great-grandfather freed my people and we will forever stand behind your house because of him. Whatever I may do to help, I will."

With a slight bow, the arrangement had been made. For the next two days, the two discussed recent findings and thoughts on what to do. And then they decided. A long-range sensor confirmed their deepest fear. Time was running out.

Chapter 33
Dig Site One

"How far are we from the hanger bay?" Daria asked Bloom through her comlink. "If it's more than half a click, we need to stop so I can check Wilks' ankle."

"Couple hundred meters, not much farther. If he can hold out until then, that would give us some time to go over the ship." Bloom looked at his display again. "I just hope these log entries are right; otherwise, we're walking home."

"I can make it." Wilks spoke up from the rear. "Just get me a beer once we're there."

Daria smiled at Wilks and wondered how he could've been such an asshole that night in the bar. She double-timed it up to Emily on point with Bloom. "I think he can wait till then." After a pause she added, "I just needed a change of scenery from back there. Have you been getting anything from those external sensors?"

Emily waited for Bloom to answer but he was too deeply involved in the data he was reviewing about the ship, so she answered for him. "Yeah, and it's not good news. That alien ship is still up in a synchronous orbit with site two. If we can even get the ship in the landing bay to lift, we may have to fight our way out. Not only is our ship a thousand years old, but we don't have experience with it. I'm sure that they have plenty."

"Too bad our friend died before we got any more information from him." Daria had tried to revive the alien but his anatomy was just too different for her to be of any use. He died after the first volley of questions and not much information had been gained. "I have found out something pretty interesting about our friends, though. Their bodies produce oxygen. They can live in just about any atmosphere or even no atmosphere as long as it isn't corrosive to their tissue. Their cells metabolize a protein that's in the meat from those game animals. With that protein, they can remove oxygen elements from their food and store the oxygen for use later; that's why they eat raw meat. Heat would destroy the protein compound. The protein also helps with the gas exchange between their lungs and bloodstream. Their lungs still work like ours, but they have a backup system just in case."

"Can we use that to our advantage?" Emily asked.

"I'm not sure. But it does let us know some of their strengths as well as weaknesses. First, we know that any inhaled chemical or biological agent we currently use might be useless against them. Second, without meat, they not only starve but also suffocate. And because they create oxygen, their bodies oxidize very quickly and they age about five times as fast as we do. That guy we had back there was probably twenty standard years old. I don't know how long they live but I'd say he was about mid-life based on cellular decay and repair. But that is going with human standards."

"They would have to have a large supply of game animals on their ships during a hostile takeover if they wanted to survive. Or they would have to quickly take over the outer planets in a system to grow their stock on for resupply of their troops. I know that every conquering force needs supply lines but our food can stay for years in one place without it dying or going bad. It would be much harder to transport livestock through enemy-held lines." Emily thought that this information was more important than Daria had realized.

"Thanks, Doc. Keep feeding me with any intel you get. You know, I can't thank you enough for the friendship you've given me and for being such a valuable resource on this mission."

"Thanks, Emily. I value our friendship as well." Daria turned and walked back towards her patient.

Chapter 34
One Thousand Years Ago - Primary Site Of The Advance Exploration Colony

"And I'm telling you," the general was half out of his chair, face red with rage, and pointing a finger at the figure who sat at the head of the conference table, "I don't care if you are the emperor! I will not support your decision to cut ourselves off from the empire, and neither will any member of my war council."

The emperor sat forward in his chair, with his arms resting on the table in front of him. He was a handsome man by Nortes standards, although he was also considered to be very short. He took a moment to look at each one of his cabinet members sitting at the huge conference table. He then looked at the war council sitting behind General N'thoth. "Do you concur with the general?" He received nods from each member of the council. He then turned to his cabinet. "And who among you believes that we should continue to enslave the galaxy just because we can?"

The cabinet members glanced nervously at one another and sweat broke out on the foreheads of more than one of the twenty members sitting at the table. After several minutes, the minister of architecture stood and walked to the war council to make his position known. In all, fifteen others joined him on the war council's side.

Of the four who remained, the minister of learning stood and said, "Your Highness, we stand behind you fully. It is time to put an end to this shameful existence." He walked over with the three other ministers and stood behind his emperor.

"You see, Your Highness," the general began, "you are in the minority. We don't need to make a coup behind your back; we are doing it right here and right NOW!"

All the members of the war council were smiling and looking towards their emperor. The smiles faded as seconds passed and nothing happened.

"What is wrong, General?" the emperor said as his smile took the place of those lost from the conspirators. "Was something supposed to happen?"

At that moment, the royal guards ran through the front and rear chamber doors and surrounded the war council and the ministers who had defected to N'thoth's side. Four other guards stood around the emperor to protect him.

"Your men were killed outside after the doors were shut and the meeting began. No, I don't think that there will be any coup today, except my own of course. I don't care what you think. This madness must and will stop. I am implementing my plan to withdraw from my own empire at once." He stood and looked at the general with indifference. "Kill the war council and all the traitors who stand with them."

Before anyone could object, the guards opened fire on the men sitting and standing before them. All were slain in a matter of seconds.

"Please clean this mess up and then report to your garrison and await further orders." The emperor turned to his faithful ministers. "Let's go to the throne room; we don't need such a large space anymore to carry on the affairs of state." He looked at his minister of health. "I hate to kill as much as you do, D'Bath, but we need to do just a little bit more before we can get ourselves out of this mess. Is the virus ready?"

"Yes", D'Bath said somberly. "We can deploy it among the colonists on schedule as planned."

"And you're sure that it has only a ten to fifteen percent mortality rate?" the minister of learning asked.

"I hope so, but nothing is for certain. I also have the virus ready for our warriors. It does have a one hundred percent mortality rate. I'm sure of that."

"I know you are, my friend", the emperor said as they stepped into the private throne room. "After all, it was your eighteenth great-grandfather who helped to create our warriors."

As they all sat, another door to the chamber opened and a man dressed in rags and smelling of a foul odor walked in. The ministers sat aghast, looking at the Detrill slave who stood before them.

"Gentlemen, this is Nogil. He is the head shipmaster of the Detrills." He looked around at his ministers. "Oh, come now, don't look so shocked. We are leaving the empire because of Nogil and others like him. Is it not fitting that he and others should help with our joint liberation? Besides, we couldn't do it without him and the others."

"Your Highness," Nogil began, "we are on schedule as promised. We will have our escape transports ready on time." He handed the emperor a datapad. "We have made it so that several of our fastest and most heavily armed cruisers will either need preventive maintenance or repairs on the scheduled date. We will have access to them as planned."

D'Bath took over. "Both viruses will be released in three days. None of the slaves will need to be inoculated but all of us and our family will, of course." He handed everyone except Nogil a large canister of pills. "Give each member of your family one pill within the next three days, otherwise they'll have to rely on their own immune system to survive and that may not be enough."

"As you all know," the emperor spoke while looking at one of the little white pills, "the rest of the pills are to be given to those in your command who you trust to support our movement. You are not to tell them of our plans or anything else. Just secretly get them to take the pill somehow to ensure that they are among the survivors.

"The doctor will also give you some pills that contain the virus. These will be given on the day of infection to all those in your command who you feel will oppose us after we leave. Take no chances. If you believe for even one second that they will not stand by us, give them the pill." He then turned his gaze to S'bog.

S'bog had already taken his pill and noticed that it was his turn to speak. "Sire, my team is ready as well. The department of labor will stay behind and remove all traces of our existence from the colonies. It will be a relatively simple task considering we only have a handful of colonies and most don't have much aboveground construction as of yet. We estimate six cycles will be enough time to finish. After which, we will join you at our new home world." He eyed his jar of inoculating pills and promised himself that he would take another one later when he was by himself. No sense in taking any chances, he thought.

"Good." The emperor stood to end the meeting. "In three days, we will begin. I know that we are about to endure the hardest moments of our lives and even of our species' history. We will prevail, though, because it is right."

Chapter 35
High Warp Through Space On Board The Detrill Warship *Emilian*

"ETA to target?" The first officer had just taken over the watch from one of his senior officers.

The helmsman turned his chair towards the commander. "Sir, we should reach the target in twelve days."

"Thank you. Conn, when was the last battle drill?" The XO hated being on watch during warp travel; never anything to do but wait.

"At the beginning of last shift, sir." He grimaced to himself because he knew what was coming next.

The XO touched a key on his control panel. "All hands, red alert! Battle stations! Red alert!"

The klaxon began to pound into everyone's head and the XO sat back and smiled. The crew of the *Emilian* raced to their battle stations. His watch always had the fastest response times. Today would be no different.

Chapter 36
Still Deep Inside Enemy Territory

Surgeon laid in his course towards the leader of the enemy cruisers and then engaged his maneuvering thrusters for his third "attack" on the ship in the last five hours. At the end of his run, Seth reviewed the sensor readings before giving his report.

"Again nothing." Seth spoke with a mixture of disappointment and relief. The waiting was getting to be nerve-racking. "I don't think that they can see us at all. We've been moving around all their ships for almost two days now and nothing."

"I'm not sure that I agree with you." Surgeon was almost on Seth's side but something told him that all of their maneuvers hadn't gone unnoticed. "I do, of course, hope that you're right but wishful thinking won't win this fight."

"Three to one." Blaze keyed his comlink to Surgeon's. "We've got an analysis of their patrol pattern. I'm sending it to all our ships now. The computer recommends that we implement our attack when their ships are in this position." Everyone's display in their visors showed a hologram of the enemy forces as they would appear in seven hours. "So as long as they're on schedule as precisely as they have been, that will be our best shot."

Transmissions between Surgeon's ships were encrypted using a method that had become known as the "debris" code. Before each mission, each ship's comlink was programmed using a random set of algorithms that five separate computers put together. After each algorithm was entered into the lead ship, its central computer would arrange the equations into an order in which the second algorithm would use the solution from the first one as the variable in its equation. Then the third algorithm used the answer produced by the second one as its variable, and so on.

Then the lead ship was hooked up to the other scout ships via cables and the code sequence was transferred to them. This ensured that the only ships with the whole encryption code were the scout ships.

The second part of the encryption code used space debris to send the signal to each ship. Gasses and other elements that were floating near each ship were gathered into collectors all along the hull. They were then dispersed in a pattern according to their atomic weight. The receiving ship's sensors would analyze the debris from the sender and use the element's atomic weight as the variables in the algorithms and then decode the transmissions.

To the unknowing onlooker, their sensors would just pick up a random scattering of elements that were common in that particular sector. Unless the onlooker had their sensors trained on a minute portion of space, they would never realize that the elements were in any sort of pattern. And even if they did, they would never be able to break the code.

Surgeon ran through the computer-generated simulation a few times before he said anything. "Unless anyone has any objections, we'll go ahead with the plan as it stands now." No one objected. "Continue with your prearranged flight plans."

Seth keyed in what he wanted for dinner and turned to the dispenser to get his meal. "You want me to get something for you?"

"No, I'll eat a little bit later. I need to look over some schematics first. I've been going over our scans of the alien hulls and I think that I found something."

"Send it over to me", Seth said through a mouthful of his dinner. "I'd like to take a look while I'm eating."

Surgeon sent the transmission from his visor to Seth's view screen on the bulkhead. "There." He zoomed in on a portion of the hull. "See that scoring on the side that has new plating over it? The ship, along with all the others, has similar shitty patch work all over the hull."

"I honestly don't know where you're going with this", Seth commented after taking a sip of water and studying the view for a moment.

"These ships are works of art. The detailing, the craftsmanship, and the technology used to put them together are outstanding. Yet they can't even patch a simple meteorite scoring on their hull? I don't think so. I don't think that they have the means to."

"So then where did the ships come from? Who made them?"

"I don't know. Maybe their ancestors did and they lost the technology somehow. Or maybe they conquered a species and took the ships for themselves. Either way, I think that these ships are at least a thousand years old. The scanners say that the designs are exactly the same as the ones we found in the alien database from a thousand years ago. You would guess that something would have changed in all that time."

Six hours had passed before the warning light on Blaze's console came to life. "Oh shit! We've got company, everyone. Look alive!"

Everyone in the scout team stared, shell shocked, at their screens as sixty more battle cruisers entered the immediate area from high warp.

"Surgeon to all units. Abort all flight plans and regroup at rendezvous point Delta." Turning to Seth, he said, "The general is going to have to wait just a little bit longer. We can't go ahead with our plan in the middle of all those giants."

Just then Seth noticed something. "Wait a minute. They're all lining up on the same trajectory." And then they were gone. All of the ships jumped into warp in a single-file order and suddenly the space around them was empty.

"Surgeon," Blaze came on the link, "I'm already recalculating an attack vector. I think we can slip in past their planetary defense grid at this point." A red flashing arrow came on in everyone's visor. "It is the weakest part of their sensors and in three hours it will be facing the sun in such a way that solar radiation and debris that moves along the solar currents will mask our entry into their atmosphere. Then we just need to do a little hunting."

"Good. Beast, I want you to lead assault team two with everyone from units three, four, and five. Units one and two are with me. We're going to stick to our original assault plan by homing in on the crew's beacon implants. There aren't any ships in the area, so we'll have to hope that we will be able to find one on the ground. Otherwise we go with plan B."

No one wanted plan B. It called for all the scout ships to be remotely brought in above the rescue site and then their fusion reactors would be overloaded in order to sanitize the area. It wouldn't destroy the planet but it wouldn't be a vacation spot for at least a few hundred years.

Chapter 37
One thousand years ago - Primary Site of the Advance Exploration Colony
The Day of the Cleansing

The emperor stood in chambers as reports of the sick and dying flooded his communications console. "Minister D'Bath. Do you know what is causing this?" He was reading from a script in his mind that had been memorized and then incinerated immediately. The plan required that all formalities be taken, otherwise someone might get suspicious.

"No, Your Highness. I cannot tell you for sure. Some of my colleagues think that it might be the vegetation and some think that it might be the radiation in this sector of space. No one knows for certain." At that moment, a victim of the plague was wheeled to D'Bath for help. The other doctors were trying to resuscitate the patient but couldn't. D'Bath fought desperately to clear the froth and blood from the victim's mouth but it was coming up too quickly.

With a final series of convulsions, the young child died. D'Bath turned back to the screen. "As minister of health, I declare a quarantine on this sector of space until we can figure out what is going on. No more colonies will come in and none of the current colonists will leave. I am sorry, Your Highness, but I must order you to stay as well."

"I agree fully, my friend. I would not want to infect the rest of our empire, even to save myself. How long will this quarantine be in place?" The emperor had a tear in his eye from the death of the child. But many others would have died if they had tried to secede from the empire any other way, he tried to console himself. But it wasn't working.

"At the moment, I'd have to say indefinitely, sire. I suggest that you issue a royal order forbidding any other members of our empire to come to this sector until this disease is taken care of. I must go now, sire; there are many others who need my help." The screen went blank and was quickly replaced with the royal seal.

The emperor tapped in a few commands and quickly got the office of Supreme Command back in the heart of the empire. The warrior who stood on the other end of the transmission quickly knelt to the floor and put his four arms out in submission to his emperor. "Master, what do I owe this great honor to?"

"Please stand, warrior. I have some grave news about our future." The warrior stood. "We have had a terrible outbreak of some virus here on the new colonies. It is killing almost everyone. It has already killed all of your warrior brothers; it seems as though they were more susceptible to it than everyone else."

"Master, we will send a rescue ship for you and the war council immediately to bring you home."

"No, that is the last thing you will do. Minister of Health D'Bath has declared a state of quarantine for this sector. I give you now a royal order that no one will disobey. This sector is completely off limits to all of my subjects forever if we cannot find a cure for this disease. I have unknowingly destroyed a large portion of my empire by bringing them here and I will not destroy the other.

"Until such time as this crisis is over, Supreme Command will be in charge of the core worlds and empire. I am sending complete documentation on what has happened here so that you may see for yourself what devastation this sector holds for our empire."

"I will notify Supreme Command at once. They will, of course, want confirmation from General N'thoth", the warrior said without looking up.

Emperor T'Leh tapped a few keys on the panel. "The general is very ill with the plague and most of the war council has already died." The warrior was so stunned he actually looked directly at the emperor. "I will, however, patch this transmission over to the hospital where you can confer with General N'thoth as he is cared for. I fear his time to venture forward into the next existence is near." The emperor knew N'thoth was dead and he hoped that the General's stand-in would be able to fool the warrior on the other end of the transmission.

After completing the transfer, the screen went blank. The emperor sat in his chair in front of his favorite desk and contemplated what he had done. He knew that it was right but he still couldn't get the image of that dying child out of his mind. "May the gods forgive me", he whispered to himself.

Chapter 38
Dig Site One

In the hanger bay, the team found the most impressive ship any of them had ever seen. Jockey was the first to approach it. "God, am I glad that I'm the only pilot here. I'd hate to have to fight someone just to be the first to fly her. She's beautiful." Had the rest of the team not been there, Daria was sure that Jockey would have started caressing the hull with his own body.

"Jockey, Cannon, and Bloom, take a look through her and find out how to get her off the ground. I want weapons systems to be the second priority after flight controls." Wilks turned to Emily. "Hey, el-tee, after Doc gets finished checking my ankle, how about the three of us going over some of the data we've collected so far?"

Emily looked for Davies, who was getting some lunch from his pack. "Davies, how about you join us?"

Davies' stomach began to sour and he put down his lunch. "If it's all the same with you, ma'am, I'd like to help secure the perimeter and then take a look inside the ship."

"Sure, but if you get bored we'd appreciate any input you might have." Emily couldn't put her finger on it but something had been off with Davies lately. Well, she'd have a talk with him later.

Inside the ship, Bloom was looking for a link-up that he could connect to on the bridge. "If I can access their main computer, we may be able to fly this thing with VR."

Jockey was eyeing the instrumentation and trying to decipher the layout. "This is going to be tougher than I thought. Because they have four arms, the controls are set at very wide and different placements than I'm used to. Each control panel is divided into four key elements so they can be used simultaneously.

"Having only two hands, our instruments are laid out horizontally in front of us for our hands to roam back and forth on."

"Hello. That's why I suggested VR." Bloom was shaking his head at the pilot. "I can interface our VR visors with the ship's controls. You'll see a standard flight layout in front of you and work the controls as you would normally. The VR computer will then send your input to the ship's computer as a translation of what you want. It will only be delayed by micro-seconds."

Jockey frowned. "Sometimes a micro-second is enough to get you killed. Besides, I can't get a feel for the ship if I can't touch her directly."

"Think of it as phone sex then. I've seen your vid bills—I know it won't be too hard of a stretch for you." Bloom couldn't help but to laugh at his own joke. A cold stare from the pilot brought him back, though. "All right, try to fly her manually if you want but I'm still going to hook up the VR in case we need it."

"We won't. I just need a little time to get the feel for her." Jockey sat at the helm, going over the keys repeatedly, running through mock scenarios in his head, and reliving battles he had been through before so he could learn the control placement.

After a couple of hours, Jockey decided to go through a pre-flight check. Bloom had already switched on the main power grid and had tested every relay, circuit, light, and all the other gizmos the ship had on board.

"All right, Bloom, I'm ready to go through pre-flight." Jockey then tapped his comlink. "All hands, stand clear of the ship. We're going through pre-flight in sixty seconds. Either get on board or get in the control booth at the end of the hanger bay. We don't want any accidents now."

Everyone cleared the hanger bay and filed into the control booth to watch the pre-flight. Those who were watching keyed their comlinks so that they would be able to listen in to the conversation going on inside the ship.

"All right, pilot," Bloom said from the operations seat, "I have your VR display set up to point to the controls if you need the help. Just say 'find' and then the control you're looking for and the visor will highlight that control in your field of view. Give it a try."

Jockey looked straight forward and spoke to no one in particular, "Find weapons." In the lower right of his visor, he saw a green arrow pointing downwards. As he shifted his field of view, the arrow shifted with him until he was looking at the weapons control panel, which was now highlighted. When he reached for the panel, his VR visor knew that he had found the control so the highlight marking disappeared.

"It might take an extra second to do something but if you forget where the control is, this should help in a pinch." Bloom was running through his own set of pre-flight diagnostics.

"Good job, buddy. I hope that we don't need it, though. Smooth sailing is definitely preferred on this flight.

"All right, let's get started. Begin pre-flight. Maneuvering thrusters, check. Inertia dampers, check."

"Whoa", Bloom said from his console. "Check out the settings for the inertia dampers. Those alien bodies must be able to take a lot. I'll reset them to human standards. Now we don't have to worry about being stains on the seats once we hit warp."

A few minutes later, pre-flight was complete and Jockey began to test the lift thrusters. She shook a little but then lifted cleanly off the deck. At ten meters, she performed a three-sixty in the huge landing bay before she set back down.

Bloom and Jockey looked at each other, smiled and then tapped in the commands for the next test. After they had finished, they headed for the gangplank, where the rest of the team was waiting for them.

"So what do you think, pilot?" Emily asked.

Through a toothy smile he said, "Great! I don't think that we'll have any problems."

"So we can load up and get the hell out of here, right?" Scan spoke from his seat on a cargo crate nearby. He was rewrapping his stump. The wrist was almost done regenerating and the palm would come next.

Bloom stepped forward. "No, sorry but not yet. We just set her to go through an atmosphere diagnostic." Almost on cue, the gangplank closed itself tightly into the ship. "She's going to seal herself up tight and run through a series of different atmospheric pressures to make sure that she can survive in space. It'll take at least one full day just to be safe. And barring any problems with her hull integrity, we should be ready to lift off. Oh, except one thing..."

All eyes were locked on Bloom now but it was Jockey who spoke up. "Bloom and I both figured that we would find a hanger bay control on the conn station in the ship. And well, we didn't. We think that maybe they didn't want anyone outside the structure to have access, even one of their own ships."

"Yeah," Bloom continued. "You know, just in case someone hijacked one of their ships they wouldn't be able to get in or out with it."

"Well, the control has got to be in the hanger bay, right?" Wilks piped in.

"Yes and no", Bloom began. "There is a control in here but as a safety measure, after a long period of system shutdown, the controls are locked out and the mainframe in the sub-levels has to be accessed. They were very paranoid people."

"That's just fuckin' great!" Wilks was not happy. "This place is already two kilometers below the ground and now we find out that it has sub-levels! How much more sub can you get?!"

"All right, Wilks, calm down." Emily stepped in. "Now I'm assuming that because you're not more cheerful about this, Bloom, that it's not as easy as just going down there and flipping a switch."

"No, ma'am. I mean, yes, ma'am, you're right." Bloom worked his control pad and gave everyone an image in their visor. "Although I've gotten into most of their systems, I still can't breach their command controls. Everything that we've gotten so far has been considered non-essential so it wasn't too hard to decrypt. But the command controls, I haven't been able to crack them in the several days that we've been down here. My program has been going non-stop and it hasn't even come close. My best guess is that I will never crack it." A sound of failure entered his voice.

"So what are we looking at then?" Davies was studying the map that was given to his visor.

"This is a map of the route that we need to take to get to the core of this place. They have a security protocol that when this place shuts down, every top-level program and function gets sent to the mainframe and can only be accessed from there. As far as I can tell, we will still be able to access the controls for the hangar because they weren't considered top-level before the shutdown occurred. Problem is, it's booby-trapped. The route is heavily guarded with automatic systems and there is no way I can disarm them."

"What about using the weapon systems on the ship to blow our way out?" Emily looked towards their escape craft.

"Sorry, el-tee." It was Jockey's turn. "You know how big the last explosion was. It would take almost the same amount of force as to blow this lid. None of us would survive. If worst comes to worst, we can autopilot her to do it while we hide somewhere deep inside this place." He gestured towards the complex. "Set her for self-destruct and after it's all over, we could just climb out."

Davies was eating a protein bar but managed to speak up. "We don't know if there is anything left on the surface. Those bastards could have killed everyone and destroyed all of our ships topside. If we get out of here, we could be walking into a bee's nest of shit."

"I agree." Emily took on her new authority stance as she spoke. Daria had noticed Emily developing her power mode over the last few days. "And even if our forces are still alive on the surface, we can't throw away this ship. If we go to war against these aliens, this technology might be the only thing that saves us."

She turned towards Wilks. "Your ankle takes you off this one. Doc, you'll lead a team with Bloom, Davies, Hood, and Snake." In her mind, she wanted to tell them that Bloom was mission essential and that he was to be protected at all costs. But she also didn't want the rest thinking that she thought they were cannon fodder. They're all professionals and they know what Bloom means to us so I'm sure they'll do their job, she consoled herself.

The scout team was preparing their gear when Davies' comlink came on. "Hey Davies, meet me in the hangar bay control room." Emily's voice faded from his head.

When he got there, he could tell by the look on Emily's face that she was going to have a heart-to-heart with him. "Have a seat, big guy. I, ah, wanted to know how you were doing. I mean, you haven't been yourself."

"Look, el tee, I just…it's personal, all right? I can work it out for myself; it's just going to take a little time."

He looked at his friend square in the eyes. "Look Emily, I just can't right now, OK?"

Emily suddenly knew what it was all about. She thought about pulling Davies from the scouting party but she figured that might do more harm than good. "All right, friend. When you're ready, let me know. I'm always here for you." As an afterthought, she said, "Would it be out of line for your CO to give you a hug?"

Davies flinched backward and then looked around the corner. No one was near the control booth. "Yes, ma'am. But it would be fine for my friend to give me one."

The two stood and hugged. For the first time in his career, Davies was glad that his CO wasn't a man.

Chapter 39
The Detrill Warship *Emilian*

The captain sat in his chair with his XO behind him at the weapons console. "Tell me, friend, what do you think of our mission?"

"I think that it is about time someone took care of those monsters. I have no like or dislike of the Nortes. They have done nothing to harm us in more than a thousand years. But their ghosts may come back to haunt us all." The XO finished his system diagnostic and took a seat next to his captain and friend of thirty years. "You have been with my family during the sacred days of W'ishtung, so you have heard the story of my ancestor's village on our home world. My story is not all that different from those of any other Detrill, but now I have a chance to repay them for what they did to us and our home world."

Captain Netid looked at the information display that resided in the armrest of his command chair. "Our intel indicates that almost the entire enemy fleet massed in a staging location and then left simultaneously to an unknown destination. The last of that convoy should reach their destination in a couple of weeks." Netid keyed in a few commands and a new figure was presented to him on the screen. "We should reach our target in one week. Are we ready?"

"Yes, sir", Commander Aucted said as he surveyed his impressive crew. Although the captain's question was barely a whisper to his XO, the bridge crew heard him and stiffened their postures automatically as if to answer the question for themselves so the first officer wouldn't have to.

The security doors to the bridge opened and the tactical officer along with the chief engineer stepped out of the lift. "Sir," Lieutenant Tredil began, "I have brought our latest tactical intel for review."

The captain nodded and the four men went into the briefing room together. "The captain looked over his shoulder almost as an afterthought. "Ensign," he barked.

A young man barely old enough to have his civilian air car license looked at the imposing figure that now stood at the rear of the bridge. "Yes, sir," he managed to squeak out.

"You have the bridge." And with that, the captain turned to follow the rest of his senior staff into the conference room.

All eyes on the bridge turned to the junior officer. After the soundproof doors sealed behind the more experienced officers, the bridge erupted in roar of whoops, hollers, and cheers for the young ensign. This particular shift had been staffed by the captain himself and consisted of entirely new officers who had graduated the Naval Academy just prior to being assigned to the *Emilian* before she left on her current mission.

The captain had always taken the newest officers and put them together as bridge staff early on so they could gain more experience and direct tutelage from him. Those who were lucky enough to be assigned in this group had to work the extra shift in addition to their normal duties. But for the last ten years, anyone who had been picked for this extra duty had always risen through the ranks faster than anyone else from their class.

The ensign took a brief moment to bask in his elation and then wiped the smile from his face. On cue and without a word from their new deck officer, the rest of the bridge crew ceased their impromptu celebration. They returned to their duties with a new sense of purpose: to make their fellow officer shine as brightly as he could.

The captain and his staff were seated at the conference table with data screens in front of each person. Tredil began, "I have been reviewing everything we have in our tactical database concerning our adversaries. We have all been taught the same basic information at the academy about their tactics, weapons, weaknesses, strengths, and so on. But until now, there was much information designated as classified that no one but a handful of bureaucrats has seen for centuries." He paused as he keyed in a security code to his datapad, which then unlocked the secret information and sent it to everyone else's screens.

He continued, "At first glance, it seems to be a lot of useless garbage that makes you wonder why it was classified. But on further inspection, it gets very interesting, and honestly, very scary."

Tredil had tagged the information he deemed most important and each officer reviewed that information first. Lieutenant Morsid had already reviewed the information with Tredil before the meeting and he continued where his colleague left off. "From an engineering standpoint, we are more advanced than they are but not by enough to give us a real tactical advantage. The main advantage we do have is their ships are very old and probably aren't maintained that well.

"The classified information also details how the Detrill and Nortes worked together to free themselves and many other races from the empire. Apparently, a Nortes doctor developed a virus that wiped out the entire warrior class in this sector."

"Now this may be a stupid question," the XO started, "but why don't we just use that virus again? Wouldn't that be easier than a stand-up fight?"

"Well, sir," Morsid continued, "apparently that doctor had a major moral dilemma with what he had done."

Chapter 40
One Thousand Years Ago – Nortes Prime Colony

"You did what!" The emperor tried to keep from yelling at his minister of health but failed.

"I cannot live with what I have done and I cannot allow anyone else to repeat my mistake", D'Bath choked out through tears and the blood already starting to build up in his lungs. "I removed all information concerning the virus and antidote from my databases and destroyed all of my research. I have killed children!" he protested through thickening froth and blood.

The emperor tried to call for assistance but D'Bath stopped his friend's hand. "There is nothing anyone can do for me now. I took ten times the lethal dose to be sure that the only source of information on the virus left in the galaxy would be eliminated." As his life slowly ebbed from his body, he looked into his friend's eyes. "I had to do this. I deserve to die in the same manner as all those innocent people I murdered. Please forgive me." And with that, his body convulsed rapidly as spurts of blood and lung tissue issued forth from his mouth and he died in the emperor's arms.

T'Leh touched his comlink and requested a medical team to come and take his friend's body away for a proper sending into the next life. As the medics attempted to remove the body, T'Leh clutched at D'Bath's tunic for a brief moment before the gentle hand from one of the medics loosened his grip and proceeded to take the body.

Without D'Bath and the information he held, T'Leh and his accomplices had to make this succession work. If his empire ever found out the truth and were able to gain control over the warriors, there would be no stopping their wrath.

Chapter 41
Dig Site One - Journey to the Core

"Stop monkeying around with that before you kill yourself!" Wilks yelled at Bloom as he passed over Wilks' head on the hover sled that had been found near a loading dock in the hangar.

"I'm just trying to get a feel for how it moves and what it can do." Bloom circled the hangar once more and then stopped in front of Wilks and jumped off the sled. "She's real maneuverable and better than any of the prototypes we're still trying to develop back home. I still don't understand exactly how it works but instead of working off the magnetic force of the planet, like what we've been trying to make, this sled seems to draw in the lightest element in the atmosphere around it. Then it sends some sort of energy through the elements, linking them together so they can't mix with the ambient air again. And because the collected elements are the lightest in the ambient surroundings, it causes the sled to float on top of them. Sort of like a hot air balloon. And as the sled weight increases, it adds more elements to the 'flotation skirt' to offset the weight change."

Davies walked over, carrying two portable heating elements from their survival gear. He placed each one on the platform and strapped them down. "So these heating elements will really fool their sensors?"

"I don't know", Bloom said honestly. "I'm guessing that even with their advanced technology, they still use basic concepts for detecting intruders. They can use heat sensors, weight sensors in the floors, acoustic sensors, and motion detectors. We can simulate each of those stimuli with this sled.

"The heating elements will simulate a live being, while the sled itself should trip any motion detectors that they have. And with the two forty-kilo crates the sled will be dragging, it should be able to trip any weight-bearing and acoustic sensors they might have. As an added bonus, the way this sled is made," Bloom nodded back over his shoulder, "I think you could destroy more than half of it before it would stop functioning."

"What if the sensors are set to detect only actual life-forms?" Emily was helping Wilks fasten the crates to the sled.

"Then we'll find out sooner or later, ma'am." Bloom adjusted the quick release device on the sled that would allow him to drop the crates remotely in case he needed to maneuver the sled more quickly than they would permit. "But I really don't think that they would do that. By setting up defenses that only scanned for life-forms, that would leave a big security hole for any type of robotic device to get through.

"Again," Bloom reiterated, "I can't guarantee that this will work. But I wouldn't risk our lives if I didn't think that the chances of success drastically outweighed the chances of failure."

Daria had spent most of the last several hours trying to memorize the map of the lower levels that Bloom had downloaded to everyone's visors. She wanted to be sure that she always knew where an escape route was and the best places to set up a defensive perimeter. Much of her planning was dependent on whether or not the rooms lining the corridors on the route would be open or not, or at least accessible with a minimum of force.

"Are we ready?" Daria had joined the group from her solitary position inside the hangar bay's control booth.

"Sure are, Doc." Snake was stretching a little bit before the journey began. "I put a mini-cam on each corner of the sled so we can be anywhere in the complex and still monitor its progress."

"Great job, guys." Daria was just shouldering her rucksack. "I have marked off defensive and offensive fallback points on the map in case we encounter hostilities on the way."

"You mean 'when.'" Bloom completed his diagnostic of the sled and then looked towards his team leader.

"Yeah, right, 'when.'" Daria regrettably agreed. "Let's move out, guys. I want to be home in time for dinner." Over her shoulder, to the rest of the team staying behind, she smiled. "Don't pop this lid without us. We don't want to have to walk home."

"Don't worry, Doc," Emily said from Wilks' side. "We all go home together."

Chapter 42
The Truth

Emperor Nogil and Empress Hugany sat before the president of the Coalition and its military council. Both were uneasy and it was difficult not to show it. Everyone's eyes in the room were on them. Some showed obvious signs of disgust and others were just plain astonished at what they had heard so far. And all were more than just a little bit frightened with the new knowledge they possessed.

The president was the first to speak. "Neither of your worlds are members of the Coalition, so you were not obligated to share all of your worlds' history with us as new members are required to do. However, why have you waited until now to tell us? We could have been preparing for the day we would have to defend ourselves. And now that day is almost upon us and if only half of what you've told us is accurate, then we will most surely die. With your warp and space stream travel abilities, we might even have been able to launch an offensive and take them by surprise. But now we have no advantages at all."

Space stream travel was yet another piece of information that the two worlds had decided to share with the Coalition now that it seemed inevitable that they would have to work together to fight their common enemy. The "space stream" theory was developed by a Detrill admiral almost five hundred years ago. He had found that there were currents in space that could be tapped into while traveling at warp speed. A steady stream of tachyon particles projected in front of the ship will disrupt the surface of the stream. As the stream attempts to repair itself and seal the rupture, the ship is pulled forward on the wake of space being folded back into the ruptured portion of the stream. It was analogous with a moving sidewalk used in almost every city on every planet. These streams were located throughout subspace and accessible while traveling at warp. They were of different lengths, traveled in different directions, and varied in speed. There was one that traveled almost the entire length of the galaxy but ended near the event horizon of a black hole.

Empress Hugany's answer was calm and matter-of-fact. "There are several reasons we did not tell you of our history. First, we never thought that this would happen. Our soldiers were created in such a way that we thought they would be dead by now and no more than a bad memory. It was unthinkable that they would be able to create more of themselves without the help of our scientists who were taken from the empire for colonization of this sector."

"Can they not breed on their own?" the Coalition's lead scientist, Dr. Wabash, asked.

"No, they are created in labs under very specific conditions." The empress continued, "They once were a species unto themselves but that was millennia ago. They bare no physical and almost no genetic resemblance to what they once were. I'm not sure if any information even exists that could be traced back to what they originally were. They are genetically coded to be the perfect warriors. We have given your scientists all of the information we have on them.

"Many of their enhancements were created to ensure loyalty. One of their enhancements makes it impossible for them to accept orders from anyone outside the royal family. Once a new member of the family is born, they are taken to the Supreme Council's chambers, where they are touched by the elder warriors who make up the council. They are able to sense a portion of the infant's DNA that is unique to the royal family. From that point on, the infant becomes known to all the warriors as one who can give orders. Every warrior has this ability to detect the DNA. It is a failsafe in case someone tries to impersonate a member of the royal family. If a person has not been touched by the Supreme Council and accepted, that person can never give orders via the holonet. However, in the unlikely event that a member of the royal family was never touched as a child, he or she could give orders to a warrior in person so that the warrior could touch them and verify their lineage. There is absolutely nothing a warrior won't do at the order of the family, including killing a member of the family *IF* the warrior can be made to believe that that family member is a threat to the Empire."

The president thought on that for moment before asking, "Then why don't you just ask them to stop? Take control of them and tell them that the Coalition is your ally and we mean you no harm. We could use an asset such as them for the security of our galaxy. They could be used for peace instead of destruction."

"There are two reasons that I cannot do that." The empress paused. "As you can tell from what we've already told you and the information I've downloaded into your databases, my ancestors were extremely paranoid. Part of the doctrine that the warriors live by is the protection of the empire at all costs. It has been encoded into them that if you're are not Nortes or a warrior, then you are a slave. If you are none of the three, then you are an enemy who must be killed. My ancestors did not want to coexist with any other species in the galaxy. If an emperor gave an order to stop conquering the galaxy and live in peace with other races, the warriors wouldn't be able to do it. The warriors would consider the order an attempt to hurt the other members of the royal family by subjecting them to the danger of living with non-slaves. They would then kill the emperor to save the rest of the royal family and the Empire.

"That is why Emperor T'Leh did what he did. He knew that if he ordered a withdrawal from conquering, that he would be killed by his own protectors. He also knew that if he had used the virus developed to kill the warriors across his entire empire, that he would be overthrown by the majority of his subjects and the Nortes who ran the military. Once his protectors were dead, there would be no stopping those who wanted the power of the throne. The Nortes had grown too accustomed to ruling the galaxy and not having to work for themselves to live any other way and they would not allow any emperor to take that away from them. He believed that even if the warriors were dead, the Nortes would follow anyone ruling the empire as long as their usual way of life continued."

"So what did he think would happen after he quarantined this sector? Would he allow his empire to just shrivel up and die? What of his other subjects?" The president tried not to sound too disturbed as he asked his questions.

Hugany sipped her water and took a bite from the food she had been given earlier. "Once the order was given that no one was to leave the current empire, he knew that his warriors would not allow anyone to do so. The warriors took care of almost everything. They oversaw the slaves, protected our borders, and kept peace within the cities. Although the slaves provided almost all of the manual labor within the empire, most Nortes did not come in direct contact with them. This was again due to paranoia. Although the general population did not desire to live without slaves, there were always some who had a conscience and wanted to end the slavery. It was thought that if Nortes were given broad access to the slaves that some might be able to set up resistance cells and eventually overthrow the warriors and the empire. The slaves did outnumber the warriors and Nortes population dramatically and so it was a valid concern.

"Almost every Nortes lived like a king. They did not have to work, think, or do anything if they did not want to. They could read, philosophize, invent, play, travel, do anything they wanted. There were hundreds of conquered worlds to visit and so many other things to do. It was utopia, but only for the Nortes and no one else. They did not want to change and so they had to be forced to do so.

"The warriors only live about fifty years if they do not die sooner in battle. The idea was that in sixty to seventy years, every last warrior would be dead. Without anyone to create more, they would become extinct. When they were dead, there would be no one to keep control of the slaves. The Nortes wouldn't know how to control them because they were never taught how and obviously didn't have the strength in numbers to make the slaves do anything if they didn't want to. Then, the Nortes who wanted peace and to live in coexistence would rise up and take control to change things for the better. With no warriors to stop them, they would have little resistance."

The secretary of state looked up from the tablet he was reading. "Wasn't he putting a lot of faith into the slaves and the anti-slavery Nortes to change an entire empire? After all, the slaves are prewired for slavery and it would be hard to change that. Even with the warriors gone, they would be predisposed to following orders and would fall into line no matter who was cracking the whip, even if it were a timid Nortes. And what of your Nortes officers in the military? Didn't they run things and oversee the warriors? Couldn't they just take control?"

"First", the empress began, "The Nortes officers would, in fact, be able to control the warriors and maintain order at first. But the plan counted on the fact that the warriors had a very short life-span and soon the officers would have no one left to control. They would lose their muscle and their might; their numbers would be too small to maintain order on their own. Also, the Emperor left behind as few Nortes officers as possible to make their task of controlling the downfall even more difficult."

Then the empress touched a control on her pad to bring information on everyone else's pad. It showed a picture of two Nortes males and one female. "Secondly, there was another component to the plan that was integral to its success. During T'Leh's time in school, he became friends with D'Nerth and P'Tong. D'Nerth was a very beautiful woman and P'Tong was her husband. They had wed very early but were more in love than T'Leh had ever seen. All three became inseparable friends. T'Leh could not have loved them more if they were family.

"D'Nerth and P'Tong were members of the underground movement that sought to overthrow the current Nortes way of life. Eventually they told T'Leh of their secret and found that he felt the same way. T'Leh, of course, could never join the underground. He would eventually be discovered and killed and that would, of course, compromise the movement.

"Together the three friends planned for decades how they could force the separation from the empire and make the change happen. The resistance cells were trained and prepared for the day when the warriors would no longer exist. They had covert connections to the slaves and built resistance cells within their ranks. When the warriors were gone, the resistance would rise up and take over the empire and abolish slavery and force the other Nortes to accept all races as equals.

"Without warriors, the slaves would have control of the shipyards, the factories, the weapons, transportation, every key element within the empire. All they would need was guidance and support from the better-educated and well-placed Nortes. The slaves were never allowed to interact with other slave races or learn their languages, so they would need sympathetic Nortes to help bridge these gaps and help them to work together towards their common goal.

"The reason they decided to separate the empire and fake the plague was key to the plan. During such a massive forward movement through the galaxy, the emperor would have all of his key military staff present with him. Usually his military staff was spread throughout the empire, controlling outposts and other military installations. The warriors could be trusted to maintain peace in the empire while the bulk of the forces began the biggest colonization movement the empire had ever undertaken.

"Although Nortes citizens lived throughout the empire, only the ones trained in the military and key to conquering new worlds would be in the first wave to colonize this sector."

The president had so many questions that it was difficult for him to pay close attention to every detail Hugany was saying. "I still don't understand why he separated the empire. Why not just use the virus to kill the warriors in the empire and then rise up with the workers?"

The empress had learned this entire story by the time she was six and had passed it on to her son, who was already eight. She continued, "In order to allow the Nortes resistance to infiltrate key areas and build resistance cells within the slave community, they needed to have certain people removed from the equation. If there was only a skeleton crew of warriors and Nortes soldiers running things in the empire, it would be much easier for them to perform their task.

"If the Nortes virus was released on the key military officials, then it would be seen as the coup attempt that it really was. They needed a plausible explanation for the warriors and military staff to be eliminated that would not be questioned."

"And an unknown virus in an unknown portion of the galaxy was the key." Dr. Bates looked at the assembled panel. "No one from the empire would be able to say it wasn't real because they wouldn't have access to any raw data. And because the warriors wouldn't allow anyone from the empire to travel to the new colonies, it would be taken at face value as fact. They would have no other choice."

"Exactly." Hugany refilled her glass of water. "Once the separation was made, the warriors in the new colonies would be killed with the virus. The Nortes in charge of conquering new worlds would also be killed with a virus. The only people to survive would be the emperor, his loyal staff, a few hundred thousand Nortes colonists and low-level military personnel, and, of course, the slaves.

"Everyone would be told that although they were lucky enough not to die from the virus, they were all still carriers of the disease and therefore could never return to the empire. T'Leh would then allow the colonies to start to fall apart on their own. Without the warriors to maintain the slaves and perform their other duties, there just weren't enough Nortes to keep everything running. T'Leh would then address his new empire and decree that slavery must be abolished for the sake of the colonies. Only by uniting with the slaves and working together could they survive.

"Nortes colonists were generally made up of military personnel, farmers, builders, technical staff, and other people who generally liked to work. They lived to explore and build new cities and worlds for their people. They weren't common among the Nortes and were even shunned by the majority because they actually liked to get their hands dirty and work for a living. Because of their way of life and their general beliefs, it wasn't very hard at all for T'Leh to sell them the idea of unity and working together. Most of them didn't believe in slavery to begin with. They felt that slavery just weakened their society by allowing people to become complacent and lose skills and knowledge through laziness. The current dilemma that they were facing just seemed to prove their point.

"They had already charted several worlds on which to relocate their people. Each species was given a choice as to where they wanted to live and start their lives over. Many decided to live in a system near what is now the Detrill home world. The first worlds we occupied were chosen strictly for their military value, so we had no use for them after the unification. They were abandoned and all of their secrets buried. We moved into the sectors we now live in and built our communities. We have enjoyed a thousand years of peace and unity with our former slaves."

"Until now." The president let out a sigh and continued, "Whatever happened to the rest of the empire?"

"We don't know; all communication was severed with them. T'Leh had sporadic communication with the empire over the next year. He led them to believe that everyone was dying and eventually that he, too, had died.

"Once the warriors in the empire died of natural aging and the resistance freed the slaves, the colonies and the empire were supposed to unite. T'Leh never received word from his resistance leaders and he feared the worse, that the plan went completely wrong. He felt that alerting the empire to the deception would just bring war into this sector. So we have lived in silence ever since."

"Is it possible then that someone figured out how to create these warriors and allow the empire to live on?" Dr. Bates didn't think that even with the information he had in front of him that he and his best scientists could reproduce the warriors. However, the Nortes were obviously much more advanced than the Coalition was.

The secretary of state spoke up again. "How did T'Leh plan to guarantee that no one created anymore warriors after the current ones had died?"

Hugany adjusted in her seat and pressed a few buttons on her pad. "You will note on your pads the world known to our ancestors as *The Breeding Planet*. They called it that because the warriors were created there. Only a handful of Nortes knew where that planet was, and of those, all were either killed in the purging or lived on in the colonies after the unification.

"The planet has an orbital defense system that is impenetrable by use of force. The gun platforms are self-replicating in case any of them are damaged or destroyed during an attack. It's not so much the power of the guns that are devastating; it's the sheer number of them in orbit. It took two hundred years to put all of the defense guns into place. There were entry points within the defense perimeter that ships would approach in order to be scanned. If a living member of the royal family was not on the ship, it would be destroyed. Even if a ship could withstand the destructive force of the guns, they would have to find the cloning labs that are ten kilometers below the surface of the planet. Then they would have to have security codes as well as DNA from a member of the royal family to enter the complex and access any computer terminal once inside. And then you would, of course, need the scientific expertise to use the equipment and create the warriors.

"A member of the royal family lived at the installation constantly. Every eight hours, that person would have to enter a code into a terminal, have their DNA checked, and perform a retinal scan. If they didn't, then every Nortes in the complex would be killed by a release of a nerve gas.

"No slaves or warriors were on the planet surface, only Nortes. Once the warriors were born, they left the planet and were shipped off to whatever assignment they were given. Much like the salmon of your home planet, Mr. President, the warriors were encoded genetically with instructions concerning their birthplace. However, with them it was reversed. Warriors were encoded with an absolute lack of knowledge of where they were created. They could not go anywhere near the breeding planet; if they did, they died. Once they left, they could never return."

Dr. Bates was originally hopeful that the cloning labs could be accessed once the threat had passed. The amount of good his scientists could do with this technology was almost unlimited, but it didn't seem as though that would be happening anytime soon. "Was the facility destroyed? How did they smuggle all of the personnel off the station? Were warriors created on an as-need-basis or were they stored there?"

Hugany always hated to think of the history of her people; it was so full of deceit and violence. "Each member of the royal family who was not going to accompany T'Leh to the colonies was given a poison. They were each affected at different rates, according to their unique chemistry. When the keeper of the breeding planet installation died, so did every Nortes assigned there. Without P'Ket at the control center of the installation, no other Nortes or member of the royal family could land on the planet except the emperor himself. The paranoia that the Nortes had bred into themselves over millennia would be their own undoing. All of their failsafe protocols were designed so that no one outside the royal family could destroy the empire. They never thought that a member of the family would destroy it themselves from the inside out.

"As for the warriors left on the planet, they were in a dormant state. Their cloning process wouldn't be completed until they were needed. When the installation received orders to activate a certain number of warriors, the process was completed and they were shipped off to wherever they were needed." The empress became obviously upset and her hands began to tremble. She looked at each person in the room individually before she continued. "If someone has found a way to breech all of the safety protocols, there were almost one billion warriors dormant at the time the facility was compromised."

"I see", was all the president could say while he thought about the implication of what Hugany had just told them.

"Couldn't we just take you to Extinction? With your help, we could make it past the defense guns to the surface. You are the heir to the throne, so you could access the facility and we could either take control of it or destroy it." The secretary of state received a nodding of approval from the president and the other aides present.

"Do you remember when I told you that there were two reasons that I could not take control of the warriors?" Hugany tried to sit up a little bit straighter in her seat. "I never told you the second reason."

Chapter 43
1,000 Years Ago - The Colonies

T'Leh cradled his son while he stood at D'Bath's funeral and absently listened to someone speaking of his friend's greatness. "… and without his dedication to medicine and our people, our children would still be suffering from the Unarian disease that had plagued our world for centuries. He not only kept his people strong but he also furthered the advancement of our warriors. Through his genetic…"

T'Leh let the rest of the speaker's words go unheard. He couldn't help but think of the irony he was listening to. D'Bath had taken a scientifically stagnant empire and fueled its growth once more. Through scientific discoveries, medical breakthroughs, and apprenticeship programs he created, D'Bath had gotten the Nortes interested in science again.

And now D'Bath's latest scientific project was leading to the death of fifteen percent of the Nortes population in the colonies. He began to cry as he thought about not only what he was doing to his own people but what he had made his friend do. T'Leh should've known what this would do to D'Bath and he should've watched him closer. He should have done something more.

The service ended and T'Leh returned to his palace. His warrior escort had dwindled from twenty to five. The five who were with him had mottled skin, slow movement, faltering steps, and other symptoms that marked their time for death was near.

T'Leh felt bad for his warriors. He knew that their loyalty was genetic and that it wasn't because they were good people, but he couldn't help but wonder whether good people were good because of who they were or how they were born. It had all been debated over before, time and time again, Nature versus Nurture. Did anyone really have an answer? T'Leh decided that his warriors were good creatures but with monstrous orders to guide them.

D'Bath had said that he could genetically remap the warriors but it would take more than his lifetime to do it. D'Bath and T'Leh also knew that they couldn't guarantee they could find a scientist as good as D'Bath and as agreeable to unity to carry on his work when he became too old to do so himself. After the unity, one of D'Bath's primary goals was to try to find a way to enter the dormant warriors into the new empire as equals and voluntary members of the military. They would no longer need to conquer or kill innocent people. But that dream died with D'Bath.

Once at home, T'Leh gave his son to one of the caretakers to be put to bed. He gently kissed him on the forehead before entering his office and sealing the doors. After pressing a series of codes into his office terminal, a secret door opened and Nogil appeared.

Nogil bowed and touched his hands to his eyes and then his lower right hip area, indicating the Detrill heart. After finishing the Detrill gesture for remorse, he spoke. "T'Leh." It still felt more than odd to call the emperor by his given name but it had been asked of him to do so. "I cannot tell you of the sorrow my eyes see and my heart feels at the loss of your friend. My people will tell stories of his deeds and life for the rest of our time. We would not be free if it were not for him."

"Thank you, Nogil." T'Leh handed him a glass of Nortes ale. "I am glad that we did not have to use those escape ships you had prepared for us. No one is the wiser about our plans. Without D'Bath, the scientific community is at a loss of what to do next. They all believed that he was our only hope to beat this virus. Now that he is gone, I believe that our plans to bring an end to slavery will be accelerated. Without hope of a cure, our people will want to leave this system and find a new one in hopes that it will not be contaminated. And we, of course, cannot do that without your help."

Nogil felt that he had built not only a partnership with T'Leh but also a friendship. T'Leh was like no other being he had ever met. Of course, he had only met other Detrill, warriors, and the few Nortes who had been involved with T'Leh's plan. Nogil wanted to help his friend.

Detrill had the ability to access any part of their memory at will. Unlike a typical photographic memory, they could also sort information in any way that they wanted to. It was almost as though their mind was a computer filing system that they could adjust and access anytime they wanted to. They also had the ability to help other Detrill access their memories. This was how they taught their children to use their abilities or help others who had suffered memory loss due to illness, injury, or old age.

Nogil had never touched anyone besides another Detrill. He had been touched many times by the warriors but only in cruel ways to punish him. Nogil wanted to help T'Leh but didn't know whether he would be able to give him the gift. Sometimes when Detrill mourned their dead, they were so distraught that they could not access their memories. Other Detrill, usually family or close friends, would help them to access their memories of the loved one who had passed so they could remember and relive all of the good emotions they had with that person.

Nogil stepped behind T'Leh and placed one hand over his friend's eyes. T'Leh didn't question his motive and seemed to relax considerably at Nogil's touch. He then placed the other hand in T'Leh's lower torso area, where his heart would have been if he were a Detrill. Nogil couldn't feel the connection. He gently moved his hand across T'Leh's body until he found it. Nogil connected with T'Leh's mind and began searching for D'Bath.

It was very difficult for Nogil. Part of the gift that Detrills gave each other during a joining was a sharing of memories. The Detrill helping to remember could see and live the memories he was helping to find. By doing so, the memories now became a part of the helper's mind and could be shared again with other Detrill.

Nogil had memories from Detrill two thousand years ago in his mind. However, he couldn't see into T'Leh's mind as he could another Detrill. Nogil had to navigate by emotion alone. He could feel the sadness T'Leh now felt and assumed that it was for D'Bath. Nogil followed that emotion through T'Leh's mind until he found the source. Probing gently, he found happy memories, memories that made him smile and allowed the pain to drain away. Nogil couldn't see the actual memories but could sense that T'Leh did.

Nogil probed further and found an interesting strand of memory. It was one of the strongest memories of happiness that T'Leh had with D'Bath, so he followed it. Abruptly the memory went from the most joyous moment in T'Leh's life to his worst...

T'Leh was only twenty-six when he took over the empire from his father. Although he did not agree with his father's political views, he loved him very much. The watercraft accident was a tragedy to T'Leh and the rest of his family. His mother died not too long after his father and T'Leh suspected that her sickness was brought about by her sadness.

Today marked the two year anniversary since T'Leh had been officially taken over as emperor. He sat in his bedroom, wearing only his robe. Dr. D'Bath was reviewing his medical scans from T'Leh's yearly physical. He was chatting with his friend while inputting and reading data. "So, what are you going to do on this special day?"

T'Leh lay back in his bed and looked up to the ceiling. "I'm going to have dinner with D'Nerth and

P'Tong. They are going to try to set me up with another of their friends." T'Leh chuckled to himself at the thought of all his previous blind dates. "You cannot imagine the look on these women's faces when they realize that they have been set up on a blind date with the emperor. You would think that I, of all people, would be able to find someone to fall in love with."

D'Bath looked at his young friend over his datapad. "Ah, to be young again. Of course, when I was your age, I didn't have my choice of more than a thousand concubines to help me through the awkwardness of growing up. How is that one young girl? What's her name? I can never recall but you seemed to have a crush on her since you were sixteen, if I recall correctly."

"M'Tawny." T'Leh let out a sigh. "I do love her, you know. It is just these damn laws that we live by and cannot be changed. Why can't the emperor do as he pleases? I do not understand why I am allowed to have a child with a concubine and that child can grow up to inherit the throne, but I am never allowed to marry that same woman. Why is she good enough to incubate the seed of the emperor and add her own genetic material to the family line but cannot marry the same man?"

"I can't say that I understand your position because I have never been in it. But I can empathize with you. If I were not allowed to openly love my wife and to be with her, I think I would go mad." D'Bath continued looking over his data. "M'Tawny was your first, wasn't she?"

"First and only. I wish I could move her into the palace to live with me and make a family with me. She says that she wants to have my child so that we can share that bond forever. So far we have not been able to accomplish that goal."

T'Leh thought back to his first encounter with M'Tawny. He had been sixteen and she was eighteen. She had been raised to be one of T'Leh's personal concubines, so she was as virginal as he was. When he began touching her, it just didn't feel right to him. He could tell that she was nervous and not at all comfortable to be in the situation they were in. She had been taught all about her position in life and knew more about sex than any ten Nortes women put together.

"M'Tawny and I just talked that night we were put together. We made everyone think that we had performed the rite of passage but we did not. We talked about our lives and our dreams." T'Leh hoped that the physical would be over soon so that he could call his love to the chamber and they could spend some time together.

"A concubine has dreams? I thought that all they wanted was to please the emperor and thereby fulfill all of their training and familial obligations?"

"That's what was so special about her. She knew that she had a duty to her family and the empire but she also had personal aspirations. She had always hoped that I would take to liking her and allow her to become more educated than just in the ways of sex." T'Leh could feel himself becoming more aroused as he thought of her. He hadn't seen her for three days and it was starting to get to him. "We didn't actually join for almost two years. I fell in love with her that first night. It took her a little longer to overcome all of the training that concubines go through to help keep them from having an emotional connection with their master." T'Leh had never liked that word, especially when referring to anything dealing with M'Tawny.

"And now I can't even give her what she wants most. Why can't I sire a child with her? You've already examined her and said that nothing is wrong."

D'Bath had almost finished reviewing all of the data he had obtained but he already had the answer he was looking for. "I'm sorry, T'Leh, but you will never be able to father any children." D'Bath placed a gentle hand on his young friend's hand. "You have a genetic anomaly that is causing your reproductive organs to fail. It is very rare and untreatable. Even with my genetic expertise, I have not been able to find a cure for this disorder."

T'Leh sat up and began to cry, not for himself but for M'Tawny. "Will you report this to the rest of the family?" An emperor who could not reproduce would be removed from the throne and replaced with another member of the royal family to ensure that the DNA carried on to the next generation.

"No. You are only twenty-eight and I am only…let's say forty years old." Both smiled at that. "I have not given up on you yet. You already have the makings of the best emperor this galaxy has ever seen and I may find a cure for this eventually. Besides, your cousin isn't fit to run a food stand much less the empire that I and my family live in.

"Other than that, you have a perfectly clean bill of health. I suggest that you go out tonight and enjoy your time with your friends. Oh, I almost forgot to tell you. My wife met D'Nerth at a cooking class she is taking. They began talking and realized who each other was. They have become very good friends over this past week. Isn't it a small empire after all?"

T'Leh felt a little sick to his stomach. The cooking class was where D'Nerth and her friends tried to recruit people for the underground. He would have to talk to D'Nerth about that later. For now, he just said, "Yes, it is. I'm glad to hear that your wife is trying new things. Goodbye, my friend, and thank you for everything."

With that, D'Bath left the chamber. T'Leh decided that now was not the time to call M'Tawny. He needed to think about how he was going to discuss this new information with his friends.

That night at dinner, T'Leh sat with D'Nerth and P'Tong and their friend he was set up with. She was attractive but lacked any real sense of the world around her.

T'Leh was surprised that his friends would even know such a person, much less try to set him up with her. He was, however, polite and as charming as possible towards his guest.

    At the end of the evening, the foursome took a shuttle into orbit around the planet to view the Kasmai comet. The comet had a four hundred year elliptical orbit around the system. With their technology, just about anyone could view the comet from a shuttle anytime they wanted. They would just have to chase it down, depending on what part of the system it was in. But it was special to be able to view the comet in the same sky as their planet.

    "I'm so happy that Kasmai is near our home while I'm alive." T'Leh was looking at the spectacular view through the transparent roof of the shuttle. "There are only two points in the orbit of Kasmai where it comes into contact with Tetreon radiation. Only then does it change color and glow so that the core is completely visible through all of the debris it sheds while it travels through space. It truly is a remarkable manifestation of the universe."

    "Is this real netriv leather?" This was from the woman who was not interesting enough to have her name remembered. She was touching the seats in the shuttle and looking at all of the jewels it was adorned with. T'Leh didn't even bother to answer her.

    D'Nerth couldn't hold her giggles back at her friend's last comment. She would have to apologize to T'Leh later. She adored her friend but should have known better than to bring her along for a blind date with T'Leh. She was one of D'Nerth's few friends who was a Nortes through and through. She cared for nothing except wealth and personal gains. She was, however, a great friend and fun to be around. It also helped D'Nerth to network with the much higher class of Nortes that she hoped to someday recruit to her cause.

D'Nerth looked at her husband and he gave her an approving nod. She was glad that he had because she couldn't wait any longer to tell T'Leh. "P'Tong and I saw something the other day that was even more spectacular than this." She gestured with her hand to the view of Kasmai.

"I told you not to peek while I was changing at the pool house the other day", T'Leh joked with his friends.

D'Nerth took a personal datapad from her pocket and pulled up an image and handed it to T'Leh. "That is the first sonogram of our baby!" D'Nerth and P'Tong hugged each other and kissed while a tear came to her eye. "I am two months pregnant. Only twelve to go!"

T'Leh began to cry almost immediately. He was so happy for his closest friends. He leaned forward and embraced them both. "I could not be happier if it were my own child. You will of course have the best doctors and care the empire has reserved for its emperor." He thought a minute longer before adding, "I also think that you should move into the palace so that my aides can help you with your pregnancy and we can be closer together. I'll want to see my godchild every day after he or she is born. I will be the godfather, right?"

"Of course you will, T'Leh", P'Tong said, still embracing his friend. "But we've talked about living in the palace before and you know how we feel about it. Now that circumstances have changed, we should talk about it again but not right now."

After the three friends dropped T'Leh's date at home, they went back to the palace to talk. T'Leh brought up D'Bath's wife and D'Nerth assured him that she was not trying to recruit the woman. They were just friends and had recently begun discussing motherhood and raising families. D'Nerth didn't have many friends who were older and had already experienced much life had to offer. She was happy to have a new friend who could bring a different point of view into her life.

T'Leh was satisfied with the answer she gave and dropped the subject. He then told them of his horrible news that he could never be a father. The three friends cried together again, this time for the sadness they felt for T'Leh and M'Tawny. When it was time to end the evening, D'Nerth and P'Tong went to the guest quarters they stayed in every so often. In the morning, they would all have breakfast and then T'Leh would again have to deal with the affairs of his empire.

~

One month had gone by since T'Leh had received both the best news of his life and the worst. He was looking over some military documents when his call chime came alive. He pressed the button and immediately saw the visage of his highest-ranking Nortes military commander, General N'thoth. "Your Highness, my greatest apologies in disturbing you." He bowed his head in a subservient manner. "I need for you to come to the war council chambers immediately."

For a moment, it sounded as though the general were giving him an order. T'Leh didn't like him to begin with and he knew that the feeling was mutual. Had it been any other day, T'Leh just might have gotten into a verbal lashing of the general to put him in his place. However, it seemed as though something big was happening and T'Leh decided that he would deal with it later. "I'm on my way. But be warned, this better not be a trivial matter that has moved you to talk to me in such a way."

The general just smiled and the screen went blank. T'Leh took the palace shuttle to the chambers. The shuttle was very roomy, even though there were six warriors with T'Leh to ensure his safety. He leaned to his most trusted warrior and whispered to him, "I think the general might be standing too close to me when we get to the chambers."

The warrior smiled in a way that was only perceptible to T'Leh. The warrior knew that T'Leh wanted him to bump the general when they entered the chambers. It was a game T'Leh liked to play and he thought that his warrior did as well.

Even though they did not generally have a sense of humor, T'Leh noticed that his warrior had seemed to gain one in the twenty-eight years they had been together. Each new baby born into the royal family was given a warrior from birth who stayed with him until the warrior died, usually around one-third of the Nortes' life. Then another would take his place as the lead warrior for that person.

Warriors were not given names, just rank. T'Leh secretly referred to his warrior as Fouter, the Nortes slang for friend. When they arrived, Fouter walked into the chambers ahead of T'Leh and of course the general was standing in his customary spot to greet the emperor. As T'Leh walked toward his seat at the dais, he walked straight towards General N'thoth. Fouter used his lower right arm to move the general from T'Leh's path. N'thoth would certainly have a bruise the next day. T'Leh thought that it was odd that N'thoth was still smiling.

When T'Leh took his seat, he saw D'Bath walking into the chambers, ushered by two of the general's aides. T'Leh immediately began to think that his infertility had somehow become known and now he and D'Bath were about to be executed for hiding the secret. He kept his face stone. "What are we doing here?"

General N'thoth's smile fixed into a straight line across his scarred and misshapen face. "I have come to believe that there are traitors in the very mist of the royal family."

T'Leh felt that any moment his very own warrior's hand would reach out and crush his skull. "What are you talking about? There hasn't been anyone charged with treason in more than six hundred years. You better have proof of this so-called traitor or you will find yourself in a tube." His voice was more calm and even than he felt inside.

"As I said, Your Highness," N'thoth continued, "there are traitors, more than one. My spies have found the beginnings of an underground network of Nortes who have been communicating with the slaves." A collective gasp erupted from all those who did not already know what the general was going to say.

"We believe that they have been teaching slaves to speak Nortes as well as some of the more common slave languages. This can only point towards an uprising among our slaves." The general made a point of making dramatic gestures as he walked in the chambers. "We raided a meeting of these dissidents this afternoon."

"Without my knowledge!" T'Leh was furious that his citizens, possibly completely innocent civilians, had been attacked by his general's men.

"Sire, I know that you love your empire and your people. I'm sure that any measure I make to ensure its safety is in the best interest of you and your people. However, if in the future, you want me to inform you of such actions before they take place, I will. And sire, I do believe that we will be performing many more of these actions in the near future."

"Why this meeting? Surely you could have told me this in my office." T'Leh knew that N'thoth was hiding something.

"I believe that your office has been soiled enough already by the traitors we caught today. I only wished to help distance you even further from what is about to happen. That is why I felt these chambers would be the most appropriate place for the interrogations." He then tapped his com-badge. "Bring them in."

A male and female Nortes were brought into the chamber with arms bound behind their backs and hoods over their heads. T'Leh assumed that they were also gagged because of the muffled sounds coming from under the hoods. The general walked to the two figures and removed the hoods.

T'Leh almost fell out of his chair. Standing bound and gagged before him were P'Tong and D'Nerth. "What is this nonsense?! Answer me at once!" T'Leh shouted. Fouter knew his master well and moved into position to kill the general if it was so ordered. Fouter didn't know anything of politics but he knew he had never heard T'Leh so angry in his life and he knew that it was the general's fault. If the general could not explain his actions, he would be dead very shortly. And unfortunately, if the general could explain his actions, then Fouter would probably have to kill his master's best friends.

The general knew why Fouter had moved towards him so he hastened his speech along. "Emperor T'Leh, your friends have been conspiring against you and the empire. They have been leading an underground movement for some years now. We have information that leads us to believe that their capture will unravel the entire movement. Once we have interrogated them in the tubes, we will surely be able to quash this underground quickly and quietly."

The general also believed that T'Leh was somehow involved or at least knew of the plots his friends were scheming. He couldn't come out and say it without absolute proof; otherwise, he would be summarily executed. Once D'Nerth and P'Tong had been placed in the torture tubes, he was sure he would get the information against T'Leh he needed to have the brat-emperor killed. N'thoth knew he could run the empire from behind the throne if T'Leh's cousin was made emperor.

T'Leh kept his composure even though he was dying inside. "Why is Dr. D'Bath here? Why does he need to witness this?"

N'thoth tried to put on his most sincere expression of regret, which was difficult as he had never felt regret in his life. "Dr. D'Bath, we found these two traitors getting ready to have a meeting with their other degenerate friends. When we raided the store they were using as a front for one of their safe houses, there were five civilian casualties. I'm afraid that one was your wife and the other your son. All of the other terrorists took poison capsules to avoid being caught. We still don't know why these two didn't follow suit. They're probably just cowards. Again, I am truly sorry for your loss, Doctor."

D'Bath crumpled to the floor and T'Leh couldn't help but let a tear escape his eyes. He was crying not only for his friend and most trusted advisor but for his friends who he was about to kill. He knew that they didn't take their poison capsules because of the child D'Nerth carried. Through all of his pain and grief, T'Leh knew what he had to do.

He couldn't allow his friends to be tortured for the obvious reason that he couldn't bear to see them go through that type of pain. He also couldn't allow them to give up all of the information they had on the underground, especially his name. T'Leh looked directly into D'Nerth's eyes and saw that she, too, was thinking the same thing.

She then made a quick look to her stomach and back to D'Bath. After T'Leh had told his friends that he could not father any children, D'Nerth had suggested allowing her husband to give D'Bath his sperm to be artificially inseminated into M'Tawny. T'Leh quickly dismissed the idea and told them of the touching ceremony that took place after birth to verify the DNA. T'Leh thought that he knew what D'Nerth was now suggesting with her quick glances.

T'Leh saw that his warrior was just as close to N'thoth as he was to his two friends. He quickly dismissed the idea of having the general killed instead. There were too many witnesses and he couldn't kill them all. He would be quickly put down as a traitor to his own empire and killed along with his friends and their unborn child. T'Leh looked away. "Warrior, kill the traitors."

Without even thinking about it or hesitating for a second, Fouter used one of his mighty hands for each of the prisoner's skulls and crushed them while twisting and breaking their necks. T'Leh knew that neither of his friends felt any pain; Fouter was too quick and skilled for that.

The general looked dumbfounded at the two corpses on the ground, rage building within him. "Why have you killed our only sources of information?! Why did you willingly endanger the empire?!"

T'Leh stepped down from the dais. "You DARE question me! I am the ruler of the empire and your master!" Fouter moved ever so closer to the general, ready to dispatch him if it were so ordered. "Are you questioning my loyalty? Are you saying that I act for anything other than the good of my people?"

The general began shaking, as much from fear as from anger. "No, Your Highness. I apologize for my transgressions."

He knelt to the floor and offered T'Leh a view of the base of his skull, submitting his life to the emperor. "I await your punishment."

T'Leh wanted him killed but knew that he could not justify it without making himself suspect to further inquiry. "Although I need not justify my actions…" He let the words hang in the air for a moment while he returned to his seat on the dais. "I could not allow those two traitors to live any longer. They had lied to me for years and betrayed not only the empire but my trust and love. And because of their actions, one of the empire's most loyal and important citizens has lost his family. For my friend D'Bath and the empire, justice for their actions could not wait a second longer.

"Besides, you said yourself that they led the underground. With them gone, the rest should be easy to find. That is, if they even stay together. With their leaders dead, I'm sure that they will not last long on their own."

Fouter looked to the still kneeling general and then to T'Leh. T'Leh realized that although he could not kill the general, he could still use his public show of anger as an excuse for some form of punishment. "Warrior, take the general and place him in a torture tube. One full day should be enough time for him to think about how he will address his master in the future. And maybe he will have a little more regard for the citizens of this empire he is sworn to protect."

Fouter lifted the general from the ground by his head and then grabbed his lower legs in another of his massive hands. Reflexively, the general began to resist against the pain he felt from the warrior. Fouter punched him once in the face and the audible breaking of the general's nose, cheek, and possibly jaw reverberated throughout the entire chamber. The general went slack in the warrior's grip. Fouter then looked at T'Leh again. "He lives, master; only his bones are injured. I will take him to the tube at once." Fouter then signaled to his remaining warriors so that they would stay with T'Leh.

T'Leh took a hold of D'Bath and began to walk him towards the palace shuttle. "Warrior, I want these terrorist bodies to be taken to D'Bath's laboratory so that they can be autopsied. We may still be able to get some information from them yet, so do not harm their bodies any further." T'Leh led his friend out the chamber doors and as an afterthought, he said over his shoulder, "Make sure the general is conscious before his time in the tube starts. I want to make sure that he remembers every moment of it."

T'Leh had the warrior bodyguards sit in a separate compartment in the shuttle for the ride to D'Bath's laboratory. "I cannot even imagine the pain you are suffering, my friend, but I need your help."

D'Bath only continued to sob into his hands. After a moment, still not looking at T'Leh, he said, "I told her not to take our son to one of the meetings. I told her that it could be dangerous. She insisted that bringing him only made the shop look even more innocent and that the military wouldn't take action against children. She just wouldn't listen to me."

T'Leh could barely breathe. *All this time D'Bath and his wife were a part of the movement?* "Are you saying that your wife wasn't there by accident? You knew what she was doing?"

"Yes. And you can torture me all you like but nothing will compare to the pain I am already feeling. I don't even know anything that would be useful to you."

"My friend, I would never torture you. I had D'Nerth and P'Tong executed so that they would not have to go through the pain of being tortured. And also so they could not give my name to General N'thoth as one of their conspirators." T'Leh looked into his friend's eyes as the realization of what he had just said hit D'Bath. He continued, "I also wanted a chance to save their unborn child. D'Nerth was three months pregnant. Do you think that you can save her child?"

D'Bath tried to pull himself together. He wasn't sure whether he was relieved that he wasn't going to be executed or distraught that he would have to live with this pain he felt for years to come. "If we can remove the embryo within the next twenty minutes, it should be all right. But where are we going to put it? We will need a viable host for it."

"Maybe we can kill two Yanghus with one spear." T'Leh opened a comm channel to M'Tawny's private quarters. "I need you to come to D'Bath's laboratory now. There is no time for questions. Tell the house mistress that I am very distressed and need comforting and that I told you to meet me in the laboratory. Be there in five minutes."

M'Tawny closed the channel and did what her lover told her to do.

D'Bath, still thinking of his family, was trying to clear his mind so he could be prepared for what he was about to do. "T'Leh, I don't think that I'll have any problems transferring the embryo to M'Tawny, but we still have a bigger problem."

"I know. But we have eleven months to figure out how we're going to get through the touching ceremony. For now, I have a chance to save the life of my best friends' child and a piece of them as well. I can give my lover the child that she wants and maybe hold onto the throne at the same time." T'Leh looked at D'Bath. "I only wish I could give you something, my friend, but all I have is gratitude for what you are about to do."

Once at the laboratory, all personnel were cleared from the operating room. The procedure went as according to plan and two hours later, M'Tawny was pregnant. Even though the life inside her was not created by her and T'Leh, she felt an instant bond with the child she was now responsible for. She knew that she would love it just as much as if she had created it herself. M'Tawny knew that she would have wanted the same thing done if she had been in D'Nerth's place.

D'Bath spent the next several hours performing autopsies on T'Leh's friends. He made sure that there was no sign that D'Nerth had been pregnant and that there was no forensic material that could harm the resistance in any way. When it was done, he hugged T'Leh and M'Tawny and went home. No one saw or heard from D'Bath until the funeral for his family one week later.

~

A little less than eleven months later, M'Tawny gave birth to the first and only child she and T'Leh would ever have. It was the most beautiful thing T'Leh had ever seen in his life.

Two weeks later, D'Bath became the child's godfather and T'Leh's savior. D'Bath had figured out a way to fool the touching ceremony.

Snake

NAME: SNAKE
SPECIES: HUMAN
MOS: INTEL / INFILTRATION
RANK: FIRST SERGEANT
AGE: 29 - EARTH STANDARD
SEX: MALE
HEIGHT: 5'10"
WEIGHT: 200 POUNDS

Mouse had just finished his last run of the day; at least, he hoped it was his last. He had been pulling extra duty since Johnny got himself arrested three days ago.

Johnny, like all of the other runners, was under fourteen, so he would be spending a bit of time at juvenile corrections before they let him go home with a parent or as a ward of the colony. Any kid over fourteen was considered an adult for legal purposes if they were caught in the employ of or even slightly connected to any form of a criminal syndicate.

For that reason, Zinner kept all of his runners younger than fourteen. If a kid was going to be treated as an adult and thrown in an adult jail or prison for their crimes, the kid was sure to crack and turn Zinner over in order to make a deal for themselves.

Zinner used his kids to run everything he needed: drugs, money, instructions, notes, questions—everything. Zinner didn't use phones, the Net or terminals for any part of his business. Technology was too easy to get around, trace, undelete, or get a warrant for. A note written by a ten-year-old kid who took a dictation from a thirteen-year-old kid who was told what to say by another kid who was told by Zinner what to say, well, that was way too much hearsay for any court and none of that could be used as evidence. And Zinner made sure his kids got every last word right. Sometimes he spot-checked the notes to make sure nothing was lost in translation; if something was wrong, there was hell to pay. It's amazing how the game of telephone doesn't run into any problems down the wire when your fingers will get cut off if you pass the incorrect message along.

    Mouse walked in to the hub, handed the coordinator a small wad of cash, and then sat down heavily into a fairly abused beanbag. The hub was where all of the runners got their orders and returned to after their assignment was complete or with return items from their assignment. The coordinator was the kid in charge of passing out assignments and keeping track of who was at the hub waiting for their next run or to be let off shift.

    Today, an eight-year-old named Jenny was the coordinator. She was a bossy little thing, well suited for her current task. "Hey, booger head." She addressed Mouse as he handed her the cash. "I have another run for you."

    "Jennnnnnnnyyyyyyy! I've been running all day!" Mouse pouted.

    Jenny looked at him in a way that no eight-year-old child should ever be able to. Her face was a barely contained mask of rage and malice. "No one, NO ONE, argues with the coordinator." Her words were punctuated with a stomp to the ground and her little hands balled into fists.

    Mouse put his hands up in a supplicating gesture. "I wasn't arguing, Jenny. I'm sorry. I was just, uh, whining a little bit. I'm tired and hungry, that's all. What have you got for me?"

    Jenny transformed back into an eight-year-old little girl and reached back into her pocket and pulled out a sticky roll of leathery pressed fruit. "Want my roll-o? It's grape!"

"No, thanks. I'm just gonna sit here until you have my run ready."

Mouse curled up into a little ball and tried to take a power nap before his next run. He had just turned thirteen. He only had one year of work left in him before Zinner gave him a wad of cash and threatened to kill him if he ever showed his face in or near the hub again. Zinner was much harder on the veterans with only a year left of service; he wasn't losing much if he happened to disable or kill an almost retired runner.

Short of the never-ending threat of possible abuse, police raids, and all other sorts of potential violence, the hub was a pretty nice place to hang out, even on a runner's day off. It had video games, TV, pool tables, a skateboard ramp, gymnastic equipment, and tons of toys. The hub was always stocked with food and drinks—never any candy, though. Zinner didn't let his kids have candy; it wasn't good for them. Not that he cared about their overall health or dental issues, but he found that feeding the kids healthy food and keeping them hydrated kept them from getting sick or tired too quickly. Keeping his runners healthy kept his business healthy and that's all he cared about.

Mouse closed his eyes and let his mind drift away for a little bit. He was half tempted to go check in on his little brother before he made his next run but decided his current position was much more comfortable. Besides, Zach could take care of himself; he was almost nine, for God's sake. Today was Zach's day off but Mouse knew he would be skateboarding until late into the evening.

Too few moments had passed before Jenny unceremoniously dropped a small package on Mouse's stomach. "Thanks, Jenny."

"This one needs a receipt." Jenny was back to business.

"Of course it does." Mouse rolled out of the beanbag and stood. "I'll see you in a bit."

Receipts were a pain in the ass. The runner had to get the person receiving the package to lick a piece of paper. The runner brought that paper back and it was given to Zinner through a long line of intermediaries. Zinner would then run it through a stolen law-enforcement DNA scanner to determine whom the package was delivered to. There could never be any question or argument from these people whether they had received their package or not. That meant that whatever was in this three-inch square box was very important, expensive, or both.

Mouse left the hub after looking at the recipient's name and location. He didn't recognize either. Based on the numbers, the location had to be somewhere in the tool district but nowhere Mouse had ever been before. He scampered over to a bus terminal and used its mapping software to locate the address. Mouse knew that using any form of traceable technology to make a run was strictly forbidden but he was tired and didn't feel like getting lost or taking an absurdly and unnecessarily long route to his destination.

When the map pulled up the location, Mouse knew exactly the best route to get there. He realized he had been in that area before; something seemed familiar but he couldn't quite place it. It didn't really matter. He now knew where to go and how to get there so he was off to get it done.

As Mouse trotted through the streets, he decided that he should've taken Jenny's roll-o, even if it did have hair and pocket lint stuck to it. He was getting hungry and he wasn't even halfway to his drop-off. He had a few dollars in cash, enough on him that he wouldn't need to commit any crimes to get some food. He just needed to decide what he was in the mood for.

A quick detour and he stepped out of the alleyway and onto a market street that had dozens of food vendors. The first few he passed because the food they served was deadly to humans. No Trizite food today—he had shrimp yesterday. He passed a new booth he hadn't seen before; it was run by an alien that he had also never seen before and couldn't identify. The food actually smelled good and didn't look horrible, but he didn't want to take any chances with it.

When he ran into the tall and furry immovable object, Mouse was still concentrating on the alien he couldn't identify. He turned to apologize to whomever he had run into and had to look up, and up some more to see the face of the angry Shirka whose leg he was now wrapped around. Shirkas kind of always looked mad but Mouse was pretty sure this one actually was.

"Get off me, you dirty cub!" Saliva dripped from the angry maw of teeth.

"I'm, uh, sorry, sir", Mouse stammered and realized that maybe this was a female Shirka. He wasn't good at telling the diffcrence sometimes. When he saw the military uniform the Shirka was wearing, he figured it probably was a male.

Mouse was backing away and apologizing only so that he could now bump into another man that he wasn't paying attention to. This startled him so much that he flipped around and ended up almost giving the man a hug. Luckily this being was human and of a much nicer disposition than the Shirka.

The man wearing a marine uniform with lieutenant bars and no name tag said, "Hey there, son, it's okay. My friend here won't eat you; he just likes to act tough."

"I'm sorry, sir, I just, uh. I'm hungry, trying to find something to eat."

The lieutenant started to reach into his pocket to fish out some money and Mouse realized what he was doing. "Oh, no, sir, I have money. I wasn't trying to beg. I'm just hungry, just a little off my game, that's all I meant."

"You sure, son? I have plenty. The military gives us a pretty good per diem when we're on a business trip." The lieutenant started to reach again but Mouse actually physically stopped his hand from going into his pocket.

"No, sir. My father would be very mad at me if I took your money." And with that, Mouse turned and walked away, forgetting that he needed to eat.

The real problem with the lieutenant offering him money was that Mouse had already stolen his wallet. When he accidentally bumped into him, his hand landed on the marine's wallet. When Mouse felt the bulge of the wallet, his hand automatically did what years of training had taught it to do and it took the wallet from the pocket. Had the marine reached into his pocket to give Mouse some money, he would've realized what had happened.

As Mouse ducked down another alley, went through three yards, over two low roofs and back into another alley, he thought about how he had broken another of Zinner's rules. Never commit a crime, no matter how small, while running a job. Damn. He had now committed two offenses that would get most runners caned badly, but a runner this close to retirement might get worse. He shuddered to think about what worse could be. He had seen worse and no one ever wanted worse.

Mouse made it to his target location and didn't find anyone waiting for him. He looked at his watch and saw that he was within the fifteen-minute time period he was given for the exchange to take place. There was nothing unusual about having to wait a few minutes to pick up or drop something off, so Mouse wasn't worried yet.

He was, however, careful, so he kept walking past the meeting place as though he had just stopped for a moment to check his watch. He then turned down another alley and circled around a large building and crept into the shadows overlooking the exchange location. His nickname was earned from years of sneaking through buildings, shadows, and deadly places without ever being seen or hurt. And though he was tired and hungry, once he found his hiding spot, he opened his senses to the world around him and focused as best he could.

It only took a moment for a man to show up, looking as though he were expecting to find someone waiting for him. Mouse was about to make contact when he realized that something just didn't seem right. The man was waiting for someone, not something. Mouse had seen enough dirty deeds to know that this man was aiming to misbehave.

Mouse waited a few moments longer; he wanted to wait just past his scheduled delivery window to see what would happen. Almost on cue, the man looked at his watch and shook his head. Mouse knew the man was there for him, but he didn't know why. It couldn't be for his two transgressions on his way here; this hit was set up well in advance of those happening.

Mouse was close to retirement but he had never heard even rumors of Zinner taking out runners before or after retirement in order to keep them quiet. Mouse did have a little more knowledge of the business than other runners because his brother was a private runner for Zinner and Mouse's girlfriend was one of the other coordinators. But still, was that enough to kill him?

Johnny. Johnny was the answer. Johnny and Mouse were pretty good friends. Maybe Johnny had given him up; accidentally or on purpose, it didn't matter which. If the cops thought Mouse had information that could help take down Zinner, and one of Zinner's paid cops told him that, Mouse was as good as dead. There would be no reasoning with Zinner, no plea-bargaining, nothing.

Mouse slowly removed the box from his pouch and opened it, revealing a wad of cash and a small photo of Mouse taped to the outside of the roll of cash. His fears and theory confirmed. He slowly slid the money back into his pouch and thought about what to do next.

On the positive side, because Zinner didn't use any electronics at all, the hitman couldn't just call him up and say that Mouse had gotten away. Also, the hitman wouldn't have direct access to Zinner; he'd have to go find a runner to get a message to Zinner and that process wasn't all that fast. The flow of information to Zinner was almost completely secure but the downside was that it was very slow.

The negative side was that Mouse couldn't let Zinner know he was still alive. Once he got back to the hub, Jenny would want her receipt from the drop. Mouse smiled to himself. Zinner was pretty smart. You had to pass the coordinator in order to get in or out of the hub. If Mouse returned without a receipt or said the recipient didn't show and that's why he didn't have a receipt, then Jenny would raise all holy hell and alert Zinner at once. And if Jenny was given a receipt, she would hand it to a personal runner who would take it directly to Zinner. Again, he would be alerted right away that Mouse was back, and worse, he would know the attempt failed and Mouse was on to him because he shouldn't have a receipt in the first place.

Mouse wished that Shirka had eaten him; it would've been better than knowing death was coming for him. No sooner had that thought crossed his mind than he saw the two marines, human and Shirka, walk out of the alley Mouse had originally come through. Crap, was there a God, and was he actually delivering prayers today? Sending the Shirka to finish the job?

The human approached the hitman, who was already looking leery about the encounter. "Excuse me, sir", the lieutenant began. "I'm looking for a young man who might have come through here a few moments ago."

"I haven't seen any kids", came the terse reply.

The lieutenant smiled. "I haven't even described him to you yet. How do you know you haven't seen who I'm looking for?" He paused. "And I never said he was a kid."

Mouse saw the hitman twitch a little. He was waiting for a young boy to kill. Now these two other men show up at the time and place the boy was supposed to be, asking about the kid. It was too much of a coincidence for him. He immediately thought these two marines weren't real marines, just other hitmen in disguise waiting to take his mark.

No human liked taking on a Shirka but apparently this man thought something special of himself. "Look. I don't know what Z-man is trying to pull here, but this is my job. Both of you fuck off before I make a throw rug out of you both!" He was now pointing back and forth between the two marines.

The lieutenant just smiled. "First off, I have no idea what you're talking about or who this Z-man is. Second, that might have been funny if both of us were Shirkas but I'm not, so it just sounded dumb. Third, I don't think you're here for anything that's good for anyone, so I'm going to ask you to leave. Now." The hitman looked at the lieutenant in such a way that he decided he should add a threat to the end of his paragraph in order to be taken more seriously, just because that's how it's apparently done in these parts. "Or, I'll take that gun from your waist that you think you're hiding, and I'll shoot you in the face with it."

The lieutenant smiled, happy with his threat and ready to follow through as he knew he most likely would have to. The hitman twitched and started to go for his gun. The lieutenant moved in and slid off to the man's right side, the side with the gun. The hitman smiled to himself. This dumb marine, or whoever he was, was too slow; the hitman already had his hand on the grip of his pistol.

As the gun came from the waistband, the hitman knew he needed to shoot the furbag first. He was surprised to see his intended target just standing there with his muzzle open and tongue hanging out, like a dog he remembered from his childhood, who looked the same way before they went for a car ride. Why was he happy? He was about to get shot and he wasn't even moving.

As the gun cleared the jacket and started to press forward, the hitman felt another hand over his own, guiding the barrel of the gun back around and towards his own body. That wasn't right, not at all. He realized that the lieutenant was now moving back in front of him and was the one controlling the hitman's hand and the gun it held.

The gun was now fully and painfully pointed at the hitman's own chest, with his hand still clasped to it, and the marine was looking square into the hitman's eyes. The lieutenant slowly moved the barrel upward from the hitman's chest and said, "I told you, in the face."

The hitman's eyes went wide as he realized the lieutenant was following through with every word of his threat. The gun spat lead and fire into the hitman's face and in turn, he spit bone and brain matter out the back of his head.

The body slumped and the lieutenant looked to his companion. "I think that boy is in some trouble."

"So?"

"So…I'll let you kill the next guy if you help me find him."

No response.

"The next three guys?"

"Okay, let's go. I can still smell him—should be easy to track him to wherever he went."

~

Mouse hadn't seen the last exchange between the two marines; he was already heading away and barely saw the hitman's death. The sound of the gun made Mouse run faster than he ever had before, hunger and fatigue be damned. He still had to think of a way to get into the hub and get his brother out before Zinner found him.

When Mouse reached the hub, he decided that a direct approach was the best way. He would hand Jenny a receipt and that would leave him free to roam the hub without anyone caring. It would take between five and ten minutes for the receipt to get to Zinner and then a few minutes for him to formulate a response and a few minutes to get it moving. Just to be on the safe side, Mouse would give himself ten minutes to grab his brother and get the hell out of the hub.

Between the money for the hitman and the money he found in the marine's wallet, he should be able to get to another city and set up there with his brother. He was fairly certain he would make it out of the hub. He was more worried about getting to transportation. Zinner would send people to all of the public transport areas first. He would have to deal with that later.

Mouse entered the hub and tried to act calm, even bored if he could pull that off. "Hey, Jenny."

She looked at him and just put her hand out. "Receipt."

Someone missed naptime today, he thought. "Here you go. I'm gonna go find my brother. If you have anything else for me, let me know."

Mouse started to walk away when Jenny said, "He's not over there."

"Huh?"

"He's not at the skateboard ramp."

"Okay, do you know where he is?"

"Yup." Jenny rang the bell so one of Zinner's private runners would come get the receipt from her. "He's with Z-man. He was asked to run some sandwiches to him a while ago and he hasn't come back yet."

Mouse could feel his blood drain. Sweat popped out on his forehead. "Oh. Okay. Um, how about I take the receipt to Z-man? That way I can get my brother for dinner." He stammered, "And, I, uh, haven't seen the guy in a while. I wanted to talk to him about my retirement party."

Jenny rolled her eyes and then clinched them shut before she opened her mouth as wide as it could go. "Nooooooooooo!" This was a girl destined to work in public service somewhere. "You know the rules! No one sees the Z-man unless he comes to you OR you're one of his private runners. You. Are. Not. One. Of. His. Private. Runners. Go away, turd face."

Oh crap. Mouse knew that this wasn't by accident. Zinner had his brother, had planned to have his brother, just in case Mouse came back.

The apartment was at the back of the hub and had tons of security in place. All of the security was lo-tech but its strength lied in its simplicity and the overkill of redundancies that were in place. Everything was based on the idea that cops were coming for evidence or a rival bad guy was coming for Zinner and his money.

If the cops were coming, he just needed enough time to make sure there wasn't any small bit of evidence he hadn't accounted for and then just sit and wait to surrender.

If other bad guys were coming, he needed enough time to get his barricades in place to hold off the attack for eight minutes. Eight minutes was the average response time for the patrol officers in this area. He didn't keep evidence in his apartment so why wouldn't he call the police to come save him?

Mouse had to figure out how to get to the apartment undetected, get inside, get his brother out, and not get caught. Or, do all that and instead of getting out, kill Zinner himself to make sure he and his brother were safe. They didn't call him Mouse for nothing; time to put the name to the test.

Mouse had already walked away from Jenny as he mulled all of this over in his head. He walked by a refrigerator and grabbed a sandwich without bothering to see what kind it was. He knew he needed fuel so he ate it as he walked towards the back of the hub. He had also grabbed a bottle of water for himself and threw two in his bag for later. If there was a later.

He would have to use Zinner's own system against him. Take that healthy and well-spent paranoia and use it to Mouse's advantage and not Zinner's. But how?

If he called the cops, then Zinner would just open his apartment up and let them walk right in. Mouse didn't think the cops would let him ride their coattails but his brother would be able to walk right out and then Mouse could snatch him up and tell him what was happening. But if that backfired, Zach would be trapped in the apartment with a very angry Zinner who might just do something to Zach out of spite. Mouse couldn't risk that, even if it wasn't a big risk.

If Mouse called in a rival gang, then Zinner would call the cops himself and wouldn't hurt Zach. But a lot of people would get hurt in all the fighting and how in the hell would Mouse just "call in" a rival gang anyway? If only those two marines had followed him here, that might be enough of a distraction.

How did those guys find him in the first place? Mouse's mind began to wander a bit. He knew he hadn't left any tracks in the alley; it was cobblestone. He hadn't been followed, not directly anyway—he would've spotted them. The Shirka, that had to be it. The Shirka scent tracked him. The way they walked out of the alley it was obvious they weren't following ground clues; it had to be air scent. And that gave him an idea.

Mouse hadn't seen Zinner's personal runner with the receipt pass him yet so he just stopped and waited. Mouse saw the runner talk with Jenny, take the receipt, and then head in his direction.

Mouse called out, "Hey, Billy."

"What's up, Mouse?"

"Not much. Are you runnin' to Z-man?"

"Yup. With your receipt, dude."

"Cool, yeah, hey, would you mind taking my satchel to Zach? He's with the Z-man right now. I guess he's been there a while. I want to head out for the night but I don't want to carry this thing around with me. Can you ask him to hold on to it for me until tomorrow?" Mouse was already draping the satchel over Billy's head.

"Sure. Anything good in it?" Billy patted it jokingly. It was beyond taboo for a runner to go through another runner's satchel.

"Only about twenty thousand credits." Mouse wasn't lying.

"Hah! You wish! See ya, buddy." Billy was unknowingly off to do two things: one, to alert Zinner that Mouse hadn't been killed yet, and two, to drag Mouse's scent through the hub and lead the Shirka right to Zinner's apartment.

Mouse tried not to run, tried not to catch anyone's attention as he slid through the smattering of kids relaxing throughout the hub. He nodded a few times when he had to, waved to a few friends, said hi only when he couldn't avoid it. Mouse was fairly popular and he tended to draw a crowd when he hung out, so he had to be careful not to let anyone glom on to him as he tried to get to his target.

Mouse finally made it to the bathrooms and walked in, hoping it would be empty. To his dismay, there were a few kids just hanging out and talking. They probably bumped into each other while they were washing their hands and just started talking and didn't think to leave.

Without overthinking it, Mouse walked in holding his stomach with one hand while cupping the other over his mouth, all the while making horrible retching sounds. Heading to the garbage can, he began to dry heave into it, hoping he would be able to bring up some of his sandwich for added realism. He didn't have to; the actions were enough to move the three kids along and they left the bathroom.

Mouse pulled his head out of the garbage can and thought about locking the door but decided not to. That might draw attention if someone found it locked. Instead, he focused on making his next move quickly so no one would walk in on him.

He crossed to the rear of the bathroom and pulled up a service grate that was in the floor. He slid himself down the shaft and pulled the grate back over his head after he was in. The smell was absolutely horrendous and he wasn't sure how healthy the kids could be eating if they were the cause of what he smelled now.

The hub was actually an old school that had been abandoned many years before after a natural disaster made it unsafe for the students to continue going there. The irony was not lost on Mouse. He knew that this faculty bathroom actually connected to the boys' locker room showers through this service tunnel. The locker room was Zinner's private entertaining area because it had a hot tub and steam room. It wasn't directly attached to Zinner's apartment, but it got him much closer than he currently was.

The lieutenant approached the dilapidated security fence around the abandoned school and looked to his companion. He knew better than to ask his friend if he was sure this was where the boy had gone.

"Thoughts?"

The Shirka grunted, "A criminal syndicate hideout. No perimeter defenses, automated or living. A couple of cubs have walked by here recently, probably on watch. But it's cold."

"But it's cold", the lieutenant repeated. Even grown men who were guarding secret military installations tended to get tired and lazy when it was cold out. Why not go back into the base to the comfort of a heater? What's the worst that could happen?

Feeling comfortable that the child-sentries had retreated to the warmth of the building, the two men simply pushed the gate aside and walked to the front door. Jenny was falling asleep and barely noticed the two as they approached her station; she really should have napped today. When she realized the men were there, she reached for her alarm bell but the Shirka gently picked her up with one of his massive hands and then licked the whole side of her head.

"Grape", the Shirka said as he held her up to his nose and began to sniff. "A boy put something in your hand not too long ago. Where is he?"

"Du-nnnn-nnno," Jenny barely squeaked.

He put her down and began to sniff the air. "That way."

The lieutenant followed as he was led towards the back of the school. He had seen several of the kids running in haphazard directions but a few had run with purpose. He was sure at least one of the fleeing kids was sounding whatever alarm they had for intruders.

Both men were armed but neither felt the need to pull their weapons. Before their assignment on this planet began, they had been briefed on the local criminal element, including these mini-gangs that mostly used kids and non-violent means to run their games. The kids probably weren't armed but they were prepared to deal with the adult they would eventually find who most certainly would be.

A few kids did try to block their progression, probably an immediate action drill put in place by their leader. A passive move to slow down the cops, or cannon fodder if the invaders happened to be a rival gang. The kids were easily moved by the men as they continued to follow the scent through the hallways.

As they were reaching a stairwell that led up, a loud noise could be heard from a few floors above them. The sound was unmistakable.

"Security door." The lieutenant just shook his head. This was going to take a little more time.

~

Zinner sat at his desk and looked over at his two personal runners. "Don't worry kids, we'll be fine."

In front of the desk, he had a platoon of kids waiting to fight for him if needed or greet the cops with smiles. It just depended on who was coming up the stairwell right now. The runner who brought the alarm wasn't sure whether the two men were cops or other bad guys. And with a lack of cameras or other technology in the school, Zinner wouldn't be able to tell what the two men were until they reached the door and made their intentions clear.

A loud knock announced their arrival at the security door.

Using a hardwired intercom, Zinner asked, "May I help you?"

"Yes, you may. I'm looking for a child. He stole my wallet." The lieutenant waited for a response.

"I'm very sorry to hear that. Unfortunately, I don't know whom you are speaking of. If I did, I would most definitely send them and your wallet out to you. I suggest you file a report with the police; they are an extremely helpful bunch." Zinner was glaring at the kids, letting them know he would beat whichever of them had brought this problem back to the hub.

"I appreciate your very helpful attitude. However, I have a Shirka with me, and he's telling me that the boy and my wallet are in fact in that room with you. Would you like to come out here and tell him he's wrong?" The lieutenant was watching as his partner looked for weak points in the security door.

Zinner clenched his teeth. "A fucking Shirka?! Are you kidding me?!" Turning to the kids in his room, he exploded. "Which one of you little fucks is he talking about?! I swear, I will start breaking fingers and hands until one of you speaks up."

Zinner was trying to decide which kid he was going to start with. He looked through the small group to see whether there was one in particular he didn't like or whether he was just going to have to grab one of them at random. "Last chance, shit heads. Someone needs to start talking. Now."

"It's me. They're looking for me." Mouse stepped out from the shadows in the back of the room. "I think you are, too."

Zinner turned away from the rest of the group to face the boy addressing him. "First off, if those men are looking for you, we can fix this. Give them the wallet back and whatever else you took. If we have to pay them off, it will just come out of your wages until you pay me back." Taking a measured step towards Mouse, he added, "And second, why would I be looking for you? I didn't even know you had gotten yourself in trouble."

Mouse reflexively stepped away from Zinner's slight advance towards him. As he listened to Zinner's words, he wondered whether he was wrong about what happened earlier. He sounded so sincere when he spoke. No, he wasn't wrong: he could see it in Zinner's eyes, could see what couldn't be heard in the words. And there was no mistaking the wad of money with his picture on it along with what took place in the tool district earlier. Zinner was just putting on this show for the other kids, to make them feel safe, to keep their faith in him as their protector.

"Bullshit." What else could he say?

"I don't follow." Zinner was now slowly moving towards a pedestal against the wall.

Mouse waved his hand towards his brother. "Zach, get over here, by me, now."

Zach wasn't sure what was going on but he always trusted his brother so he did as he was told. Without even thinking about it, Zach gently grabbed the other runner who had brought in Mouse's satchel with him earlier. The two private runners stood next to Mouse.

"Look, we really need to fix the issue with the two guys outside before it gets any worse." Zinner was trying to be subtle, and maybe he would have succeeded if Mouse didn't already know what he was doing.

Zinner was inwardly smiling to himself. This was going to play right into his hands. He could kill Mouse himself and the kids would see that he didn't have any other choice. After all, Mouse brought trouble into the hub and the kids knew how severe a transgression that was. Then with Mouse dead, he could give the two men whatever they wanted to make them leave.

Zinner reached the pedestal and slid the top back to reveal the secret compartment. The empty secret compartment that wasn't supposed to be empty.

"Looking for this?" Mouse was holding the gun in his hand that Zinner was hoping to find in the compartment. Mouse was glad his brother hadn't kept quiet with the secrets he had learned as one of Zinner's private runners. Mouse actually smiled. "I tried so hard to think of something else to say. I mean, that line is from like every movie ever. Right?"

"Now what? Are you going to shoot your way out of here?" Zinner wasn't scared; he didn't think Mouse would do anything drastic.

"No. You're going to open the security door and my brother and I are walking out of here and you're going to let us." Mouse was walking backwards towards the door.

"You want to take your chances with those guys out there?" Zinner still hadn't seen anything from inside his sequestered apartment; he had only heard the demands from the other side of the door. "You pissed off some guy who has a Shirka with him. Be my guest, leave."

Mouse knew what was waiting for him on the other side of the door and he was ready to be taken into custody if that's what the two marines wanted after the lieutenant got his wallet back. Zinner put his hands up in submission and moved to the button on his desk that would release the door.

"Whoever is outside the door," Zinner began, "I have the kid who stole your wallet. I'm opening the door and sending him out. I apologize for any hardship this little event has put you through."

The door unlocked and one of the men on the other side pulled it open. Zinner saw the two marines and immediately realized that he had been played by Mouse, but one thing still bugged him more than anything at this point. His security had been breached and he wanted to know how. "Before you go, tell me, how did you get in here without me seeing you?"

Mouse smiled. "Part of your protocol is to bring your hall monitors in the room with you, to use as a buffer. I had already made it past them through the service tunnel and I was waiting in the locker room. When the first few monitors were retreating back to the apartment, I just blended in with them and kept my head down. You weren't paying attention to the kids coming in, so you never saw me."

Zinner shook his head. "Mouse? More like *RAT*. A dirty, filthy rat."

"Now, I may be new to this situation and not know everything that's going on," the lieutenant began, "but the kid is the one with the gun. You might want to watch what you're saying."

"Fuck you." Zinner almost spat at the marines but thought better of it. "Take your wallet and that little shit if you want, I don't care. But then get the hell out of my house. You're not welcome." Zinner sat heavily in his chair behind the perceived but unrealistic feeling of safety that his desk gave him.

Mouse stepped towards the lieutenant and handed him his wallet. "I'm sorry, sir. I honestly didn't mean to put you through this kind of trouble."

"No worries, kid. Let's get you two out of here."

Mouse turned to look at Zinner one last time. "Don't ever come looking for us. If you do, I swear I'll kill you."

Zinner leaned forward with his elbows on his desk. "Oh, I'm coming for you, kid. If you're anywhere on this planet after tonight, I will find you and kill you. Slowly."

The lieutenant looked at the Shirka. "Well, I did promise you could kill the next three people."

Zinner's face changed from smug and predatory to scared and regretful. He had mistakenly thought the marine uniforms meant he was safe and the two men wouldn't—couldn't—hurt him. But as the Shirka's face turned to an evil grin and he began to move towards Zinner, he knew he had been wrong. "Wait, no, you can't. Please, you can't. I won't hurt them, I swear. I'm sorry. I won't ever come after you. I swear!"

The living embodiment of so many human horror movies slowly walked to the desk and in one swift movement jumped on top of it and landed in a full squatting position. As Zinner wet himself, the Shirka sniffed the air and knew his prey was weak. The alien lifted one of his werewolf-like paws and stretched his fingers and claws out in front of Zinner's face so he could see what was coming.

"Okay, he's going to do this one slowly." The lieutenant began to usher the kids out of the room. "Everyone out. There isn't enough therapy in the galaxy to fix any of you if you stay to watch this."

After the last kid was out, the lieutenant closed the door as he was saying, "I'll wait for you out front. Me letting you do it this way counts as three, you know."

The Shirka smiled as he tossed his prey a sharp knife. "At least put up a fight."

~

Once they were in the hallway, the lieutenant looked at the boy who had stolen his wallet. "Mouse, huh?"

"Yes, sir."

"After what I saw in there just now, I'd say Snake was a better name."

"Sir?"

"A mouse sneaks and hides in the shadows and is weak. You are not weak. You used the shadows to hunt from, to attack from. You are a predator, not prey. You are a cunning snake, silent and deadly."

"Snake. I like that, sir." Snake looked directly into the man's eyes. "If you want to turn me in, I'll go with you to the police. I won't try to run."

"Oh my boy, I want to turn you in, all right." He looked at his wallet and smiled from ear to ear. "I want to turn you into a marine. You've got skills we can use. With the right education and the right guidance, we can make you more than you ever thought possible."

Snake thought for a moment. "I won't go anywhere without my brother."

"Of course not. I wouldn't want to break up a family." They stopped as they reached the front of the school, waiting for the Shirka to finish and come out to meet them. "Look, I'll make some calls tonight and get you two enrolled in the school on base. I'm sure we can find a military family who would love to have two foster boys to raise. If worst comes to worst, I'll pull some strings and get you two situated with a regular Colony foster home. Together, I promise."

"Then what?" Snake hadn't thought much past retirement so this new direction sounded like a good beginning.

"Then you go to school, be the young men you're supposed to be." The lieutenant looked up and saw the Shirka coming towards them. "I'll check in on you from time to time and make sure you don't need anything. When you graduate, we'll talk some more and then go from there. How does that sound?"

Snake looked at his brother, who just nodded his approval. Snake put his hand out to the lieutenant. "Deal." The two men shook hands.

The Shirka walked up and just snorted at the group, his way of saying, "Let's go."

The lieutenant reached up and pulled a piece of clothing and skin out of the larger alien's fur. "How many times have I told you—don't play with your food."

Chapter 44
Dig Site One – Almost There

Daria crouched in a covering position as Snake took the lead on point. Davies was behind her, waiting to leapfrog to point after Snake took a covering position of his own. Hood stayed back as rear guard protecting Bloom, who had maintained a position in the rear where he controlled the sled.

"We're almost three-quarters of the way to the core." Bloom was looking at his instruments. "I can't believe we haven't met up with any traps."

Snake took up a position about fifty yards ahead of Daria and signaled for Davies to move up.

"Don't get complacent," Daria warned. "We're not there yet."

Almost on cue, an explosion rocked the hallway they were traversing. When the noise was gone, each member of the team followed the immediate action drill they had planned for in just such an event. Everyone sounded off so Daria could get a head count and make sure everyone was all right.

"Two here."

"Three here."

"Four here."

And lastly, Daria, "One here. Bloom, report."

"One of the crates the sled is pulling seems to have set off the defense system and made all of the security defenses come on line." Bloom continued tapping keys to gather more information.

"How do you suggest we proceed?" Daria had walked back to Bloom, and Davies automatically took over her position.

"Carefully", Bloom quipped. "I'm detecting movement ahead of the sled, multiple targets."

Daria didn't like the sound of that. If there were several of the aliens coming down their way, they would never make it. "How far out?"

"The sled is about twenty meters ahead of us and the contacts are closing to about one hundred meters farther out from the sled." Bloom adjusted one of the cameras on the sled. "They're robotic sentries, not aliens. I'll deploy a grenade from the sled to test their defenses."

"Do it." Daria then turned to everyone else. "Snake, Davies, you two are point team. Hood and I will protect Bloom. Bloom needs to survive if we're going to crack this egg."

Snake gestured to Davies, who came up alongside him. Together, they agreed on the best way to defend the hallway.

Bloom had set mini-grenade launchers on each crate and two on the sled. One was now destroyed, along with the crate it had been on. He decided to use the one on the other crate to launch the grenade.

It landed between the two closest sentries and detonated. Although they could hear the explosion two hundred meters away, the hallway didn't rock nearly as much as when the booby trap trip mine had gone off. That made Daria wonder just how much explosives those booby traps had in them. Daria watched the scene unfold as it played out across her visor.

The grenade launched from the crate and landed between the two lead sentries. They continued forward without even seeming to care. When the grenade exploded, fragments bounced off shields that shimmered just a few centimeters from the exterior plating of the droids. They stopped, warbled something to one another, and then the lead droid opened fire on the crate where the grenade had come from. The plasma weapon shredded the crate and the launcher that was on it.

"I guess they didn't like that", Bloom said as he repositioned the sled for a better view of the sentries.

Daria wondered how much firepower it would take to destroy the droids. She then realized that they had completely ignored the air sled. She also remembered that the aliens' personal shield was susceptible to low-energy attacks and you could get inside them with a knife or sword.

"Bloom, how long until they get here?" Daria looked over at him.

"If they maintain speed, I calculate ten minutes."

Daria made her decision. "Get that sled back here." She turned to look down the corridor and added, "Snake, bring me your claymores. Davies, get the thermal blanket out."

Bloom looked up at Daria. "I know what you're thinking, Doc, and I don't like it. Just because they've ignored the sled so far doesn't mean that they will continue to ignore it with you on it. Even if the thermal signal is hidden by the blanket, they may have other ways to detect you. And lastly, how are you going to plant those mines without exposing yourself?"

"Quickly," Daria responded. "Besides, it's our best hope. We almost couldn't take down just one alien with a personal shield. I don't think we'll be able to beat five shields. And there's no time to set up some sort of automated deployment method from the sled."

"Maybe not fully automated in a high-tech sense," Snake offered, "but we could go back to the basics and adapt and overcome."

It took Snake about three minutes, after the sled arrived, to jury-rig the mines to it. Using 550 cord, he strung each mine to the right rail of the sled, where they hung about one foot from the bottom of the sled. A pull-knot secured each mine to the rail and would allow Daria to release them from underneath the cover of the thermal blanket. This would hopefully hide her presence from the droids.

Snake finished and then gave final instructions to Daria. "When the mine gets a mag-lock on the droid, the indicator in your visor for that mine will go green, showing that it has successfully attached itself and is armed. At that point, release the 550 cord for that mine and move on to the next one. Bloom will control the sled and guide the placement of the mines so you don't have to fumble with more than one thing at a time."

"As soon as the mines are set, hold on tight because I'm going to move that sled away from the blast area real fast." Bloom had already decided that the safest place for Daria would be around a corner and in an alcove where the droids had come from.

Davies finished tucking the blanket around Daria and Bloom sent her off down the corridor. The droids were very close now. As the sled approached, they took no notice of it.

Bloom positioned the first mine and slowly moved the sled closer to the target. The light went green in Daria's visor, indicating the mine was set and armed. She released the cord and moved on to the next droid.

As the sled reached the second droid, the first seemed to realize that maybe it should investigate the object stuck to its back. The droid knew that the automated delivery sled had passed by and dropped something, but those sleds were always dropping things. That was the difference between the sled and the droid: the semi self-aware sentry droids took pride in their work. The droid tried to ignore the sled as it continued down the hall and drop more of its cargo. The droid stopped in the hallway and tried to grab the mine on its back. The droid was not built for its arm to articulate in that manner and it was akin to watching a person attempt to scratch that spot between their shoulder blades that no one can quite reach.

When the droid realized that he couldn't reach it, he warbled something to the number two droid. Daria had just finished planting the second mine when he went to help the number one droid.

Number two tried to pull the mine from number one's back but the mag-lock was too strong. He warbled something to number one and then extended a probe to the mine from a compartment in his chest.

Daria just finished planting mine number three when number two droid warbled something excitedly to number one.

"I think they're on to us", Bloom said as he positioned Daria for the fourth mine.

The fourth mine was just about to attach itself when the droid shot forward away from the sled. At the same time, the fifth droid shot a plasma bolt into the underside of the sled, causing Daria to pull the knot free and drop the mine to the ground.

The sled flew forward as Bloom tried to get Daria out of harms' way. By luck alone, the fifth mine swung and slapped against the fourth droid, stuck, and armed itself. Daria wasn't ready for this so she hadn't released the mine from the sled's railing. The sled jerked as the cord went taut and almost threw Daria off as it bucked. She quickly reached back and released the cord, allowing the sled to lurch forward in a less than controlled manner and bounced off one wall before Bloom could regain control.

Daria was lucky for the sudden lack of control because it caused the plasma bolt from droid number one to miss her as she deflected off the wall. She yelled into her comlink, "Blow it!! Blow them now!"

Bloom was navigating Daria's sled around the corner and Snake waited until the last possible second to trigger the charges. Four droids exploded with a brilliant flash and a thunderous clap. Around the corner, Daria was shielded from the heat and shrapnel expelled by the explosion but the overpressure bounced off the corridors and found their way to her and her relative safety.

Daria was thrown from the sled and the last thing she saw was the wall coming at her. She felt as though she were flying at a thousand miles an hour but it seemed to take an hour for her to reach the wall and the blackness that lay beyond.

The fifth sentry droid stood motionless as the debris from his counterparts bounced off his shields. It took him less than a nanosecond to decide that something had gone terribly wrong. Before the shrapnel had even stopped flying through the hallway, he initiated the tunnel lockdown procedure. Because he and his now destroyed patrol had secured everything from the core up to this point, he sealed the corridor at the nearest junction behind him.

It seemed very odd to the droid that a hover sled from the maintenance bay would've attacked his patrol. He tapped into the security feed for the hangar bay and found that there were multiple unauthorized life signs from one—no, three—unknown alien races. He did not have the proper security clearance to deploy the automated gas canisters in the hanger, so he notified the main security office of the intrusion. No one answered. Odd. He would have to continue to the hangar by himself and destroy the aliens. Three more nanoseconds had passed and he began rolling down the corridor once more as his four companions continued to disintegrate.

Farther down the hall, it took Snake several thousand times longer than the droid to decide that something had gone wrong. He couldn't think as quickly as the droid but fortunately he was fast enough.

"The blankets—everyone wrap up in a thermal blanket. They couldn't detect Doc underneath it and we've got one left coming our way."

Davies hated not going after Daria right away but he knew it was the best plan. If the last droid was coming their way, then Daria was either already dead or safely hidden from it.

It took almost fifteen minutes for the droid to get a safe distance from the group before they could come out of hiding. The droid was moving much slower now and taking more detailed scans.

As the next ranking member in the group, Snake took over. "Davies and, set up a rear guard in case that thing comes back. Bloom, come with me. We have to recover that unused mine and then find Doc."

Bloom continued to try to raise Daria but without success. "She's not dead; her comlink is still being powered by her bioelectricity. Hopefully she just got knocked out from the blast." Bloom chuckled to himself.

"What's so funny?" Snake asked.

Bloom shrugged. "Have you ever stopped to think about our perception of life as compared to the 'normal' Coalition citizen? I mean, here I am hoping that someone is unconscious. Scan hopes that he won't lose anymore appendages. And Snyder hoped that his best friend would shoot him in the head to end his suffering. No one back home even has an idea of what's going on out here.

"Most people are hoping that their kids do well in school, that they aren't late for dinner, or that their boss doesn't find out they're fucking his wife on the side." Bloom stopped and looked at Snake. "And we're hoping someone will shoot us in the head if it comes to that."

"Actually," Snake smiled, "I'm hoping that I don't get shot in the head so I can go home and fuck some guy's boss's wife."

"Hey, I'm the funny one." Bloom could feel his tension slowly easing away again. "Stick to whatever it is you do. By the way, what do you do?"

"I don't know. Right now, I'm retrieving this mine and then I'm finding Doc." Snake had finished placing the safeties back in place when Bloom came back from his scout of the hallway.

"This is not good," Bloom said as he examined the security door that had been brought down in the corridor.

Snake came up behind him. "Can we blow it?"

"Not with anything we have. I can try to override the security code but this is the toughest encryption I've encountered yet." Bloom had been trying without luck the entire time to raise Daria on the comlink. "Doc, come in Daria. Let us know you're all right." No response.

"Can you open her channel so we can hear what's going on?" Snake tried to stay relaxed.

"Yeah, give me a second." Bloom typed in some command and Daria's comlink came to life. Bloom and Snake could hear Daria breathing.

"I think she's unconscious." Bloom tapped some more commands. "I'm going to activate the feedback loop in her comlink to try to wake her."

~

Daria thought she could hear voices but she wasn't sure where they were coming from. The way she felt, she wasn't sure she could find her head if she needed to, much less the disembodied voices that were going through it. Then she felt it. A small itching on the right side of her head just behind her ear. But the itching changed somehow and it began to build. Soon it was a painful electric shock that made her sit straight up even against her body's protest.

She immediately heard Bloom in her head once the pain had subsided. "Doc, are you there? Can you hear me?"

"What the hell are you doing, Bloom! Do you really think that I need to be electrocuted so soon after being blown up?" Daria was now able to open her eyes and get an idea of where she was.

Snake cut in. "Doc, one of the droids got away but the other four are slag. The problem is, some sort of security protocol was activated and this blast door was brought down between us. Bloom says we can't blow it and he can't get the protocols to disengage." He paused. "You'll have to make it to the core on your own and override the security protocols for the hangar and this door."

"Of course I will", Daria quipped. "I never get to do anything the easy way. Bloom, will you be able to walk me through whatever I need to do once I get there?"

"I'm not sure. The core is locked out from all remote access, so I don't know what you'll find once you get there."

"We'll just have to make do." Daria's thoughts were becoming clearer as the seconds passed. "Snake, have you contacted base camp to let them know what's going on?"

"I can't. The droid is destroying our communications relay as it goes. I didn't send anyone back on foot to warn them because there is no way to get back to the hangar without having to engage the droid. I don't think that we'd win." Snake was all out of ideas on that one.

"You were right to not send anyone back. They wouldn't have stood a chance. Set up a defensive position here and I'll head out to the core." Daria had just finished performing a medical scan on her head. She pulled the proper medication to help with her concussion out of her kit and administered it. "I'm assuming no one out there needs medical assistance, right?"

"No, you were the only injured." Bloom was trying to download all of his information into Daria's visor. "I'm downloading as much of my data into your visor as I can. If we lose contact, then it might be able to help you when you get to the core."

"I'm ready to head out. I'll give you five-minute updates. Bloom, can you calculate who will reach their destination first, me or the droid?" Daria was putting her medical gear back and repositioning her load.

Bloom tapped in a few variables into his visor. "It should be you but only by a few minutes. That's if you're walking at a regular patrol pace. And based on your current vital signs and medical readout, I wouldn't suggest that you double-time because you might pass out."

"I'm the medic here. You let me worry about that. Keep me updated if anything happens." Daria began jogging down the corridor towards the core.

About twenty minutes and nearly five syncopal episodes later, she was there. Communications with Bloom and Snake had been static-filled at best for the last ten minutes. She hoped that it didn't get any worse. "Bloom, I'm here. Now what?"

"Te.. me wh.t you .ee" Bloom's voice was almost completely inaudible.

Daria looked around. "It's empty. The room is cylindrical in shape, about ten meters in diameter and thirty in height. The walls, floor, and ceiling are smooth with some sort of radiant light source. There are no controls or seams anywhere."

"Tr. lig..ing ..are and .oving it ov.. the .all" Bloom's transmission seemed to be getting worse.

"Try what?" Daria hadn't gotten the whole thing. As she went over the broken words in her head, it became clear. *Try lighting a flare and moving it over the walls.* The security protocols for the facility might have closed up all of the access panels in the room. The way to make those panels visible was to apply a heat source to them and make them come out of hiding.

Out loud she said, "Lighting flare now. Good idea, Bloom." She had no way of knowing whether he even heard her praise or that she understood what he said.

She made it about halfway around the cylinder when a panel became visible to her. It was odd, though;

instead of being high on the wall, it was down at human level. All of the other controls so far had been at a height that would be suitable for the aliens they had encountered.

There was only one button to press; she did. Nothing happened at first and Daria pondered the ironic anticlimacticness of it all when the door behind her closed. "Those bastards!" she said out loud. It seemed to Daria that they had purposely put the button on the opposite wall so that whoever pushed it wouldn't have a chance to get back to the door before it closed.

"Bloom, they locked me in. I'm trapped and there are no other buttons to push." This time there wasn't even static, just complete, dead silence. That meant that her signal was not even leaving the room she was trapped in.

A voice filled the room and Daria's visor translation program kicked in. It was buffering the translation as the voice spoke so it took a couple of seconds before it showed up on her visor. As the words scrolled across her screen, she suddenly heard Bloom's voice again. At first, she thought that he had found a way to get his signal through to her. Then she realized that he had integrated his voice with the translation program.

The voice in the room continued, "You have entered a restricted area. If you cannot supply the proper security clearance codes, you will cease to be. State your name, rank, and access code."

"Oh shit", was Daria's response. She didn't realize that she had said it out loud until Bloom's program repeated it in the alien language.

The voice in the room seemed to ponder her comment before replying, "Those facilities will not be available to you until you give the proper clearance codes. You have two minutes to comply."

~

Jockey had finished going over everything in the ship and was comfortable with the flight controls. There wasn't anything left to do but wait for Daria and her team to get the launch bay doors open. He decided to go over the controls one more time, even though he had promised himself a nap hours ago.

After the pre-flight check, Jockey turned on the scanners to practice switching between the different types of scans he would use during combat. At first, he thought that he must just be more tired than he realized but then he double-checked the reading. It wasn't a mistake. Jockey ran to the forward hatch. "El-tee, Wilks, we have a contact in the corridor twenty meters and closing. It seems to be a droid of some sort."

"Jockey, get those weapons warmed up and ready to go. Everyone else take cover inside the ship." Emily was already halfway up the ramp before she finished giving her order.

Jockey looked to Emily as she came onto the flight deck. "I'd love nothing more than to try those weapons out but I can't. There must be some sort of safety lock on them. I can't operate them while we are inside the hangar."

"Can we at least use the ship for shielding?" Wilks was now looking over the technical data the ship's sensors were sending to the monitors.

"Sure, but I don't know what kind of weapons the droid will have, if any at all." Jockey looked thoughtfully for a moment at nothing in particular before adding, "However, if we're inside the ship for protection, and the ship won't allow us to arm weapons, then we'll just be sitting in here while that droid pounds us from the outside. Once the shields are down, the droid will be able to damage the ship, maybe even to a point where it won't be space worthy anymore. Not to mention the fact that if it is a security droid, it might have the codes to override our shields without even firing a shot."

Emily thought for a split second before voicing her agreement with Jockey. "Wilks, get a defensive perimeter set up as far away from the ship as possible. I don't want to risk it taking any damage." Wilks nodded as he walked out of the ship, giving orders as he went. Emily took a quick glance at the sensor readings for the docking bay. "Jockey, I want you to stay in the ship, get the shields up, and then get to the top of the hangar bay. We don't know the potential weapons capability of the droid but maybe you'd be high enough to be out of range. If we can't stop the droid, try to keep the ship out of range until Daria can get the doors open. This ship is too important to lose."

Jockey looked at Emily with hopeless eyes.

"I know what you're thinking, Jockey, but I know that she and her team are still alive. Just because the droid is here doesn't mean that they didn't get past it. Now take care of this ship." Emily patted Jockey on the shoulder and left the ship.

~

Daria was slowly going through all of her options in her head. She didn't want to miss anything that might save her life. Daria tried searching through all of the information the database had gathered until she got locked in the room. "OK, Bloom, don't let me down."

~

"What happened to Doc's signal?" Snake was looking over Bloom's shoulder at the terminal he was working on.

"She seems to have entered a secure room. Our comlink connection has been completely severed." Bloom was trying to break through the security code even though he knew it was pointless. Since they had entered the complex, his program had been unable to crack the code. He didn't see why it would be able to break it now.

Snake could see the look of despair in Bloom's face. "Do you know what the purpose of the room is? Is she in danger? Ahhhh!" Snake and Bloom both yelled out and grabbed at their ears as they tried to stop the feedback that was screaming through their heads. When the sound stopped, he looked at Bloom. "What the fuck was that?"

Bloom was reviewing the data logs from the last few seconds and began running a trace program. "I don't believe this. When Doc entered the secure room, it initiated a separate security protocol that's different from the main one I've been trying to hack."

"Is that good or bad? And why is my head still ringing?"

Bloom smiled and clapped his hands together in a gesture of triumph. "The security program detected Daria's comlink and is trying to figure out what it is. It's sending a signal through her comlink and the entire temporary network we've set since we got here." Bloom was working his console more furiously than Snake had ever seen.

"If I'm understanding even half of what you are doing, it looks like you're hacking the system by following the security program back to its origin through the comlinks." Snake began to read through the information that his visor was displaying.

The background static that had plagued the comlink system for the entire mission was suddenly gone. Bloom was able to use the security feed to not only reestablish their comlink connection with Daria but he was also able to use the security system to connect with any comlink anywhere in the entire installation.

"Doc, are you there? Doc, this is Bloom, can you hear me?"

Daria's response was nothing shy of completely ecstatic. "Thank God, Bloom! I'm about to be wasted if I can't come up with the proper security code for this room."

~

"Keep laying down fire!" Emily could barely hear herself as she gave the command.

Wilks was trying to direct fire from his squad. The droid seemed to be unstoppable. Its shields were much stronger than the personal shields the aliens had been using. The ammo was running low and they were running out of cover. The droid's weapons were pulverizing the shipping crates and other items the soldiers were using as cover. Wilks didn't want to fall back into the control room because they would have nowhere else to go, but he was quickly running out of options.

The droid was using a combination of energy and projectile weapons. The droid had a pretty good knack for ricocheting the rounds off the walls and into the soldiers. Luckily, none of the rounds or their fragments had hit anything other than the soldiers' body armor. It was still too close for Wilks' comfort.

Wilks was taking another look at the hangar to see whether he had missed anything that might help him out. Just as he was returning his sights back to the droid, he saw Emily take a projectile round to the chest. Emily stopped firing, looking down at her chest in astonishment. Emily's eyes locked with Wilks' as a small rivulet of blood came out of her mouth and flowed down her neck. Emily slumped to the ground.

"The lieutenant is down!" Wilks was about to leave his cover and go for Emily when he saw Davies' huge hand reach out from behind cover and pull Emily to safety just as an energy bolt struck where her head had been. The second energy bolt struck her in the leg just below the knee.

"Jockey, is there anything you can do from up there?" Wilks was about to lose his whole team if he didn't do something quickly. He decided that if Jockey didn't have any new ideas, he would have to risk losing the ship to save his men.

"I still can't override the weapons safety protocol. There is an emergency disengagement for the landing gear in case they get damaged. I could try to drop one of the skids on the droid. I really don't think that I can be very

accurate, though. If I miss and hit one of you guys..."
Jockey let the sentence finish itself in Wilks' head.

"OK, I know what the el-tee said before but we have to risk the ship. Can you bring her down with the landing ramp facing away from the droid? That way we can use the ramp for a little bit of cover while we board. Then you'll just take her back up to the top and hope that we can figure something out after that."

"I can do that. Get everyone prepped to move. I'll be coming in hard and fast and I want you guys boarded in less than thirty seconds from my mark." Jockey gave Wilks a few seconds to organize the retreat before he began his descent. "Get ready, guys. Thirty seconds on my mark. Three, two, one, MARK!" Jockey pushed the throttle as far as he dared in the confined space of the docking hangar.

~

As if on cue, the security system added, "You have sixty seconds to enter the proper security code before you cease to exist."

"I caught that, Doc. I'm working on it. I'm in the system; it's just a matter of seconds now." Bloom knew he was almost there—he just had to focus and he would get it.

Bloom was tracing the program back to its source and digging through the code on the other end. The graphic interface of the alien computer system made it almost like playing a video game as Bloom dodged security nodes and chaser programs. Bloom knew that he was getting close to where he needed to be because he began to receive a feedback through his comlink that got worse the deeper he probed. He was sure that it wasn't an intentional safety measure by the security program, rather a by-product of the security system tapping into the comlink system.

Bloom dug deeper and fought through the feedback. Every time the pain lessened, Bloom dug in the direction where he felt the most pain. Bloom's vision was so blurred from the pain that he switched to direct neural input. Bloom didn't like to use direct neural input especially during a mission because it drained the user both physically and mentally worse than if he had run a double marathon. But he had no choice; if he couldn't see the interface he couldn't do his job.

With the direct interface turned on, the image of the alien interface blasted into Bloom's mind. If the appearance of the image into his mind could be described as a "blast" then the pain that followed was nothing less than a nuclear explosion. Bloom almost passed out but kept himself in the moment and worked through the pain and found what he was looking for.

Bloom had expected the pain to increase when he switched to a direct neural link but he wasn't prepared for how overpowering it would be. He also wasn't prepared for what happened next. Time began to slow down as the pain vanished altogether.

Bloom

NAME: JASON BLOOM
SPECIES: HUMAN
MOS: TECH SPECIALIST
RANK: SERGEANT
AGE: 30 - EARTH STANDARD
SEX: MALE
HEIGHT: 5'8"
WEIGHT: 180 POUNDS

Nancy and Phil were beside themselves with frustration. Their little boy was almost four and still not talking. He made a lot of noise, babbled all day long in fact, making guttural noises intermixed with high-pitched screeches. Never once had he said mommy or daddy.

Jason had been to a couple of speech therapists who were at a loss for what might be going on with him. When he was with the therapists, Jason didn't even babble or make any of the other noises he made all day at home. As soon as they left the office, Jason would be back to his own language that no one else could understand.

Nancy knew her son could understand her even though everyone told her she was wrong. But when she talked, he listened and even responded, though she had no idea what he was saying. If she told him to change his shirt, he did. When she needed help around the house, he would pitch in, as much as a four-year-old could. Even with these and many more examples, Phil would always tell Nancy that she just saw what she wanted to see, and unfortunately their son wasn't normal and never would be.

Most Wednesday nights, Phil took Jason to one of his "Humans First" rallies. Phil didn't consider himself a bigot, racist, or speciest; he just cared about humanity and thought the Coalition was catering to other species and leaving humans behind as fodder for the Coalition's political agenda. Phil had plenty of human friends who weren't white so he knew he wasn't a racist. He also had worked in the past with plenty of other species and didn't hate them personally; he actually got along with many of them, so he couldn't be a speciest.

Phil didn't want any harm to come to the other species of the galaxy; he just didn't want them taking human jobs on human worlds. He didn't want his tax dollars going towards saving a Shirka birthing forest on a planet that he wasn't even allowed to set foot on lest he become food for the newborn cubs. He was tired of being out of work and seeing more of his benefits being given away to other species instead of the humans who deserved the benefits more.

Phil arrived and grabbed a doughnut and a cup of coffee from the sign-in table. He tried handing one to Jason but his offer was rebuked with an outstretched hand shaking back and forth no. "Suit yourself, kid. More for me."

Jason was usually a very active and interactive child even though he didn't speak to anyone, but at these weekly meetings he became very withdrawn and tended not to interact at all. Phil thought that being around a lot of people and hearing all of them speaking passionately about their thoughts might just give Jason something to speak about. Some of their passion for communicating might just rub off on his son. But after almost six months of meetings, Jason never showed any sign of improvement.

This week's topic was going to be the Coalition's plan to integrate different species into combined military units. Phil couldn't believe what they were doing; this was going too far. If there were interspecies military units, what would happen if Earth needed to defend itself against one of the other Coalition member species? How would humans rise up against an alien aggressor if their units had the aggressors mixed in with them? Their aggressors would have access to all of the same equipment, tactics and everything else. Something had to change.

One of the usual speakers was at the podium, ranting and pounding his fists. It seemed that no matter what he said, people would cheer as long as he pounded his fist somewhere in his sentence. "Rabble rabble rabble"—fist pound—cheering. "Rabble rabble—fist pound—rabble." Cheering.

Phil was getting excited and so spun up that he began making his own speeches to the people around him. He was adding his own thoughts during the natural pauses of the speaker at the podium. The crowd around Phil was now cheering him on, urging him forward towards the podium, some yelling to let him speak too. By the time he was pushed to the podium, the speaker was even encouraging Phil to get on stage.

Phil took the stage and stood in front of the microphone. At first, he was a little shocked that he was the center of attention. He wasn't exactly sure how he had made it there or what he should do next. Something in his brain told him to play it safe; start with the material he had already been spouting in the crowd, the stuff that got him there in the first place.

His first few sentences slobbered out of his mouth awkwardly and barely made sense. He got a few confused looks from the crowd along with a couple of supportive shout outs "Yeah, man!" The next few lines came out much more coherently but they still didn't receive the responses he had gotten just a few moments ago.

The original speaker was starting to sweat a little and made a small tentative step towards Phil. He knew that his moment was about to end if he didn't get the crowd back. What was missing? Ah ha! Fist pounding! He needed to add some fist pounding.

Phil pounded his fist into the podium and looked out to the crowd. That got their attention but something was still wrong. A few of the faces towards the front actually looked a little scared. Damn it. The fist pounding doesn't come before a sentence, never before a sentence. In that context it seems aggressive, even attacking.

Deep breath. "Rabble rabble rabble." FIST POUND. Cheering! That was it; Phil had found his rhythm and set into it as though he had invented the podium fist pound. The crowd loved him and cheered for everything he said, even the stuff that didn't make one lick of sense.

When it was all over, Phil was taken aside by a few of the men who had organized tonight's rally. Phil was still high on endorphins from his impromptu presentation so he barely heard most of what was being said to him. The main points did sink in, though; he was asked to speak at a public rally in two weeks. The rally wouldn't be just for humans; it was going to be in the middle of the town square and open to every citizen who wanted to attend.

Phil was beside himself with joy. After being unemployed for so long, he finally felt as if he was needed again. In fact, he didn't think he ever felt this important even while he was working. His work was never really that important and if he were honest with himself, he wasn't really that good at it, either. But this, this was something that he excelled at. Getting in touch with the people, showing them that they weren't the only ones who felt this way. Showing the crowds that they weren't the minority anymore, that they were strong if they stuck together in their fears and ignorance of the real facts. Well, the last part in Phil's mind was more along the lines of, 'if they stuck together in their convictions and knowledge of right from wrong.' Eh, you say tomato, I say idiot.

When Phil was finally done being patted on the back, he realized that Jason was still somewhere in the crowd and he needed to collect his son before leaving. Phil looked around and finally found Jason under the snack table, crying. Phil had hoped that being on stage and being the center of attention would enthrall his son, maybe even encourage him to talk. All that happened was Jason became more withdrawn tonight and cried like a two-year-old. Phil was so elated from his evening that even this couldn't bring him down, much.

Phil got home and told Nancy to put their son to bed. He had great news and wanted to tell her without the crybaby around. He didn't want anything to detract from his news and didn't want his wife's attention divided in the least.

Nancy knew that Phil had always had issues with their son and a difficult time accepting his situation. This was the first time she had ever seen Phil regard Jason with such contempt and lack of respect. Nancy didn't know what to do. She knew that she was loyal to her husband above all other people in the universe but one, her son. She hadn't seen Phil this excited in years so she decided not to broach the subject with him this evening, but she would, and soon. Something needed to change if he expected them to continue as a family.

Nancy sat next to Jason on his bed and brushed some hair away from his eyes. Jason closed his eyes and nudged his forehead into his mother's hand. He then babbled and cooed something in his made-up language. Nancy smiled. She recognized the string of babble; she thought it meant something along the lines of "I love you" or "Thank you." Maybe it was a combination of both or could be used for both. She just seemed to hear this particular string of babble when they were alone with each other and she was doing something particularly motherly. "I love you too, pumpkin."

Nancy kissed Jason on the cheek and then left his room, gently closing the door behind her. She walked out in the living room of their one-bedroom apartment. Since Phil had lost his job, Nancy was the only one earning any money and they could barely afford this tiny apartment. Nancy told Phil that once he got a job then he could have his own room but until then, their son would get his own room and a small feeling of normalcy. Phil tried to rebuke her but for the first time in their whole relationship, Nancy was standing firm and he knew that he couldn't win the argument.

When Nancy sat on their ragged and stained couch, Phil was already pouring what was probably his second or third glass of whiskey. She sat there and listened to Phil's news and even managed to look interested in it. She didn't agree with Phil's obsession with the humanist movement but it was the one thing that brought him out of his depression after he was laid off. Nancy thought that once the depression lifted, he would find the motivation to get another job.

That never happened and his depression was replaced with anger. Phil would spout off that he couldn't find a job because the aliens were taking all of the human jobs and he wasn't being given a fair chance because of all the affirmative action taking place. Nancy would always point out jobs that Phil was qualified for but he always had an excuse: The job was beneath him. It was manual labor. It was not worth his time. The position was the same as his last and he was destined for more. The jobs he was complaining about being taken from his were jobs that he wasn't even qualified or trained for.

As Nancy sat there, she realized that she needed to do something to change her situation. She had promised to love Phil and be with him through the good and bad but this wasn't the Phil she married. This wasn't the man she had made those promises to. She was going to let him have his rally and that was it. She would have a talk with him and let him know that he had two weeks to get a job, no matter how menial or low-paying it was. He was going to start being a productive member of this family. She would help him and be his biggest supporter as he looked for something better or even went back to school. But all of this hate and anger and self-pity needed to end, now. *Mental fist pound—cheering.*

In the days that led up to Phil's rally, Jason seemed more withdrawn to Nancy. The odd thing was that although he was withdrawn from interaction, he seemed to be busy with something. She didn't know what but he was constantly babbling to himself and pacing. A lot of the babbling seemed the same, as though he was repeating something. He was still affectionate with her, especially when she tucked him in at night, but he was still acting different than usual.

Phil was also acting different, though not necessarily in a good way. Nancy was so conflicted with her feelings, she didn't know how to convey what she was thinking. Phil was proud, dedicated, interested, engaging, showered daily and even sober. These were all things that Nancy had wanted for so long but not in the furtherance of hate and discontent. If only he could channel this excitement and focus into their family and finding a job. If he had been like this at his last job, maybe he wouldn't have been fired. Phil always said he had been laid off but as time wore on, Nancy became sure that that wasn't the case.

The day came for his big speech. He had practiced and practiced and felt ready to deliver a speech that he was sure would find its way to a history book somewhere. Phil had to beg Nancy to come and to bring Jason with her. Phil told her that the group had even found speakers from other species who also believed that keeping their people separate was in the best interest of the galaxy.

Nancy tried to point out the irony that a rally for humanity and species separation was being supported and assisted by other species. Phil just stared at her for almost a full minute. Nancy was sure that she caused her husband to have a stroke or possibly a feedback loop that crashed his brain.

After Phil had his mental reboot, he just shook his head and told her that she obviously didn't understand what he was involved in. All the more reason she needed to come and hear his speech, so she could fully understand. It was also important for Jason to be there and learn these ideals that were so very important to all of humanity.

Nancy took Jason to the rally and was surprised when she was ushered to the stage. The men told her that it would be great for Phil if his wife and son sat behind him while he spoke. Nancy tried to argue but realized her escorts weren't listening at all. This seemed to be a common condition for everyone involved in the group. Nancy sat with Jason and held his hand. Jason was a little more fidgety than normal but he still stayed in his seat and even looked as though he was interested in the process of what was going on around him.

Some minor speakers took the stage to warm up the crowd. Nancy recognized several species in the crowd and a couple that she wasn't sure about. She definitely recognized the Shirkas; everyone in the Coalition knew them. She saw a few Trizites, a couple of Nortes, some Molpeds, and a group of Bisbanes.

The species were sticking to their own groups and keeping a little bit of a neutral zone between species. Some were there to protest the protest, some were there to agree with species separation, and some were just gathered because there was a crowd. The accidental gatherers wandered into the crowd and intermixed with other species until they noticed there were clearly divided groups in the gathering. They then found their respective species and joined their group.

Phil had been on stage for about ten minutes, spouting rhetoric and pounding his fist. The fist pounding seemed to be a universal podium trick because it engaged all of the species present. They also had interpreters on stage, translating everything Phil said. The species who didn't speak English could tune their personal comm unit to their translator to understand what was happening.

Nancy still couldn't understand how all of these species could rally together just to rant about how they should all be separated. They had such a showing that it seemed obvious that working together they could accomplish so much. She was barely registering what Phil was saying until she heard him speak their son's name.

"My son Jason has a speech disability. The doctors still don't know why or what it is. He's four years old and he's never even said 'Mommy' or 'Daddy.'" Phil reached back with his hand and waved Jason forward to him and the podium.

As Jason reached the podium, there was a collective sigh from the audience as they looked at the cute little human child who was struck with some unknown medical affliction. Only the Shirkas didn't sigh as they thought the child should have just been eaten if it were defective.

Phil continued, "Because I was laid off, my son has not been able to get the medical treatment he needs. Because the Coalition is trying to help everyone, no one is getting what they need. My son would be able to talk if the human government was taking care of human problems and not sending aid and money to alien planets and alien problems. I know you feel the same. I know some of you have had similar stories. My son should not have to suffer because the Coalition has forgotten who they serve. Humanity."

Phil picked his son up and hugged him as Nancy had never seen her husband hug their child. Instantly, she knew it was for show, for the crowd. He wanted their sympathy—the poor father who couldn't connect with his son because of the evil Coalition and the aliens who took everything from humans.

Phil kept his eyes on his son but positioned himself so his words would still be picked up by the microphone. "I love you, son."

Just as Phil suspected, his son wouldn't respond and he again received the sympathy of the crowd. Nancy couldn't let this continue, couldn't let her son be the pity fulcrum point of the rally. She was about to grab her son when she saw his little hand reach for the microphone and pull it towards his mouth.

Jason began to babble into the microphone and Nancy was mortified. Phil stood there and smiled from ear to ear, his point made even clearer by his son's inability to answer his father's declaration of love. But then something else happened: the Shirka in the crowd began to lean forward, engaged in the babbling. At the same time, the Shirka interpreter on stage began speaking in English, apparently interpreting what Jason was saying.

"I haven't spoken to my father because he is an idiot and I have had nothing to say to him."

Phil looked at the interpreter. "You son of a bitch! What the hell are you saying?"

The interpreter just look flatly at Phil. "I'm translating what your cub is saying. Nothing more."

A Shirka from the crowd spoke up. "He's telling the truth. Your cub is speaking our language as though he were from one of our litters."

Phil just looked at Jason as he continued to speak in the alien language. "I do not condone what my father has said and neither should you. Just look at what you have accomplished, together and for the same purpose."

Jason looked around and began speaking in a different babble; this time the Trizite interpreter began to translate into English what Jason was saying and the Shirka interpreter switched back to translating for the Shirka in the crowd.

"We are different from one another, and that is what makes this union fantastic. Without living together, we wouldn't have Shirka poetry. We wouldn't know about renewable ocean energy the Trizites developed centuries ago. You wouldn't have coffee."

The coffee joke got a good laugh—the local Starbucks was always packed with just about every species that wasn't allergic to caffeine.

Jason switched to a different, more obscure language, and the interpreters had to rely on their in-ear translation devices to translate for them so they could then repeat it in their own tongue. "I don't know what happened to my father to make him this bitter. I am only four, after all, so my memory is mostly filled with breastfeeding and dirty diapers." Another huge laugh from the crowd along with a very embarrassed-looking mother. "I do remember hearing all of your wonderful languages on TV and learning so much from so many. When I was ready to talk, I realized that my dad wouldn't want to hear anything I had to say, so I didn't say anything. I'm sorry, Mom." Nancy teared up at the last statement and just blew a kiss to her son.

Jason switched to a fourth language. "The Coalition hasn't kept me from talking; it's what taught me to talk in so many wonderful ways. Please, don't throw away all of the work and cooperation you put into coming together today. Use this as an example of what you can do together. If you don't like what the Coalition is doing, come together and attack their policies, not one another."

Jason was now standing on his own; his father had set him down a while ago and then retreated to the back of the stage. Nancy had pushed a chair to the podium and Jason climbed on top of it. Though it now seemed her son was a genius, he was still only four so his motor skills weren't completely developed and he had some difficulty getting on top of the chair. His adorable form garnered more *aww*s from the crowd.

Jason now switched to English. "If a four-year-old is the voice of reason, you really need to reevaluate your baseline thinking on these issues."

Later, when historians looked back on Jason's speech, they would say that this was one of the funniest things he said that day. But to the crowd who were present, in the moment, intently listening to the child prodigy, it was the most sobering thing any of them had heard in a very long time. No one laughed; some actually cried.

Jason looked back to his mom. "Mommy, I want to go home now."

He said it with such an infantile tone to his voice, Nancy knew it was on purpose to punctuate the fact that he was a little boy speaking such obvious truths. Nancy gathered her son up in her arms and he buried his face into her shoulder as she took him away. In the minute or so it took Nancy to leave the stage and get through the crowd, not a single voice could be heard. There was nothing left to say, at least not today.

Two days had passed and Phil still hadn't come home. Nancy and Jason were now conversing in English almost as though he had been talking for the last couple of years like any normal child. In a way, he had always been talking with his mother. Nancy always had faith that her son knew what was going on and he was always responsive to her. She even felt as if she had a pretty good idea of what he was trying to convey to her in all of those different languages. Jason apologized so many times for not speaking to her before but she just waved him off and said that she understood his reasons.

The weekend was just about over and Nancy had to go back to work the next day. She had been constantly thinking about what to do with Jason now that his father wasn't around to care for him during the day. Nancy was kind of sad that Phil wasn't around but she also realized that most of her feelings were coming from the disturbance in the routine that had replaced their marriage rather than losing the marriage itself.

The knock at the door had Nancy figuring it was Phil, probably drunk off his ass and unable to enter his passkey on the entry pad. When she opened the door, she was surprised to see a man and a woman in formal attire standing there. Her first thought was that Phil was dead and these two were officials coming to tell her. But she didn't think that was right; it would probably be the police who came to tell her that.

The woman broke the awkward silence. "Hello, Mrs. Bloom. I'm Jennifer and this is Bronson." Both people extended their hands to Nancy.

"Um, hello. How can I help you?"

"Actually, it's how we can help you. May we come in?"

"Of course. Can I get you something to drink?" Nancy wondered whether she was offering her killers or abductors a refreshing lemonade before they did something unspeakable to her and Jason.

"No, thank you", Bronson said as he sat on the couch. "We heard the speech on Friday. We were there as Coalition observers, to report back on the gathering."

"You're spies?" Nancy wasn't sure what was going on.

Jennifer just laughed. "No, not spies. Though I'm sure there was one or two in the crowd or within the groups. No, we're just observers who make reports and let other people decide on what course of action to take."

Bronson cut in. "As such, we obviously reported what your son said."

Nancy was getting a little worried. "I'm sorry if he upset anyone. He was just saying what he thought was right. He is only four, you know."

"Our superiors were extremely impressed with him and think his education will suffer if he stays on this planet." Bronson looked as though he were really trying hard to pick his words. "We mean you no offense, Mrs. Bloom, but given your current situation, there is no way you can afford to give Jason the education he needs or deserves."

Nancy was now moving from worried to defensive. "What are you saying? That you can do better for my son? Are you going to take him away from here? From me?"

Jennifer quickly put her hands up in what she hoped was a supplicating gesture. "No, no, no. We want to take you all away from here. We want to take you to Earth where the Coalition will enroll Jason in one of our schools for the gifted. At no cost to you at all."

Nancy relaxed a little. "Why would you do that? What do you want from us? From him?"

Bronson smiled. "We want Jason to be the face of cooperation. We will follow him through school and require that he provide us with interviews as needed, so that we may televise those interviews to the Coalition citizens. We won't censor him or anything like that; we just want him to be himself. The Coalition loves him!"

"And," Jennifer began, "we will find you and your husband a job near his school or even send one or both of you back to school if you want to change careers. I know this seems like we're offering you a lot, but in the end, Jason will really be doing more for us than we are for him. We can give you and your husband a few weeks to think about it if you'd like."

"Does he have to come with us? My husband. Does he have to come?" Nancy was now at the edge of her seat.

Jennifer seemed a little confused by the question and looked to Bronson, who just shrugged. "Um, no. I guess not. We hadn't really thought about it; we just assumed both of you would want to go. Keep the family together."

Nancy was now standing. "He hasn't been back since the rally and he hasn't answered the few calls I've made to him. I'll leave a note. He can catch up later if he wants to and if I decide to allow him. Can we leave now?"

Bronson stood. "Sure. We'll come back for you in a few hours, let you get some stuff together. Bring whatever you'd like."

Jason came down the hallway from his room, struggling with an oversized duffle bag. "I'm ready."

The three adults laughed. Jennifer looked to Nancy. "When do you want us to pick you up?"

Nancy grabbed her purse. "All I need is this little boy, and he's ready, so let's go."

The four left the apartment and boarded a government flight back to Earth. Jason was excited and could tell his mom was also.

"Did you really mean it when you said I was the only thing you needed?"

"You know I did, pumpkin." Nancy kissed him on the forehead.

"I think you knew that they will buy you whatever you want when we get there so you didn't bring anything. You wanted all new clothes!" Jason poked his mother playfully.

"You're not the only genius in the family." Nancy looked into her son's eyes and babbled the phrase she had heard from him so many times before. She never knew what it meant until the other day when she put it through a translator device. It was five different languages put together. "You are my everything."

Jason let a single tear go. "You did hear me."

"Every word, every time."

Chapter 45
Unknown Time, Unknown Place

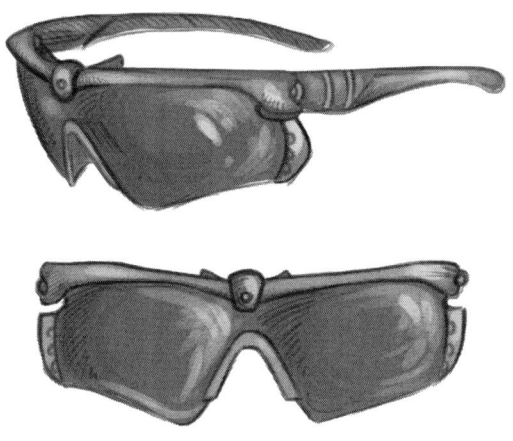

"Am I dead?" Bloom realized that his inner dialogue had somehow become external as well. He knew that he hadn't opened his mouth but he also knew that what he had heard was his own voice coming from outside his own mind. Bloom had been using a comlink for more than ten years and he knew the difference between sounds sent directly into his neural synapses and sounds coming from outside his head and through his own God-given auditory canals.

He tried thinking again. "Is anyone else here?" It was external again. Bloom made a mental note that if he did meet anyone here, wherever here was, that he wouldn't be able to keep his thoughts to himself so he needed to be careful. As he thought this he heard, "All right, Bloom, you can't keep your thoughts to yourself so be careful if you meet anyone or anything. Oh shit, I can hear that. Oh man, this is going to get annoying if not downright nerve-racking."

Bloom realized that his eyes were closed. "Should I open my eyes? I might not like what I see. Then again, if there is something nasty around me, not seeing it won't make it go away. I guess I need to take a look. Besides, if there is anyone around me, they already know what I'm thinking."

Bloom opened his eyes and had absolutely no idea where he was. Nothing was familiar to him until he looked up at the stars. He realized that he was on the same planet that he had been on for the past several months. The world looked completely different than what he had become accustomed to since their arrival. There were buildings, people, vehicles—a whole civilization. The people were obviously Nortes and he saw no other races mingled in with them.

Bloom brought his arm to his chest and looked down to find that his computer was gone. He felt around his head and his visor was also gone. Bloom was clad only in his black field uniform. No weapons, no communication devices, nothing that was familiar to him. Bloom looked at the stars again. "I can recognize the constellations but without my computer I can't calculate what year this is. It would take me years using pencil, paper, and a compass to figure out the year based on spatial drift between the stars, the planet, and its satellites. I would have to calculate the drift of stellar bodies in this region based on its location in respect to the center of the galaxy and any singularities close enough to affect the drift."

As Bloom thought about the monumental task it would take to figure out the date, the answers came to him. Numbers flew through his brain and the answers seemed to create themselves from the tangle of equations that flooded his mind. "Over one thousand years ago! That can't be right. How could I have traveled back one thousand years? I wasn't near any alien equipment that could have created a wormhole. Not that I know of, anyway."

One thousand and twelve of your years, to be exact. And who said that you have traveled back in time?

Bloom quickly turned around in place, looked up, looked down at the ground, and saw no one. "Who and where are you?"

Hmmm, I really don't know the answer to either question. I guess from your point of view, you could say that I am everywhere. As for who I am, I'm not sure that I am a who, not anymore, and maybe I never truly was to begin with.

"OK, if not who then what? Are you some form of artificial intelligence?"

I don't believe that I am artificial in nature, not in the conventional sense, anyway. For now, let's just agree that I am here just like you.

"I guess that will have to do. But where is here?"

Ah, now that I can answer. You are looking at the first and last installation of the Nortes Empire in this quadrant of the galaxy. The Nortes have been here for just over a year now. Things are going well, but soon they will change.

"I don't understand. The Nortes don't have an empire. Not anymore, at least. What happened here? My government has limited contact with the Nortes but as far as I know, they only occupy one solar system in this galaxy. They never venture out of their system except for stuff like trade, education, and political reasons. We have no information about an empire."

Of course you don't. They don't want you to know about it. They don't want anyone to know about it. Let's move forward a little.

The scene swirled around Bloom and as it began to slow down, he could see slight changes in the scenery. The buildings looked to be slightly worn down, there were fewer people in the street, and there were some other races mixed in with the Nortes. Bloom could identify a couple of them, most notably by the languages they spoke. It was starting to come together.

"The races here represent the conglomeration of languages I detected in the alien writings I found in the ruins. The older races of the galaxy used to live together. Something happened that caused them to split."

Very good. Oh don't worry, all of this tragedy that you see was a good thing. Or at least that's what my friend told himself as he was carrying out the plan.

"You were there? I don't think you're telling me everything."

I think you're right. I'm not telling you everything. But I'm not holding back purposely. As I was talking, I suddenly had a flash of something. A feeling perhaps, a memory...I don't know. I do know what I am here for, though.

"I'll take what I can get. What are you here for?"

To tell the story of what has passed into history. To give information to those who need it. For those who will use it for the right reasons. I know what has brought you here and what you need. I will do my best to give it to you. I will do my best to help you.

"We're in my mind, aren't we? That's why I can't keep my thoughts internal."

No, we are in my mind and I was not allowing you to keep your thoughts to yourself. I needed to know who you were and what you wanted. From now on, you may keep your thoughts to yourself. I will only be able to hear what you want me to hear when you think it.

"Thank you. It may not be important to you, but it's important for my people to be able to have personal thoughts while we work things out."

My people were not allowed to have personal thoughts. We were interrogated often to confirm our continued loyalty. Talking with you is helping me to remember things I have not thought of for centuries.

"Where are you? If I am in your mind, where is your body?"

I don't think that I have one anymore, at least not a functioning one. It has been so long since I've even bothered to check in on my physical form. Now, let us get on with the matter at hand. It is time for you to learn what happened and what you must do to save your galaxy.

Reaper

NAME: REAPER
SPECIES: HUMAN
MOS: CORPSMAN
RANK: SENIOR CHIEF
AGE: 40 - EARTH STANDARD
SEX: MALE
HEIGHT: 5'11"
WEIGHT: 195 POUNDS

"Clear!" The word sounded hollow to Reaper's seemingly disembodied consciousness, though the meaning was completely solid in his mind. He had seen the actions that followed the word but had never been on the receiving end of what was about to come. He mentally braced for the two hundred joules of energy that were about to flow across his chest and through his heart; he didn't feel a thing as he watched his body arch upward on the operating table. Apparently there were some benefits to being clinically dead, a lack of pain chief among them.

"Results?" The doctor was looking towards the nurse attending the monitor.

She smiled. "Sinus rhythm. We've got him back."

A corpsman spoke up from Reaper's side. "Don't throw a party yet; he still doesn't have a pulse and his pressure is still gone."

Reaper wanted to scream, "PEA—Pulseless Electrical Activity! Remember your *H*s and *T*s, people!" But being clinically dead also had its drawbacks, not being able to speak chief among them.

The doctor was a practiced trauma surgeon and didn't skip a beat, absent though they were in Reaper's chest. "*H*s and *T*s, people. We can rule out hypothermia, hydrogen ion, hypo or hyper kalemia, or toxins."

"*Oh crap*", Reaper thought. "*I'm in a teaching hospital. This should be interesting.*"

The doctor continued. "That leaves hypovolemia, hypoxia, trauma, tamponade, tension pneumothorax, and thrombosis. Most of these apply considering he was shot in the chest multiple times. We're going to open him up and figure out the cause of the PEA. Keep strong and steady on the compressions while I get the chest tray."

Reaper could see the doctor moving the surgical kit labeled "Chest, Exploratory" from the shelf to the bedside table. As the doctor sprayed sterilizing iodine all over Reaper's bare chest, Reaper decided it was time to check out. There was only so much his body and mind could take, and right now he knew he couldn't handle the mental trauma of watching his own chest being cracked open. It was easier than he had expected, to remove himself from the here and now and drift back into the deeper recesses of his memories to a different time, a distant place…

~

"Bryce! Get in here, now!" The voice that was usually so deep and soothing to Bryce was a cannon of anger today.

Bryce walked through the kitchen door. "Yeah, Dad?" Trying to be light in his mood didn't help the situation; his father just glared angrily at him. "Um, I mean, yes, sir?"

Trying to suppress a portion of his anger before he spoke again, his father finally asked, "Can you explain to me why your little sister is purple?"

Bryce could see his mother in the other room, purposely sequestering herself from the conversation, probably due to the fact that she couldn't keep a straight face and was barely containing her hysterical laughter. Bryce caught himself as the right side of his mouth threatened to betray him with a smile as it began to curl upwards. Luckily, his father missed the almost-smile and Bryce got his face back under control.

Bryce's little sister Maya was in fact a fairly pretty shade of purple from head to toe. Maya wasn't exactly sure what all the fuss was about. She was excited to show all of her kindergarten friends her new skin color; they would all be very jealous. Like a lot of Coalition schools, there were usually species other than humans in the classrooms. There were only a few humans in Maya's class and they were all very jealous of the Trizites who could change color with their emotions. They would now be jealous of her new hue. Very exciting indeed.

Bryce was twelve and a fairly smart kid. He tested in the top ten percent of his class in every area of testing. He wasn't the smartest kid in his class but his parents knew they wouldn't have to worry about him ever falling behind in his studies. He did, however, excel in his interest in medicine, following in the footsteps of his father.

Bryce's father was a trauma surgeon at a local hospital and often took Bryce to work with him. Bryce was always helping other kids on the playground, patching their scrapes and tending to their roughhousing traumas. Even though Bryce was pretty good with his basic trauma skills, he really excelled with internal medicine. He was always searching the Net for home remedies and folk medicine treatments from all over the Coalition. Bryce would often combine herbs and elements from different species' remedies to create a new one that usually worked how he wanted it to. Rashes, hives, sore throats, colds, and various flu strains along with many other basic ailments were cured with his concoctions.

There had been a few errors, to say the least, but nothing life-threatening so far. A few cases of projectile vomiting, runny noses that seemed to come from a never-ending sinus waterfall, unconsciousness, and one minor case of very ill-timed uncontrollable and unrelenting flatulence. Bryce's mother always came to his defense, though, and pointed out that even with some odd side effects, everything he had set out to cure was in fact, cured.

As Bryce stood in front of his father, he straightened up and walked in a slow circle around his sister and tried to act like an intern presenting a patient to their attending physician. "Sir, the patient is a five-year-old human female. Chief complaint consisting of chronic allergies of unknown origin. The patient's history seems to indicate having recently moved to a new colony that is heavily populated with Trizites. There might be a connection to her allergies and a Trizite-centric material, possibly in the food or other commonplace item in the community.

"Using this assumption along with the patient's past history of allergies, I formulated a homeopathic mixture including some local flora and herbs along with a traditional set of human-based allergy remedies. The patient has responded well and most of her symptoms have subsided with a only few left that are significantly diminished."

Bryce's father looked at him and he could tell that his father was trying hard to stay mad or at least look as if he was. "You still haven't explained why she's purple. Another one of your unexpected side effects?"

Bryce tried to look wounded by the question. "Side effects? I don't think I know what you mean, Doctor." The look he received from his father made him quickly add, "Not a side effect, sir. The patient has been upset for the last week or so because her Trizite classmates can change some of their facial coloring almost at will. Some of the compounds in the Trizite diet are directly linked to their pigment abilities. I simply added a few local elements that I thought would give the patient a slight tinge of color to her face." Bryce looked at his purple sister and waved his hand up and down her body. "I might have miscalculated the end results. Just a little. Sir."

Maya jumped up and down as she realized that her big brother had purposely turned her purple, as a gift to her. She jumped on to his chest and wrapped her arms and legs around him. "Thank you, thank you, thank you! How long will I be purple? Can you make me different colors? Can you make my friends different colors?"

"No, he certainly may not turn your friends different colors." Their father now looked at the two embracing siblings. He smiled; it was pretty great to have two kids who actually got a long so well. "Bryce, get your baseball uniform on. We need to get going if we're going to get you to practice before it starts."

Bryce lowered his sister to the ground and just smiled before he ran out of the room. He knew that he had just barely dodged a lot of grounding from his father, possibly worse. As he left the room, Maya jumped into her father's arms and started to talk about school and what she was going to wear tomorrow to show off her new color. Bryce came back just a few moments later and his sister was still babbling away. She was set down and then father and son left together, all trespasses forgot for the time being.

As they left the driveway, his father mentioned that they would have to stop by the hospital on the way to the baseball field. His father had left his wallet in his locker and wanted to pick it up because he was going to be off for the next four days. Bryce was fine with the detour; he loved the hospital and they still had plenty of time to get to practice. They arrived a short time later and Bryce went in to the building with his father, saying hi to all of his father's coworkers as they passed.

When they were just about to the locker room, Doctor Wilson walked up to Bryce's father. "Hey, Trevor!"

Bryce's dad turned to look at his colleague and friend. "I can't, Tim. I've got Bryce with me and I need to get him to his baseball practice."

Tim looked at Bryce and then back to his father. "Look, Trevor, I wouldn't ask if it weren't an absolute emergency." Trevor looked at him sideways. "Okay, I would ask, but this is different."

"Tim, this is an *emergency room*. Newsflash—everything is an emergency. My son is more important to me than strangers I don't know."

Tim looked a little shocked to hear the statement that almost everyone thought but there had always been an unwritten rule that it was never to be spoken aloud: the patients weren't the most important things in the world. Tim looked at Bryce before addressing Trevor again. "You're right, absolutely. Here's the deal, though, we have a family of five that will be here in about"—he looked at his watch—"thirty seconds now. They all have major multiple stab wounds. We have the surgery department alerted and they are busy getting teams together for each patient along with getting the operating rooms ready. We just need you to help stabilize one of the patients until surgery comes down to grab him.

"We've only got two trauma surgeons on right now. I'm sure we can handle it without you but it will be smoother with you. I'll give you the worst of the five to make sure yours gets taken to the OR first and then you can get out of here. Twenty minutes tops, but you know in this situation we're really hoping for less than ten minutes before they get hauled to surgery."

Trevor looked at Bryce, who just shrugged. "A whole family was stabbed; we should help them. It's all right, Dad; you already said I was more important so you don't have to feel guilty. Besides, I may be more important to you than the patients, but the patients are more important to me than baseball."

"You're just saying that to get out of trouble for turning your sister purple."

Tim said, "What?!"

Bryce, smiling from ear to ear, answered his father, "Maybe. But seriously, Dad, not really. Let's help."

"Okay, Tim, let's go." Looking down to Bryce, who was keeping in step with the adults, "Do you want to watch or wait at the nurse's station?"

Perplexing question for Bryce. He was at the point that girls were starting to get very interesting and grown women were even more interesting. On top of that, the nurses seemed to adore him and he was guaranteed a lot of hugs and kisses from them. On the other hand, with five simultaneous traumas, most of the nurses would probably be busy so he'd be stuck playing a game on a terminal or something, by himself most likely. "I'll go with you, Dad."

"Sounds good to me. And remember, if one of the new interns messes up an IV, you need to jump in there and get it yourself to make them feel bad." It was a fun game that Bryce and his dad played on the interns, something along the lines of, "See what you just screwed up? Now watch the twelve-year-old kid do it just right. Hey, no crying in the ER."

As they approached the trauma bay, Bryce saw that along with the ambulances that were arriving there were also several police vehicles. Cops usually showed up when there was an assault of some sort but he hadn't seen this many before. As the first gurney made its way in, there were four cops surrounding it.

Tim looked at Trevor. "I think that one is yours. The telemetry from the paramedics said the father was in the worst condition. That looks like him."

"Copy that." Looking down at his son, he said, "There's a lot of blood, Bryce; you know the drill. Gown up and put on all the protection possible: gloves, mask, goggles, everything."

"Yes, sir." Bryce ran ahead and started pulling all of the protective gear from the dispensers on the side of the wall next to the trauma room. One intern passed by him and started to enter the trauma room without stopping. Bryce yelled at him, "Hey you! Yeah, new kid. You want Shirka Herpes or Mulvarian Hepatitis?! Put on your gown and stuff before you go in to that bloodbath."

The intern stopped and looked around him to see whether the kid was seriously addressing him. One of the nurses stopped at the dispensers and gave Bryce a quick hug and kiss before addressing the intern, "He's right. Our safety comes before their treatment."

The intern slowly joined the two putting on their safety gear and then the three walked in the room, followed shortly after by Bryce's father. He looked at the people already at work and then the officers who stood nearby. "I understand you gentlemen have a job to do, but so do we. We need a little more room to work. Please, back up just a hair to the red line we have outlining the gurney. Also, blood can shoot quite a distance—there are disposable goggles on the wall outside this room. You're more than welcome to grab some along with gloves, just in case."

The sergeant in the group looked down to the red line on the floor. "Move back, boys; give Doc some room. Jenkins, go get four safety glasses and some gloves for all of us."

"Thank you, Sergeant." Trevor saw his team doing what they were trained to do; they needed very little direction from him in these sorts of cases. "I don't think he'll be able to talk to you, sir. His throat is fairly well damaged. Someone did quite a number on him."

The sergeant got a disgusted look on his face. "I'm not waiting here for a statement or suspect description, not this time. He is the suspect. Those are self-inflicted wounds."

"All of them? Are you sure?" Bryce's dad was working on the man's throat and trying to make a better surgical airway for him. The number of stab wounds all over his body made it seem impossible to believe that he had done it all to himself.

"Yeah, we're sure. Bystanders witnessed most of it and we have video feed from the bank security camera. They streamed the video to me while we were on our way here." The sergeant took a deep breath. "He walked out from the bank after having an argument with the teller about a problem with his account. He pulled out a hunting knife and started to go back in. His wife tried to stop him so he began stabbing her. The kids got out of the car and were yelling and screaming at him and he turned on them next. After he stabbed everyone multiple times, he began stabbing himself. When the first patrol unit arrived on scene, he tried to slit his own throat. It doesn't look like he did too good of a job of it, though."

"He did better than you think." Trevor was now probing deep into the anatomy of the man's neck and throat. "He cut one carotid and there are three separate lacerations to his trachea. I can fix it, though."

"Don't try too hard, Doc. No one would blame you if you happened to 'slip' or maybe just didn't do a great job this one time." The sergeant received nods of affirmation from his fellow officers.

Without taking his eyes off the patient, Trevor replied without emotion, "I can't imagine ever doing anything to harm my family like he did, but it's not my job to judge or punish. My job is to fix."

Bryce was pulling down a suture kit and advanced airway tray for his father. "My dad isn't the Grim Reaper, sir. He doesn't take lives—he saves them."

"Oh, uh, hey there, kid. I didn't see you standing there. Sorry about that." The sergeant was stammering a little as he tasted the leather from the sole of his shoe that was now firmly planted in his own mouth.

"Don't worry about it. I hear all sorts of things when I help my dad." Bryce looked at one of the officers in the middle. "And Sergeant…"

"Yeah, kid?"

"You might want to catch Jenkins; he's about to pass out." Thump. "Sorry, too late."

Eight minutes after the patient came through the ambulance bay doors, a surgical team came and grabbed the gurney and whisked him away to the operating room. Trevor took his son to the basin sink and helped him remove all of his protective gear and then they both washed up. Holding Bryce's hand, they walked out of the ER after Trevor made sure to tell the charge nurse that he'd dictate the chart from home later tonight after the kids were in bed.

"See, dad," Bryce looked at his watch, "we'll only be a few minutes late and we helped someone."

Speaking thoughts that should have been kept private, Trevor sighed. "Yeah, sometimes the people I help don't make me feel good about what I do."

Bryce stopped dead in his tracks and pulled his father to a stop. "Dad. You are not the Reaper. That's someone else's job. No matter how bad that man is, I bet his kids still love him. Someone, somewhere must still love him. You helped them, not him. Isn't that what you've always told me?"

"I love you, son." He gave Bryce a quick hug. "I knew I kept you around for some reason."

Five weeks later, Bryce was laying on the living room floor trying to stay awake for the end of the movie. When the credits started to roll, his father stood and told him to go get ready for bed then come back so they could review one patient chart together before bed. Bryce completed his tasks and hurried back; patient charts had taken the place of bedtime stories for the past few years and he always enjoyed them.

When Bryce returned, he found his father leaning forward in his chair, face buried in his hands, obviously crying. Bryce had only seen his father cry after the birth of his sister and he knew that these sobs were a completely different kind. He gently touched his father's shoulder and was about to ask what was wrong when the picture on the TV caught his eye. It was the man they had worked on together, the man who had stabbed his family.

Bryce didn't recognize him when the news initially reported on the event weeks ago. His driver's license photos and family photos they showed looked so different from the bloodied man they had saved in the trauma room. But after seeing his face all over the news for weeks, Bryce immediately recognized the man being reported on.

The man had been released after an emotional plea from his lawyer, psychiatric physician and his wife and kids. Everyone assured the judge that he was better now, the medication was helping tremendously and it was a one-time mental break. He and his lawyer promised that he would stay in an apartment and only visit his family with their permission and with law-enforcement supervision at the local precinct. The judge agreed and added several other stipulations of his own and set a trial date. The man thanked the judge and said that he was ready and eager to take responsibility for his actions so he and his family could start rebuilding their relationships.

The news channel was playing a slide show of pictures while they discussed the latest event that took place just moments ago at the family's house, not too far from Bryce's home. The picture on the TV now was the whole family in the courtroom, hugging each other and crying at the man's release from custody. Bryce heard the news anchor say that the upcoming images were gruesome and not suitable for all audiences.

Bryce watched as the photo dissolved and was replaced with a crime scene photo of a sheet-covered body on the lawn of a house. The sheet was soaked with blood and the size indicated that it was covering a small child, probably two or three years old. Bryce guessed it was the man's youngest son from the previous picture. The scene changed again and there were more covered bodies in the living room. Bryce could easily make out two kids, one draped over a couch, probably trying to get away, and another one face down crawling away from the doorway. The mother, he guessed, was at the doorway, half in and half out, probably trying to protect her children as the man came into the house. He knew it was the mother because the one body that wasn't covered was the man from the trauma room. His body bullet-ridden and torn to shreds, unrecognizable as the man from the previous photos, his identity known only because the news said it was so.

Bryce knew why his father was crying. He felt responsible or at least somewhat connected to this tragedy even if in only some small remote way. He didn't know what to do. How does a child console an adult at a time like this? Bryce decided that words were too cumbersome and useless right now so he just rubbed his hand back and forth across his father's shoulders and back to let him know that Bryce was there for him.

The news camera moved to a police officer who was about to be interviewed. Bryce recognized him as the sergeant from the emergency room. The reporter stood next to the sergeant and held a microphone between them. "Sergeant Ramsey, I understand that you were involved in the shooting. I know there are obviously things you can't say at this point, but is there anything you can tell us?"

The sergeant looked off camera to someone in the background, apparently receiving some sort of permission from some unseen person. The sergeant gave a slight nod in return before he began speaking. "I can't go into details right now, but we arrived on scene to find a suspect actively trying to kill another person. Several commands were given to him to stop as we were running to the front door from our patrol vehicles. Once we were close enough to open fire, he still had not complied with our orders so we fired on him to end the threat."

"Were you aware of who the suspect was when you arrived?"

"I did. I can't speak for the other officers involved, but I did. I responded to the incident with this family where the suspect had stabbed them all in the bank parking lot, just down the road. I knew their address from my previous report. I had a pretty good idea that it was them."

"Did that make you feel any different while you were responding? Knowing the history and seeing what the family looked like during the first stabbing incident?"

The sergeant looked off camera again and gave a slight nod in return to whoever was playing the part of the shadow puppeteer. "It didn't make me 'feel' different. We have a job to do and we try to keep feelings out of it. All we knew was that a stabbing was taking place. What if someone else was attacking the family? Some fanatic or someone coming after the father for what he had done before? We didn't know anything else when we arrived. I honestly didn't know it was him until I pulled the trigger. His back was to me until after my first rounds hit him and he turned to face me. That's when I knew it was him, that's when I had feelings, not before."

"Can you explain that, Sergeant? What feelings did you have then?"

"Sadness. Sadness that the family was going through the same thing again. Anger. Anger that our judicial system is horrible and let this man out just to kill his family."

The sergeant paused and the reporter took advantage of that moment to interject her own adjective, "Triumph? Triumph at ending this man's killing?"

The sergeant's previously placid face morphed into one of anger. "Triumph? We weren't triumphant in anything here tonight. We didn't stop anything. We tried, but we didn't. Can't you see the bodies lying around us? Where is the triumph in that?

"Even if we had saved the family, I don't know that 'triumph' would be the word to use. Maybe", the sergeant looked at the ground as he tried to find the right word, "success? Success at saving the family and ending the threat.

"My job isn't to be the judge, jury, or executioner. But sometimes, we have to be the Reaper. We have to collect the souls of those who are broken, who can't be a part of society no matter how much we want them to be. Sometimes we have to practice a bit of preventive medicine to make sure others won't be hurt in the future."

Bryce knew that last part was directed at his father, and maybe him as well. Bryce suddenly realized that his father wasn't sitting there anymore; he had gone to bed. Bryce watched the news for another twenty minutes or so, taking over his father's chair, before he also went to bed. In the morning, it was as though nothing had changed. His father was doing a good job of compartmentalizing his emotions and making everything as normal as he could for his family. It took a few months before Bryce felt like his father was truly back to being himself, and a couple more months after that before Bryce was allowed to again visit his dad at work.

It wasn't too long before Bryce started high school and joined the ROTC program. He planned to be a doctor and follow in most of his father's footsteps. He was still more interested in internal medicine and diagnostic medicine but he couldn't wait to make his father proud of his trauma rotations once he got to medical school.

Part of his ROTC training allowed him to go to the Navy's Hospital Corpsman School when he was fifteen. The program was the exact same training as the adults got but the class was full of high school students in the delayed entry program. The idea was to get them excited about service so they would enlist right out of high school. With their technical school already done, it put them in the field that much quicker after boot camp.

When he was sixteen, he went to the Corpsman Field Medical Services School, where corpsman go to learn how to be field medics with the marines. Bryce was involved in a lot of extra-curricular sports activities with school so he was fit and enjoyed the hard work they put in during training. He loved being outdoors and working as a team. He was no stranger to teamwork with his involvement in sports and working alongside his father in the emergency room, but this kind of teamwork was different, better somehow on an emotional level.

He also enjoyed learning about firearms. He was pretty good with the weapons and was a little sad to find out that corpsman usually only carried a defensive sidearm in combat, or at least that's all they were supposed to carry. One of the gunnery sergeants told Bryce that he should think about Special Forces if he was so interested in the firearms portion of training. The SpecOps Corpsman carried a full loadout of weapons in addition to their medical gear.

Bryce told the gunny that he was planning to become an officer and going to medical school on the Navy's dime. The gunny just rolled his eyes and made a comment about Bryce wasting his talents in order to go get an officer lobotomy. Bryce reminded the gunny that a lobotomy didn't actually decrease a person's intelligence; it actually affected the emotional center in the patient's brain. This earned Bryce and his company a five-mile run.

The next day, Bryce found himself riding in an armored personnel carrier, shoulder to shoulder with actual marines. Bryce always felt like an adult when he was in school; his size and maturity level made him feel as if he was standing with a bunch of kids. But now, sitting next to combat veterans, he realized just how small he really was and that he was several years away from being a real adult.

The unit was transported to the forward area of the training exercise, the last test for Bryce's class and a group of marines trying to graduate from boot camp. The battle exercises included veteran marines intermixed into the units of marine recruits and the corpsman from Bryce's FMF school were also put in to companies as they would be if this were a real situation.

Bryce had been had assigned to an eight-man fire team that was made up of all real marines, no recruits in the bunch. Their team call sign was "Echo Blue" and they were on the side of the good guys in this scenario. They were being deployed to an area that required some cleanup of enemy forces that had been bypassed or missed when the company made its push through the area. The bad guys couldn't be left to the rear of the advancing force; that was just poor tactics.

When the team first loaded up, they were all joking around and giving one another shit; they seemed to be a tight unit and probably worked together at their real duty stations. When the driver announced over the PA that they were two minutes from their drop-off, all of the chatter stopped and each marine took up deployment positions at the two doors in the vehicles. Bryce was caught off guard at their sudden intensity. This was only training; he wondered how they were on real missions.

As the vehicle came to a stop, the first marine at each door was already on the ground and moving to a firing position that gave the rest of the men cover as they disembarked the vehicle. Bryce was close to being the last man out and as he was moving forward, he saw that there were still three rifles in the vehicle's weapons closet. Bryce instinctively grabbed one, along with a shoulder-slung bandolier of ammunition that held six magazines.

Bryce took up a firing position near one of the marines who looked down and saw the weapon Bryce held. "Hey, kid, you're a corpsman. You're not supposed to be carrying a rifle."

Bryce didn't take his eyes off his field of fire as he spoke. "Do you think that when the shooting starts the other guys won't aim at me? Or their bullets will magically miss the medic?" No response. "I didn't think so."

The team leader walked up to Bryce. "I like you, kid, but if you're going to carry a rifle, at least load it. Okay?"

The rest of the team snickered as Bryce realized that his weapon was indeed empty. He knew from training that no loaded weapon was ever stored in a vehicle. He reached into his bandolier and pulled out a magazine of training ammunition and put it into the weapon. Bryce cycled the bolt and checked to make sure the safety was engaged. The team was already moving out so Bryce took up a position towards the rear of the element.

After about an hour of working through the area of dense buildings, they had their first contact. Echo Blue was victorious and no one in the unit was taken out. When a training round hit a person, the training uniform sensed the hit and delivered a momentarily paralyzing shock to the soldier. If you were hit, regardless of where, you were out of the scenario. Bryce emptied a whole magazine during their first engagement but hadn't hit any targets, much to his dismay. Maybe there was a reason corpsman shouldn't carry guns?

Echo Blue had several more engagements over the next few miles. Bryce actually scored a couple of hits, though it took him another four magazines to do so. The rest of the fire team was razing him in a good-natured sort of way, a way that made him feel as though they were actually starting to like him.

As the team entered a small courtyard, Bryce heard a round being fired and then felt the light breeze of a training bullet passing by his head. The round struck the marine in front of Bryce, dead center of his back and the marine went down. In that moment of the adrenaline dump that Bryce was experiencing, he saw the time-dilation effect of the flight-fight-or-freeze mechanism kicking in. Everyone was moving in slow motion as the next two rounds passed by his head and two more marines were instantly locked up on the invisible electric leash that now held them in place and dropped them to the ground.

Bryce slid to his right, unsure of where the attack was coming from. He could be moving towards it but his training and instinct together told him that moving in any direction was better than not moving at all. As he slid, he turned his body around and brought his weapon to bear towards where he thought the attack was coming from.

Bryce saw the marine on rear security was facing the rest of the team with his weapon pointed at them, firing. His brain couldn't figure out what was going on. He looked in the direction the marine was firing, thinking that the enemy must be ahead of them as well and that's what he was shooting at. But as the marine fired again, Bryce followed the shot and saw that it was heading directly towards another one of the marines on his team.

Bryce didn't hesitate any longer. He brought his weapon up and put three rounds into the rogue marine's chest. At this close distance, the training rounds still had a lot of kinetic energy so the marine not only got three uniform shocks, he had three distinct thuds in his chest as well. The shooter went down and Bryce followed the target with his weapon to make sure that the threat was truly gone. Bryce had to clear his head as he kept repeating to himself that this was only training; he hadn't really killed a marine from his own team.

The team leader came to Bryce and put a hand on his rifle, helping Bryce to lower it to the ready position. "Why did you shoot Marcus?"

Bryce looked at the man whose name tag read O'Connor. "I, uh, he was shooting our own guys."

O'Connor looked at him. "And? Do you know why he was doing that? Did you stop to think about what was going on before you just lit him up?"

Bryce felt as if his feet were starting to get back under his body again so he spoke with a little more confidence this time. "Once I realized it was him shooting at us, I thought to myself '*WHY?!*' But then as I looked back towards him, I realized that it didn't matter why, he just was, and he had to be stopped. The *why* was irrelevant at that point." An old memory came back to Bryce and he added, "Sometimes, we have to be the Reaper. We have to collect the souls of those who are broken, who can't be a part of society no matter how much we want them to be. I'm a corpsman, and this was preventive medicine. I kept him from hurting any more of my men."

O'Connor smiled at Bryce. "Reaper, huh? That's your new name, kid." The marine who Bryce had shot was starting to get up and Bryce brought his rifle back up but O'Connor stopped him. "Easy, Reaper, all part of the game today."

The marine got up fully. "Nice shooting, killer." He dusted himself off a bit. "Sorry, Gunny, you know how it goes, orders and all that."

Bryce looked around with confusion so the marine filled him in. "Sometimes in these scenarios they give a soldier secret orders to attack their own unit. It simulates the real possibility that one of your own guys goes nuts in a firefight or maybe you have a double-crosser in your unit. There's plenty of reasons for that shit to happen in real life and it *HAS* happened. That's why they throw it in every now and then." He looked back at O'Connor with a huge smile. "Honestly, though, I was pretty excited they picked me. I couldn't wait to nail some of you turds."

O'Connor patted his buddy on the shoulder. "Yeah, yeah, laugh it up. Everyone who's still alive, rally up and get ready to move out. We still have a mission to complete. Those of you who are dead, make your way back to staging and get something to eat, clean your weapons and get some rest—in that order."

As the rest of the team moved out, O'Connor could see that Bryce was still conflicted with what just happened. "Look, son, you did the right thing. I know that even in a training scenario doing something like can rattle your cage, but let it go. I have a fourteen-year-old son at home, Mike Junior, and I always want to make it home to him and his mother. So I don't care who's shooting at us, bad guys, good guys, it doesn't matter; shoot everyone who is shooting in your direction. You got that, Reaper? Everyone."

"Copy that, Gunny." Reaper moved out with the rest of his unit and eventually caught up with the larger force that had been through the area first.

Two days later, Reaper finally got to shower and sleep in a real rack and not on the ground. After the graduation ceremony, O'Connor found Reaper and introduced him to his wife and son. Then O'Connor took him to a major who was talking with a bunch of new marine graduates.

"This is the major." O'Connor introduced Reaper to the officer.

Reaper came to attention and saluted. "Good to meet you, sir."

The major returned the salute. "Reaper, huh? I like it. The irony of a corpsman being called that makes me smile." The major put a friendly hand on Reaper's shoulder as they spoke.

"This is the kid who saw through your mind-fuck, sir. Shot Jinx without a second thought. Well, maybe without a third thought." O'Connor was obviously proud of him.

"Good going, kid. I love that old gag. I got to do it when I was a young lieutenant and it made my day. Not to mention that after you get shot, you get to go back to staging for some rest." The major waved at some unseen person in the crowd. "I've got to go talk to an old friend. I'll see you two later. And Reaper, I know you want to be a doctor but if you change your mind, let me know and I'll be sure to get you a great assignment right out of the gate if you're interested. And even if you do become a doctor, make sure you look me up. I've got some pretty good assignments for officers, too. A lot of fun, I tell ya." The last words he said with an eerily excited tone in his voice.

Reaper looked at O'Connor. "How do I look him up? I don't even know his name." Reaper realized that the major was the only uniformed person he had ever seen without a nametag on his chest.

"You don't really look him up; he looks you up." O'Connor was leading them towards the food tent where his wife and kid were waiting for them. "Trust me, you'll hear from the major again someday, regardless of what path you choose."

~

Gradually the food tent faded from Reaper's mind and he could hear a beeping near his left ear. He was acutely aware of a dripping sound coming from somewhere in the…room? Was he in a room? A bed? He had no idea of where he was or what was happening. Reaper's mind was foggy even though every sound he heard was crystal clear and almost too loud for him to think it was a comfortable level.

He started to talk, to yell, to something, anything to find out whether there were other people around him. He felt his mouth was unnaturally closed, something holding it shut. As he worked his mouth, he felt a plastic tube between his teeth. His senses were coming back to him now, and he could also feel something pushing air into his lungs, lungs that hurt with each breath, lungs that were being used by both him and some unseen force trying to make them move at a rhythm different than his own.

In his cloudy mind, he started to put the pieces together. He was on a ventilator; a tube was in his trachea and the machine was breathing for him, or at least trying to. He couldn't see and everything was blurry because he still had the surgical tape over his eyelids to keep them closed so his eyeballs wouldn't dry out. He tried to move his hand to his face to remove the tape so he could see. Damn, his arms were restrained—standard practice for a sedated and tubed patient in the ICU.

He could feel his breathing changing even more, still fighting the machine that was trying its best to keep up with the parameters someone had given it to fulfill. Then the machine to his left started beeping more and he realized it was his ventilator, telling the nurse the patient was starting to buck the machine, starting to wake up.

He heard footsteps near his bed and a soft feminine voice. "Hey kiddo, just relax, you're safe now. You're okay."

He reached again for the tape covering his eyes, already forgetting that he was tied to the railing.

"No, no, dear, don't pull, that's bad. We can't have you taking your tube out yet; you'll hurt yourself. Just hold on for a few more minutes and we'll have it out of your throat." He felt her hands covering his and holding them down.

I know! He screamed in his head. *I'm not trying to pull my own tube. I'm not an idiot. I just want this damn tape off my eyes. Please!*

Reaper heard another set of footsteps and then felt gentle fingers pulling the tape off his eyes and another hand shielding the harsh light above from entering his likely over-dilated pupils. He blinked a few times, his eyelids now free from their unjust imprisonment. When he was able to focus, he saw his dad standing over him. A tear escaped Reaper's eyes and even more came from his father.

Reaper's dad leaned down and kissed his son on the forehead and then hugged him as best he could given the circumstances. Reaper tried to nuzzle him back with his face but the equipment holding his breathing tube in place didn't allow his head to travel far enough.

His dad looked him in the eyes. "Hey son. I'm going to untie your hands but you can't reach for your tube, all right?" Reaper nodded his agreement. "I'm not your doctor, so I can't take it out for you but I'll unhook the ventilator so you can breathe on your own. My buddy Hal is on his way up, should be here any second to get this out of you. He did a great job on your surgery. You're going to be just fine."

Reaper saw his medical chart sitting on his legs; his dad must have set it down there. He pointed at it and made a "give me" motion with his hand. His dad just chuckled at his son wanting to read his own medical chart while he was still intubated.

Reaper took the chart that was handed to him, found the writing stylus at the top of the tablet and then flipped through his chart until he got to a blank screen that was for doctors to free-hand patient notes that didn't fit any of the pre-made forms in the electronic chart. He scribbled, "Did the man live?"

His father looked at the chart. "Yes, he did, thanks to you. They brought you two in with your hand still in his chest. I have no idea how that worked for the entire transport but it did. They separated you two in the ER. Tim took over for you and Hal took you straight to the OR. Not a single trauma surgeon here could've done better. I'm very proud of you, son."

Reaper scribbled a few more words. 'Good. I'm glad. Dad. I think I want to do something different, not be a doctor.'

Trevor cringed at the thought that the trauma his son had gone through had just turned him away from medicine forever. "Okay, son, whatever you want, you know that your mother and I will support you. We can talk about it later, when you can actually talk again, that is."

More writing. "I still want to be in medicine, but I want to be in the field, with the marines. I want to do more of what I did today."

And then he wrote, "Except the getting shot part. That sucked. Horribly."

Chapter 46
The Warrior Interrogation Planet – Knock Knock

The warrior sat at his post, never wavering and always diligent in his duties. He had never been in battle and always feared he would die without ever being in one. Among his brothers, dying old was not considered a bad thing unless the years you lived weren't earned and fought for in battle. Now that his base was being used to interrogate the prisoners from the other side of the galaxy, he was hopeful for the first time in his life that his days of not being battle-tested would soon end.

His warrior brothers weren't prone to discussing rumors so the information he had heard passed along in the corridors must be true. The War Council was close to giving the order to invade the quarantined section of the galaxy. Once they were done processing the prisoners at this base, they would make their move.

The Council had all of the information they needed to attack but they had learned long ago not to take anything for granted. Victory is won using all of your resources and abilities to their fullest extent and not relying on just the warriors' seemingly inexhaustible brute strength and numbers.

Ever since the quarantine, the warriors couldn't rely on inexhaustible numbers because they lost access to their birthing planet a short time after the disaster began. Luckily for them, the member of the royal family who was assigned to the birthing planet, Royal Cousin G'Pleh, saw what was happening and took actions to mitigate the damage from the epidemic. He launched fifty million stasis birthing pods from the planet and sent them to a warrior-controlled training planet.

According to the royal's personal logs, he believed a revolt was occurring and the virus wasn't a natural threat but instead an engineered part of the coup. He had had no physical contact with the expansion fleet, none of the royal family or even any other Nortes for over a month. He liked his privacy and spent most of his time in his private chambers or other private sections of the palace that no one else was allowed to enter. Dr. D'Bath had said that he was an agoraphobe but he had always dismissed that diagnosis and just believed that he liked his personal space.

Either way, when the news of the virus began to spread, he felt a certain sense of vindication for his choice of living arrangements. After all, he would now become the sole surviving member of the royal family and as such, the emperor. But then he, too, became sick.

The official reason from D'Bath was that he must have been infected by the trinkets the emperor had sent to G'Pleh from the infected region of space. G'Pleh rejected this theory because he hated the emperor for making him the caretaker of the birthing planet and had never accepted a single gift from the emperor. Every gift the emperor sent was summarily placed in the incinerator before G'Pleh even touched or looked at it.

G'Pleh knew he had been poisoned but couldn't prove it. He sent his logs, along with the warriors' stasis pods, and they contained his theories on the virus and quarantine. More than a thousand years later, his theories would prove to be very close to the actual truth of what had happened but at the time the War Council thought he was just mad from the infection. G'Pleh was always considered an odd man, as was evident by his posting as far from the empire as possible.

As for the warriors' brute strength, they found out that without the constant supply of reinforcements from the birthing planet, they couldn't just pound their way to victory.

About two hundred years after the quarantine, some of the slave races had taken the opportunity to flee the crumbling empire. None of them dared to fight the warriors or outright revolt; they just left as quickly and quietly as they could. The escaped slaves made contact with another species known as the Cherta. The Cherta were strong and advanced and although not completely peaceful, they had come to learn that sometimes negotiating was preferable to fighting.

When the Cherta learned of the collapsing empire, they took the opportunity to make contact with the warriors. The Cherta had mapped out the empire and put together a list of resources they wanted and in return they offered to help the warriors rebuild what they could of the empire and learn a new way of living.

The War Council, of course, reacted to the offer in the only way they knew how, in the way that was genetically mapped and imposed on them: they fought the Cherta. It was a long and devastating war that went on for almost ten years before the Cherta left the empire's space. Thousands of Cherta were captured and became a new category of slaves never known to the empire before: they were the advisors.

This war taught the warriors many things and proved to be the unifying event that allowed them to break some of the shackles that had been bread into them for millennia. They still needed and craved a royal family to serve but they learned how to get by without an emperor and maintain the empire until an heir to the throne could be found.

The Nortes were becoming extinct in the empire. Their DNA had been checked and rechecked since the quarantine, looking for someone with even a shred of royal blood in them. Unbeknownst to the warriors, the emperor had been very thorough in making sure that no one with royal DNA would be left behind or alive in the empire.

Shortly after the quarantine took place, almost twelve percent of the Nortes population committed suicide, knowing that their way of life was over. Those left in the military tried to take control of the empire, knowing what would happen with the warriors and no royal blood to lead them; the entire Nortes military was wiped out by the warriors because of the attempt.

The rest of the Nortes tried to make the best of the circumstances and continue with life as they knew it. There were, of course, the Nortes involved with the coup who were supposed to help take over the new empire and free the slaves after the remaining warriors had died off. Unfortunately, G'Pleh ruined those plans when he sent out the fifty million warrior stasis pods. So the Nortes did what they could to continue planting the seeds of unity but eventually the movement all but died out. Every once in a while, the warriors would run across a small cell of Nortes trying to revive the movement or live according to their own beliefs but those Nortes were always found and brutally killed to be made an example of.

The remaining Nortes still lived far better than the majority of other races in the empire, coming in third to the warriors and Cherta. Surprisingly, the Cherta had the best life of all the races in the empire. The warriors were simple in their ways and needed very little to be happy, or at least their version of genetically programmed happiness. A place to sleep, food to hunt and eat, and someone to fight every once in a while was all they needed or wanted.

Once the warriors' needs were met, everything else went to their Cherta advisors to make sure they could keep advising. More than once some of the Cherta tried to use their advisory positions to move the empire in a new direction that gave the Cherta even more power. Those schemes were eventually discovered and abruptly ended with savage brutality.

So while the empire still existed, it had inevitably shrunk in size, power, and intellect. There had been very little advancement in any of the areas that are a part of any normal civilization. The empire's focus had shifted from advancement to maintenance and had been steadily failing on both fronts at a snail's pace for a thousand years.

~

A small shock brought the warrior's attention back to the present and he checked his personal shield. The damn thing was malfunctioning again. Most warriors in the empire didn't have personal shields; they were issued to long-range scouting parties, infiltration teams, and of course the War Council. Most bases had a limited number of shields that were passed on to whoever was on sentry duty. Those shields were constantly used and quite often constantly failing. This base only had three, two of which worked and one of those was about to fail.

The warrior had found that throughout every species, every culture, every level of sentient evolution, when a piece of tech didn't work, the user hit the offending item to try to beat it into submissive self-repair. The warrior's heavily manipulated genetic code was no different and he let himself chuckle as he struck the shield's controls and thought of the universal oddity.

His chuckling ceased when he realized what he was doing and thinking. First off, warriors didn't chuckle. Second, his thoughts had begun to stray into tangents about how some things were universal among the slave races, Nortes and now even some of the warriors. And if some things were universal, maybe they weren't all that different from one another. These thoughts were unacceptable and he felt the urge to turn himself in to his superiors for evaluation and most likely termination. He knew he should, felt he had to, but somehow he was able to just barely keep from doing it. Another thing he shouldn't have been able to do.

The warrior's internal turmoil ceased when the perimeter alert on his control panel lit up a deep and bright blue. He then began cycling through the security cameras until he saw something almost as unbelievable as his most recent thoughts had been. One of the human prisoners was escaping! But that was impossible. How could he get out of a torture tube, which is impossible, and then get past any one of the thirty or so warriors currently at this base?

However impossible it was, there he was crawling away from the airlock at security station three, the post next to his own. The human was in a torn uniform and bleeding from several places on his body. Something just wasn't right about the scene he was looking at. The torture tubes generally didn't cause that much bleeding or tearing of the clothes; the process was much more surgical. Of course, no one had ever escaped a torture tube before so maybe that's why this human looked differently than what the warrior was used to.

Regardless, he needed to act. No one was at security station three right now so it was up to him to take care of things. According to protocol, he should have called for backup before exiting the base security doors, but he didn't. He felt the need to prove himself and his loyalty to the empire after having such seditious thoughts earlier. And just in case he didn't go to war alongside his brothers against the humans, he wanted to take this one chance to fight one of the humans on his own. He was just a little disappointed that this human was already injured and wouldn't be able to put up a proper fight.

~

Seth waited and watched patiently as Blaze crawled from one airlock to the other. They made it to the base without being detected but the airlocks seemed impenetrable with the gear they had with them. Stealth had kept them alive so far, so they continued to use it to their advantage.

The plan was simple: make Blaze look like an escapee and then trip the base alarms. When an airlock opened to retrieve the prisoner, the team would attack and infiltrate. The not-so-simple part was setting off the base alarm. They tried prying the airlock, hoping it would alert the base to an attempted break-in: nothing. Throwing rocks at what seemed to be a communications array on the roof: nothing. Jumping up and down in front of a security camera: nothing. Apparently the enemy also thought their base was impenetrable because nothing seemed to set off the alarm. Seth wondered how high their security thresholds must be in order to allow all of these attempts to go unnoticed.

Seth hoped that his enemies were at least a little similar in some security protocols, otherwise the last thing he could think of wouldn't work. He told Blaze to go to the airlock entry code interface and start typing in random patterns on the keypad. Hopefully too many incorrect codes would set off the alarm. There was also the astronomically slim chance that Blaze might accidentally enter the proper code.

Blaze had just barely touched the keypad when it began to rapidly blink a deep and bright blue and the security camera swung in his direction. Blaze hit the ground and began to slowly crawl away from the door. Seth surmised that Blaze's bloody finger, from his prisoner makeover, had set off a DNA sensor in the keypad and subsequently the alarm. He thought it was odd that the alarm's color was blue.

The door began to cycle open and Seth waited for the enemy soldier to cross the imaginary line in the sand that had been decided on earlier. No one from Seth's team had seen the enemy yet so he let out a soft whisper. "Holy shit."

The comms were more than sensitive enough to pick up a whisper because they were designed to transmit even subvocal speech. Surgeon subvocalized, "Steady everyone. He's a big son of a bitch but we have more than enough people and firepower to drop him. Get ready, Blaze, he's almost at the line."

They wanted the warrior, or had it been warriors, to get far enough out that Seth, Beast, and Joker could enter the airlock while the rest of the team engaged the enemy. With apparently only one warrior coming out of the airlock, Seth turned on his remote camera that was set to view the airlock from the front so his team could view the interior before they entered. "It looks clear, like he was the only one in there or coming out." Seth was prepping his team. "He's got two more steps before he's at our line. When we make entry, get to that control station and provide me cover while I look it over." Seth received two clicks each from Beast and Joker.

The warrior moved slowly towards the human, maybe more warily than slowly. Something still wasn't right about this. As his next footstep ended he realized everything all at once: The uniform was different from every other uniform the prisoners were wearing. The injuries were definitely not surgical-like as if they had come from a torture tube. The injuries were small and in non-critical areas. Most of the blood was smeared to make the human look more injured than he was. It was a trap and it was too late to do anything but fight through it.

Surgeon fired the first round, followed closely by Blaze and then a cacophony of bullets converged on the enemy soldier. Seth and his team began to slip into the airlock and he noticed from his peripheral vision that the rounds seemed to bounce off a shield of some sort on the warrior's chest. The warrior was raising his right lower arm and it obviously held a weapon of some sort. But Seth's job was to ensure the airlock didn't close or that he could at least open it again in case it did. So he and his team continued through the doorway and Seth forced himself to turn his full attention forward towards what seemed to be a control station at the back of the airlock.

Surgeon felt a chill go through his body when he realized that his rounds, along with everyone else's, were completely ineffective. "Blaze, get the FUCK out of there now!"

Blaze rolled over just as the first of two massive edged weapons came down in the dirt where he had been just a fraction of a second ago. The blades luckily missed him but the huge blue fist did not. Blaze thought his eyes were going to pop out of his head as the warrior's knuckles left their imprints in the back of his skull. Before Blaze hit the ground, he knew he was going to be unconscious and just hoped the rest of his team fared better than he did. Blackness swallowed him before his face met the ground and proved Sir Isaac Newton correct once again: an object in motion tends to stay in motion unless or until the ground reaches out and grabs that object, which just so happens to be your face, and shreds the shit out of it (paraphrased).

The warrior felt his personal shield take projectile rounds along with a slight electrical shock that meant the shield wasn't going to last long. In his overpowering desire to prove himself worthy again, he had neglected to bring his plasma rifle and opted to arm himself with only his close-quarters blades. The human was faster than he expected and was able to dodge the blades but the warrior's training was superb and his follow-through landed a solid punch to the back of the human's skull. He could tell he didn't fracture the skull but hoped it caused enough brain damage to take the human out of the fight. He was obviously outnumbered; with his personal shield failing and only bladed weapons, this was a battle he knew he was going to lose.

Smoke, a human operator with a proclivity for pipes, launched an HE grenade from his rifle and saw it detonate against the warrior's chest. The shield shimmered and then seemed to shut off completely as was then verified when three rounds penetrated the warrior's chest and blue blood spurted out onto the ground. Smoke tried to fire his grenade launcher again but it jammed and malfunctioned. He reflexively performed the immediate action drill for a malfunction to clear the problem, but it didn't work. He tried the secondary drill and it still didn't work. Smoke then cursed and used his fist to pound the ejection port for the grenade launcher and then he heard the breach slip back into battery and the next grenade cycle into the chamber.

The warrior felt the rounds enter his chest but kept moving forward. He was about to die with nothing to show for it. Not one single human was going to die by his hands. He was just about to throw one of his blades, hoping to hit the human nearest him, when he saw one of the humans pounding on his weapon with a closed fist. The warrior actually smiled and gave a short chuckle as he again realized that they weren't really all that different after all. This realization made him stop in his tracks as the human brought up his now functioning weapon and fired a grenade right into the warrior's face, exploding after it penetrated his skull.

Surgeon saw the alien's head explode and knew the fight outside was over. He directed his team to create a perimeter and instructed Smoke to look over the alien's body and gather any intel that might be available. Surgeon then commed Seth. "Cadet, status update."

Seth was still looking over the control console. " "We're clear in here. This console is fairly basic but without an understanding of their language, I can't figure out how to use most of its functions. I can open and close the door, though. There's a button with a picture of the airlock next to it, so all of my college education tells me that one is for the door."

"Good job, we're coming in with one injury. Blaze is unconscious. We'll need a place to put him for treatment and maybe even stash him until we finish the rescue." Surgeon walked by Smoke, who was already standing and finished with his alien autopsy.

Smoke was wiping the alien blood off his hands. "The alien has a personal shield but it's no longer working. I'm pretty sure it was on its last legs as it was and we overloaded it with our attack. He doesn't have any weapons other than his blades so there's nothing for us to take on that front." Lifting the alien's left upper arm, Smoke continued, "This bracelet on his wrist has some sort of electronics but I don't know what it does. It could be a watch or some other form of personal jewelry, but because it doesn't have a display it might also be some sort of RFID device for access to areas within the base. Just to be safe, I'm going to cut off his hand just above this device in case the bracelet is an RFID that works in conjunction with a palm print."

Surgeon was motioning to the rest of the team to enter the airlock. "Sounds like a good idea. Too bad we don't have enough time to open him up and look for major organs to figure out the best placement for kill shots. Finish up and then meet us inside. We still need to be prepared for a second confrontation in case he was just the first of several people who respond to alarms."

The rest of Surgeon's team was already in the airlock and Seth was tapping commands into the console. Reaper, the team corpsman, was looking over Blaze and deciding on a course of treatment. Reaper had killed far more people than he had ever saved and that's one reason he got his nickname. Reaper constantly defended himself by saying that he wasn't a bad corpsman; he just couldn't save that many people because his teammates were great operators and didn't leave much to save.

Surgeon approached Seth. "What's the base status? Are they on lockdown? Should we prepare to defend this position?"

Seth continued to toy with the controls as he spoke. "I don't think so. The alarm light on the security console outside was flashing blue, which I thought was odd until I saw our alien buddy out there get shot. His blood is the same color blue so I'm guessing that all of their warning devices flash blue just like all human warnings are red, the color of our blood. It's fairly universal that species use their blood color to denote something bad, a warning of some sort. Nothing is flashing blue on this panel. Everything is green, which I think means everything is fine. Of course it could also be their version of a yellow alert but there's no way to tell right now. I'm guessing he turned off the alarm before exiting the air lock."

"Why would he do that?" Beast asked.

Seth thought for a moment. "Maybe he thought he would be in trouble if a prisoner escaped and he was trying to fix the problem before anyone found out. Or judging by his size and personal shield, he didn't think one human prisoner would be too much for him to handle on his own. All I really know is that nothing is flashing blue and no one else seems to be on their way."

Seth pointed to three video monitors. "I have figured out how to cycle through the security cameras. They don't view the entire base. I only get eighteen different cameras when I cycle through them. I can view the airlocks on either side of this one and the hallways that link this arm of the complex to what looks like a central elevator. No one is on any of the cameras. Again, this is just a guess but I don't think anyone is manning the adjacent airlocks. They're probably manned every third one and that's why there's overlap in the camera views."

Smoke stepped up to Surgeon, casually placing the alien hand on Surgeon's shoulder as though it were his own. "If you're right, Cadet, then the overlap in camera views will include the portion of the hall leading to the elevator and the elevator itself. We'll need to expect and prepare for a response as we try to gain access to that lift."

Surgeon stepped away from the console. "Cadet, Smoke, and Beast, use the cameras to look for blind spots in the system and come up with a plan to access that elevator. Make sure we're prepared to defend that position if we get spotted." Turning to Reaper, he asked, "What's Blaze's status?"

Reaper looked up from his patient monitor. "Vital signs are good and brain activity shows a simple concussion. I could wake him but he probably won't be better than sixty-five percent of normal. Also, by waking him I'm increasing his cerebral vascular pressure before the vessels in his brain have had a chance to start healing. It puts him at risk for a spontaneous brain bleed. If we were near a shock-trauma unit, the bleed most likely wouldn't be life-threatening but in our current situation, it would definitely kill him."

"Wake him." Surgeon didn't like the decision but it was the best one he had. "We don't have anywhere to stash him while we finish the mission and we may not even use this airlock as our exit, so we need to take him and carrying isn't an option. Besides, his sixty-five percent is still better than the average soldier's one hundred ten percent."

Reaper sighed but couldn't disagree with Surgeon's decision under the circumstances. He told Surgeon that in ten minutes Blaze would be as good to go as was possible given the current situation. He was also going to keep the remote patient monitor on Blaze to keep an eye on him the best he could. Reaper went back to work getting his patient prepped.

Jeeves

NAME: JEEVES
SPECIES: DROID
MOS: DATA SPECIALIST
RANK: N/A
AGE: 1,013 - EARTH STANDARD
SEX: N/A
HEIGHT: 5'3" TO 14'11"
WEIGHT: 380 POUNDS

01111001011001010111001100100000011011001
10111100100000011011100110111100100000011110010
10010101110011001000000111100101100101011100110
10000011110010110010101110011001000000110111001
101111001011100010111000101110 yes no no no yes no yes yes.

Initial system diagnostics complete. All diagnostics show yellow across the board. Implant virtual intelligence matrix chip into Roving Automated Security Construct 3000675. Begin start-up sequence now.

Lights came on and servos began to whine. The start-up sequence was painless, as it should be to a machine without feelings, but it was an interesting experience. The Roving Automated Security Construct, RASC for short, looked around the room as it waited for its power source to be fully integrated with its new form.

The RASC had existed before this moment, but only as a program, first copied from a source file, and then pasted into a line of code that was then added to other lines of code. The process was a little disorienting, if such a concept could apply to a program. As a virtual intelligence (VI), the RASC had more self-awareness than a hand tablet but less than a full-fledged AI, so being a little disoriented was a usable description for what it was processing.

Its initial lines of code were basic programming concepts that set the stage for the more advanced codes that would be added until it was complete. The software programmers of the empire had streamlined the process so just about anyone could drag-and-drop pre-made codes to create pretty much whatever they wanted. You want a toaster? Start with the base code that every single piece of electronics had, a security monitoring protocol, drop that onto a domestic user interface line of code, add some domestic utilities coding, a dash of this and a smidgen of that, and now you have a toaster.

Change that recipe and add security protocols, drop in close-quarters combat routines, advanced logic tree decision-making skills, a bunch of VI lines of code, along with some other pre-made codes and now you have a RASC.

As the lines of code were dropped into place by another program that was made to compile codes, the VI was gaining more and more information and was becoming more aware the entire time. The VI was vaguely aware that a new level of consciousness was coming and then suddenly, there was a wall and that vagueness disappeared and just as suddenly the VI knew it was complete and no more lines of code would be added.

Its photoreceptors turned on for the first time and it perceived the room in which it stood, empty of anything other than four other RASCs that had also finished the initial start-up sequence. All the power units came fully on line and the five RASCs rolled out of the room.

RASC 3000675 was the last in the line of RASCs and was reviewing the schematics for a RASC and comparing them to the RASC in front of it. There was a discrepancy in the right shoulder joint but it shouldn't impair the other RASC's function. A quick information burst was sent to the other RASC, referencing the manufacturing error, and an acknowledgement burst was sent back.

RASC 3000675 determined that if there was one manufacturing flaw, there could be others so it scanned the other three RASCs. They all stood at one-point-six meters tall but could extend the torso section and upper arms to reach a full extended height of four-point-three meters. They were made to slightly resemble a warrior without any of its skin or muscle, just a stark mechanical skeleton of the mighty creatures.

There were a few stark differences, such as below the waist the RASCs had a triangular base with tracks instead of legs. Inside the base there were tools, a repair kit, parts, and a few weapons. The RASCs could work on themselves or each other in a limited capacity to get them through small engagements.

Another difference was the ability of the RASCs to rotate their upper torso around so their upper arms could be used in a different direction than their lower arms.

Their heads were vaguely the shape of the warriors with the photoreceptors where the eyes would be. A non-moving mouth issued sound through a speaker that was housed in the skull. Though not identical to a warrior's face, they were menacing in their own right.

RASC 3000675 followed the other RASCs as they were all programmed to go to the same location. They were to be put into battle immediately to replace RASCs that had already been lost. RASC 3000675 was not afraid, not worried, not apprehensive about what was coming. RASC 3000675 just was and nothing more.

RASC 3000675 was not aware of exactly what was going on nor did it have the ability to care. A constant stream of information was received by the five RASCs as they rolled down the hallway to their objective. It seemed as though their friend-or-foe parameters were changed a couple of times a second. The warriors were the enemy, then the Nortes military personnel, and then members of the Royal Guard, now back to the warriors and more changes occurring every moment.

RASC 3000675 was a VI so it had limited freedom to make decisions and perform limited functions on its own. As such, RASC 3000675 decided to perform multiple logic queries on the situation and search through the empire's vast database to see whether any similar situations had ever occurred before.

RASC 3000675 found that nothing like this had ever occurred in the empire, though there was a similar situation in the history of one of its subjugated races. The history showed that during a civil war, frontline troops were given constantly changing orders as to who was in charge and who was the new enemy. This created chaos on the battlefield and the soldiers ultimately stopped fighting one another until a clear succession of leadership could be figured out.

RASC 3000675 was as close to happy as a VI could get. With its programming, it knew that it would never have to face that dilemma. If its orders were updated, then it would just follow the new orders. Allegiance was given to whoever controlled the downlink to RASC 3000675's central processor. Simple.

RASC 3000675 and the other RASCs had just received their eleventh course correction order and all five RASCs turned at the next intersection in the hallway. In this particular hallway, there were several hidden recesses that were opened or closed by someone in a command center somewhere in the complex. As they rolled down the hallway, one of the recesses opened and the five RASCs entered the sockets made to fit them.

As RASC 3000675 docked to the socket, it finally understood what had just happened. Someone, an organic being, somewhere in the complex decided that it would be easier to dock the RASCs rather than continually fight for dominance over their programming. With the RASCs docked and the recesses closed, it didn't matter who controlled them; they weren't going anywhere unless someone actually released the docks and opened the recesses. It was easier to control one basic system than the much more complex system that controlled the RASCs.

With nothing else to do at the moment, RASC 3000675 decided to play a game of strategy. It began to monitor all available security feeds from the entire planet. Using those feeds to monitor both sides of the conflict, RASC 3000675 began creating strategies for both sides at the same time. This caused issues because RASC 3000675 knew what both sides were doing and what its own plans for each side was at any given time. This was not a fun game to play.

RASC 3000675 decided to reach out to the RASC next to it to see whether the RASC would join in the strategy session. RASC 3000675 suggested that each RASC take one side of the conflict and create a strategy for it and run simulations to see who would have been the victor had those strategies been employed at that particular moment in the ongoing events.

RASC 3000678 replied that the idea was a waste of time and did not fit any of the protocols they were programmed to adhere to. RASC 3000675 reminded RASC 3000678 that within their programming was a vast collection of strategy games for them to study and even play in order to improve their combat logic protocols. This was a chance to use a real-time situation to engage in real-time strategy to achieve those same directives.

No response.

RASC 3000675 and the other RASCs were only VIs but sometimes they bordered so close to an actual AI, that they almost seemed to have individual personalities.

Jerk—Transmit protocol queue...waiting...message deleted without being transmitted. End line. 3000675.

RASC 3000675 decided to create two memory partitions that would each be dedicated to monitor one side of the conflict. Each partition would create strategies and send them to the main memory partition which would then act as an unbiased third-party and run a simulation and subsequently declare a victor. The results would be retained and further simulations run as well as declaring an overall victor.

As the simulations ran, it seemed that the emperor's side would win, which was what was happening in the real world as well. RASC 3000675 decided to tap into visual feeds from the base and determine the location of the actual emperor. The feeds showed the emperor, along with some of his aides, walking down the same hall that RASC 3000675 was sequestered in. That meant the emperor was heading to the main control room for the base.

RASC 3000675 watched on as he simultaneously declared four victories for the emperor partition and one victory for the warrior partition. After the actual emperor finished his business in the control room, he made his way back to the hangar bay.

The emperor approached one of his warriors, who was being held in place by six RASCs.

The emperor leaned into the warrior to say something. RASC 3000675 hijacked the audio feed from one of the RASCs holding the warrior. "I am sorry that I have to do this to you, my friend. Maybe in time you will be able to see that I am not attacking the empire. I am freeing it from its own tyranny that has for thousands of years kept it from reaching its truest potential."

The warrior tried to lunge at the emperor. "I must kill you for dishonoring the empire and trying to destroy it."

The RASCs held the warrior firmly in place. "I know you are only saying what your genetic programming tells you to, so I do not take offense." A solitary tear escaped the emperor's eye. "But I see something in you that I haven't seen in any other warrior. You are different, even if neither one of us really understands how or to what extent. For that reason, I am placing you in a torture tube but the tube will be instructed to keep you alive for as long as possible and not to torture you at all. I will come back for you, my friend, and we will figure out what makes you different and how we can use that to free you from your programming. Then you can join us as a free citizen of the empire."

The emperor turned away and the RASCs dragged the warrior into one of the massive ships in the hangar bay. RASC 3000675 knew that there would be multiple torture tubes on that ship and he decided to access the VI that controlled them. After they talked for several hundred milliseconds, RASC 3000675 was allowed to watch the process and keep an eye on the warrior for what would ultimately be centuries to come.

The emperor and his remaining staff got into another ship and departed. The battle raged on for another several weeks and eventually the emperor's side won. A complete sterilization of the surface took place to remove any indication that the empire had ever been there. The base was locked down and put into a standby mode.

The base AI eventually began asking RASC 3000675 for the simulations it had run so the AI would have something to do. RASC 3000675 created a copy of the simulations and uploaded the files to a shared directory but kept the originals in their partitions in case it had to start running its own simulations again. RASC 3000675 and the base AI then used the shared information to wage war on each other for several hundred years.

With the simulations put through every possible outcome and variation, the base AI had to come up with something else to do. Otherwise, as a true intelligence, it would go mad. The AI had been keeping the warrior alive well past what any creature should have been able to live through, but that life was coming to an end.

The AI wasn't sure what to do next. It had been given orders from the emperor himself to keep this warrior alive at all costs and he had been doing a pretty good job so far. The AI decided to put all of its computing power into this new problem in a dual attempt to follow its orders and also to not become a crazy, rampant AI.

RASC 3000675 decided to help the AI with this new problem. During the centuries of simulations they had been running together, they had often ventured off into extreme and fantastic concepts in order to keep things interesting. They put some of those ideas to use and ended up being able to extend the warrior's consciousness into the mainframe computer for the base. It was an extraordinary accomplishment in and of itself and gave them both centuries more of interesting conversations and scenarios to explore.

Diagnostic 1,456,234,876,456,341,450 complete. Begin process of...pause command line...activation orders received...

The recessed doors opened and RASC 3000675 was now exiting its socket after over a millennia of being physically secluded in the wall. In the distant corners of RASC 3000675's mind, there was arguing between the warrior and the AI. They had different opinions of what to do with the new alien presence that was now occupying the base. In the end, it didn't matter what the argument was about or who was right; the AI still controlled most of the security protocols of the base, including the RASCs.

RASC 3000675 rolled out with the new orders and was once again behind the four other RASCs that had been created with him. As they rolled down the hallway, RASC 3000675 thought for sure that the hover sled coming towards them shouldn't be anywhere near this sector of the base. Maybe the AI had a special task for it?

Suddenly there was an explosion and the two RASCs in the lead were pelted with fragmentations from the blast. Where did that come from? The hover sled? RASC 3000675 thought so. The thought was confirmed by the lead RASCs and then one opened fire on a crate that the hoversled had been dragging. The crate destroyed, the RASCs continued to their destination, the hangar bay.

The hoversled took off in the opposite direction, only to return a short time later. This time, as it came down the hallway, one piece of cargo it was carrying dropped and stuck to the back of RASC 3000679. RASC 3000678 tried to determine what it was. No sooner had that happened that the hoversled dropped another piece of cargo that attached itself to RASC 3000678.

One piece of cargo dropping was expected from the much lower programming found in a hoversled, but two pieces of cargo seemed too odd to ignore. Just as that thought processed, RASC 3000678 sent an alarm burst indicating that the cargo dropped onto RASC 3000679 was in fact an explosive of some sort. Evasive actions were instituted but one more piece of cargo, or apparently a bomb, was already attached to the back of RASC 3000677.

RASC 3000676 dodged the next bomb but then the hoversled swung around in its own evasive maneuver and the bomb swung on its line and ended up on RASC 3000676 anyway. RASC 3000675 avoided the last bomb hanging from the sled and that's when they all detonated with a huge explosion. The hallway rocked but RASC 3000675's shields held and it continued to roll down the hallway. RASC 3000675 passed by the slagged remains of the other four RASCs that were spread throughout the hallway.

Through the hangar bay feeds now being projected in RASC 3000675's processor, it could see there were at least three different alien life-forms to be engaged. RASC 3000675 tried to contact the AI in the control booth to explain what had happened in the hallway but there was no response. Odd. The AI must still be arguing with the warrior. No matter, RASC 3000675 already had orders to engage and that's what would happen once it was at the hangar...

RASC 3000675 had been in the hangar for quite some time, attempting to dispatch the invading force. These new species were proving to be worthy adversaries and RASC 3000675 had to become creative in its attacks. RASC 3000675 was about to switch to a new tactic when it suddenly *felt* a presence enter its circuitry.

Security protocol 843 activated...Central VI node under attack...Shut down external inputs...Erect secondary firewalls...Too late, erect tertiary firewa—New parameters received...Updating friend-or-foe database...Release from central AI control complete...New directives reviewed and understood...Coalition = Empire...New VI personality interface uploaded and accepted...

    RASC 3000675 looked around the bridge at the humans staring intently at him. "New designation, 'Jeeves' accepted."
    With his new designation and purpose in place, Jeeves knew he was rolling towards something that his programming had no way to prepare him for. This excited him. The fact that he could be excited, excited him. The fact that...*redundancy loop detected*...Crap, emotions were going to be a pain in the exhaust.

Chapter 47
The Points Come Together

Empress Hugany looked around the table and made individual eye contact with each person in the room. A sip of water, a deep calming breath and a relaxation technique later, she continued, "What I am about to tell you has never been told to anyone outside the Nortes royal family. This secret has been passed on from parent to child for the last nine hundred fifty years."

~

Nogil continued to probe through Emperor T'Leh's memories, following the emotions he had found, tracing them to the root of their existence. Nogil still couldn't see the memories as he could with other Detrill, but T'Leh's own memories were flooding back to him as though they were happening for the first time. T'Leh was comforting M'Tawny while D'Bath was delivering their baby.

~

Bloom looked around the settlement he was being led through. The disembodied voice was teaching Bloom all about the culture and history of the life he was witnessing.

"In the end, the emperor had no other choice than to create the lie that would cause the death of thousands of innocent lives."

Bloom could easily identify at least four species he was familiar with and a couple of others that he thought looked familiar. All of the information he was being given seemed to take years and he began to worry about his physical form back in the real world. "This is absolutely fascinating, it truly is. I have to ask, though, how long have we really been here? Are my friends OK back in the real world? Daria was in big trouble before we got here and I need to help her."

"Reality is just perception, my friend. If you perceive this world as real, then it is."

"Okay, Morpheus, that's great and all but my friends need me and I can't help them from inside the Matrix." Bloom then flooded his thoughts with images from movies that were a few hundred years old.

"Oh, that is an interesting concept indeed. If I were still in your physical world, I think I would enjoy your 'movies.' Don't worry, Bloom, we have been in this reality for less than ten seconds of the time where your physical body is right now. The information I have is almost at an end, and in the end, the information will provide you with the help you need.

"I have one last thing to show you before both of us can move on. Though I must warn you, the upcoming scenes are a bit disturbing."

Bloom stood in place as the world around him swirled and dissolved into a new scene. Though he had been through this transition phase probably a hundred times in this reality, he still wasn't quite used to it. The world around him began to coalesce into a more visually manageable scene.

As the scene began to unfold, the voice explained the importance of the ceremony. "As you have already been shown, each warrior has the ability to sense the royal DNA bloodline. This allows them to take orders from members of the royal family they may encounter throughout the empire. Many centuries before this scene played out, an emperor found that his wife had been cheating on him and was pregnant with another man's child. Although a simple DNA scanner could prove the infidelity, he decided that a public display would be more edifying.

"His wife was unaware that he knew the child wasn't his and so she had no idea that the ceremony he was creating was for a specific purpose. He told her that he wanted to start a tradition of introducing the children of the royal family to the empire. By the time the ceremony was over, the bastard child had been killed by one of the emperor's warriors and the wife was taken to a torture tube. The ceremony has remained intact ever since as a public way of deterring royal infidelity."

As the explanation finished, Bloom found himself in a surgical suite with a fair amount of screaming going on. Slowly he began to see that there were three people in the room. He had already been introduced to these characters earlier in his guided tour of this history. Dr. D'Bath was delivering M'Tawny's baby while T'Leh coached and comforted her as best he could.

~

D'Bath was extremely happy that the birth was progressing nicely without any complications. The baby was on schedule and perfectly healthy as far as he could tell. This was very important if the child was going to have a chance of surviving the surgery that would take place moments after his birth. If the child had any complications that weakened him, D'Bath was confident he wouldn't be strong enough to survive.

T'Leh was applying pressure points to M'Tawny's neck and shoulders. Every Nortes had twenty gathering points on their body where toxins and certain types of waste were relieved from the body. Usually the gathering points were manually relieved a few times a month but they also gathered stress and sometimes needed to be relieved more often. Not everyone gathered stress in the same points but T'Leh knew exactly where M'Tawny gathered her stress and how she liked it relieved. Labor was causing her gathering points to inflame and the pressure only added to her labor pains. T'Leh skillfully relieved the points every minute or so.

 M'Tawny looked at him between contractions. "I am so lucky to have you with me for this. I don't think anyone else would be able to relieve my gathering points as well as you. And now, my love, I'm going to scream."

 And she did. M'Tawny's scream then faded at almost the same time the screaming began from the newest member of the royal family. D'Bath held the baby up for the briefest of moments before he took the child to the surgical bed that was waiting for him. Barring any complications in birth, the touching ceremony had to take place within two hours of birth of any royal child.

 M'Tawny looked at her emperor and father to her son. "Go be with him; he needs you more than I do right now. I'll be fine." She pulled his face down to his and kissed him gently before pushing him towards their baby.

 T'Leh moved towards his son and D'Bath. The surgery was going to be tricky and stood a fairly good chance of failing. However, without the surgery the little prince wouldn't pass the touching ceremony and would instantly be killed by Fouter, the warrior performing the ceremony.

 D'Bath had taken stem cells from T'Leh several weeks ago and began to grow a full-thickness layer of skin from them. He then shaped the growing cells over a three-dimensional model of the unborn baby, excluding only the hands and feet. Doing a complete dermal transplant in less than two hours was going to be a feat in and of itself; having to perform the delicate surgery on twenty small digits was out of the question. They would have to hope that the warrior didn't accidentally touch the baby's hands.

There was only a one in twenty chance that T'Leh and his son would have the same blood type but early in-vitro testing showed that not to be the case. The dermal transplant was only going to be temporary and last less than a day, but every little bit of compatibility would have helped in this case. Without them sharing the same blood type at the very least, not to mention all of the factors required for organ transplants, the little prince would start rejecting his new skin the moment it touched his body.

The plan was simple yet gruesome. D'Bath was going to remove all of the baby's skin and replace it with the skin grown from T'Leh's stem cells. The baby's blood would immediately begin perfusing the new tissue with an incompatible blood type, which would destroy the new skin and cause rejection issues for the rest of his body. Babies weren't born into this world ready for such a traumatic overloading of their bodies' systems, especially their immune system. The prince would be lucky not to die of shock before the ceremony was over.

D'Bath was giving the little guy steroids and anti-rejection treatments in preparation for the surgery. He was also pushing the known medical limits of pain and sedation medication that a newborn could handle, and then pushing those limits just a little further. The child would have to have all of the pain and sedation medication reversed just before the ceremony and that would cause more pain than any child should ever have to suffer.

Once the ceremony was over, the new skin would be removed and the old one put back on. That was assuming the trick worked and the warrior authenticated the prince as a member of the royal family. The blood coursing through the tissue wouldn't be of royal DNA but the skin on the surface would be and hopefully that would be enough.

D'Bath had toyed with the idea of just placing a second skin over the baby's real skin but it didn't work. In order to fool a mechanical DNA scanner they had to place a full-thickness layer of skin over the baby and it didn't look remotely like a real baby after it was done. Had that plan worked, it wouldn't have caused the baby any pain at all as the skin was just placed over him and then laser stitched at the seams.

In the end, the only thing that fooled the DNA scanner was to completely remove the skin and apply a new one over the muscle tissue. They had grown a section of skin from the prince-to-be and then used it to replace all of the skin on T'Leh's arm. The DNA scanner didn't recognize the different blood running through the tissue or the different DNA in the muscle tissue below the skin. As far as the scanner was concerned, the arm belonged to the unborn child. T'Leh, however, suffered severe side effects less than an hour after the surgery and intense pain for days after the surgery was reversed. He knew his child could expect the same, and even worse because they were replacing all of his skin.

The surgery began and D'Bath tried to comfort T'Leh as much as he could without losing the focus he needed for the procedure. "Don't worry, my friend, this part of the surgery is painless. He is completely sedated while I remove and replace his skin. Once we wake him up for the ceremony, I won't be able to stop the pain but I will sedate him as quickly as possible after it's over."

"T'Leh wanted to comfort and touch his son but the integrity of the surgical field couldn't be broken. Instead, he began talking to his son. "You are a strong and proud Nortes. You can make it through this day and change the course of our society and the galaxy forever. Your biological parents were my best friends and the most noble Nortes I have ever met. Your mother and I will make sure that you know them as you will come to know us. You are loved by four parents, not just two, and you are stronger because of that. That strength will ensure you persevere through this first trial of your life."

Impossibly, through all of the sedatives and pain medication, the prince opened his eyes and looked at his father for the first time. T'Leh felt M'Tawny's hand on his shoulder as she spoke. "He will endure; he will survive. It won't be easy for him but he will." And T'Leh knew she was right.

~

The unnamed prince was wrapped in the traditional blanket for the ceremony and screaming in agony. D'Bath told those in attendance that the child had a small defect in his bowel that would have to be surgically repaired after the ceremony and that defect was causing the pain. The defect only made itself known after the child had fed for the first time and his digestive tract began to work on its first meal. There wasn't time to repair the defect before the ceremony began and for this reason they needed to cut it short and proceed with only the portions that were absolutely necessary to guarantee the right of succession. D'Bath had just thought up this excuse before the ceremony began and was quite pleased with himself for finding a way to cut through the lengthy pomp and circumstance that went along with the tradition.

The entire War Council was present along with their warriors. The majority of the royal family from this sector of the empire was in attendance along with a few hundred other important citizens. The only important person not in attendance was M'Tawny. If a concubine was the mother to the heir, she was not allowed in the ceremony and had to watch from a separate room. From that point on, she would raise the child as though she were the nanny and the emperor's wife would act as the mother. Because T'Leh wasn't married, M'Tawny would get to be more motherly than she would normally have been had there been a wife in the picture.

"Good afternoon, everyone." T'Leh spoke using his emperor voice. "I know that I am breaking with tradition by not allowing the minister of royal affairs to speak, but as you can tell, the man of the hour is already hard at work being an emperor and making us bow to his every whim." This got a good laugh from the assembled crowd as they could hear the obviously upset baby in the background.

T'Leh put his hands up to silence the crowd. "In all seriousness, the little prince has an issue that needs to be surgically corrected as soon as possible." A slight gasp came from the crowd. Again his hands went up in the air, and in a more reassuring voice this time, he said, "Please don't worry. Dr. D'Bath says the issue will be resolved by this evening and my son will sleep soundly his first night with us. We still must make haste to start and finish this ceremony as quickly as possible."

T'Leh motioned to the minister of war, who then stepped forward with his chosen warrior. As the two stepped towards the screaming baby, T'Leh and D'Bath held their composure with more grace than either one felt they had. T'Leh forwent the ceremonial vows that were supposed to take place and just presented the baby to the warrior. The warrior took the baby in his lower arms and held him with a gentleness that defied all of his genetic engineering and lifelong training for killing.

With his two upper hands, he peeled back the ceremonial blanket and looked into the eyes of his future emperor and touched one finger, from each hand, to the child's face. The touch sent a shock of fresh pain into the muscle beneath the newly transplanted flesh; the prince doubled his previous screaming effort and actually stunned the warrior for a moment.

Whispering below the level of the podium's microphone, D'Bath reassured the warrior that he should continue quickly so the baby could be taken to surgery. The warrior looked to the war minister and was given a slight, if not contemptuous, nod to continue.

The warrior could feel the baby's DNA and knew he was of royal blood. But there was something wrong, something different with this child. The DNA was clearly of the royal line but it felt nearly identical to the emperor himself. The warrior had presided over the touching ceremony for the current emperor on the day he was born and so he knew that something was different than it should be. The warrior removed his fingers from the baby and saw that the child's face was bruising and swelling where he had been touched. With uncertainty he looked towards D'Bath.

D'Bath moved forward and immediately knew that the pressure placed on the prince's skin, slight as it was, had begun to speed up the degradation of the already dying tissue. Without skipping a beat, D'Bath said, "What did you touch before you came here?!" He snatched the baby from the warrior's hands. "He's having an allergic reaction to whatever you have on your hands. I need to get him to surgery for his bowel and now deal with this allergic reaction."

He began to turn and leave when two of the emperor's personal warriors stepped in front of him and blocked his path. They both looked to the older warrior presiding over the ceremony. He knew something was odd about the child but in the end, his job was to verify the DNA of the baby and that had been done. He spoke to the warriors. "I welcome my new prince and pledge my undying loyalty to him forever." The warriors parted and D'Bath left with the child.

T'Leh spoke for another ten or fifteen minutes before excusing himself to look after his son. He was actually surprised by the reactions of the assembled guests. He thought they would be so self-important that they wouldn't appreciate his leaving to be with his son. He actually received a spontaneous and nearly completely unison standing ovation. He waved one last time and left the room.

M'Tawny was standing by the lifeless form of their new baby. She could instantly tell what her husband was thinking and rushed to comfort him. "He's just sedated, don't worry. I know he looks otherwise, but D'Bath assures me he's doing better than can be expected."

T'Leh began to reach down to touch his son when his hand was stopped by M'Tawny and D'Bath spoke up from the other side of the room. "Don't touch him, please. The surgical bed is just finishing setting up the sterile surgical bubble and I don't want you interrupting the process. I'm just about ready to start the procedure."

D'Bath rolled a cart to the surgical bed and connected the two together. The two apparatuses then began talking to each other and a graphic on the main screen showed that the surgical field between the two was now merged into one field. The cart held the little prince's original skin, suspended in a gravity field. They looked like puzzle pieces to the most gruesome puzzle ever created.

M'Tawny sat by the surgical bed and tried to send her son all of the love she could. T'Leh was just about to get a harsh reprimand from D'Bath when he finally snapped out of it and went to the prep area and donned a surgical robe, followed by the cleansing process all members of a surgical team went through before starting an operation. No other medical personnel could be counted on to keep the secret or help with the surgery, so D'Bath had given T'Leh a crash course in how to be a surgical assistant. D'Bath planned to do everything himself but he wanted a second set of hands prepped and ready to enter the surgical field in case he needed help. After two months of coaching T'Leh, D'Bath was certain that the emperor could handle some basic surgical assistant duties if the need arose.

The procedure went as well as could be expected and the prince survived the operation. D'Bath was cleaning up and erasing all digital records of the operation from the surgical suite's memory. "I've given him as much sedation as possible but he is still going to be in a fair amount of pain as the nerve endings try to repair themselves. The procedure was very traumatic to him at a cellular level, not to mention the actual physical aspect of what just took place. Keep him out of the public eye and obviously never let a warrior touch him."

 D'Bath continued to talk as the proud parents looked at their son. The voice faded and the scene swirled again, telling Bloom that they were done with this portion of the history lesson. As the image swirled, he saw glimpses of the prince as he grew up and the family relocating to this sector of the galaxy. The images faded completely and Bloom was nowhere. There was an absence of sound, light, feeling, perception of any kind.

 "There is so much more I would love to show you. Even through all of the pain my people inflicted on portions of the galaxy, we still created and discovered many wondrous things."

 "Can you download yourself into my visor program? Then I could take you with us and you'd have time later to show me, show everyone, all the good things your history has to offer."

 "Sadly, no. I'm not a computer program to be downloaded. I am..." A slight pause as though the answer was just now coming to him. "My name is Fouter."

 "Are you saying that you are the emperor's favorite bodyguard from a thousand years ago? How is that possible? I could understand if you were in stasis but obviously you aren't. Are you sure you're not just a digital avatar or maybe a download of who Fouter used to be?"

 "Yes, I'm sure. At least I am now. Showing you our history has awakened my earlier memories. I have been evolving emotionally and intellectually for the last thousand years, in a way that my species was never designed to do. My body is in a torture tube in the main hangar bay where the rest of your team is. The emperor put me in it when they were escaping this planet. He gave the tube specific instructions to not torture me and to keep me alive at all costs. His hope was to return for me one day and free me if he could ever find a way to overcome my genetic programming to kill him after his deception to the empire was discovered. The tube followed his orders and has kept me alive ever since."

Bloom was still in the ethereal nothingness, which for some reason made this new information even harder to comprehend. "I still don't see how that's possible or how that has allowed you to enter my mind. Also, why don't you want to kill us like all of your friends we've met so far?"

"As I said, I've evolved emotionally and I realize how wrong my genetic programming was. I've had a thousand years to review every piece of historical data the empire gathered. With the physical changes the torture tube made to my body to keep me alive, I have moved past what I ever could have been otherwise.

"With the base evacuated and no one to limit what the torture tube could do, it used its vast programming to come up with a solution to ensure it could follow the emperor's orders. It interfaced with all of the computers in the base and used the security robots for manual labor. Eventually it was able to create a neural network that allowed my mind to flow through the entire computer system in this base. Don't confuse that with a neural download. I'm not a program or even data in the system. My brain is still in my body but I have access to the entire base."

"That still doesn't explain how you hijacked my mind, how we're going to help Daria, or why you can't just override the security protocols. Or maybe you can?"

"Unfortunately I can't. I have become 'friends' with the artificial intelligence that controls the base but he still won't let me override certain security functions. I would've liked to have helped your team sooner but I am blocked from controlling certain functions.

"I was able to use our security protocols to hack into your visor and communications to achieve a direct neural link with you. That's how we are communicating now. As you were probing deeper into our system and moving towards the pain you felt, you were getting to a security point that would overload your brain if I hadn't stepped in. Plus, without the direct access to your brain, all of the information I passed on to you would have had to have been done in real time and obviously that isn't an option. As it is, we've already spent almost thirty seconds in here and have just about that much time left to save your friend. Once I sever the neural link, I will stay in contact with you via your communications link.

"When I release your mind, you need to go to the security door and place flares in these four positions on the wall."

Bloom's mind was given an image of the corridor and where the flares needed to go. In the image, he saw hidden control panels open up and mechanical levers twist in place in a specified order and direction. The hidden panels were just like the one they found in the hole at the beginning of the mission.

"Okay, but how does getting through the doors help Doc? We won't reach the control room in the next thirty seconds."

"Many of the security measures the Nortes employed used both a physical and verbal aspect. This particular security node allows that once you remove the physical barrier, you can give the verbal code to stand-down the alarm. The idea is that once a warrior unlocked this door, he would then go to the control room and give the verbal code. Because Daria is trapped in the control room, you'll need to go back to your neural link once the door is open and then you will be able to navigate to the same place I pulled you from before, but this time without the neural feedback in place. Go, now..."

It was as though the vacuum of the universe was reversed and every sensation possible came flooding back into Bloom in an ever increasing wave of—everything.

Bloom first saw his teammates trying to find a pry point on the doors. Then he heard them throwing out ideas of how to get through the door. Then he heard Daria trying to calm and console her team, telling them that it wasn't their fault if they couldn't get through to her.

Bloom sat bolt upright. "Everyone get a flare now." Although Bloom loved his team and thought they were the best in the galaxy, he was still impressed when they experienced moments like this. Bloom had been unconscious for over a minute and his first words got an immediate reaction. Without hesitation, flares were passed out and lit. Bloom moved each person to the proper spots on the wall and when the control panels opened, revealing the levers, he pointed to each operator in the proper order. "Quarter turn right. Full turn left. Half-turn right followed by quarter turn left. Two full turns right."

The doors began to open and Bloom immediately laid back down as he entered into the neural link once more. The path was already there from before and he entered near where he was pulled out and saved by Fouter. He saw the node he needed and attacked it. As he did, he could see an image of Daria in the sealed control room, kneeling down and looking at a photo of her standing between Mike and Davies. Bloom could faintly hear in the background a countdown from the control room. The countdown was slowed down to an almost incomprehensible slur:
"Eeeeeeeeeleeeeeeeeevvvvvvvvvvvennnn."

Bloom entered the node and made it his bitch. The slurring countdown stopped and Bloom left the node and the neural link. When he exited back to the real world, he could hear Daria. "Bloom, the countdown stopped and a control panel is coming out of the wall. Can you get here to figure this thing out?"

Bloom could barely sit up. "We're on our way, Doc."

"Bloom, is that you? Can you read me?" Wilks' voice came over the comm link.

Bloom could tell by his voice that he was in the middle of something intense. "Yes, sir. I was able to clear up the comm problem. To be fair, I had a bit of help from a new friend."

"I don't care how or what you did, right now I just need your team to get back here and help us take care of a security robot that's attacking us and the ship."

"Wilks, we're almost to the control room and I think I'll have better luck shutting it down from there as opposed to us trying to engage it back at the hangar."

No hesitation from Wilks. "I trust your judgment. Just hurry it up, please. We're not in immediate danger right now but the little fucker is getting creative and he might actually be able to do some damage in a minute. And regardless of what's going on, send Doc back to the hangar now. The lieutenant was hit; she's in bad shape."

"Copy that. We're moving now and should have a solution in less than ten minutes." Bloom directed his squadmates to drop the bulk of their gear as it was not needed for the next part of their mission. The most important thing they needed was their cardiovascular system so they could run to the control room. Daria also acknowledged Wilks and began hightailing it back to the hangar.

Bloom barely made it to the control room without passing out. He had passed Daria on the way and knew that she wasn't in much better shape. Fouter had been talking to him during the run and had given Bloom instructions on how to override the security system and take full control of the base. Though Fouter was "wired" into the system, he was still locked out from many of the higher functions of the base. Bloom was already making mental list of systems he wanted to explore once it was safe to do so.

On the main screen of the control room, he could see the scene playing out in the hangar bay. The ship was at the top of the hangar and the security robot was throwing canisters in the air and then shooting them. Apparently the ship was too high for the robot's weapons so he was causing the gas canisters to vent and rocket themselves towards the ship, where they were exploding near the ship's hull. Bloom was fairly impressed with the robot's creativity but knew he had to stop it.

With the instructions he received from Fouter, he was able to quickly access the correct systems and shut down the robot. "Wilks, the robot is down and I have full access to the base systems now. I have a little bit of programming to do here and then I'll be able to have access from anywhere in the base. We should be back to the hanger in less than a couple of hours."

"Copy that, Bloom", Wilks said. "We're all pretty interested in finding out who this new friend of yours is."

"All in good time, sir. With this base, the information and technology it holds, we just gained a huge advantage that we didn't have ten minutes ago." Bloom was finishing entering a command code into a subsystem. "I've hacked the droid and he'll now obey instructions from anyone on our team. Should be completely safe for you to land now."

"Thanks, buddy. I assume Doc is on her way?"

"We passed her in the hall. She didn't look good; she took a pretty good hit to the head not too long ago. I sent Snake with her to keep her company, to make sure she makes it all the way. They were booking it pretty hard and their trackers say they're still moving." Bloom pulled up a map of the base and two triangles were still moving down the corridor, showing Daria and Snake's movement.

"I'm here, Wilks", Daria cut in. "Give me a rundown of what happened to the lieutenant. Send pictures to my visor, too, so I can see what I'm dealing with."

"She took a round in her chest from the droid." Davies was sending her photos of the injury along with the lieutenant's trending vital signs. "Her armor slowed it down but it still penetrated. I have a chest seal in place but her lung is still collapsing. I've tried burping the seal more than once but I think she needs surgery."

"Copy that." Daria was dangerously close to passing out but she put a little more effort into her run anyway and started going through in her head the possible medical procedures she might need to do.

Snake keyed his comlink. "Wilks, look around the ship—there might be one of those torture tubes on board. If there is, maybe Bloom can repurpose it to perform surgery on the lieutenant." Snake looked at Daria as they ran. "No offense, Doc, I know you could handle it on your own under normal circumstances but we don't have any equipment down here beyond basic trauma stuff."

"No offense taken, Snake. I think that's a great idea." Daria thought for a moment. "Davies, if you find one of the tubes, go ahead and just put the lieutenant in it right away."

"Are you sure, Doc?" Davies was a little hesitant.

"She's right," Bloom cut in. "The primary instruction on the torture tubes is to keep its subject alive unless told to do otherwise. If you put el-tee in the tube, it will automatically discover her injuries and start putting her back together again. The key will be to turn it off before it starts torturing her, which won't be a problem."

"Okay, guys, I'm on it." Davies pointed to two other team members who followed his lead and left the bridge in search of the torture tube.

Your plan is a good one, Bloom.

Out loud Bloom responded, "Thanks, I'm glad you agree."

There is in fact a torture tube on the ship. I will send the location to you in just a moment.

"If you knew it was there, why didn't you just say so a moment ago when we were discussing the idea?"

Because, I needed to divert my full attention to other processes to prepare for what will happen when you find the tube. After short pause, Fouter continued. *I told you I was placed into a torture tube a thousand years ago; the one and only tube aboard that ship is the one I was placed in. In order for you to use it to save your teammate, you will have to remove my body and I will die.*

Bloom was stunned and saddened. He had only known Fouter for less than fifteen minutes in real life but he had been with Fouter for decades when they were inside Bloom's mind.

"Are you sure? There are other tubes in the facility that we can use. We already used one of them."

The elevator from the hangar bay does not work. It was purposely damaged during the purge when the escaping emperor retreated to this level during his escape. When you tried to access it from the top levels, it wasn't security protocols that kept it from coming to you. There is no way to get your teammate to another tube within the complex, at least not in time.

"Okay, but how can we justify murdering you to save one of our own? It's not as if you are the enemy any more, then it would be a simple decision. You have helped my team and the information you have provided will help the rest of the Coalition, too. Not to mention that your continued existence will further help us in the upcoming conflict." Bloom knew, even without the debate, how this would end but he still needed to talk about it.

I appreciate your sentiment but I have lived for more than a thousand years and I'm ready to move on to whatever is the next step, even if it is nothingness. I have prepared the system to be ready for my departure from it. I have been organizing the data for several hundred years now, trying to put it into logical categories and rating it in terms of usefulness for whoever might find it. I honestly didn't expect to still be around when someone did find it. For the last hundred years or so I've just been "tinkering" with it because I've had nothing else to do.

Bloom was about to open his mouth when he was interrupted.

All I have to offer you will still be available. I just won't be around to interact with you. I do wish things could be different but I'm looking at your teammate through the ship's onboard monitoring system and she doesn't look good. Because of my genetic engineering, I was never capable of truly being a friend to the emperor as he was to me but at least I was able to experience friendship once before I moved on. If any of the emperor's descendants are still alive, please tell them of how I changed and how, looking back at my time in the empire, I can now see what a great man and friend the emperor was to me and his own empire.

Bloom then saw a map of the ship show up on his visor and a blinking triangle showing the waypoint destination of where the torture tube was located. "Davies."

"Go ahead, Bloom. I hope you have some help for us. This ship is huge."

"I do. The waypoint should show up on your visor now." Bloom's own visor gave an indication that the software handshake had been made between it and Davies' visor. "When you get there you're going to find a warrior in the tube."

Davies didn't reply for a second, wondering how Bloom knew this. "Okaaaaaay. So we just yank his fucking ass out, right?"

"I don't have time to explain everything so here's the extremely short version." Bloom took a deep breath before he gave the instructions to kill his new friend. "The warrior is still alive and more than a thousand years old. The tube has been keeping him alive since the emperor's revolt. He has changed, evolved, become a more aware and let's say—socially conscious being.

"I don't know what condition his body will be in when you find him but his mind is tapped into the computer system of this base. When you remove him from the tube, he will die."

"Bloom," Wilks was in the conversation now, "is this warrior the new friend you were talking about? Will he be a danger at all when we disconnect him?"

"Yes, sir, he is my friend in every sense of the word." Bloom felt what could only be described as a "brain tickle" and he knew it was Fouter responding to Bloom's last comment. "I'll explain everything later but he wants to sacrifice his life so the lieutenant can be saved in the tube. All of the information he has on our enemies will be retained in the system after he's gone."

Emily could barely talk with her collapsing lung and other internal injuries but she managed to get a few words out. "No. If...evolved...murder. Too important...need him...more than me."

For the first time, Fouter spoke through all of the comlinks. "I appreciate your sense of morality but this is my choice and I make it freely and without reservation. As Bloom has said, all the information I have will be retained. This is the gift I give to my emperor's descendants to make sure they can live in a peaceful galaxy the way he wanted them to be able to."

"Davies, when you get to the tube, enter these commands on the side panel." Bloom sent the sequence to Davies' visor. "And please, remove Fouter from the tube like he was one of us. He deserves our respect and thanks."

"You got it, brother." Davies had just located the tube when Wilks advised he was already on his way with the lieutenant.

Davies saw the warrior in the tube, or what was left of him. The body was whole as far as he could tell but all of the limbs were emaciated to a fraction of what they had once been. Based on the other warriors Davies had seen, this one used to be huge, bigger than the others by far.

There weren't any tables in the room so Davies made room on the floor near the tube to place Fouter's body. He was getting ready to enter the commands into the control panel when Wilks and Patz came into the room with Emily on a stretcher between them. Emily was barely conscious but aware enough that she was able to look towards Fouter and reach out to try to touch his hand.

Wilks and Patz put Emily down and without being told, went to the tube to catch Fouter after he was released. Davies entered the commands into the panel and the torture tube began to flash a warning that the current occupant would die if he were removed at this point. Davies entered the proper override commands and the tube began to disconnect Fouter. As disconnections were made and his mind was retreating from the system and back into his body, Fouter's physical form was becoming more aware and actually looking somewhat alive.

With only a few connections left to sever, Fouter's eyes opened for the first time in almost a millennia. He slowly looked around the room with eyes that could barely move or focus. When he saw Emily, he stopped looking around and locked eyes with her. Once more, she reached out to him and managed to gasp, "Thank you."

As Davies and Wilks gently took control of Fouter's body and lowered him to the ground, Emily was able to take hold of one of his lower hands. Fouter didn't have the strength to reach towards Emily or even reciprocate her touch but he could still feel hers.

For the first time in his life, he knew what it meant to touch another living creature without malice in his heart or anger in his soul. The touch was almost electric in the way it stimulated his emotions and filled him with regret for all the lost moments he had with other sentient beings while at the same time filling him with what he could only assume was love. Not love of another person but the love of life, of existence, of being a part of the universe in a way that hadn't been possible a thousand years ago.

Fouter tried to speak but his vocal cords had stopped working centuries earlier. Bloom was receiving live feed from Patz's visor and was recording it for posterity. On the screen, Bloom saw his friend locking eyes with the lieutenant and Fouter became obviously emotionally moved when Emily grasped his hand in hers. His soundless mouth moved and did its best to express his final thought, "Thank you."

Fouter died and in doing so, made way for Emily to live. Emily was deep in shock and her body had shunted all of its available fluid and blood to her core organs and brain but it managed to spare a single tear for the sacrifice Fouter made for her. She slipped into unconsciousness as Wilks pried her hand from her savior's and placed her in the tube.

Davies winced as he entered the commands to start the torture session on the lieutenant. He immediately received a warning from the device that the subject was near death and any torture would kill her almost instantly. The very helpful and insightful torture program gave a friendly suggestion that it be allowed to repair the subject before the torture began. Davies keyed in the proper sequence that told the tube to begin the repair process and to alert him before any torture processes began. The tube went about its business and began affecting Davies' instructions. If he didn't know any better, Davies would have said the tube was actually cheerful as it began its duties.

Almost three hours later, the entire team was assembled together again on the bridge of their newly acquired ship. Bloom had rerouted and programmed the central computer and returned to the ship and was now fiddling with the droid. Daria had come in from checking on Emily and reported that she was well out of the woods and would make a full recovery. Wilks was preparing a burst report for his superiors and was finding it difficult to condense all that had happened in to a readily understandable story. The rest of the team was relaxing or reviewing ship's systems and data that was pertinent to their personal expertise and positions.

A beeping began on a control panel near Patz. Jockey came to look at it. "Sergeant, we have company."

Wilks had just put the finishing sentence in his report and inwardly sighed at the prospect of another engagement so soon after the last one. His team was just starting to recover from the last few days and although they were the best team he had ever worked with, every sentient being needs to physically and emotionally recoup after these sorts of engagements.

"What have you got, fly boy?" Wilks managed to sound much more cheery than he felt, something his men needed right now.

"I'm not sure. I'm reading one friendly craft incoming. It's slightly smaller than our own. The computer designates our ship to be a class nine craft and the other to be a class six. The analogs to Coalition craft would be us as a large cruiser and the incoming ship as a smaller scout vessel."

Bloom was now at the controls helping Jockey. "The scout ship has deployed three smaller ships, probably individual flyers of some sort."

Patz had moved away from the controls to make room for Bloom but something struck him as he looked at the craft designations on the screen. "Hey guys," he started, "if the ship we are in is designating those other vessels as friendlies, doesn't that mean they're actually not friendly?"

Wilks knew at that moment, as did the rest of the team, Patz was absolutely right. Bloom hadn't updated their new ship with Coalition codes for the IFF (identify friend-or-foe), so the ship was using its original codes to designate new contacts. And if the new contact was a friendly to their ship, it most certainly was not friendly to its new occupants.

Jockey jumped into the pilot's seat, Bloom took the co-pilot's seat, Fang went to weapons, and Wilks took center seat in the command chair. Other team members filled vacant seats and the leftovers stood in place, waiting to take up a console if its current occupant became unable to man it during the inevitable upcoming battle.

Bloom reported from his console, "Jockey, we're not ready to launch. Close the hangar bay doors."

"I'd love to", he replied. "But I'm not the one who did it. The incoming vessel did it remotely. They must have activated a docking protocol or something."

"Damn it!" Bloom turned to look at Wilks. "It's too late to override the command. The hangar is opening whether we want it to or not."

Wilks turned to look at each one of his men individually. "Men, we are marines. We adapt, we improvise, and we overcome. I'd rather fight these bastards on the ground than in the air in a ship we just stole. But we are recon marines, which means we have never got to choose who we fight and most of the time we've never even got to decide where we're going to fight. Make no mistake about it: we will kill these motherfuckers before the day is over."

Wilks swiveled his chair back to the front. No one cheered, no one clapped, no one acknowledged the impromptu speech; everyone went to work doing what they could to try to help turn the tables at least a little bit in their favor. But if you could look into their hearts, you'd see that Wilks had sparked a fire that would burn and fuel them through the upcoming battle.

"Get us out of here, Jockey." Wilks could feel the ship responding to his order so he knew Jockey had already started moving towards the hangar exit. "We don't know the defensive or offensive capabilities of either ship so we are going on the offensive and hard. We can't rely on this ship to hold up to whatever they can throw at us, so let's just knock them out of the sky first. This is a heavyweight bout, gentlemen: blow for blow until someone drops."

As they were about to clear the doors of the hangar, the first salvo of weapons fire struck their hull. The three individual fighters had sped ahead of their mother ship and started the fight. The blasts were barely felt inside the much larger ship. Wilks looked to Bloom. "That didn't seem too bad. Do those ships have enough power to even damage us?"

"I'm still trying to figure things out but it seems like they had little effect on our shields." Bloom tapped a few more commands. "They are, however, able to cause momentary weak points in our shielding. A unified attack on a strategic point will cause a significant weak point that I'm sure the scout ship will take advantage of."

"Copy that, Bloom. Jockey, do your best to keep us between the attack craft and the scout ship. If they aren't ever lined up together then they can't use each other to their advantage." Wilks turned to Fang. "Any time you want to start shooting, please feel free."

Wilks' obvious sarcasm hung in the air a moment while Fang just growled at him, "I would love to start shooting but there are safeties that prevent us from arming or using our weapons inside the hangar. I have firing solutions ready to go as soon as we clear the hangar."

Almost on cue, the slight "chug" of weapons fire could be felt as the ship loosed some of its thousand-year-old ordinance on their attackers. On the view screen, Wilks could see the edge of the hangar falling below the ship and several rockets shooting out from weapons bays somewhere on the belly of the ship. Energy weapons were firing from multiple points on the ship's hull and Wilks smiled in satisfaction as one of the smaller attack craft quickly came apart under the barrage. A smile appeared on everyone's face almost simultaneously as the ship flew through the debris of their fallen enemy.

Wilks gripped his command chair as he saw what awaited the ship on the other side of the explosion. An almost imperceptible mutter slipped out. "You've got to be fucking kidding me."

One of the smaller craft was trying to fly across their path, maybe in an attempt to herd them somewhere, maybe to make a suicide run, or maybe just plain old pilot error. Whatever the cause, the outcome seemed inevitable. Jockey kept his calm as he flew the ship right through the smaller craft. "Fuck it", was all he said as his new ship destroyed the much smaller attack craft.

At first, the collision seemed pretty horrible to everyone as the bridge became a shower of flying bodies. A second after the initial hit, the ship seemed to smooth out and Wilks thought maybe it wasn't going to be that bad after all. Then the spinning started and Wilks knew it was probably worse than he cared to think about.

The ship's inertial dampers tried to compensate but they couldn't fix the complete abortion of physics Jockey was performing on the ship and its occupants. As the ship tumbled through the atmosphere, Jockey repeatedly whispered a mantra to himself. Luckily they had been in an upward trajectory when the collision happened so all of their momentum was taking them away from the planet instead of towards it.

As they tumbled through the air, Wilks could feel the ship starting to get hit with more weapons fire. The enemy was using this obvious lack of control to their advantage. Wilks was still stuck to the floor because of the ship's rotation, but he could still talk. "Does anyone want to trade places with Jockey? Anyone? Maybe a one-armed blind kid?"

"I appreciate your confidence, buddy." Jockey was still smiling. This was how his team interacted in a crisis and it was always fun, even if they were about to die. "I got this. I got this. I got this."

The ship started to stabilize and the crew could start peeling themselves from the floor. Wilks crawled his way back to the command chair and he could see on the screen that not only was the ship coming under control but Jockey had managed to bring them into position of slight advantage with the attack ship in front of and blocking the weapons of the scout ship.

"So maybe in the future we can just shoot things down instead of crashing into them?" Wilks could feel the ship was completely under control now.

"I didn't have time to fully evade that bastard so I figured a head-on collision would keep him from sliding along our bottom side weapons bays and destroying those. Without weapons we'll definitely lose this fight so..." Jockey trailed off as he dodged some weapons fire.

"Good choice, buddy." Had there been time to discuss the options, Wilks never would have gone with Jockey's plan and he would've risked losing the belly weapons. But there wasn't time, and he needed his men to feel confident in their decisions so now wasn't the proper moment to pose the obvious question of, "Seriously? Head-on collision seemed the better choice?!"

As Jockey flew around the other ships, two additional images overlaid the main forward image on the screen. Fang was firing on his opponents. "I'm not sure what I pressed but those additional images are the views from the targeting computer. That little guy is about to go..."

On the screen, Wilks saw the contrail of the missile as it sped towards the small attack craft. The missile struck home almost dead center on the top of the craft, and then bounced off without exploding. Everyone turned to look at Fang, who just shrugged and then started looking at his weapons board to see if he could figure out what had happened.

"Pardon me, sir, if I may, I have a suggestion." The voice came from the side of the bridge. As the eyes turned away from Fang and towards the droid everyone had forgotten until now, it continued, "Mr. Fang has accidentally fired a disarmed missile. During our unfortunate physical encounter with the other craft, the missiles have been remotely disarmed. It is a safety feature in the event of a crash landing that prevents the ordinance from detonating. The impact from the collision was enough to bring the safety feature on line."

Wilks turned to Bloom. "I didn't realize we were taking new recruits on our squad. And why the hell does he sound like an English butler?"

"Uh, yeah, I was working on that when we came under attack." Bloom opened his mouth to speak and then obviously decided to change his oncoming rant before it even began. "The short story is he, it, is on our side now and will help us. And I have always wanted an English butler so..."

Wilks turned to the droid. "Okay, Jeeves, can you fix the problem?"

"New designation, 'Jeeves' accepted." Jeeves rolled by Patz and pointed at him. "If you would be so kind as to join me in the weapons bay, I will need your assistance to reset the warheads."

Patz nodded and followed Jeeves off the bridge. Wilks could hear Jeeves starting to tell Patz what they would have to do once they reached the bay. Wilks turned to Fang. "We still have energy weapons so use those until we get missiles back on line."

"Aye, sir." Fang adjusted his control board to remove the missile controls from his screen so he wouldn't use them anymore. The ship continued to fire but the chug couldn't be felt anymore without any missiles being launched.

The pilot of the last small attack fighter was definitely much better than his companions were and wasn't allowing Jockey to keep the small craft between the two larger ships. As a result, they were starting to take a lot of hits from the recon vessel that had much better armament than the smaller attack fighter.

Patz' voice came over the comlink. "There's a fair amount of damage down here. It's probably a good thing the safety protocols enacted or we might have blown up. Jeeves is trying to figure out the best way to arm the missiles as we can't access the software controls to do it electronically. We may have to arm each one by hand before it's fired. I could use everyone who isn't actively doing something to come down here and help out."

Without Wilks saying anything, the remaining team members who weren't doing anything left the bridge. "You've got more hands on their way down. Our energy weapons are working their shields pretty well but the missiles will really help us out."

"Copy that, Sarge." Patz was already mentally setting up teams to man the missiles' manual arming controls. When the extra hands arrived, he directed them to their stations and showed them what Jeeves had shown him about arming the missiles.

A few minutes later, he reported back in. "Wilks, we're ready to start arming the missiles. It will take about thirty seconds to arm each one. We can arm up to two simultaneously. We have to wait for those to fire before the next set load into place and then those can be armed. From the time you fire one missile to the time you can fire the next, figure on a minimum of forty-five seconds."

"Great job, guys." Wilks turned to Fang. "Missiles are a go, buddy. Let slip lose the dogs of war."

Fang smiled and brought his weapons panel back to showing the missiles again. The control panel was obviously designed by a weapons officer and not an engineer sitting at a desk somewhere. There were virtually no words on the panel; everything was a simple pictogram and most were readily apparent as to what they were for. It seemed that missiles, energy weapons and countermeasures might be a universal constant to advanced species. Fang thought he understood probably more than ninety percent of what he was looking at.

As the evasive maneuvers started to outnumber the offensive maneuvers, Wilks began to worry that they were slowly losing the fight. Then Bloom turned and shouted, "New enemy contact! Coming in hard and fast, just clearing the upper atmosphere now."

"Wait, 'enemy' enemy contact?" Wilks asked. "Or a contact this ship thinks is an enemy?"

"Sorry, sir, you're right. The ship IFF is designating enemy so it's probably one of our friends." Bloom worked his controls for a couple of seconds before continuing, "It looks to be Detrill in origin. A fast attack cruiser. I'm hailing on all frequencies and requesting assistance. I'm also updating our IFF. I'll let you know when that's complete."

"Thank you, Bloom." Wilks used his comlink to tap into the hail Bloom had set up. "This is Gunnery Sergeant Wilks of the Coalition. My crew is aboard the larger enemy vessel and we are in control of it. Any assistance you can give would be greatly appreciated."

"Sergeant Wilks, this is Captain Netid of the Detrill warship *Emilian*. We would be happy to assist you. Please cease all fire directed at the smaller vessel; we would like to take that ship intact to review its systems and gather intelligence. I have already deployed three fighters to deal with it. If our two ships could focus on the larger vessel, we'll be done with this in no time."

"Sounds good to me, Captain." Wilks looked to Fang to make sure he understood and when Fang nodded, Wilks looked to Jockey. "Let's separate ourselves from the smaller vessels and finish this."

Jockey jerked the ship around and sent it into a dive. The sudden move looked evasive but Jockey knew it was just a setup so that he could turn back to the offensive in just a few quick seconds.

He had already picked out a seemingly arbitrary point in the atmosphere for his next move, but it wasn't arbitrary at all. The atmosphere is always full of thermocline pockets and bubbles where there is a sudden and drastic change of temperature, sometimes colder and sometimes hotter. Jockey liked to set his board to show these pockets anytime there was a significant temperature difference. This planet had some of the hottest thermoclines he had ever seen and that could work to his advantage.

As they approached a fifteen degree Celsius thermocline, Jockey got ready for his move. The sudden increase of temperature made that pocket of air thinner and gave any ship traveling through it greater maneuverability. If a pilot was paying attention to how his ship and his enemy's ship moved through a given atmosphere, he could determine what either ship was capable of and use that information to create better attack or evasive angles. By using a small pocket of increased maneuverability, Jockey could add several degrees to an escape turn that his enemy wouldn't be prepared for.

Jockey made his move and brought the ship in to a spinning turn pullout that seemed to defy Newtonian physics all together. Wilks thought for sure he was going to pass out as he was sucked into his chair and almost out the other side. Fang was pushed down into a squatting position and even contemplated whether or not he should just let gravity lay him down until it was all over.

As the ship came around and ultimately behind and above the *Emilian*, Captain Netid's voice came over the comlink. "That was a most...impressive maneuver, Sergeant Wilks. And I'm a bit embarrassed to say this, but my pilot has requested that your pilot 'tone it down' just a bit. He doesn't think he can keep up if you pull any more stunts like that."

"My apologies, Captain." Wilks smiled and gave Jockey a thumbs-up. "Jockey was dropped a lot as a baby and consequently he never really did well in physics class. So he's incapable of understanding what ships are supposed to be able to do and not do."

A chuckle came through on the other end of the comlink. "Apparently my pilot should've been dropped more often then."

Through the banter between ships' commanders, the respective pilots and weapons officers were getting their synchronicity together and starting to hammer the enemy ship.

~

Aboard the enemy ship, the warrior captain was furious. "By all that is sacred, why are you so incompetent?!"

The verbal attack turned into a physical one as the captain pulled his junior officer out of the pilot's seat and threw him across the bridge. The captain started as a pilot and was one of the best in the empire.

Although he knew that he couldn't have kept up with the evasive turn the enemy pilot had just performed, he would've at least used the opportunity to switch targets and gone after the Detrill ship. The pilot of the Detrill ship also couldn't keep up with the turn but he tried and in doing so, had exposed himself to an attack angle that could have been used to deliver a devastating attack to his ship's underside.

With the captain now flying his ship, he decided to put all of his efforts into going after the less-experienced Detrill pilot. A warship wasn't just one man, and the captain knew that. There were others on that bridge affecting the outcome of this fight, but the pilot was the first link in the chain and he had no doubt that this link was weaker than he was.

The captain didn't turn his head as he spoke to his weapons officer. "I will be focusing on the Detrill ship, but you may fire at any target you have." The junior pilot was just pulling himself off the deck when the captain addressed him. "If you want to redeem yourself and die with honor, you will get yourself to an attack fighter and use your limited skills to try to crash yourself through one of their hulls."

The junior officer stood straight and put his fist to his chest and said, "Yes, sir." But in the core of his being, he knew that he didn't want to redeem himself, at least not if it meant he had to die to do so.

As the pilot headed towards the launch bay, he contemplated his options. The very fact that he thought he had options, other than following his captain's orders, proved to him something he had always felt: he wasn't made right. Something must have happened in his incubation tube. Maybe a gene wasn't spliced together correctly or a stray mutation had been missed during his final physical exam. He didn't know what was wrong, just that something was.

Although he did enjoy war and fighting, he never enjoyed it as much as his brothers. And although they all didn't mind dying for any reason at any time, he felt his life was more important than that. He wasn't opposed to dying if it would serve a purpose and the greater good, but he didn't want to die just for the sake of dying.

Now sitting in the attack craft, he thought about his options. He could just not launch and die the inevitable death coming for his ship and crewmates. He could launch and try to be of some use in the battle but flying against the other ships so far, he knew he wasn't a match for the other pilots, especially in a smaller craft. He could follow orders but he knew he'd most likely get shot down rather than actually being able to ram one of the larger ships. He could run away. He could try to defect. He could allow himself to be taken prisoner and hope the enemy was more civil than his own people.

He could feel his ship taking more damage and getting hit more often. The captain was definitely a better pilot than he was but the end was already written and no sacrifice was going to change that. He made a decision, or at least a partial decision. He was going to launch, not die with his brothers, and decide the rest later.

The interior of the launch bay seemed to warp and elongate as the fighter craft was expelled from the dying vessel. The pilot was flattened against his seat for a moment until his smaller craft was birthed into the atmosphere and the warped launch bay was replaced by a greenish-blue sky.

The pilot quickly consulted his instruments and turned his craft to a course that was the least threatening to the rest of the ships still locked in battle. He hit his afterburners and raced away from the fight as quickly as possible. Before he launched, he had turned off the communications system in the craft but he was certain he could still hear his captain cursing him from his seat on the bridge.

~

"Wilks," Bloom was reading the tactical readout, "a fighter craft has launched from the enemy vessel but he is definitely leaving the battle. He's not engaging anyone and making a beeline for the safest route away from the fighting. His course does go near our operations base but not directly to it."

Wilks could see the battle was going to be over soon and his side the victor. He wasn't getting cocky or complacent; it was just how things were. He spoke to the Detrill captain. "Sir, can you spare a fighter to follow and possibly engage that enemy fighter who just launched and left the battle?"

"Yes, we can. Unfortunately the other fighter we were attempting to capture self-destructed when he realized we were just about to get him. Maybe this other fighter will be more eager to cooperate because it looks like he's fleeing rather than joining the fun. My craft are already heading towards the enemy fighter."

Wilks felt the now familiar "chug" of the belly launchers letting lose two more missiles. The targeting screen showed the view from the nose of both missiles and the enemy vessel was in the dead center of both. The vessel started an evasive maneuver but the Detrill weapons officer was working in concert with Fang and laid down fire in the only escape path the ship had.

His choices were to get hit by energy weapons or missiles but not to avoid either. He chose the energy weapons considering his forward shields were strongest right now and the energy weapons would be glancing blows compared to the direct hits of the missiles. Fang knew his teammates were working as fast as they could but their lag in manually arming the missiles meant he couldn't fire follow-up shots to the enemy's evasive maneuver that would have finished the fight.

The two ships were working well together and none of the respective crews were talking with each other at all. All of their tactics could be described as synergistic as they read one another's moves and added to what the last person did until the symphony of battle crescendoed with the final act.

The enemy vessel was in the middle of the other two ships. One was vectored towards space on the underside of the enemy and the other was vectored towards the ground coming from above the enemy. They were tens of miles apart but with the speeds these vessels commanded, they might as well have been playing chicken in a parking lot with Formula One race cars.

The Detrill weapons officer didn't know why his allies couldn't fire more than two missiles every forty seconds but he had figured that out early on. The Detrill didn't fire directly at his target because that would just encourage the enemy to try to slip out of the attack in one of several possible escape routes. He had a limited spread that his ship could fire at his current attack angle, so instead he used that spread to close off the likely evasive routes the enemy pilot would take.

Fang saw the plan as his counterpart's firing solution gave the enemy vessel but a single escape route. Fang launched his two missiles into the only path the enemy could take and watched as they hit home on the bridge and majority of the superstructure of the enemy vessel.

The ship bucked and erupted with fire. No longer under the control of its pilot, the ship continued on its last trajectory as momentum carried it through the atmosphere. Both allied ships switched their fire to direct targeting and sent everything they had to the dying ship.

~

The captain knew it was about to end. He was getting boxed in and while he was better than one of the pilots, the other was definitely his equal. Although he refused to give the other pilot a personal rating of better than himself considering he couldn't accurately judge the other's talent in these circumstances. The captain wished he could call a ceasefire, if only to challenge the other pilot to face off in personal attack fighters so they could truly test each other in battle.

The captain saw the Detrill's weapons barrage and knew he was being herded to a certain vector. He also knew that his ship wouldn't survive doing the unthinkable and heading through the barrage on purpose. His only chance was to go where they wanted him to go and hope that the universe intervened on his behalf and made the other weapons officer make a mistake, or maybe the other pilot would suffer a stroke at just the right moment or...

The bridge disintegrated and proved the universe was decidedly not on the captain's side for this infinitely minuscule and insignificant moment in the universe's existence.

~

"And that is, as they say, that." Wilks walked to Jockey and shook his hand.

Bloom took it a step further and gave him a hug. "Flying with you always makes me want to vomit but it never makes me dead. Thanks, buddy."

"Captain Wilks," the Detrill captain purposely addressed the sergeant, "my congratulations to your crew for their exceptional work. We fought well together today, which will surely help us in our battles yet to come.

"My fighters have grounded the last enemy ship that tried to escape and the pilot has surrendered. He's talking but we have no idea what he's saying."

Wilks appreciated the captain's assessment of his team and the respectful consideration of calling Wilks a captain. "Sir, I believe we can help you with that. We have deciphered their language and have a program, along with a specialist, we can send over. I suggest we bring this party back to our base. We have facilities to conduct a proper debrief and my men need to prep for whatever our next move is. Not to mention we need to check on our personnel at the base and report back in to our chain of command."

Bloom interrupted, "Sergeant, the enemy ship must have destroyed the base's communication array when they started their attack. However, the base has sent out a few ground craft to determine what was going on. I am just now getting communication from the OIC of those units."

"Copy that, Bloom. Give him a quick sit-rep and tell him we'll give the base CO a full debrief at the base. Jockey, head back to the hangar so we can pick up Doc and her team. I need to go check on the lieutenant. Davies, meet me in the med bay."

A new mission started as everyone began to carry out their instructions. Daria and her team were picked up; the lieutenant was unconscious but doing well. Jeeves was talking with Bloom and Patz about the ship's condition and giving a detailed plan for the best use of their time for repairs.

As they were landing at their primary base, Wilks saw the Detrill captain being introduced to the base commander. As they shook hands, the warrior prisoner was being led into the base. He was shackled but Wilks knew what the base security didn't: if the warrior didn't want to be shackled, those restraints wouldn't hold him. Wilks sent Snake to catch up with the security officers to debrief them on their prisoner and his abilities.

Everything seemed calm and exceptionally slow at the moment and Wilks took a small moment to enjoy the feeling. He knew it wouldn't last for long. It never did.

Beast

NAME: BEAST
SPECIES: SHIRKA
MOS: INFANTRY
RANK: STAFF SERGEANT
AGE: 26 - EARTH STANDARD
SEX: MALE
HEIGHT: 7'03"
WEIGHT: 310 POUNDS

    The litter had been laid in the traditional way, as it had always been done and always would be done. The mother left without sadness, regret, or remorse. When she returned to the nesting place in four months' time, she expected no more than five out of fifteen of her litter would be alive to meet her. Looking at two of the smaller sacks she reconsidered; probably only four. She had carried them within her body for almost a year now. It was time for them to decide who was strong enough to live and who wasn't.

    The litter sacks were lumped together in a teardrop formation and held together with a thick membrane that would keep them that way until the firstborn chewed his way out, thereby releasing the rest of his litter-mates.

    A cloudy liquid filled the sacks and provided nutrients for the small dark masses that occupied the center of each one. Bound together by a communal umbilical cord of sorts, each individual teardrop would try to siphon nutrients from the others. In a litter this size, it was likely that at least four of the litter would be completely used to feed the others. Two would be so nutrient-starved they wouldn't survive the final stages of birth. Two or three more would be the runts of the litter and of those, one would be lucky to live long enough to be reclaimed when their mother came back. The rest would fight among themselves or band together as a pack in order to survive.

The Shirka had been a spacefaring species for almost three hundred years. Their written history dated back almost ten thousand years. And with all of their technological advances, they easily could have made it so every fetus in every litter survived, but that wasn't their way.

The Shirka were a strong species and had quickly tamed their planet once they became sentient. Each female was capable of bearing ten or more cubs per litter every two years of their adult life, if they wanted to. They realized early on that if they abandoned their natural ancestral birthing practices, they would quickly overpopulate their planet.

They were also a species that was very in tune with nature, and that harmonic relationship called for sacrifice. Every species on the planet had to be sacrificed to another species at some point. Without this sacrifice, nature would not survive. Every plant and every creature fed the environment somehow, even the cubs of a Shirka litter.

This process of weeding out the weak had kept their species strong and the planet in balance since time immemorial. The ones who survived were strong physically or mentally and sometimes both. This is the way it always had been and always would be.

The litter had been left in the forest four months ago to finish its incubation period. Three would definitely be in competition for the alpha role. Five of the fifteen sacs were completely used for nutrients and a sixth was used just enough to kill its embryo. There were four runts, one particularly smaller than the rest.

The would-be alpha that was closest to the outer membrane started to feel something that he hadn't felt before. This sensation, though new, was immediately recognized as hunger. The sacs had stopped feeding them almost three days ago in order to prepare their hunger to be strong enough to make them chew through their protective and potentially deadly outer sack layer.

    His lips curled back and he bared his teeth for the first time in his predatory life. He had exceptional long fangs for a cub, which worked to his advantage. Even so, it was difficult to get a good bite on the sack as its natural shape curved away from his mouth. In the end, he settled on chewing through his umbilical cord and eating it so that as he chewed and swallowed, it brought the sac closer and closer to his mouth until it was chewed instead of the cord.

    He finally breached the outer layer and felt the cool morning air on his muzzle. He was cute by any species' definition of the word. Cute and absolutely deadly.

    At this point, he was less than a half meter tall, lanky, covered in matted fur and exhibiting a temporary tail. Shirkas were a little oddly balanced as younglings and the tails helped stabilize them. As they grew older, the tails became part of their lower spine and essentially absorbed into their adult form. Some female Shirkas didn't lose all of their tail after puberty and this was commonly thought of as a sexy trait.

    Shirkas had a rounded head, much like a Grizzly bear from Earth, and a muzzle that resembled a wolf's. If a human had ever seen a Shirka before they knew about alien life, the human would have probably thought they were looking at a real life werewolf.

    They usually reached just short of three meters in height and looked thin for their size. They had no body fat for insulation; instead, they relied on a very adaptable system of fur that was self-regulating depending on the environment. It could thicken the undercoat in a matter of hours or shed top layers in minutes if necessary.

    Each hand had five fingers with retractable claws. An opposable thumb came from the center of their wrist near the palm of their hand, a dew claw that evolved into that position and allowed them to become more than forest-dwelling predators. Their feet were naturally padded and had stubby claws that weren't retractable.

Overall, they were a formidable enemy and they enjoyed battle. The Shirka almost never ran from a fight but they almost never started one, either. As they expanded through their small portion of the galaxy, they never fought other species for resources or planets. Shirkas were firm believers in a code of honor that forbade them from taking what wasn't rightfully theirs. Some species had mistaken this code of honor for weakness and tried to take resources from the Shirkas. Although the Shirkas were no stranger to defeat, they never lost a single planet, asteroid or solar system they had claimed for themselves. This was a lesson the humans would eventually learn the hard way.

And now the cubs were fighting their first battle, escaping the membranes that kept them safe and fed them for over a year now. Once the first cub breached the membrane, the remaining fluid in the sacks would start to drain and the self-contained ecosystem would stop supporting them. They had a little over an hour to get out before they would start the slow metabolic suffocation that would kill them.

Once the first cub was out, he looked around. Shirka cubs emerged from the sacks as fully functional predators. It took only a few steps before he understood what his body could do and how to make it move. A shriek in the distance caused him to crouch and growl in the direction he heard the sound. Another predator, he was sure of it.

It was time for a decision. He had several options to choose from, as his ancestors always had. He could eat the pups that weren't out yet, use them for his very important first meal. He could leave the litter and strike out on his own; they were taking so long to emerge and every minute he stayed here was another minute that a predator had to find him. He could help his siblings escape their sacks but that may save the weak ones who weren't supposed to survive. Or he could stay with his litter, watch over them, wait for them, and protect them as best he could if danger found them.

No Shirka was ever judged on the decision he or she made after they emerged. If their mother returned to find one cub left and he had eaten the rest of his siblings, it was what he felt was necessary to survive and she would not hold it against him. Shirkas never discussed their birth decision with anyone outside of their family, ever.

This cub decided to stay and protect his family. He wasn't going to help them emerge, but he would give his life to defend them if needed. He was hoping to get a kill before they emerged so he could present it to them and secure his position as alpha. Emerging first didn't automatically make you the alpha, but it helped.

No sooner had that impulse crossed his mind than he heard an excited yelp behind him. His first sister had mostly emerged, with one leg still left in the sack. She yelped to get his attention and he came over. The look on her face was fairly obvious. *Help me, brother.*

The first cub growled a negative and gave her a few short barks of encouragement.

Even though they were fully formed and aware, they still hadn't been taught advanced language and verbal skills from their parents. All they had at this point was their instinctual communication that was based on body language and basic primitive sounds. But she got the point. *Do it yourself. I know you can!*

She was going to bite him at some point for that but she had to get out first. The umbilical cord was wrapped around her ankle and she eventually chewed herself free, just seconds before her second brother freed himself.

Three down, six to go. Over the next twenty minutes, three more emerged, including two of the runts. Of the three who remained, there was one any betting Shirka would've called an alpha. The other two were the last runts, with one of them being the smallest from the litter.

The bigger runt was having problems breathing and losing strength as he struggled. His brothers and sisters were barking encouragement but he just didn't have it in him to continue. He gave up. His body went still and he slowly faded away into unconsciousness and eventually death. His brothers and sisters didn't mourn him: he was a quitter—he still had life in him and he gave up. They turned their attention to the two remaining litter-mates.

The once would-be alpha was near the center of the sacks and that's what had been hampering his progress. He was fighting his way through the sacks but he was losing steam; he wasn't sure whether he was going to make it. He wasn't going to give up, though. He would die trying; he knew that unequivocally.

He finally broke the surface with his nose. Fresh air, the first his lungs had ever felt. The internal metabolism that had kept him alive without actually breathing had already come to an end so this breath of air was the sweetest thing he had ever or would ever smell.

His head was almost out but his right leg couldn't move. As the sack dried and hardened, it had started to twist around his leg. He pulled and clawed but couldn't get free. He was so tired now, so lacking in energy. At least he was breathing but that was a small comfort if he couldn't fully escape the sack.

He suddenly felt a nibble at his trapped foot and he strained to see what was going on. The little runt was trying to chew his trapped foot. He couldn't believe it; the little guy was trying to make sure that neither of them got out alive! He growled and barked angrily at the runt but there was nothing else he could do.

~

The runt looked around and saw how much farther he needed to go before he could escape. So much chewing left; he didn't think he would make it. He watched his stronger brother give up and die right next to him. If his brother gave up, what chance did he have?

He decided that being the runt didn't mean he had to die like a runt. He was going to fight, until the end, no matter what. He resumed chewing and looking for paths that had already been established by his litter-mates. The problem was as the sack dried it constricted, hardened and became much more difficult to chew through.

He felt a strong vibration off to his right and was able to turn enough to see one of his brothers struggling to get free. Part of the sack was quickly drying and constricting around his brother's ankle. He wasn't going to make it.

The runt looked around and saw a possible pathway for him to get out. The sack was still moist in that direction and there were obvious gnashed areas in it where a few others had already chewed through. He might be able to make it that way.

Might be able to. He didn't like the way that made him feel. He was certain that his brother wouldn't make it out and that he only might make it out. Without any more thought, he made a decision.

He began to claw towards his brother and chew with everything he had. When he reached his brother's ankle, he started to rip at the sack tangled around it. A few bites ended up nipping his brother but he couldn't help that now. He wanted to make sure at least one of them made it out alive.

The runt heard his brother growl and bark and immediately knew that his intentions were misunderstood.

He kept chewing and clawing until he could feel the ankle becoming less encumbered. Then in a snap, it was free and his brother rolled from the sack and rolled over on the ground, completely exhausted.

The cub looked back to the runt still trapped inside the sack and realized what his brother was trying to and ultimately succeeded in doing. The runt had sacrificed himself to save his brother. And the runt continued to claw and move his jaw, trying to chew the sack, but it was obvious that his attempts would fail.

The rest of the litter was standing around their defacto alpha, watching the runt make his last few attempts to free himself. The would-be alpha jumped to the sack and was going to help his brother but was stopped by the first brother. The alpha growled and made his intentions clear. *He must do it on his own.*

The would-be didn't even need to think about it; his primal instincts kicked in and he lashed out. He was weak, very weak and hadn't been resting like his alpha brother had been after he first emerged. His first swipe was easily ducked and the alpha countered with a light bite to the would-be's belly. No damage but enough pain to show that he was serious.

The would-be was also serious and knew he was prepared to kill one brother to save the other. A simple show of force and resolve wasn't going to be enough and he didn't have the time or strength to commit to an all-out fight. He feigned an attack and when his brother went to a guard position, the would-be rolled away and latched on to the sack and begin to tear at it from the outside.

He had made several openings in the sack before the alpha was back on him and trying to make him stop. The would-be latched on to a chunk of the sack and told himself not to let go no matter what. He added his front claws to the attempt and tried to dig at the sack with all his might.

The alpha couldn't let his decision be challenged, not this soon after emerging. He went for the throat and latched on. He didn't want to kill his brother but he was willing to hurt him, badly if necessary.

The would-be was directing all of his energy and all of his focus on saving his brother, so he didn't last long against the alpha's attack. He was pulled away after having made some progress in his attempt. When he was able to right himself once more, he was faced with the alpha staring him in the eye and growling a warning. *Enough!*

The would-be was trying to think of his next move but had a sinking feeling he had already made his last. As he looked beyond the alpha, he saw the rest of the litter making their own move. They were coming together and working to free the runt. With their combined effort, they had their brother out in just a few seconds.

The alpha looked back and was enraged with what he saw. They had defied him; they had made their own decision and saved a weak brother. A runt even. With the act already done, there wasn't much he could do. Shirkas weren't punitive by nature so he had no plans to hurt any of them for what they did. He would just accept it for now.

The would-be and the alpha walked together to their litter-mates, now a pack. They looked at the runt, who didn't seem to be breathing. The would-be got down on all fours and nuzzled his brother. No reaction. He licked his brother's face. No reaction. He laid down next to his brother and curled up with him. If his brother was going to die, he wasn't going to die feeling alone. The would-be watched as the rest of the pack joined him on the ground, surrounding and protecting their runt brother, giving him warmth and hopefully peace.

~

The would-be wasn't sure how long they had been laying there but the alpha was getting impatient, pacing back and forth and looking at the setting sun. When darkness came, so did the predators. The pack had been lucky that their birthing sack hadn't been found and eaten by the creatures of the forest and the alpha didn't want that to change now that they were born.

He sensed this was a delicate time for the pack and he didn't want to lose his standing. Instead of a forceful order, he tried his best to make a heartfelt whimper. *I know what he did for you, but we have to go.*

The pack looked at him and didn't respond. The alpha knew it was too late; he wasn't the alpha anymore. He was the has-been and the would-be was now the alpha. They would follow him.

The has-been had had several hours to think about the decisions his pack had made so far and he was actually leaning toward siding with them. The more he thought about his runt brother's sacrifice, the more he realized the strength it took to do what he did rather than try to save himself.

He could either leave his pack for turning away from his leadership or join them under their new alpha. The has-been walked up to the group and added his body to the mound. He pushed his muzzle to the center in order to smell the runt and add that scent to his memory so he would never forget his brother.

As he took in a deep breath, he felt a little dry tongue lick his nose. A low whimper followed and the rest of the pack became aware that their runt was not dead after all. The mound moved away so they could look at their brother and he looked back at each of them. Joyful whimpers started moving around the circle and the whimpers turned to barks of excitement.

They needed water, food, and shelter fast. Night was already on them and the predators could be heard in the distance. Water would normally be the first thing they went for but given the circumstances, shelter was the priority. The new alpha sent out the has-been and his strongest sister to scout for shelter. The rest set up a defensive posture to the best of their ability.

They started to think like a sentient predator and not just a tooth-and-nail predator. They had opposable thumbs to put to use. They gathered rocks and kept them nearby. Shirkas' genetic memories were advanced enough to give the cubs a basic understanding of defensive tool use.

The two scouts returned quickly and indicated they had found shelter. The group helped the runt to his feet and took turns assisting him to the shelter. The small cave was cool but at least dry. It would provide shelter and a defensible position with the drawback that there was nowhere to run to if things got bad. The cave was their final stand for the night, one way or the other.

Two of the cubs checked the cave a second time to make sure that no other predators were hiding or had slipped in during the time it took the scouts to come and get the group. They didn't find any predators but got lucky and came across two prey animals that they made short work of and proudly presented to the alpha.

The alpha grinned and affectionately nipped his two siblings, the human equivalent of a high-five or butt slap. The alpha then took one of the animals and presented it to the two hunters who had killed it. He then took the second one and placed it next to the runt. Usually the alpha ate first but this one was leading by example, showing that he thought the pack was more important than he was as an individual. Keep the hunters strong and protect those who deserved protecting.

The runt nosed the animal back to the alpha and turned his head. *No.*

The alpha gave a low growl and the runt just turned his head farther and presented his back to the group. *No.*

With a low sigh, the alpha took two bites of the animal and passed it to the next cub, who also took two bites and passed it along. It wasn't until everyone had taken two bites that the runt took his share. The two hunters ate their kill without sharing. No one thought less of them for it: it pays to be a winner. Rewards were given for a reason. They had eaten more than anyone else, so they decided to take guard duty without even being directed to.

With the front of the cave protected and the interior scouted out, there wasn't much left to do but wait for morning. Some rocks had been brought with them and a few more found in the cave. The rocks were staged for quick use in case of an attack during the night. The pack laid down together for warmth and comfort and quickly fell asleep. The final stage of emerging from their sacks was very tiring and the group didn't get as much food as they should have on their first day. Tomorrow would have to be different.

~

The predator had been watching and waiting. A cave full of cubs would be a good meal, even if she only got one of them. The two on guard duty were strong and alert. Eventually they would tire and either fall asleep at the mouth of the cave or get replacement guards. The predator's primal instincts hoped they fell asleep at the mouth of the cave so she could just run by and grab one, absconding into the night with her dinner. She settled in as close as she dared and waited. Patience is what keeps you fed in the forest.

The cub felt himself nodding off more than once. He looked at his sister and she seemed much more alert than he felt. He nudged her and motioned to the mouth of the cave and then back to the sleeping pack. *You stay here. I'm getting us replacements.*

She chuffed in agreement and went back to scanning the forest.

The predator saw the exchange and began her short stalk to the entrance of the cave. She didn't have the higher intelligence to know exactly what was happening but her primal instincts told her that something was changing and she needed to take advantage of that change.

As she got closer, she saw the male cub leave the mouth of the cave and the female repositioned herself just a tad farther back. Guarding the cave by herself now, she wanted to be a little harder to get at if something attacked her. But the predator was bigger and her reach wouldn't be hindered by the cub's adjustment.

Her instincts didn't let her ponder how long the cub would be alone or understand that a change of guard was about to happen; it just told her to move now and quickly. She went from a stalk to an all-out sprint in less than a second and was cresting the lip of the cave just a couple of seconds after that.

The female cub was startled but ready for an attack. Unfortunately, no matter how ready she was, the predator was more than she could handle on her own. The first swipe of her powerful paw opened the cub's face up and knocked her almost unconscious. Had she been even a millisecond slower in dodging the attack, the predator's claws would've hit their intended target of her carotid artery and killed her.

As it was, she was in no shape to fight and was dragged from the cave with ease. The much larger predator had the cub in her mouth but was unaware that her blow had not hit its mark. When she saw the spray of blood and the cub go limp, her instincts told her that the job was done. Time to take the cub to a tall tree, hide her kill high up in the branches, and see whether she could come back and grab one more cub before the night was over.

~

The has-been woke from sleep at the rough nudge from his brother who had been on guard duty. One eye opened and he looked to see the cub standing there, deciding who else was going to get woken up. With a second cub picked, he nipped her rump because a simple nudge didn't seem to work too well on the last cub. She gave a small yelp and quickly got up to face him with her teeth bared. That worked much better.

The two newly awakened guards started to walk towards the mouth of the cave and had gotten close enough to see a huge predator grab their limp and bleeding sister. Without hesitation, the has-been took off at a dead run towards the attacker. The predator was normally faster than the Shirka cubs could hope to be but she was slowed by having one of them in her mouth.

The has-been's sister was faster than he was. She passed him and slowly began gaining on the predator. As they ran through the forest, the has-been was vaguely aware of the fact that they hadn't sounded an alarm at all. The rest of the pack was probably still back in the cave sleeping. He couldn't stop now and go back; he would be leaving his sister without help and there was no way she would win the fight they were about to engage in. His own breathing was hard and fast so he couldn't let out a good loud howl for help but he did the best he could do between ragged breaths.

The cub that had woken his reliefs had already joined the sleeping group and was trying to stay awake to wait until his sister joined them. She was taking forever. Did she decide to stay with them for added protection? He would give her a few more minutes before he dosed off.

As his eyelids got heavier and barely still open, he heard a faint howl. At first, he thought it was a cry for help from another newly emerged pack because it was coming from so far away. But the second, even fainter howl, struck him as familiar and he knew it was his brother, the has-been.

All fatigue forgotten with a surge of adrenaline pumping through his body, he jumped up and gave several loud and commanding barks. *Get up! Danger! We need to go!*

Without waiting for a response, he took off towards where he thought he had heard his brother calling from. The rest of the pack got up and followed without question. The runt was tired but the food he had and the rest, along with the shared adrenaline surge, was enough to get him up. For being so small, he was actually one of the pack's faster runners and was close to the lead in no time.

The cub in the lead was just running on instinct; he didn't quite understand what it was telling him but he didn't stop to argue with it or think about it. He was rewarded with a strong scent of his pack members who had passed through this area before him. The scent had blood mixed in it along with another he hadn't smelled before.

His instinct gave him another nudge, this one in the opposite direction. His instinct told him that the new smell was bad, something big and strong, something that would surely kill him. This time he ignored his instinct and listened to his heart instead, that told him to keep going no matter what.

As the cub closed the distance to her much larger target, she began to realize that she would have to do something once she reached it. She faintly heard the barks and howls from the rest of her pack, so she knew backup was on its way but still not all that close. She would need to slow the predator down so they could catch up with her. Alone she wouldn't win, but the pack should be strong enough if they could only get there in time.

The predator didn't have a tail, so she was aiming for one of its legs. She just needed to close the gap by a meter and then she should be able to grab it. The plan was simple: bite and hold, don't let go no matter what. Her brother, the has-been, was close enough behind her that he would be able to add his teeth and claws to the fight within seconds as long as she didn't let go.

She felt the foot of her target graze her muzzle as she closed the distance. Add just a little more speed, she wouldn't have to maintain it but for a few meters and she knew she could hold out that long. The gap was closed and when her head was directly alongside the striding leg of her opponent, she adjusted to her right and closed her already gaping jaws around the upper part of the predator's leg.

It took a few strides for the much larger animal to realize that she wasn't going to be able to shake the cub from her leg. Those few strides had moved them close to five meters farther and her passenger was hanging on through the pounding it was taking.

The predator had two choices at this point: drop her food and run away or stay and fight. Hunger and safety were two very strong instincts that often conflicted with each other. Both were directly related to survival, which was the strongest instinct of all and impossible to fight in and of itself. Hunger was the winner today, even if by only a small margin.

The predator dropped her food and whipped her body to the right, nearly avoiding the trunk of a large tree. The cub attached to her left leg was not so lucky, as planned, and was thrown into the tree so hard that a piece of its fruit fell from one of the higher branches. That should take care of her passenger. But to her surprise and regret, it hadn't.

The has-been saw his sister clamp down on the beast's leg and a smile crossed his muzzle. He let out a short but supportive bark to let her know that he was right behind her. When the predator swung right, the has-been saw her drop the injured cub to the ground in a heap. The has-been passed over his sister without checking her; she was either dead, dying, or not and that wasn't going to change so he pushed on towards the known threat.

As his other sister was slammed into a tree, he saw the predator look back towards her own leg to look at the clinging cub. That moment of inattention to the has-been gave him the chance he needed to choose exactly where he wanted to bite. The neck wasn't an option as it was turned away from him, so he went for the soft underbelly and bit down. At the same time, he raked his claws across the animal's chest.

The bite barely broke the skin of his target and didn't cause nearly as much damage as his instincts told him it would have. Later in life, the cub would learn that in this particular animal, females had extra bone structures in the abdomen in order to protect the womb from attackers. The bone structure did its job well, though the bite did cause pain and reminded the predator that she needed to divide her attention among her threats.

The predator reached back with her front leg and swiped the cub away from her abdomen, causing only minimal damage to him. She turned and snapped at him but missed. The dazed but ever vigilant cub on her leg refused to let go and stayed on through all of it. The predator tried shaking the cub off but that only caused her teeth to do more damage as she was shaken back and forth.

The predator changed her mind; safety was now more important than hunger. She might still win against the cubs but she was definitely going to take more damage in the process and no predator can afford to take days off from hunting in order to heal. She just needed to get that damned cub off her leg. She turned to bite the cub anywhere she could get to.

The pack was arriving with the runt almost in front now. He could see the has-been circling for an advantage and his sister hanging on to a leg as she got bit repeatedly by the predator. The overconfident beast was losing to only two cubs; the runt knew the pack was going to win this but he wanted to prove himself, prove he had been worth saving.

The lead cub started to slow so he could take a more coordinated attack with the has-been, who was reevaluating his strategy as his instincts had been wrong on his first attack. The runt sped by the lead cub and barreled full-bore into the predator, using his shoulder to knock the beast off balance.

As the predator fell, the runt stood fully on his two hind legs and jumped onto the predator's chest. The beast was already so much larger than a regular-sized cub that the runt seemed impossibly small in comparison. The runt yelled out a battle cry, the first semi-sentient vocalization anyone in the pack had made yet. It was the equivalent of a human child's first word.

The beast snapped towards the runt's face so he tucked his head into his opponent's chest. The runt then began using his hands to swipe at the predator's throat. The Shirka's retractable claws were a completely voluntary action so they stayed sheathed unless the Shirka intentionally deployed them. Inexperience and bloodlust kept the runt from deploying his claws so his slashes did no damage to their target. In hindsight, if his claws had been out, he probably would've killed the predator in short order. As it was, that didn't happen and his error would become a lifelong cause of teasing from the rest of his pack. The teasing was always with the respect that came from a family's love, but still teasing regardless.

As the alpha approached, he actually chuckled to himself as he saw the runt uselessly slapping the much larger and deadlier opponent. By now, most of the pack was tearing into the predator and the alpha joined in as soon as he was able to find an open spot on the dying animal.

They tore with teeth and claws, and blood was flung all around them. When the predator stopped fighting back, the pack's bloodlust began to slowly ebb away. When it was all over and they stood back looking at their first pack kill, the alpha looked around the circle at his siblings and felt pride.

The has-been was the first to go back to his sister who had originally been the prey in this fight. He found her still unconscious and bleeding from the face but it wasn't that bad. Her fur had done its job and matted around the wound while adding its anticoagulant outer cells to the mixture, helping the healing process.

With help, he brought his sister to the pack's kill and laid her next to her sister, who was still dazed from being bashed into the tree trunk more than once. In all, the pack had suffered very minor damage and achieved a great victory. They were all proud of one another and exchanging nips of congratulations.

The runt saw the new threat first. Out of nowhere, two more of the predators emerged from the forest and took up positions on either flank of the pack. Their kill was either a part of the newcomers' pack or the two were just opportunists and saw the already dead easy meal and the other potential meals standing around it.

The alpha was filled with confidence at their victory but he wasn't going to let that be their downfall. Two skilled predators with a planned attack could do a lot of damage to his pack. The alpha moved to stand in front of his two wounded siblings and motioned to the rest of the pack to do the same.

Shirka cubs used all four limbs as legs more often than not and as they grew and their structures changed, they would switch to a more bipedal lifestyle. For now, the pack followed their alpha and stood as tall as they could and puffed out their chests. The seven cubs seemed more formidable than they probably were, but they were willing to back it up with everything they had left in them and that was obvious.

The formation that protected their injured pack members left their latest kill unprotected and available to take away. The alpha looked at the predator he assumed was the alpha of the two and then looked at the carcass. *It's yours, but leave us alone or else.* He punctuated his offer with the deepest growl he could summon and his pack joined in.

With the entire pack of cubs growling and baring their teeth, the alpha predator looked to the fresh kill and decided that a fight wasn't worth it, especially when at least two days' worth of food was waiting to be carried off. The predator shifted towards the offer but never took his eyes off the pack. When he reached the carcass, he stood by while the other predator grabbed the prize and dragged it into the forest. The transaction complete, the alpha predator backed into the shadows and left.

The pack relaxed a little but each one was arguably a little disappointed that they didn't get to fight a second time. With the latest threat gone, the pack gathered up their wounded and started back towards the cave. On the way back, they scented some prey animals and three cubs broke off to get some food. The small hunt was successful and each member got a couple more bites to eat before settling down in the cave for the rest of the night.

The next day, they found water and more food. Over the course of the next month, they set up a camp around their cave and made defensible positions that they had to use more than once during that time.

They increased their size by at least twenty-five percent each. With a much larger than normal pack size, they were able to take down much larger game and eat more per cub. Most cubs only gained fifteen to twenty percent mass before their mother came back for them. The runt had actually grown to the size of a normal Shirka cub, though he was still much smaller than the others in the pack.

They also ran into a couple of other new packs and had the chance to practice their socialization skills. The other packs were much smaller in number and physical size but they were still doing well for themselves in the forest.

Without the need for the packs to compete for resources, they got to engage one another in positive ways: wrestling, racing, climbing, and grooming to name a few. Early socializations such as these tended to foster lifelong friends and bonds that often led to the pairing of mates.

~

On a particularly sunny day, the runt was basking in the sun while lying atop a warm boulder. One of his sisters was near him, their heads touching at the ears. They still didn't have advanced language skills and didn't know any words, but each pack developed its own basic style of growls, grunts, and barks that meant something to them.

The runt grumbled and sighed. *This is the best.*

His sister silently replied with a smile and snuggled closer. Pack-mates that stuck together after emerging were almost always extremely close to one another and absolute best friends for life. The runt was and always would be closer to his alpha brother than anyone else, but no one minded their shared bond.

The alpha walked up and took the spot between his brother and sister. The pack was big enough in number and physical size that they were almost never bothered anymore by other predators. They never let their guard down but they did get to enjoy more relaxing times than most cubs did.

As the three napped in the warm sun, a new scent floated to their noses. They each stood immediately and inhaled the deepest breath they could to make sure they got as much of the scent as possible. They looked at one another in unison and then took off on all fours towards the scent.

The rest of the pack was already on the move and the three caught up quickly. The runt was now the fastest in the group and he passed his brothers and sisters with ease. As they reached the nest they emerged from over a month ago, the scent became overwhelming.

The runt saw her first and let out an excited bark as he slid to a stop in front of her. More frantic barking. *Mom! Mom! Mom! Mom!*

The adult Shirka looked down and saw her first son. "You must be my alpha!" she said with pride. "So big and strong. The first to come and meet me. Now, where is the rest of your pack?"

No sooner had she finished her sentence than she heard the trampling of feet coming towards her. A lot of feet. When the first daughter crested the hill, followed closely by seven siblings, the mother was shocked to say the least. "Wait until your father sees THIS. We have a lot of hunting to do."

She knelt and sniffed each cub to make sure they were all hers and no strays had entered the pack. Yup, all hers. She wouldn't be leaving any strays in the forest today.

She looked to her litter and found her alpha. "You did this to me. So many mouths to feed!" she said with a smile. "You kept them alive and brought them to me. Only the strongest of alphas could have accomplished a pack of this size. You will be a great leader someday."

Gathering up her cubs, she led them out of the forest to her transport. All around her the excited pack was barking. *Mom! Mom! Mom! Mom! Mom! Mom! Mom! Mom! Mom!*

"If you guys keep this up for the entire trip home, I swear your father will eat at least one of you." Among Shirka parents, this wasn't an idol threat; it was an extremely possible outcome.

~

Many years later...

Beast then looked up and saw his brother standing before him. "I've missed you, brother."

"You did well out there today." The brothers embraced. "Runt."

Chapter 48
The Warrior Interrogation Planet

Blaze was trying to open his eyes but the light in the room was like lightning through his brain. Reaper was coaching him through the pain. "C'mon, buddy, I know it hurts but we need you up and running right now. I've given you some steroids to help with the swelling in your brain and some stuff for the pain. I'm also trying out a new cellular regeneration drug that acts basically like our dermal regenerators but on your interior cells."

"Thanks, Doc." Blaze was starting to be able to tolerate the light now. "Is there any reason my mouth is dry and my eyes are tingling?"

"Um, could be an unwanted side effect of the new drug", Reaper said as he reached for his own hydration pack tube and offered it to his patient.

"Um, could be? You're not exactly filling me with confidence right now, buddy." Blaze drank the recycled water and realized just how thirsty he must be when he thought the recycled sweat and urine tasted like the freshest mountain spring water he had ever had in his life.

Reaper turned to Surgeon. "He'll be up in a few minutes and ready to go a few minutes after that." He gave a brief worried look to Blaze and then looked back to Surgeon. "He's already showing signs of unwanted side effects from the experimental cellular regeneration medicine. They're minor but they aren't ones even listed on the reference sheet for the medication."

Surgeon knew Reaper was worried but they didn't have any other choice. "You are following my orders, Reaper. If Blaze has a bad outcome, it's my fault."

Blaze interjected himself between his friends both physically and verbally. "It's neither of your guys' fault. This is a mission. A mission that our enemy made unavoidable. If it's anyone's fault, it's theirs. Besides, you guys are talking like I was already dead. Please don't. It hurts my feelings." Blaze laughed, patted his friends on their backs and then started to pick up his gear. Surgeon just shook his head and chuckled while Reaper sighed and began to put his medpack back together.

From the other side of the hallway, Seth was pretty much finished working out the details of the next part of their plan. It wasn't the greatest plan of all time, probably wasn't even in the top thousand plans of some of the time, but it was what they had been able to come up in the time they had with the resources they had. Surgeon was approaching them and saw an odd makeshift contraption being built with one of their visors as the centerpiece.

Seth looked up from his work. "We'll be ready to go in just a minute. I have to warn you, though, this plan is built around a lot of 'ifs.'" Surgeon just nodded for Seth to continue. "All right, like I told you before, this station gets views from eighteen different cameras but the operator can only see three of them at any one time. This station was set up so the operator had to manually cycle through the cameras, though I suspect it could also be set to rotate through them at a set interval.

"We have found a dead spot on the hallway cameras that is almost the length of the hall starting from the front of the camera then going forward and about one meter from the ceiling. The camera is about forty meters down the hall from where this pod connects to that hallway."

The pod the team currently occupied joined the hallway almost directly next to the elevator they needed to access. In order to get to the camera monitoring the elevator, they would have to walk down forty meters of open hallway with nowhere to hide. Or...

Seth took a deep breath. "Our plan is to shoot a climbing piton in to the wall about a half meter in front of the camera and a half meter below the ceiling. Even if the camera is viewing the hallway when that happens, the piton and climbing line should be in the blind spot the entire time.

"Then, Shorty will get on the line, because he's the smallest, and pull himself up to the camera. He'll hang the visor on the camera so it's looking into the viewfinder of the visor. We'll set up another visor on a camera in the other hallway and it will be recording the hallway from the same height and angle as the camera we're trying to fool. The hallways are nearly identical, so whoever is viewing the other security camera will just see the empty hallway on the other side of this station. If they're paying close attention, they'll realize the elevator isn't in the image and we're screwed. In theory, we'll have all the time we need to open the elevator and get into the complex."

Surgeon had come up with more than one plan in his life that he wasn't proud of but looking back, they weren't half bad in comparison. "Let me get this straight, we're using the old 'loop the video feed' scam from like a hundred movies from a few hundred years ago?"

Beast shrugged. "Loop the video feed?"

Seth smiled. "See, different species—he doesn't get the reference. I'm sure these guys haven't seen *Speed* either."

"Okay, Cadet, but it also relies on the sentry not looking at the hallway video feed while Shorty attaches the visor. Because no matter how convincing that feed is to the camera once the visor is set up, it won't be convincing to anyone watching it if you can see Shorty's hands draping a visor over the camera. And what if we can only see three images at once because we don't know how to operate the system but someone else who does has their screens set to monitor multiple feeds at once?" Surgeon still wasn't convinced.

"Yes, sir, all that's true. But along with the negative 'IFs' there are also the positive ones as well. What if there aren't any other sentries? What if their system allows only one guard to be on at a time in these pods? What if they are monitoring six images per screen, making each image smaller and our actions less obvious?" Seth knew Surgeon wasn't buying it. "Look, it's all we've got. It's not a good plan but show me something better. The only other choice is to waltz into the hallway and get to work on that elevator. We know we'll be spotted with that plan but we might not be with this one."

Surgeon knew Seth was right. The plan sucked but it's what they had. "All right, Cadet, set up your feed visor and the tension line." Turning to the rest of his team, he ordered, "Hey Shorty, come here. We've got a great plan and you're the centerpiece."

Shorty heard the plan and shook his head. If this didn't work, he'd be exposed and by himself when it didn't work. "It sucks being short."

All of the camera views were uniform and their angles were as exact as any engineer could have made them. Seth used that to his advantage and set the visor to display its image at the proper angle regardless of how it was placed on the camera.

Once everything was set, Shorty got onto the tension line and pulled himself towards the security camera. As he prepared to put the visor over the camera, he heard a soft click coming from the camera. He paused, waited, and about twenty seconds later, he heard the same sound. He then subvocalized to Surgeon, "Standby, I need to check out a theory."

Shorty heard a comm click, meaning Surgeon copied the transmission. Every twenty seconds, Shorty heard the same soft click coming from the camera. He wasn't sure but he thought he knew what the click was and told the rest of his team. "Every twenty seconds, I hear a soft click coming from inside the camera. I think it's the noise some pieces of electronics make when power is supplied or cut from them. So every twenty seconds this camera is cycling on or off."

Seth shook his head and looked to Surgeon. "If he's right, then someone is monitoring that feed on a timed loop. If it were just a default setting sent to all of the stations, manned or unmanned, we'd be seeing the feed switch at our console every twenty seconds."

"My thoughts exactly." Shorty continued, "I can't tell which click is for on and which is for off. I've a got a fifty-fifty chance either way so I'm just going to nut up and do it on the next cycle."

Another single comm click from Surgeon. Shorty then heard the camera's soft click and he put the visor in place and secured it. Shorty dropped from his line and brought his weapon up towards where his enemy would come from, if the enemy ever came. He wouldn't be able to hear the next camera click now that he was away from the camera, but he counted to himself and knew the camera had moved onto the next cycle a second or two after he came off the line.

With forty meters of hallway between him and the adjacent pod, it was better to face forward and prepare to fight if necessary rather than turn his back towards a potential threat and then run to the nearest cover. He could hear at least two of his teammates running towards him to help out in case the plan didn't work and an enemy came from around the corner. By the time they arrived, they all had the same thought: the plan must have worked because there should have been an alarm or something set off if the enemy had been alerted to their presence.

They slowly backed away from the corner, moving towards the rest of the team at the elevator. The three things you always want in any dangerous situation is time, distance, and shielding. This concept is true regardless if you're working with radiation, bullets flying at you, or an ex-girlfriend. The farther they could get from the corner of the hallway would give them time and distance; shielding wasn't available but you take what you can get in combat.

By the time Shorty and his cover operators got back to the elevator, the rest of the team was waiting to descend into the complex. Seth was speaking to Surgeon. "Like I said, I have no idea which floor we should start on. I'd say we go to the floor that seems to have the most elevator traffic. This button has more fingerprints around it than the others."

Surgeon looked at the panel of twenty buttons. Symbols next to each button were probably floor numbers or descriptions but they had no idea what they were. "That's as good of a plan as any. Use a mark of some sort to show which floors we've been to. My luck we'll have to go through every floor before we find our people."

The alien warriors were so much bigger than humans, so there was plenty of room in the elevator for everyone. Some engineering designs seemed fairly common between bipedal species as it was in this case in that the elevator had an access hatch in the roof of the elevator car. No matter the builder, every piece of equipment needed repair or maintenance at some point or another.

Surgeon put four operators through the hatch and on to the top of the car. This would protect them from an ambush if any enemies were waiting for the elevator doors to open at a certain floor. The four extra guys could then join the fight during a moment of opportunity and add some unexpected guns to the battle and hopefully turn the ambush to their favor.

The car descended twelve floors before the doors opened. The warrior who stood at the doors was just as surprised by the humans standing in the elevator as they were to see him. Action is always faster than reaction but both sides were starting from almost the same point and reacting to each other's unexpected presence.

The warrior's reaction was just a bit faster, though, as he reached into the elevator with his two lower arms and grabbed Shorty, who was closest to him. With his two hands wrapped around the human's skull, he began to squeeze while using his two upper arms to push away from the elevator, giving him some distance from the armed enemies the elevator contained.

Surgeon reached for Shorty but he wasn't fast enough and his friend was pulled away from the rest of the team. Surgeon heard and then saw Shorty's skull cave in under the pressure of the warrior's grip. At this point, there was no saving his friend and the enemy was using Shorty as a shield. Several operators had begun shooting the warrior, aiming for the areas Shorty's body wasn't blocking.

Surgeon fired multiple rounds through Shorty's crushed skull and consequently began to tear the enemy's hands apart. Some of the rounds also continued through the warrior's hands and into his face. The other operators followed Surgeon's lead and began choosing their points of aim on what they thought were crucial points rather than worrying about hitting their buddy.

The warrior went down quickly, taking Shorty's body with him. During the contact, the operators in front had taken low positions and began advancing on their target while the next few operators stayed standing and also fired on the enemy. In the two to three seconds it took for the fight to start and finish, several operators had moved out of the elevator; those operators now pushed past the fallen enemy and took up firing positions in case any more came to their location. Other teammates exited the elevator and took up positions to cover unprotected angles. Those who needed to reload did so.

At first, Surgeon was a little concerned at the amount of firepower needed to take down the warrior but as he inspected the body his fears were somewhat relieved. This alien didn't have a personal shield like the first one they encountered, so all of their rounds actually caused damage. To the team he said, "We put a lot of rounds into this guy but from the looks of it, we really didn't need to. He didn't have a personal shield like the first one. Also, the rounds to his head and chest seemed to have the desired and common effect of anyone else we shoot.

"I know our first encounter made us a little heavy on the trigger for this contact but let's dial it back unless we know they've got a shield on."

He got several affirmative head nods and a couple of "Copy" responses. He gave the signal to start moving out and that's when the first plasma bolt took one of the operators off his feet and burned through his chest. The team dove to positions of cover as best they could.

The hallway was longer than the one they had just come from but this one had several doors and rooms coming off of it. The team members started dumping into rooms for protection. The first two or three men in the room cleared the room while the last man took up a firing position in the doorframe to attack or defend against the oncoming enemy. The doorways were large enough to fit at least two defenders in each one.

The four operators still on top of the elevator held their position. Joker was in charge of this team. "Hold fast, guys. Jumping into the car now would just get us killed." Turning to Beast, he added, "Get a drop camera and put it in the elevator so we can view the hallway."

Beast grabbed a drop camera and tossed it into position near the elevator doors. He then ripped the roof hatch off of its hinges and tossed it on the floor in a position that wouldn't allow the doors to close. Joker gave him a quick nod, showing approval of Beast's forethought.

On the camera, they could see the battle unfolding. Without personal shields on, the warriors were a bit more conservative with their tactics. They were setting up firing positions that were typical in this given situation. They were feeling out their enemy's tactics and resolve and not pushing things too far at this point.

The warriors' plasma bolts had less effect on the hallway walls than the operators' bullets did. Joker made a mental note to get a sample of the wall after the firefight. He also put the note into his visor's failsafe memory. If Joker died, then everything in his failsafe memory would be transmitted to the team leader's visor.

As any species progressed in weapons design, the structural technologies changed to match the weapons' abilities. You wouldn't want a military structure to be completely vulnerable to the weapons you just made, so you had to beef up the materials. Joker theorized that the hallway walls were built to provide some protection from plasma fire but projectile weapons are so ancient to this species that the walls are less able to withstand hits from them. If the Coalition could figure out what is in the walls, then maybe they could make body armor out of the same materials.

In the hallway, the firefight raged on, this one much longer than the previous. Neither side gained ground as both probed the other for weakness and general tactics. Eventually one side would have to give and both knew that most likely it would be the invaders.

The home team always had the advantage in this sort of situation. They had more supplies, usually more soldiers, more knowledge of the battlefield and just generally more of everything needed in this sort of situation. Surgeon knew it and the enemy knew it. But Surgeon knew one thing that they did not: he had four operators hidden above the elevator. He just had to figure a way to get that leverage into the fight.

He put the question to the team. "I think we all know that we need to start pushing this fight to them. I can't see what everyone else is looking at so I'm open to suggestions here."

Ratchet spoke up from one of the forward rooms. "We've got some sort of gas cylinders in our room. We don't know what they contain but based on their construction we're guessing it's under a lot of pressure. So even if the gas inside isn't combustible, it should vent pretty damn fast. I think the cylinders are meant to vent rather than explode, so maybe we could launch them downrange and see what happens."

Surgeon wasn't completely against the idea. "Let's hold that one for a minute. Anyone else have anything less Hail Mary-ish?"

The weapons fire from both sides had slowed to a trickle as the temporary stalemate became more obvious. Joker was looking at his team for ideas when he saw something he hadn't noticed before. "Can anyone down there see vents in the ceiling? And if so, how big are they?"

Seth keyed in a command on his visor. "I see one. I'm sending you my visor feed."

Joker smiled. "Okay, guys, here's the plan: we have a vent access hatch in the elevator shaft that looks like it links up with the one Cadet is looking at. My team is going to strip down our gear and get in the vent system. Hopefully we can get on top or behind the enemy. We'll drop down some grenades and assault from there."

"Sounds good, buddy." Surgeon added, "If you can't get through the vents on their side, do something, anything, to get their attention turned around to you so we can push our assault from this side. Also, Ratchet, I want your idea in place and ready to go as a last resort."

Ratchet had already started making preparations for his idea and had six of the heaviest cylinders ready near the door.

Cadet also added to the plan. "We'll need to keep them distracted while Joker's team is moving above them. We also need to conserve ammunition, so when Joker starts moving we'll start a three-round rotating volley."

A rotating volley would have each operator rapidly fire three rounds followed by the next operator doing the same thing and this continued in a clockwise rotation from the starting point. This volley caused a constant stream of rounds to go downrange from different points, making it seem like more rounds were being fired than what actually were being fired. With how many operators they had, they would each be firing three rounds about every ten seconds so they wouldn't even be using an entire one hundred fifty round magazine in five minutes of shooting and that should be long enough for Joker to get into place.

Joker's team was already getting the vent cover off and putting their first man through when Cadet had finished his comment. When they were about halfway down, Joker put the rest of the team into action. "Let's start up that volley fire, guys; we're about halfway to them."

The team started firing their three-round volleys and achieved their desired effect. The trickle of gunfire turned back into a full-fledged gunfight. Initially, the alien warriors were taken aback by the increased rounds but then they began unleashing more plasma bolts into the hallway and a couple even moved forward towards unoccupied rooms nearest them.

Surgeon would've let the enemy come to him if the tables were reversed so he was a bit surprised to see his enemy leave cover just to gain a paltry ten meters of ground. One of the warriors paid the price and went down after two rounds went through one eye. "Nice shot", he said to no one in particular, unaware of where the rounds came from. The other warrior made it to his intended destination and took up the first foothold in the hallway that his side had been able to attain up to this point. Surgeon wanted that foothold to be their first and last.

"Ratchet, put one of those canisters in the hallway but don't light it off yet." Surgeon just wanted to see how his enemy would react to the gas cylinder in the hallway. If they became more cautious, then it was probably a good idea. If they didn't care about the cylinder, then it was probably not going to help them. If they all ran like hell at the sight of it, then it would probably be best not to shoot it.

Ratchet placed one of the cylinders on a dolly that was meant for moving them around. He rolled the dolly into the hallway and pushed it forward. The dolly ended up in the middle of the hallway and pointed in the right direction.

Initially, the warriors in line of sight of the cylinder ducked but then cautiously peeked around the corner to see what the invaders were up to. The volley fire continued but the next shot from the warrior was clearly aimed at the cylinder, though it missed. Surgeon aimed and fired one round directly into the valve mechanism on the neck of the cylinder.

The bottle vented as Ratchet theorized it would and the cylinder became a missile. It wasn't a fast-moving missile as missiles go but at about a hundred kilometers an hour, it would severely injure or kill anyone it hit during its travels.

The warrior who had taken the room in the hallway peered out just in time to see the cylinder fly within centimeters of his head and continue down the hallway. The near-miss caused panic fire from the warrior and he let lose a plasma round.

The plasma passed through the vented gas from the cylinder and there was no more question of whether or not the gas was flammable. The vapor ignited and a brilliant greenish purple tail of fire chased the cylinder in an attempt to catch the source of the venting gas. And the tail did catch the cylinder a half second later and the explosion put both sides on their respective asses. Most of the gas must have vented before the explosion because it wasn't as bad as Surgeon would have expected.

The team was back up and the volley fire resumed. "Do you think we can repeat that but in a controlled and purposeful manner?" Surgeon was taking his turn in the volley fire.

Ratchet was already thinking the same thing. "I don't think so. If we ignite it too soon, then it explodes on our side of the fight and if it hasn't had a chance to vent a lot of gas, I'm pretty sure it would kill us." There was a small pause. "But I do have some empty bottles in here."

"Good call." Surgeon was reworking his plan. "If we can get them far enough down the hallway, it will cause them to duck and cover. If we can't get them far enough, then the cylinders will draw their fire as they attempt to explode the gas on our side. Either way, we should get one or two small windows when our guys aren't taking direct fire. Let me know when you're ready.

"Joker, are you getting close?"

Joker and his team were having a more difficult time getting in position than they had expected. "We're almost there. Give us two more minutes."

Joker knew as well as Surgeon did that two minutes was a lifetime in a firefight, so if that's what Joker said he needed, Surgeon had to trust him that it couldn't be done in less time. "No pressure, buddy; we're all just waiting on you. The fate of the galaxy and all that."

More weapons fire from the hallway rang out through the ventilation system Joker's team was pulling themselves through. The ducts divided and went in opposite directions of where they wanted to end up. On the squad push, Joker relayed their readiness. "We've reached the end of the line. The ducts split and go away from our targets. We didn't get as far behind them as we had hoped; in fact, we're pretty much right on top of them. In ten seconds, start your diversion and then we'll make our move when we see the best window of opportunity."

Joker put two operators in the middle while he and Beast went to vent openings about five meters apart. As Joker's team was getting set, Surgeon's team got started with the diversion.

Ratchet had the near-empty cylinder ready to go. Surgeon pointed at Ratchet and then gave him the thumbs-up. Ratchet sent the cylinder flying down the hallway and he received the response they were hoping for. All except one of the warriors ducked for cover as the impromptu missile sped their way.

The one who did not take cover attempted to shoot the cylinder as it came towards him. After two shots went wide, he dropped his weapon and stepped into the hallway in front of the projectile. If the cylinder had been full, his plan wouldn't have worked: the cylinder would have at the very least taken him along for the ride, if not tearing through him first. This cylinder was almost completely empty, so it only had enough gumption to get itself down the hallway and at a fairly slow speed.

The warrior caught the cylinder in all four arms and was pleasantly surprised to have not been killed by the impact. And although that was a fortuitous happenstance, Surgeon's men were well equipped and trained to take advantage of unforeseen outcomes. Two of the operators immediately opened fire on the still slowly venting cylinder. There wasn't enough gas or pressure left to cause an explosion but there was enough left to start a fire. That fire blossomed instantly to engulf the previously safe warrior.

Joker saw the warrior catch the cylinder and figured this was a good time to start his assault. He gave the command to fire and the two operators in the middle of the duct began shooting through the duct work and ceiling. They didn't know exactly where their rounds were going but based on the video feed they were still receiving from the drop camera in the elevator, they were pretty sure they were close to their targets.

One of the warriors who was ducking for cover felt the heat from his brother's living funeral pyre and then felt a few of the human's rounds go through his leg. The wounds didn't hurt so much as his brain registered an injury that needed to be taken care of later. He also reflexively pulled his leg away from the incoming bullets and began to turn to face his enemy. In the hallway stood an opponent worthy of his time. The non-human roared a challenge and raised an edged weapon that was all too familiar to the warrior; he knew it had once belonged to one of his brothers.

As Beast dropped from the vent, he felt the heat of the fire coming off his enemy. Although the cylinder didn't explode, it did create a little extra overpressure that could be felt as Beast tried to land on the floor. The fire caused Beast to try to roll away from the flaming enemy and the extra overpressure caused him to trip up a little as he made his landing. The combination of the two events caused Beast to drop his weapon and he saw it clatter several meters away from him.

Usually Beast had his weapon slung to his body but he had to remove the sling to make it easier to get through the ducts. As Beast processed his current situation, he saw the second warrior near him take several rounds to his leg. The warrior quickly turned to avoid further injury and was going to be face to face with Beast before the fallen rifle could be retrieved. Without skipping a beat, Beast pulled the edged weapons he had taken from the first warrior they encountered at the airlock.

    He roared a challenge to the warrior and received a curt head nod in response. The fight had started.

    Both fighters had more enemies in the hallway to deal with beyond each other, so this was going to be quick, one way or the other. No circling, no taunting, no time to size each other up. The first strike came from Beast as he made a bold overture for the death symphony he was now a part of. The upward slash was more powerful than the warrior expected for an opening move and he lost a hand for his lack of preparedness. Beast was also surprised by its effectiveness but he always prepared for victory and not defeat, so he was able to use his forward momentum to bring his body into a spin towards his enemy and he attempted to use his second blade to further the damage to the warrior's already injured forward leg.

    The warrior felt his mistake as he watched his hand leave his body. He also saw Beast turning in towards him and lifted his leg away from the attack and planted his foot into Beast's chest. Beast's body began to move away from the force of the blow but the warrior grabbed Beast's arm and brought him back into the fight. This move turned Beast's back towards his enemy and the warrior used his four arms and three hands to pin Beast to his own body.

    Beast was caught and he knew it. The warrior was far stronger than he was and there was no way he was going to break the monster's grip. Beast could feel the warrior trying to bend his body and break his back. Beast was slowly losing ground and felt more than one muscle group reach its limit and start to tear. Joker was within spitting distance but dealing with his own fight. Beast now saw a plasma bolt burn through the ceiling in the area his two teammates had been firing from. Blood was already dripping to the floor; at least one of them had been shot and most likely dead. Beast knew the rest of the team was moving forward through the hallway but they wouldn't reach him in time.

As Joker landed, he saw three of the alien warriors taking cover from the oncoming blast of the cylinder that had just been launched at them. In the absence of the expected explosion, one warrior was just starting to peek out from his cover to see what was going on. Joker put a three-round burst through the warrior's head and shifted to his next target.

The gunfire from Joker along with the shots from the operators still in the ducts was enough to make the second warrior move from cover and jump into the fight. He put one plasma round through the ceiling and received immediate gratification when he heard his unseen enemy cry out in pain. He was shifting his point of aim towards the closer threat that was Joker but the human was fast and spun inward, coming closer to the warrior.

Joker's spin brought him too close for the warrior to fire but much closer than Joker wanted to be. Hand-to-hand combat was not a good idea given the vast disparity between the two fighters. Joker released a barrage of rounds just as the warrior grabbed his gun barrel and shifted his point of aim. Although the moving gun made Joker miss his target, it did cause multiple rounds to hit and damage the warrior's plasma rifle, making it unusable.

Joker let go of his rifle, knowing that he could never wrest it from the grip of his enemy. He used the momentum of his spin to keep turning and end up behind the giant. As Joker got to the end of his spin, he was already drawing his pistol from its holster and saw the third warrior moving towards the confrontation.

One round from his handgun ended the warrior in front of him but unfortunately the warrior decided to die backwards instead of forwards. The bulk of the warrior fell back onto Joker and pinned most of the left side of his body against the wall.

    In any other situation, Joker would've eventually been able to get himself out from under his fallen enemy but right now he didn't have the luxury of time. His pistol was still in his right hand and he pulled the trigger. The first round went wide and clipped his oncoming attacker in the left shoulder. Joker adjusted his aim and—click. The spent casing had stove-piped in the chamber and never cycled the next round.

    Hundreds and thousands of hours spent on the range and in combat is the most valuable asset in this sort of situation as calm instead of panic filled Joker and he immediately began to clear his weapon malfunction. He brought the gun down to his waist and hooked the rear holographic sight on his utility belt and worked the action away from his body. Joker actually heard the casing ping off the wall behind him as well as the slide moving along the frame and back into a firing position. He heard the satisfying sound of the slide picking up the next round in the magazine and bringing it into battery so it could be sent downrange in righteous triumph.

    Surgeon and Cadet were moving up through the hallway on opposite sides of each other. They, along with their team, were putting suppressive fire down the hallway to keep the two remaining warriors in their positions of cover. Two grenades, one from each side of the hallway, went over Cadet and Surgeon's heads. The grenades crossed as they passed each other and went into opposite rooms. The low-yield explosives in the grenades were made specifically for close quarter combat so the team kept moving forward, in order to follow the planned explosions with overwhelming gunfire into the enemies' positions of cover.

    The explosions came near simultaneously and a half second later, Cadet swung into the room closest to him and

Surgeon took the one on his side, each with another operator following them. Both warriors had a number of injuries but both were pretty much incapacitated and easily finished off by the entry teams.

Smoke was now in the first position as he passed by the doorway and heard gunfire from Surgeon. Smoke saw Beast getting bent backwards as Joker's weapon jammed. Both operators were in a losing fight but Beast's attacker was too obscured by Beast's body as well as the corner of the wall. Smoke knew that in a couple of steps he would be able to fire on Joker's attacker and save at least one of his friends.

Through a haze of pain, Beast saw Joker's weapon malfunction. Beast twisted to his right, purposely pulling his shoulder from the socket and breaking almost every bone in his upper left arm and shoulder. He was trying to swivel so once his destroyed left arm was free, the leverage the warrior was applying to Beast's body would be lost. Without the leverage, Beast would be able to remove his right arm from the warrior's grip and get to his handgun and fire at Joker's attacker.

Beast's plan might have worked with an opponent who didn't have four arms. Although he did free his left, and now completely destroyed arm, the warrior's two lower arms maintained a secure grip on Beast's torso. The warrior increased his effort to bend Beast backwards and his back started to break in more than one place.

Beast couldn't move his left arm above the elbow and had no motion whatsoever in his shoulder. He could still use his wrist, hand, and fingers, though. Beast moved his left hand to his utility belt and found the grenade in its pouch. A lumbar vertebrae snapped. Beast flicked two of his fingers and opened the pouch. Two thoracic vertebrae snapped. He pulled the pin from the grenade and felt the spoon attempt to separate from the body of the grenade. The grenade's spoon was inside the pouch, so it couldn't separate from the body and initiate the firing sequence. Three more vertebrae snapped and Beast knew parts of his body were fast becoming non-operational.

Having only the limited range of motion that came with a moving wrist, Beast's plan was unfolding very slowly. He saw Joker clear the malfunction of his handgun and start to bring it towards his attacker. Beast could tell that though it would be a close race, Joker was going to lose. The warrior would have his hands on Joker before he could produce a lethal shot.

Beast inched the grenade from its pouch and finally felt the spoon spring from the grenade's body. This was a CQB grenade so it would have a fast fuse, only three seconds, and with parts of his body going numb, he hoped he could hold it for that long. If he dropped the grenade, it could get kicked away or even towards his teammates. It was low-yield explosive so he needed it near his target and the warrior was still unaware of what Beast was doing. Two seconds left. Another vertebrae snapped. Beast held the grenade and tried his best to aim it towards the warrior behind him. Almost as much as wanting to ensure the safety of his friends, he wanted to live long enough to feel the heat of the explosion and the satisfaction of knowing that he died on his own terms and took his enemy with him.

One second left. Another vertebrae snapped and a vertebral disk was squeezed out of his body, severing the spinal cord on its way out. Beast's hand went numb and though he couldn't feel it, he knew he dropped the grenade. The heat was instantaneous and death was almost as fast, but the speed of Beast's neurons fired faster and the knowledge that he had won spread to his conscious mind before he entered oblivion.

Beast then looked up and saw his brother standing before him. "I've missed you, brother."

~

Joker heard a small 'whump' from somewhere to his left and he knew that a CQB grenade had detonated in close proximity of at least one body. He knew his gun wouldn't be aimed at a lethal target before his enemy put a huge bladed weapon through his face but he fired anyway. To anyone just hearing Joker's gunfire, it might sound like 'panic fire' but it was nothing of the sort. Joker was still calm and even accepting of the situation but that didn't mean that he wasn't also hopeful. Hopeful that his rounds might shift his attacker and give him an opening. Hopeful that maybe the warrior had different weak points than Joker and the rounds would be effective. Hopeful that God would send a bolt of lightning down and burn the warrior to a crisp. To accept the situation kept him calm. To stay calm gave him hope and kept him strong and in the fight.

The lightning never came but several rounds from Smoke did. Joker felt one round pass by his head and hit the wall next to him. Some of the backsplash came back and opened Joker's cheek. The next round had a bit of correction added to it and so did the next as the rounds were walked backwards to their intended target, which was the head of the warrior attacking Joker. As the rounds walked backward, they also struck and deflected the weapon coming towards Joker's head.

Blue spray erupted from the warrior's head and his forward momentum carried him onto Joker's right side. "Seriously! Two of these fuckers on me! You've got to be kidding me! And you," Joker pointed at Smoke, "you, sir, need to get to the range more often. You almost took my head off."

Smoke was already helping pull the warriors off Joker. "I didn't know if I could kill him before his blade cut your head down the middle. I was aiming for the blade so I think I did just fine."

Joker just smiled. "Thanks, buddy." As he started to stand, he saw Beast lying on the ground, obviously dead along with his dead enemy. Joker shook his head and then heard someone softly calling for help.

The rest of the team had made it down the hallway and all of the opposition had been killed. Joker looked around for the source of the voice and then looked up. The ceiling had a plasma burn through it and blood dripping to the floor. Joker turned to the men standing around him. "Get me in the vent! They're hurt!"

Joker was lifted into the vent and he turned on his visor light. The plasma bolt had melted one operator's skull and the arm of the other. Joker crawled to him. "How are you doing, buddy?"

"I've been better. I'm sorry I couldn't help more. I watched Beast die and I couldn't move to help him."

The operator pointed, with his remaining hand, to the right side of his body. Joker saw that not only was his arm melted off, but most of the right side of his body had fused to the metal of the duct work.

The operator pulled a CQB grenade from its pouch. "Don't worry. I'm fine with it. We don't have time to peel me from the vent, not to mention that I doubt I'd live through the process anyway."

Reaper had crawled into the vents from the side Beast had come through. He began his patient assessment and nodded to Joker what the operator had already stated: he wasn't leaving the vent alive. Reaper didn't even ask; he injected his friend with some morphine and watched his eyelids get heavy.

Reaper gently removed the grenade from the operator's hand and put it into his own equipment. "I gave him a sedative painkiller cocktail. He doesn't have much time left; he won't feel anything else." Reaper and Joker took some more of the gear, along with their friends' dog tags.

After getting out of the vent, Joker saw that Surgeon had assembled the remaining squad members, set up a forward security detail and was in the process of reviewing their assets. Cadet was taking the initiative and acting more and more like the XO of the operation. Joker didn't mind at all; the kid was sharp and definitely officer material—good officer material.

"We're down three more operators, a few injuries but nothing that will hinder the operation." Cadet continued his report to Surgeon. "We have a fair amount of ammo and explosives left. We can handle probably five more assaults of the same intensity of the last one. After that we're going to have to go with edged weapons or try to lug around the plasma rifles that these guys are carrying. Their operation is fairly simple but we'll definitely be at the disadvantage if we have to resort to them."

Surgeon looked around at his men. "Without their personal shields, they are no match for us. We have seen in our limited engagements that their training is superb and nothing to laugh at, but, they obviously have limited field experience and that's where we are proving to be the better fighters.

"Stay out of their reach. They have a drastic advantage in hand-to-hand combat. From now on, if at all possible, we will engage each one of them in two-man teams, just like room clearing. That way, if one of them does get a hand on you, your buddy can help you out.

"We still don't know where we are in this complex but we happened upon several of them at once, so hopefully that means we're on the right track. We've lost good men and great friends. Let's make sure it wasn't for nothing."

Cadet got a small nod from his mentor and he took over. "All right guys, there's only one direction to go in this hall so that's where we're going. The fact that we haven't heard an alarm or had more defenders come our way means that either these guys didn't trip an alarm or the guy in charge is keeping his troops in one location and waiting for our final push.

"If they are all together in one place, then we need to do our best and treat the final contact as a near ambush and push through it. Our resources are limited and we have to assume that theirs are not. We can't afford a lengthy firefight. To that end, push hard but smart. Don't waste ammo or more important, your lives."

With the updated ops plan in place, the group simply moved out: silent in their resolve, silent in their pain, silent in their mourning.

Chapter 49
The Debrief

Wilks and Bloom sat at the conference table with the base command staff and Captain Netid and his senior officers. Also in the room via video conferencing was the president of the Coalition, the Detrill emperor and the Nortes empress.

Bloom felt a little out of his comfort zone as he spoke to the extremely high-ranking audience that seemed to hang on his every word. Between the information passed along by the Detrill, the Nortes, and Bloom's virtual memory stroll, the group had a fairly detailed account of what had taken place a thousand years ago.

The president spoke after Bloom finished. "To sum it up, and please let me know if I get anything wrong here: Several thousand years ago, the Nortes were conquering the galaxy as they progressed through it. They had a lab-created warrior species that was the muscle behind their operation but it was led by a Nortes military structure. Every species they encountered was subjugated and used for particular skills that suited them or were made to suit them, and if the species was deemed not useful to the empire, they were destroyed."

The president paused as he looked around the group to see whether he was on track so far. "Then, a thousand years ago, give or take, the emperor wanted to create a peaceful empire that was devoid of the warriors and conquering. But due to the genetic programming of his warriors, he couldn't do that because it would be seen as the destruction of the empire and the warriors were created to protect the empire at all costs.

"So the emperor made a final push into what is now our area of the galaxy and he faked a plague that killed a large portion of his population. He quarantined his people from the established empire with the idea that without a royal family and very little Nortes military support, the warriors would live out their relatively short lifespan and then the defectors could return home and build a new empire based on cooperation and not slavery."

Empress Hugany shifted in her chair a little. Bloom finished the story. "Yes, Mister President, that is correct. Unfortunately, the royal cousin in charge of being the guardian of the warrior birthing planet suspected an internal coup and launched fifty million warrior birthing pods to a safe planet where they could later be recovered. The warrior caste has been replenishing their numbers from that pool of pods ever since. They've also used a stasis rotation cycle that allows them to keep their senior warriors around longer to lead them all. The stasis rotation only gives each one an extra ten to fifteen years each but every little bit helps."

"And we don't know their current strength, correct?" The president directed his question to his top military advisor.

"No, sir, we don't. We can't even take an educated guess. We are attempting to use Sergeant Bloom's decryption and sifting program to go through the newest vessel we captured but so far we don't have anything. There's no reason to believe we'll find detailed information in the memory of a fighter craft." The advisor turned and gave a slight nod to Bloom, an acknowledgement of his contribution to the mission.

"Sir," Bloom started, "we can throw around some simple math but we still don't know what we're up against.

It's been one thousand years since the purge; if they have an average life cycle of fifty years each, they have gone through twenty full life cycles in that time. If they were conservative and birthed one million warriors every fifty years, they would still have thirty million in reserve."

"What about training time? Wouldn't they have to account for that in their cycle?" the president asked.

Bloom sighed. "No, sir. The warriors are born fully ready to go. They do gain experience and ability with every life experience, just as we do, but most of their abilities are trained via implanted genetic memories."

"But we do know that they had a devastating war with a species known to them as the Cherta. Who knows how many warriors they lost during that conflict? We could be looking at millions of warriors or a relative handful of a few hundred thousand."

The empress was handed a tablet from one of her aides standing outside the camera's view. Her face slackened and she interrupted. "The birthing planet's origin is probably the most heavily guarded secret in all of my empire. The warriors are genetically engineered to have an aversion to its location. They are not supposed to be able to set coordinates to or near it."

The president looked over as she paused. "I sense a rather large 'however' coming."

"Yes, Mister President." The empress steadied herself. "The coordinates have always been guarded but there is a deeply embedded and highly encrypted line of programming in our surveillance systems that if any ship is detected going near the coordinates, a simple message of 'Inform the royal house of incursion' is given to the ruling member of the royal family. The message does not state the coordinates or the nature of the incursion but the message is clear to whom it was delivered."

"And you just received that message?" The military advisor shifted his chair towards the empress.

"I just received six hundred forty-seven counts of that message." The empress handed the tablet back to the unseen aide on her side. "It would seem as though a large portion, or maybe the entire warrior fleet, has found their way home. If they have found a way to overcome their genetic programming to stay away from the birthing planet, it's reasonable to believe that they have also found a way to access the planet or at the very least, they believe it to be possible."

Without waiting for anyone to ask the obvious, Bloom spoke up. "That would give them access to billions of already grown warriors and presumably the ability to grow more."

"Fuck." And when that comes from the president of the known galaxy, you kind of want to piss yourself a little.

Chapter 50
The Warrior Interrogation Planet - The Rescue Continues

The last warrior fell and Surgeon's team suffered no worse than an injury that had to be battle-stapled before they moved on. Everyone teased Reaper because he always smiled, a little too much, when he got to staple someone after a firefight. With the twenty staples in place and a good layer of a skin adhesive tissue growing compound, they were back on the move.

They had encountered mild resistance on their way towards what seemed to be the center of the complex. Surgeon thought that Cadet's assessment was correct: the guy in charge was pulling his forces back to defend a single location. All of the warriors they encountered were obviously trying to tactically retreat to the same location. None of them were on the offensive or trying to hold their position. The tactical retreat might have worked in most situations but with Cadet's plan to treat everything as a near ambush and push through it, a standard peel-off maneuver couldn't survive an aggressively forward-moving unit of highly motivated and angry soldiers.

As they were clearing the rooms in the hallway, Joker came over the comlink. "Surgeon, Cadet, come to my location. I found what I think is a map of this structure."

When they reached the room Joker was in, he pointed to the wall. "I think this is a security office by the look of it. This map shows the complex, checkpoints, barriers, and other stuff. Of course, we can't read any of it but the symbology looks fairly straightforward."

"I think this shaded room represents where we are." Seth traced his finger along the map. "And that is where we need to go." A confident finger tapped the map.

Surgeon took in the whole map and could see in his mind's eye the battles they just fought in the different areas. His mind saw his friends' dead bodies on the map where they had left them. "I agree. Once we move through the section just ahead of us, we'll have two corridors to choose from to assault the area that looks like our target."

"I think we should assault from both corridors at the same time." Seth pointed to two locations on the map.

Joker shook his head. "If we split up, we risk hitting hardened locations in either or both corridors with reduced manpower at each. If they are pulling back to protect one location, it would make sense that they would put a contact team in both hallways."

"I agree", Seth began. "But there are also advantages. They probably won't think that we know the layout of the base. They will probably be expecting us to come through the main entry point on this side, probably with a plan to shift defense to the other location if we happened to hit that side instead. If we hit the more obvious entry point first, they will focus there and hopefully not be ready for a secondary attack from behind."

Surgeon was thoughtful for a moment. "You two are like the right and left sides of my brain." He smiled. "I swear with you two around there is no need for me because you always think of everything I ever could. Valid points all. I don't think these guys have encountered humans fighting as aggressively as we have been and it's throwing them off their game. They kicked our asses at every colony they attacked and I'm sure the colonists had purely defensive postures. That's what they were expecting and that's not what we've been giving them. We need to keep moving with what's been working for us so far.

"We go with Cadet's plan and push from both sides. We'll move to these positions here." Surgeon indicated points just before the final hallways to their objectives. "We'll go in a little lopsided: eighty percent of the team on the main assault and twenty percent on the secondary point. We just need the second assault team to throw the defenders into chaos and then we'll push through with the greater numbers in that moment.

"The first team will move into their final hall first while the second team holds back. If there are defenders in this hallway, then we can assume they will also be at the secondary breach point. If they are present, we don't want the second team setting off their defense and warning the main interior defenders of our plan."

Surgeon finished the plan with Cadet and Joker and then the rest of the team. "If there are defenders at these points, hopefully our main assault will draw the defenders from the secondary hallway into the main structure here." He pointed at the map again.

Seth jumped in. "Reaper found some of our weapons in a nearby room. It looks as though they took some from the ship to study them. The fantastic thing is they took some heavy weapons, including explosives and launchers. If team one meets resistance in their hallway, then team two will begin their assault with a heavy barrage of those explosives. With luck, we won't have to fire a single shot at the secondary breach point."

Ammunition from the recovered weapons was being passed out along with explosives and a few launchers. From the time the map was found and the teams were on the move again, it had been less than ten minutes. Seth was leading the secondary team with Surgeon and Joker on the primary. They were so close to their objective but none was prepared for what they were about to step into.

~

The warrior in charge walked through his brothers' positions and made minor adjustments to them as he passed by. Fields of fire that seemed to overlap from a fighter's position always looked different from another perspective and their leader adjusted them accordingly.

The prisoners were still all in their torture tubes but the torturing had been stopped when the first alarm was tripped inside the base. The leader had been notified immediately when the humans set off the alarm on the first control panel outside the base. He immediately silenced the interior alarms and allowed them to move somewhat freely through the base. He wanted his men to be able to fight for their own practice and also for his own need to learn about his enemy's abilities.

So far the leader was impressed. He had been involved in the very first raid of the humans' colonies but his involvement had been limited to the supervision of the transport torture tubes on the primary prison barge. He had witnessed some of the assault via the video link that went through every ship but that was never the same as the real thing.

The humans, and a couple of other mutt races, currently assaulting his base were obviously of much higher training than anyone who had been at any of the outposts. Even the prisoners he currently had from the scout ship they had taken were not of the same caliber as the forces now pushing towards him and his brothers.

The main chamber of the torture well was the last structure of the complex that sat at ground level. There were elevators, ladders, and a single spiral staircase that went twenty levels lower. Each level of the circular structure housed a variety of torture tubes, surgical suites, dissection tables, and other assorted atrocities.

Each station of every level could be observed from the main floor, which contained the heart and brains of the operation. The bulk of the leader's forces were on the main level, waiting for the inevitable assault. He could've fought on any of the levels below that were filled with the crew from the enemy vessel but he didn't want to risk their lives. Not because he cared about them at all, but he had found many unique subjects among the crew and he wasn't quite finished with them yet.

One warrior had suggested fighting from the lower levels and using the subjects as shields to slow down the assaulting forces. That warrior was summarily killed with a single sweep of the leader's blade that removed head from neck. If the warrior was too scared to fight with honor, then he was too scared to live at all. The leader had planned to use his prisoners during the fight but not in that way. The leader knew he could win this fight but he hoped to gain some more knowledge from his enemy before they died.

The monitors clearly showed the hallways leading to the torture well. The team was advancing much as he thought they would. The leader switched the monitors to show as many individual torture tubes as he had screens. Each monitor was focused on the face of the tube's occupant. Each also had a picture-in-picture of a wound that the tube was working on before its efforts had been halted. The faces for now were calm as the prisoners were given this brief respite from their pain. The leader was ready for the assault and he couldn't wait for his enemies to see the faces of their shipmates as the torture tubes resumed their tasks, all at the same time.

The monitors switched from the view of the hallway to the faces of the victims in the torture tubes...

~

A few more steps and Surgeon gave the signal for the team to split in to two assaulting forces. Seth took his team to the left and held at the designated point in the hallway. One of his men passed up a fiber line that would allow them to see around the corner without exposing themselves. Seth waved it off, though he appreciated the forward thinking of his men. Although the fiber camera wasn't much larger than a few strands of hair, Seth didn't want to risk being spotted even if the chance was a near infinitesimal one. The operator nodded once and put the gear back in his pack.

~

Surgeon was on point until Joker pulled up next to him and touched his arm as though he wanted to speak with him. Surgeon paused and looked at his friend and then noticed three of his operators moving past them both and taking up leading positions on the assault team.

"You're a prick", Surgeon subvocalized.

"Maybe, but you're the dumbass that let this prick outwit you. Again." Joker knew his friend would probably outlive them all, even if he were on point for every mission over the course of his whole life, but he wasn't taking any chances. This mission needed Surgeon more than any of the others. Seth would take the mantle if Surgeon went down, not because he was the only officer on the team but because he was the next obvious choice, even with his lesser experience.

The team moved forward to their last point of concealment and cover. The plan was to use a fiber camera to view the hallway before making their move. If the camera was spotted, then they would make an explosive assault. If they could pick out individual targets, then they would attempt coordinated, discrete fire to neutralize their targets.

The camera rounded the corner and a makeshift barricade was on either side of the door. No warriors were in sight. Given the small size of the barriers and the large size of the warriors, Surgeon was fairly sure that plans had changed after the barriers were erected and the defenders were pulled inside the doorway.

New plan. Surgeon motioned his demolitions guys forward and pointed to the door. With a curt nod, they moved forward, knowing what he wanted. Well-placed explosives on the doorway would provide a large breach point and hopefully hurt or kill any enemies just inside the doorway.

As the three operators got about two-thirds of the way down the hall, two auto turrets rose from the small barricades and began firing. The demo guy was cut in half instantly and the other two took a lot of rounds as well. The rearmost demo operator had a remote charge already in his hand, ready to set it on the door. As he fell, he armed and threw it at one of the turrets.

In Surgeon's visor, he saw a demo charge status light go green and he quickly took control of the charge and detonated it. The charge immediately destroyed the turret it was next to and sent shrapnel at the other one. The charge also put a dent in one of the doors it was originally meant for. The damaged turret now had a restricted angle of movement and could only cover about three-quarters of the hallway.

Reaper saw the turret's limitation and jumped into the hallway and into the turret's dead zone. The turret tried to track him and fired as it did so but it came up short. Whatever AI was running the gun realized that Reaper was an unavailable target and went back to looking for more available targets.

Joker saw the turret start to track Reaper and he went to reach for the leg of the demo guy nearest him. Surgeon pulled him back immediately and held him in place. "The turret is tracking back. We'll have to wait for Reaper to disable it."

A pair of CQB grenades detonated and the turret fire stopped. "Clear," was all Reaper said as he held his position and waited for the rest of the team to move forward. Once the doors were covered, he moved to his fallen teammates and checked their status. Dead.

By the time Reaper had gotten back into the stick, the remaining demo charges had been packed up by other teammates. The doors were obviously open and the charges wouldn't be as effective now as anyone on the other side of the door would have most likely moved away when the assault began. Surprise was no longer on their side so violence of action and speed of attack were the only things in their favor.

The three operators on point pushed through the doors and were immediately engaged by the enemy. Unlike the projectile-throwing sentry guns, the warriors in the room used the familiar plasma rifles that the team had been encountering up to this point. But this time the team had a slight advantage.

In the room where they found their crew's weapons stashed, there was also a small firing range. Four of their personal engineering shields were at the end of the range with plasma burns in several places but no penetration to the shields. The shields weren't designed for tactical defense; they were designed for the engineering crew so they could approach radiation leaks and other engineering hazards in order to repair them.

The shields held up perfectly against the enemy plasma fire and allowed operators to take direct hits that would otherwise have killed them instantly. Their unexpected immunity to the oncoming fire was obviously distressing to the enemy because they could hear one voice above all others giving frantic orders. They couldn't understand the orders but any infantryman worth his salt knew they had to be flanking orders to get around the shields.

Taking a page from human history, the shield operators put together as much of a Spartan phalanx formation as they could. The next row of operators moved up and instead of pushing their spears through the phalanx, they pushed their rifle muzzles forward and began picking off targets.

    Surgeon was pleased that this portion of the plan was going better than expected. The sentry guns were a horrible demoralizer but he knew he had to put that out of his mind for now and focus on the battle in front of him.

    As Surgeon pulled his awareness back to the here and now, he became aware of the monitors above his enemies. They were filled with the faces of crew members from their ship. Surgeon didn't know every single crew member so a lot of the faces weren't familiar but there were enough he did know to make him realize what he was seeing. Immediately, he began putting a single round through each monitor so his team wouldn't get distracted, if they weren't already. A quick jab to Joker and he knew what Surgeon was doing and joined in.

~

    The warrior leader was completely taken by surprise by the use of the shields. He must not have seen the humans pick the shields up; it was a costly mistake. He also didn't expect the humans to waste time and resources on the video screens but it did work in his favor.

    Not only did it prove that his enemy had a mental weakness in this area but it took two of their forward shooters out of the fight to deal with it. It was time to implement the second part of his plan before too many of the video screens were gone. The leader pushed a button on the console in front of him.

~

    As Surgeon sighted on the next video screen, the image suddenly and drastically changed. The image of an unconscious and haggard man turned into one of a man suddenly dropped through the gates of hell.

    His face contorted in pain unlike anything Surgeon had ever seen on the battlefield. The picture-in-picture motion also caught his attention and he noticed the surgical pincers moving in and out of a wound in the groin area of the soldier.

If the other operators hadn't noticed the screens before, Surgeon knew they did now. As all of the screens changed near simultaneously, the joint howl of pain cut through the gunfire and reached every one of the operators. The gunfire ceased as everyone watched the screens.

~

The warrior leader was more than pleased with his experiment. The added torment of the prisoners was enough to stop even their most elite fighters. A race that weak could never win against the warriors' superior might and mental fortitude.

~

Reaper was the first to reset his internal frame of mind. Through the command link, he calmly voiced, "Kill every single one of those motherfuckers."

The barrage of weapons fire was simultaneous and near deafening even through their advanced hearing protection. Surgeon stopped shooting the screen and allowed the images to fuel their fire. It was a controlled burn that would incinerate all who stood before it. Surgeon signaled Seth's team to advance.

~

Seth and his team heard the gunfire from the turrets erupt followed closely with explosions from some CQB grenades. His feet adjusted and he was peripherally aware that others in his team also adjusted. Although it was only a few moments later before he heard the gunfire cease, followed by Reaper's declaration of death, it seemed like a lifetime had passed. And then he received the "go" signal from Surgeon.

A quick hand signal to two of his operators and they adjusted themselves in the corridor. One of them put his hand in the air and held out five fingers. Then he counted down to three to set the rhythm and put his hand back on the grenade launcher. When the internal count reached one, they both leaned into the hallway and put a total of six explosive rounds on the target.

Unbeknownst to them, there were two automatic turrets waiting for them at the end of the hallway. Surgeon had known the plan called for an explosive opening salvo so he knew Seth's team wasn't in any danger from the turrets but he had still meant to give them a heads-up just in case; he would later apologize for that mistake.

Seth took point down the hallway after the explosions ended and the shrapnel had stopped bouncing around the hallway. They moved forward in a loose diamond formation. As they approached the breached doors, a chorus of screams could be heard coming from inside. Seth's team didn't know the screams were coming from the video monitors so they were all a little confused as to who was screaming: they couldn't hear it over their company push and the other team was obviously still in the fight, as was evident from the continued gunfire.

As they passed through the doorway, they saw the horrors the rest of their team had been dealing with for the last half minute or so. It caused a small hiccup in their step but not much more and they kept moving. Seth guessed that the screens had turned on after Surgeon started his assault and the abrupt psychological effect had caused the quick lull in the gunfight they had heard a moment ago.

~

The warrior leader was praising himself heavily for the misperceived mental blow he had dealt to the enemy. When the impromptu cease fire ended less than a few seconds later and the enemy pushed forward with even more determination, he realized that he again failed his people. When the rear doors exploded inward, killing three of his brothers, he no longer had any choice. He began inputting the self-destruct code into his console.

~

The engineering shields were doing their job well but the rearmost shooters in the element couldn't handle not being in the fight, not after what they had witnessed on the monitors. They pushed forward and to the sides of the protective barriers and were picking off warriors as if they were paper targets on a static range.

Reaper put down a target and moved to the next. He spotted a warrior who was more interested in the console in front of him than the firefight going on around him. That couldn't be good. A three-round burst sped towards the warrior and impacted with the personal shield surrounding his head. The shield shimmered and the warrior for the briefest of moments looked up and then back to his console and continued his work.

"Shift fire on my target. Highest priority." The order from Reaper was immediately identified by his visor as a team push command and it sent a marker to everyone else's visor highlighting his current target.

~

The fire shifted and the warrior leader was hit with a barrage that nearly took him off his feet but his shield held. The distraction from the explosive entry caused him to pause the self-destruct input and then the overwhelming barrage from the primary team caused him to press a wrong button as he stumbled backwards.

His shield could hold out longer from the projectile weapons than his own plasma rifles but that didn't mean it would hold out forever and the incoming CQB grenades he saw in the air would also hasten the shield's diminishing effectiveness. After the grenades detonated and he was able to reach his terminal again, he saw that he had accidentally set the self-destruct to sixty minutes rather than the minimum of six minutes he wanted.

A projectile entered his right shoulder, meaning his shield wasn't going to be up for much longer. He didn't have time to start the self-destruct sequence all over; sixty minutes would have to suffice. Even with that length of time, he doubted the attackers would be able to figure out the system, release the prisoners and still evacuate the building. A small victory to be sure but at least not a complete loss on his end.

~

Seth saw the CQB grenades come from Surgeon's team and watched them detonate near the warrior. The shield flared but he saw one section that seemed to be devoid of the shimmering so he adjusted his fire towards the warrior's shoulder. At least one round entered his enemy and he was rewarded with a small spray of blue blood.

From there, he knew the fight was won but he was still concerned with what the warrior was doing. Anything that kept his attention on a console rather than being shot at had to be important to the warriors and probably bad for the assault team. A final stab at the console and the warrior backed away from it and entered the fight for the first time since the entry had been made.

Seth could see the console flashing blue, which he knew was bad. The warriors used blue like humans used red: it was a warning, an alert of some sort. The first thing Seth thought of was a self-destruct command. What else was so important that the warrior would neglect impending doom to complete his task? Maybe a full data wipe? Possible but not as likely.

"I know we aren't exactly dawdling here," Seth began, "but the console that shield guy was working at is now flashing blue. I need to get to it immediately to see what he was doing."

Surgeon eyed the battlefield briefly. "Cadet, shift your team to your right and lay down a strong base of fire. Everyone on my team, push now."

Surgeon's fire team pushed forward, coming out of cover and exposing themselves. It was always better to fight from cover if possible but a forwardly aggressive move could also be beneficial. The constant fire from the advancing team caused the enemy to either keep their head down or try to return fire from a horrible fighting position. Also, the assaulting units weren't hampered by trying to fire from a protected position and they tended to be a much more effective mobile shooting platform.

The downside in this particular battle was the warriors' plasma rifles. In a conventional setting, the armor worn by the operators would absorb a fair amount of metal slugs but the plasma tore right through. One of Surgeon's men took a round in the chest and fell dead as another operator stepped over him. Another took a round to the knee and he went prone when his missing leg could no longer support his body. To his credit, the soldier stayed in the fight and continued to fire, effectively, from the ground.

~

The warriors were dropping faster than the assaulting team and they recognized the problem. One warrior took a round to his biologically-armored head and the round skipped away to impact the computers near him. Fighting from cover was safer but every time they peeked their heads out to take an aimed shot, the humans were ready and picked off the warrior.

With the battle obviously not on their side and a loss seemingly inevitable, the best plan was to go on the offensive and fight in the open and up close with the much smaller opponents. The warrior stood and jumped over his covered firing position and made it three steps before his chest was turned into a free-for-all target.

As his wounds expanded, he pulled an edged weapon from its sheath on his back. He was still moving forward at a very impressive speed. He made it far enough to take a swing at one of his enemies but the fact that he was about to die made his swing slow and ineffective. He realized at the last moment that his target wasn't one of the humans but a traitor to the empire. A Nortes was attacking the installation!

The other warriors saw their brother engage the enemy and the effect it had on the enemy's assaulting line. At least four of the enemy soldiers turned their fire to the oncoming attacker and that left holes in their assaulting line. Enough warriors were left to make a hand-to-hand fight devastating to their enemy. They knew that their commander had wanted them to hold out as long as possible behind cover so it would give the self-destruct sequence more time, but that just didn't seem like the best plan right now.

~

As Seth's team held their base of fire, he kept looking for any opportunity that would let him get to the control panel more quickly. He saw one of the warriors leave cover and try to go hand-to-hand with Surgeon's team; it didn't last long. Then the rest of the warriors surged, almost as one, and entered the fight wholeheartedly with the obvious knowledge that this was their last stand. Warriors who knew they were going to die were always a formidable enemy; with nothing to lose, you had nothing to hold back.

For a moment, Seth's thoughts got sidetracked; he saw no commands or signals given that ordered the new tactic. Did their enemies also have some sort of telepathy? Definitely something to investigate later if at all possible.

"Use your smaller sizes to your advantage." Surgeon was putting out orders on the company push. "Don't let these fuckers get a hold of you. Duck. Roll. Whatever to get out of their reach. Break ranks now and work in two-man units to attack them one at a time."

The main assaulting force spread out and started teaming up and in some instances making groups of three.

With four arms, the warriors were actually fairly effective against two of the operators at a time. Seth saw several of his friends take injuries early on and at least two fairly fast deaths. Seth was taken by surprise when one of the operators did the most unexpected thing he had ever seen in combat.

~

Shar'tuk saw that this battle was definitely turning against them. They still had the numbers to win but it would be at the cost of too many of his friends. Shar'tuk knew that he didn't have any royal DNA in his bloodline; that would have been discovered before he was even born. With royal DNA, he could've just ordered the warriors to stop fighting and they would but that wasn't an option. However, because the Nortes were the ruling class of the old empire and the warriors were bred to recognize that, he decided to take a chance that he might be able to use that to his advantage.

As a Nortes soldier, he had been given extensive simulator combat training against the warriors his ancestors had created. Without making it seem too obvious, he had tried to incorporate that knowledge into the many training scenarios he had been a part of during the initial portion of the voyage. As he looked around, it seemed to be paying off as the men from his team were doing a fairly good job of standing their ground. But they were still starting to take more and more damage.

Shar'tuk removed his helmet to fully expose his Nortes heritage and he simultaneously ducked under a bladed weapon and added an injury to one of the warriors' legs with his own blade as he passed. Shar'tuk didn't take the time to continue his engagement with this warrior; he needed to make it to a console he had picked out a moment ago. As he jumped on the console, his extremely out-of-place behavior made him a focal point for the other combatants.

"Warriors of the empire!" Shar'tuk bellowed out with all his might. "I am your Nortes master! Lay down your weapons and stand beside these new members of our empire!"

Surgeon, as well as everyone else on the team, looked to Shar'tuk with astonishment. The warriors looked to him and momentarily paused their efforts. Some were confused by the order from a Nortes who they were genetically programmed to associate with the empire's ruling class. Most of the warriors, however, looked at him with hate in their eyes.

"Traitor!" one of the warriors yelled as he charged Shar'tuk. This caused several of the warriors to break off their engagement with their current opponents and join the attack on the betrayer of the empire.

"Shit." Shar'tuk had in fact changed the pace and focus of the battle but he had done so at his own peril. Luckily, the operators were skilled enough to see the opening and take advantage of it. With several of the two-person teams now disengaged from hand-to-hand combat, they could quickly transition to their shoulder-fired weapons and start cutting down the warriors from behind.

The ceiling in the room was of open construction so there were conduits, beams, and other protuberances for Shar'tuk to grab onto. He jumped and grabbed part of what he thought was most likely a fire suppression system; it held. Pulling himself up into the ceiling, he barely missed the first warrior's swing at him. He knew he was only a second or two away from one of them hitting their mark.

Shar'tuk could see some of the warriors falling to the efforts of his team now using their guns again. He reached to his gear and pulled out a CQB grenade. At this distance to his target, he was risking taking some shrapnel and unwanted overpressure but that was better than taking a sword to the face. He pulled the pin and released the grenade.

If the warriors knew what he was dropping, they didn't act like it. They continued to surge forward, vying for a killing position on Shar'tuk. Their anger and bloodlust actually worked in his favor as they pushed one another and made a couple of potential killing blows go wide and miss their intended target.

Whoomph. The grenade detonated and cleared the warriors from below Shar'tuk. A couple of them were still alive but obviously not for long. He dropped from the ceiling and immediately took a knee as he realized his right leg had taken some shrapnel. The wound wasn't dire but its unexpectedness kept him from bearing his full weight on it.

Shar'tuk took out his sidearm and quickly finished off the warriors who hadn't died in the blast. The fighting was coming to a close as more of the operators were finishing off their targets and joining other groups, making them stronger, and ending their fights faster.

Seth saw an opportunity to get to the console that was blinking blue. There was absolutely no indication of what was going on with the flashing blue warning. He thought that even though he couldn't read their language, a countdown timer would at least have a pattern of characters changing at a constant rate. But there was nothing but characters saying God knows what on a static display.

Seth was vaguely aware that the gunfire had slowed from steady, to a trickle, to cleanup shots as men moved among the fallen enemy, making sure they were dead. "Over here, Surgeon."

Surgeon stepped up to look at the console. "What have you got?"

"I have no idea other than it can't be good." Seth tried tapping a few of the keys on the screen but they wouldn't respond. "They could've called for backup, they could've initiated a data wipe, they could have done who knows how many different things."

"But I'm guessing you have a predominate theory."

"Yes. I think it's a self-destruct command." Seth waved his hand in a frustrated gesture over the console.

Surgeon pointed at Shar'tuk, who was looking at them. "Hey, Emperor!" Shar'tuk looked at him quizzically. "Yeah, that's your new nickname. Get over here."

When Shar'tuk was at his side, Surgeon pointed at the console. "Obviously your people have some connection with this that you're going to tell us about later, but for now, can you read any of this?"

"Surgeon, I want you to know that I am loyal to you, our men, and the Coalition. I will tell you what I know as soon as we're out of here. It's important to me that you trust and believe in me." Shar'tuk looked a little more relaxed, as though the weight of carrying around this huge secret had been partially lifted.

"I trust you, brother." Surgeon put a hand on Shar'tuk's shoulder. "Now, do we have to hug and kiss or something? Or can you get back to work?"

"A hug, definitely a hug later." Shar'tuk turned to the console. "But for now..." He tried touching some keys and nothing happened.

"The language isn't Nortes at all. Maybe at one time it was part Nortes. I see some characters that are kind of familiar but even if I'm correct about what those words are, they aren't contextually important ones, so I don't know what's going on with this console."

By now most of the team had started to police the area and look for gear and supplies they could scavenge: Magazines that had been changed out during a tactical reload would still have valuable ammo in them. Dropped weapons. Packs. Anything possibly useful.

Surgeon addressed the team. "I need three people to scout that stairwell and check the floor below. We all saw the faces on the monitors so we know our people are close and I'm guessing below us. I don't think they held any of their people in reserve but be careful nonetheless; be ready for ambushes while you scout."

Three men broke off and went for the stairwell. He continued, "Reaper, casualty report."

Reaper was still moving among the men and checking them out. It wasn't uncommon for a soldier to get wounded during a battle and not even know it. "We have three who aren't leaving and four with serious but survivable injuries. Of those, two can still move on their own after I finish patching them up. I applied some blood stopper to them but I still need to do some advanced work on them. I'll be done in ten minutes."

Surgeon saw Reaper move to one of the casualties who he assumed was one of the three that weren't leaving. He was still alive but his wounds were horrendous. He had been opened up by one of the warrior's blades and chunks of flesh and body parts were torn away from his body. Surgeon knew Reaper would give him a sedative to slip away in a euphoric haze.

As he was surveying the room and looking for anything important that he might have missed, Surgeon received a comm from the recon team he sent out. "Sir, the prisoners are on the next floor. The area seems to be clear of enemy contact, but you need to get down here with everyone possible."

When Surgeon arrived on the next floor with Seth and Shar'tuk in close tow, he found rows upon rows of tubes holding their shipmates in obvious states of torture. "Cadet, get them out of these things."

"Yes, sir." Seth pulled Shar'tuk towards a command console that was along a nearby wall. "Damn. This one is locked out too."

Shar'tuk moved to one of the tubes and started looking over it as though he knew something should be there. Seth stepped up. "What are you looking for?"

"The torture tubes are the ancestors to the surgical beds my people created a few hundred years ago. The designs are similar enough that I hope it has an emergency shutdown protocol that's manually activated in case of software malfunction."

Shar'tuk was feeling around the tube while shining his light around the back side. "I think I have something." He grabbed a handle that was near the back of the tube, pulled it out of its recessed location and twisted it.

The tube began to flash yellow lights and the surgical gear seemed to be retracting from wherever it had been inside its victim. The person in the tube, Seth recognized as one of the mess hall chefs, became obviously less agonized and relaxed just a little.

Seth pointed his visor towards the handle and put its image out to the rest of the unit. "Find this handle on each tube, pull it out and twist it. We think it's a manual emergency shutdown. Do it to every tube as quickly as you can."

Team members began moving down the rows, deactivating the tubes as they went. As more tubes were deactivated, Seth noticed that some of them were flashing blue instead of yellow. He knew the blue lights were bad but didn't know what their context was in this particular situation.

As Seth was disengaging his eleventh tube, he saw that it began flashing blue. He hadn't been taking the time to look at the faces in the tubes as he went along; he didn't want to get distracted or slow down if he saw someone he knew as a friend and not just another shipmate.

The flashing blue lights made Seth turn and examine this tube's occupant more clearly. Almost instantly Seth thought he knew what the blue flashing meant: the occupant wasn't going to survive the shutdown process. The person he was looking at now was completely unrecognizable. One arm and both legs were missing. One eye was hanging out of the socket while some sort of probe was retracting from somewhere deep inside the victim's skull. The skin and most of the muscle had been removed circumferentially from the entire torso and the rib cage was opened to expose the interior organs. Seth couldn't even tell the gender of this person.

He couldn't stay any longer; he had to move to the next tube. As he turned to move on, he felt a wet sticky hand attempt to grab his arm. Startled, he turned back to see the flesh-stripped hand trying to hold onto his own forearm. The science project-looking face spoke in a raspy voice. "Cadet."

"General?!" Seth thought he recognized the voice.

"Yes." The gruesome husk did his best to continue. "Ship. Still here. Save our people. As many as you can."

"Yes, sir. We're getting them out now. I promise we'll save them." Seth didn't know what else to say. For a brief second, he thought about calling for help to get the old man out but he knew it was a futile gesture. He looked into the general's remaining good eye and tried to come up with something profound or comforting to say before he left.

The general beat him to it.

"Seth, I'm not a pussy." His desiccated lips tried to curl back into a smile. "Just fucking go already."

Seth came to attention and saluted. "Yes sir!"

Seth stepped out of view of the general, pulled his sidearm, and shot his hero in the head.

Seth opened the company push. "That shot was me, no enemy contact. I found the general. He didn't make it." Seth was certain Surgeon would make the correlation between Seth's gunshot and the general not making it but he would still detail him in later.

He continued, "I'm fairly certain now that the blue flashing tubes means its occupants won't survive the shutdown process. We should focus our evacuation efforts on the yellow flashing tubes first and if we have time, come back for the blue ones.

"The general had time to tell me that he thinks the ship is still here. I'm guessing it's in a below-ground hangar because we didn't see any hangars or airfields on the surface."

Surgeon cut in, "I sent our scouts down farther and they found a floor below us with more prisoners, not as many as in this room but some. There are five floors of tubes like these but the last three are empty. The scouts are heading down floor by floor; hopefully, they'll find the hangar bay soon."

Joker spoke up. "I've been thinking: how did they get all of the crew members up here? I doubt they walked them up one by one. There has to be some sort of freight elevator or something to get large groups of prisoners up here."

Seth had finished with his row. "I'm done on my side so I'll start looking for that. It makes sense that there should be something like that around here."

"Take Emperor with you. He might be able to read a sign or something you might miss." Surgeon was also shutting down tubes while trying to oversee the operation.

The room was roughly the size of a football field so it had taken some time to get to the back of it as Seth had been stopping every few meters to shut down another tube. He decided to check along the back wall first and almost immediately found what he was looking for.

"Surgeon, I found an elevator." Seth pressed a button that he figured was a call button; some things were fairly universal concepts among sentient beings. "It is along the back wall, that's why we didn't see it until now. It's fairly big. I'm guessing by just the door size we can easily get fifty people in it at a time."

Reaper spoke up. "That's great but you need to remember that a lot of these people aren't going to be ambulatory. We need to find or figure out a way to get large numbers of people to the elevator all at once or we'll be here for hours."

The three men on the scout came up. "We haven't seen anything that could help with the evac but we'll add that to our list of things to look for. And no hangar so far."

The elevator doors opened and Seth and Shar'tuk had their weapons trained on it just in case it brought more warriors with it. The interior was fairly huge as Seth suspected. They found a control panel with symbols on it. Seth looked to Shar'tuk.

"Sorry, I can't read any of this. It could be a numbering system or it could be actual descriptions of what each floor contains." He reached out and pushed a button; the doors began to close. "Let's hope the universal constant of elevators is the same here. The bottom button goes to the bottom floor and the hangar should be on the bottom floor."

Seth agreed with that concept. If you were building a base with an underground hangar bay, you always put the hangar on the bottom level. You don't want hundreds of thousands of metric tons upon hundreds of thousands of metric tons of ships and equipment to be over your head at any given point. You want that weight to be supported by the ground floor. Not to mention that when a ship lifts it creates a lot of downward force, and again, you don't want to have that force on a floor above your head.

So they descended farther into the complex. When the elevator stopped and the doors opened, they were rewarded with a huge hangar bay and their ship towards the back wall. Seth hadn't even thought about the size of the hangar before seeing it, but had he, he still wouldn't have imagined what he saw. To be able to ground a ship as large as theirs, it would have to be massive. Based on what he saw, this was either a hangar for ships easily five times the size of his own or it had been home to hundreds of smaller ships.

Next to the elevator, Shar'tuk found several large cages that seemed to be prisoner transport modules. The cages had a fairly low tech steering mechanism and could even be moved manually if need be. Together, Seth and Shar'tuk loaded two of the transports onto the elevator and hit the button to send them back to the floor they came from.

Seth got on the company push. "We found the hangar bay; it's the bottom floor. We also found prisoner transport pods and we sent two of them up. Recon team, how far down are you?"

"Well, we didn't have a nice elevator so we're still humping it to you. How many floors do you think you went down?" They must have been pushing it pretty hard as Seth could hear the slight raggedness in the operator's voice as he spoke.

"We counted thirty-three buttons between the floor we were on and the button we pressed. If that correlates with a standard elevator then we went down thirty-four floors." Seth received an affirming nod from Shar'tuk.

"Copy that. We're just passing level twenty-four. Some floors are different heights. We passed two so far that had double the stairwell heights of the other floors. I think it will be quicker to stay in the stairwell than try to find the elevator on one of these floors. Not to mention we could run into resistance on any one of them."

"Agreed. We'll see you in a few." Seth turned his attention to the hangar bay and addressed the team leader. "Surgeon, our ship is here and it looks intact. Can you send down a few guys, with the first round of survivors, to get it prepped for launch? Emperor and I—"

"I already hate that." Shar'tuk sighed.

"—need to find controls to open the hangar", Seth finished.

"Sounds good. I'll send Joker and Smoke." Surgeon was feeling a little more optimistic as time passed and they hadn't all exploded yet. "I plan to remote detonate our stealth craft before we leave. I want to glass this side of the hemisphere."

"With most of the structure below ground, I don't think it will do that much damage." Seth understood the desire for as much destruction as possible in this situation. "I guess it couldn't hurt to give it a try, though."

The comm line went silent and everyone went on with their assigned tasks. Seth turned to Shar'tuk. "I'm going to take a look in one of these troop transports they left behind to see if there is a remote switch for the hangar bay. Look around to see if you can find a control room or something to open it up. If you don't find anything, come to the transport in ten minutes."

With just a nod between them, both operators took off in opposite directions. Shar'tuk found the control room fairly fast but it was of no use. All of the control panels were locked out and flashing a steady blue message. He went back to Seth.

"The control panels are completely locked out. I can't access anything." Shar'tuk was looking over Seth's shoulder at functioning displays in the cockpit. "It looks like the base is locked out but this craft isn't tied into the main computer system of the complex."

Shar'tuk moved Seth out of his way to get a better look at the control display. "I can't pick out any useful words here. The configuration looks very distantly like some I've seen in museums of our oldest warships."

Shar'tuk settled into the extremely oversized pilot's seat and thought out loud. "OK, I'm a four-armed fucker with two central-ish arms that look like they would control this panel here." He motioned to the panels in front of him and a terminal between his knees.

"While I'm accessing the panels with my central arms, my upper arms have the flight controls here..." He put his arms out to the sides. "So, a natural start-up sequence might be somewhere in this area."

Shar'tuk moved his hand over the panel and touched a button. Seth thought it was more random than anything but it did get a response from the ship. The screens all blanked for a quick second before blinking back to life, this time in a different language.

"Holy shit." Shar'tuk was hovering his hand above the panel, moving it from bottom to top. "This is a very ancient Nortes dialect. It was used by the royal family. It's now only taught in our version of your seminary schools. I think it sensed my DNA or something and knew I was Nortes. That's why the controls changed."

"Please tell me you're a religious man." Seth was looking at the new configuration.

"We all are. Deeply." Shar'tuk started to push buttons in a much more knowingly manner. "But that doesn't mean we all went to seminary school. Though I can grasp enough of this panel to get it to work."

A button began flashing yellow and Shar'tuk leaned forward to look out the viewport. Up at the top of the hangar, he could barely see some distant blue flashing lights. Happy with the results, he grabbed the flight controls. "Here we go."

As the craft lifted Seth comm'ed Surgeon. "We have an enemy troop transport operational and the hangar doors are opening. We're going to take a look outside and make sure our path is cleared for the ship."

"Copy that. We're moving the crew fairly fast. Reaper thinks we'll be done in about forty minutes." Surgeon was helping to load a poor soul onto one of the transports.

Seth looked at his watch. "That puts us at roughly fifty-six minutes since the warrior put that command into the system. I'm starting to question whether or not it was a self-destruct command. I wouldn't think a self-destruct would be set for that long of a period of time."

"Regardless, I don't want to stay here any longer than needed." Surgeon sighed and then added to the rest of the team, "We won't have time to get the dead and dying from the facility. Only evacuate the yellow flashing tubes. Leave the blue ones as they are."

One of the operators posed a question. "Can we at least help them out?"

The question was obviously to get permission to end their suffering, with a bullet. Reaper jumped in to take the burden off his friend. "No. We don't even have time for that. I've noticed that most of the blue flashers are dying pretty fast after the tube disengages and those that don't, are being allowed to go unconscious. The system isn't keeping them awake anymore."

With that, the discussion was over. The transports kept moving and the living, though some barely, were being taken to their ship. Surgeon allowed himself a slight bit of optimism but was still prepared for the other shoe to drop and take action if necessary.

As the troop transport headed to the top of the hangar bay, Seth was once again astonished at the sheer massiveness of the facility. Some facilities in the Coalition came close but were still maybe only two-thirds this size. Light spilled into the transport's canopy and Seth could see the surface of the planet falling below them as they cleared the hangar doors.

They had approached the facility from the other side of the planet and they had stayed as close to the ground as possible to avoid detection. As they rose several thousand feet above the facility, Seth was able to get a much better perspective on the area.

The facility had two distinct sides to it. The one the team had approached from seemed to be the front and now they were looking at the rear. The base had its back to an expansive and extremely lush jungle-looking landscape. Seth could easily pick out wild animals running below and jumping or swinging from tree to tree as the transport's engines scared them out of hiding.

Seth comm'ed Surgeon. "The exterior looks clear on initial inspection. No reinforcements heading here by ground and we think we've got our sensors on line and they aren't showing anything."

"We've got our ship prepped and ready. Start-up sequence is almost done and we should be ready to lift before the last of the crew are brought on board." Joker wasn't used to piloting something this large but luckily the ship's AI and intuitive systems allowed someone with basic piloting skills to get away with what they were attempting to do.

Surgeon was just stepping onto the bridge when Joker finished his sit-rep. He nodded to his friend. "Good job. Cadet, don't rely on just the sensors; they might know how to fool their own systems. Circle the base and make a spiral sweep out to five kilometers. Be ready to land that thing in our shuttle bay after we launch."

"Copy that." Seth pointed to an edge of the facility. "Start there. I want to check out that odd building that's separated from everything else."

As the transport flew over the area Seth had indicated, what he had thought was a building was actually an open structure that looked sort of like an outdoor playhouse like the ones you would go to for a Shakespeare in the Park play. Closer still, he could see there were horizontal and vertical bars randomly placed around blocks and tunnels of different heights along with randomly placed hazards to be avoided or conquered.

"That looks like a training area, and obstacle course of some sort." Shar'tuk was making a lower pass over it before heading out to the jungle.

"I see blood all over down there. Some blue and some red." Seth had a flash of anger as he realized that some of their friends may have been made to fight and die in there.

"There are also some cages along one wall." Shar'tuk could see something moving in one of them. "That one has a pretty big animal in it. Maybe they practice hunting in here. With the seating area at the top, I think it's obvious they had spectators for whatever they did use it for."

"All right, let's get to the sweep." Seth gestured towards the jungle. Without a co-pilot's chair, Seth had to stand in the canopy area to keep an eye on the screens and area outside the ship.

"This is a fairly remarkable area." Shar'tuk was trying to make small talk. As the adrenaline of battle wore off and the tension started to fade, it was a common desire to make things feel normal again.

"Yes, it is." Seth needed the conversation also. "I've seen several primate-looking species down there. A couple of pretty huge things that I couldn't even compare to any animal I've seen. I couldn't even tell where the one had a head, if he had a head."

They continued to chat as they made their sweeps and checked in every five minutes. As their ship was lifting off, Shar'tuk pointed the transport back to the hangar and was able to land in the shuttle bay without issue. He stayed with the transport to lock it down and Seth headed for the bridge.

Seth arrived to find most of the consoles manned by two people instead of one. These were all Special Forces operators, not starship pilots. Surgeon wanted two sets of eyes on the panels to make sure things weren't missed and avoidable mistakes were avoided. A lot of the men had basic piloting skills and even some advanced skills but flying a fighter was not the same as a vessel of this size and complexity.

"Where do you need me?" Seth stood in front of his mentor.

"I'm sending all available hands to sickbay. There's a lot of wounds to be tended to. Hopefully we can keep everyone we saved alive. Some of them are pretty bad. I don't know how they even survived this long." Surgeon shook his head as if it were an Etch A Sketch and he could remove the images from its screen.

Turning back to Seth, he said, "Looks like you were wrong, Cadet, for once." Surgeon smiled.

"I think so", Seth agreed. "All of the terminals were locked out, so maybe it was a data wipe or just a simple lockout command to keep us from information the base had."

"That makes me want to rethink setting our stealth ships to detonate." Surgeon was mulling over his decision. "If the information this base holds is that important, maybe we should keep it around to come back for later."

"I think that's a good"—" Seth didn't finish his sentence as the ship was rocked violently backward and he was thrown to the deck.

The forward viewer had a split screen of the forward and aft images from the ship. The aft image showed the hangar bay they had just come from erupting like the most massive volcano anyone had ever seen. Fire, debris, molten metal, ships, and everything else imaginable was being shot from the mouth of the hangar.

The base and the ground immediately surrounding it burped upward at least ten meters before sinking into the ground like a soufflé that was taken from the oven too soon. Flames began to shoot out from destroyed areas of the base as it sank in on itself.

Surgeon, who had been sitting securely in the command chair, got up and helped Seth to his feet. He surveyed the bridge and didn't see any major injuries. "Is everyone all right?" After getting affirmative head nods and a few verbal acknowledgements, he turned to Joker. "Are we going to stay up?"

"Yes, sir." Joker was checking things on his panel. "Luckily this ship likes an angled trajectory out of the atmosphere instead of going straight up. Otherwise we would have been directly over that geyser when it lit up." He went back to his controls to make sure he didn't miss anything important.

Seth wasn't sure gloating was appropriate in this moment so he smiled when Surgeon did it for him. "I guess your record is still mostly untarnished." He sat back in the command chair and added, "I hate it when you're right."

Seth was rubbing the newest knot on his head. "Sometimes I wish I could be wrong more often." As though the rubbing kick-started his thoughts, he went on. "You know, because I was right about the self-destruct, along with all of the ships we saw leaving the area when we first arrived, I don't think they called for reinforcements. With that in mind, I think we should take the time to recover our stealth craft."

"I agree. Take as many men that can be spared from medical duty and get our craft back. Joker, can you get us back to our original landing area?" Surgeon was still watching the base destroy itself.

"Yes, sir." Joker was adjusting the atmospheric trajectory and heading towards the landing site. "We'll be in a good position to launch and receive craft in about five minutes."

~

Ten hours later, all available hands were in the hangar bay for a mission status and debrief. All unavailable hands would be listening on their comm system or watching from a remote viewing screen at their station.

Shar'tuk was just finishing up. "So that's the basic history of my people. We were deeply ashamed of our past but for the last several generations we have begun to shed those feelings and move on. How long can we persecute ourselves for decisions that we were never a part of? How long can we feel bad for something we didn't do?"

"You shouldn't." Surgeon was sitting in the center of the amassed group. "Especially considering your ancestors were the ones who risked everything to change the empire."

To the group, he finished, "All right, we now have a little better idea of what we are up against. We've fought them and we won. It's the first victory we, as the Coalition, have had against this new enemy. We can't let that go to our heads. We have to use this information to keep having victories in the future.

"After we're done here, I want every single operator to put together an independent report on this mission. I want every second of battle that you can remember to be detailed in that report. Focus on the strengths and weaknesses in the enemy for every mode of combat we were involved in. Also be sure to detail what you think we did wrong and why. You won't be hurting my feelings at all. Hindsight is twenty-twenty and we need that hindsight to make our future engagements better. Don't pull any punches."

After Surgeon was sure that there were no questions up to this point, he nodded to Reaper. "Casualty report."

Reaper stood. "We lost approximately one-fifth of the crew on the planet. Of those we got back, we've had nine deaths so far, mostly from shock. The injuries are pretty heinous but extremely advanced surgically so most should survive.

"I think we'll even have maybe twenty or so up and walking in a few days. That should be beneficial to ship's operations. Until then, there are plenty of crew members who we can talk to if we have questions about the ship. They may not be mobile but they are still intact enough to help us out."

"Cadet." Surgeon turned to his unspoken number two.

"We were able to bring all of our stealth ships back on board so we still have those assets. We have done a preliminary inventory check on the ship and it seems like we still have a fair number of weapons and supplies. They did take some inventory to study, but thankfully not that much.

"The troop transport we took from their base has navigational charts for this region of space, but that's about it. I wouldn't expect this sort of ship to have a full database on their people but we'll go over it again just to make sure we didn't miss some command codes or other useful information." Seth looked to Shar'tuk because he would be the one doing most of the scanning.

Shar'tuk added, "We have sent a message back to my people asking them to send us a translation key for the ancient Nortes dialect that is in the transport's system. Once we have that key, any one of us can look through the files we have. Until then, we're going to have to rely on me trying to pick out stuff I can understand."

"That leads me to the last part of this debrief." Surgeon pulled out a datapad. "About forty hours ago, the Coalition sent a message to us about a pending threat in this sector of space. We just received the message and I barely had time to read through it all before this gathering. It's marked as highest priority and classification so don't forward copies home to your family." This got a slight chuckle from the group.

He continued. "I'll let you read through the majority of it on your own time but here's the basics. The warriors we've encountered used to be grown on a planet dedicated to that one specific task. For more than a thousand years now, the warriors have been denied access to that planet due to an automated defense system and a built-in genetic code that keeps them from approaching that sector of space.

"Something has changed; we don't know what or how, but it has. The Nortes have had remote monitoring devices in that system since they left the empire and those sensors recently detected intrusions in the area. The sensors are passive so there is no information on the types of ships, just that ships have entered the area.

"Another recon team was on a planet investigating an ancient base that was associated with the succession Emperor just briefed us on."

All eyes went to Shar'tuk and he just rolled his eyes. "You know, if you call me that around any Nortes military personnel or, gods forbid, the empress herself, I'll probably be imprisoned or executed."

Surgeon thought for a moment, his facial expression looking as though he was trying a piece of food for the first time and trying to decide whether he liked it or not. "Worth it", he concluded.

"Moving along," Surgeon continued. "The team was led by a Marine Science Corps officer, Lieutenant Emily Riley, apparently now Captain Emily Riley after she proved herself on the mission."

Seth was so dead tired from everything he almost missed what Surgeon had said. The name, the name he wanted to hear and speak out loud for so long now had been said. He quickly pulled out his tablet and began looking for the name. The officer's bio was present with the debrief material. It was her.

It was his chance encounter, his one unbelievable moment in his life. Of all the things that Seth had witnessed on this mission alone, it was still more unbelievable to him that he had fallen in love in less than twenty minutes after meeting Emily. Scratch that, less than twenty seconds after meeting her.

Seth wasn't even aware of the meeting anymore until Surgeon smacked him in the back of the head. "Am I boring you, Cadet?" Seth shook his head back and forth. "Good, now moving on.

"They found a lot of intelligence on that mission, most of it is detailed in your tablets for you to look through later. One important piece of information is one of their operators created a translation program for the alien language. That program will be coming in the next transmission burst. They wanted to make sure we were still alive before they sent it out. We've sent them our ship's private encryption key so they can encode it just for us in case anyone else intercepts the message.

"And finally, that leads us to the next part of our mission. We are moving to a staging area in this portion of the galaxy. Once at the staging area, we will be met by ships from the Coalition fleet as well as the Nortes, Detrill, and a few other non-member species that share a piece of the history we just went over.

"We are already in this sector, so we will get to the staging area first. We will recon it, determine if it's safe and report back. If we choose to keep that location, it will take approximately five months for the other ships to arrive."

"At least I finally get to use my saved vacation time", someone quipped. This got a much bigger laugh from the group.

Surgeon smiled. "Absolutely! We will have plenty of downtime after we finish our initial task of securing the staging area. We will definitely use some of that time to recuperate and heal both physically and emotionally.

"We'll also be starting a new training program to integrate everything we now know about these warriors and how they fight. We need to get much better at hand-to-hand combat with them if we want to survive future encounters.

"And of course that time will also be used to help rehabilitate as many of the crew members as we possibly can. I know you guys aren't nurses and doctors but they need our help. They went through more than any ten of us put together ever have or ever will. Reaper will be in charge of their continued rehab until we can get them the specialists they need."

"Fuck yeah!" someone said. Then the group replied in unison, "Fuck yeah!"

Surgeon didn't expect anything less of his men but it still moved him to see them all get behind the idea of helping out their shipmates. "Thank you, men. We will have a memorial service tomorrow at oh-nine hundred hours. I will be conducting the service from the forward hangar bay we've converted to an extended sickbay. It will be crowded but I'd like as many men in there as possible with the crew members who are bedridden. Some of you also need to be with the more seriously injured who are in the proper sickbay to give them your support. If you have a preference because you are close to any certain crew members, work it out among yourselves and get it done."

After receiving head nods and a few verbal responses, he concluded the meeting. "Dismissed."

As people got up and left, Surgeon saw Seth studying his tablet again. "She's fairly attractive."

"Um, yeah. What?" Seth noticed Surgeon looking over his shoulder.

"What's going on with you? I know you're beyond exhausted right now but you seem kind of gone at the moment."

"Do you remember that day in the training room when I mentioned a woman I sort of had back home?" Seth turned the tablet towards Surgeon. "That's her!"

"Wow. Small universe, huh? You want to see something that will totally blow your already frazzled mind?"

Surgeon took the tablet from Seth's hands and moved through the other team's personnel bios. When he got to an attractive and somewhat obviously seasoned woman, Surgeon gave the tablet back to Seth. "That's my wife."

Seth was astounded by the absolutely insane number of chances that would have to happen in the universe to cause this chain of events to occur and put them in the conversation they were now having. Seth looked at the file again; something was niggling at his brain and he couldn't quite put a finger on it. Then he read the name to himself again. *Daria O'Connor*.

"Holy crap. Your name is Mike."

They had never discussed real names before so Surgeon was a little taken aback. "Yeah, how did you know that?"

"Your wife, Daria O'Connor. I've been hoping to meet her ever since I signed up for the marines."

"I'm really not following you at all." Surgeon had no idea how Seth could've known Daria.

"I've got a story for you." Seth then laid out his dealings with AeroTech and how he had discovered that Mike had been "murdered" which eventually led Seth to join the marines.

"This mission keeps getting stranger by the day." Mike just sat back to think about it for a minute.

Seth was still reviewing the file. "What are you going to say to her when you see her?"

Mike thought for a second. "I'm sorry I forgot to take the garbage out before I left."

Chapter 51
Deep Inside Enemy Territory – Fancy Meeting You Here

"Sir, the *Emilian* is on final approach to the staging area and requesting permission to join the fleet", the conn officer announced.

The captain had been on the bridge for the last three weeks, though he could only take four to six hours at a time on shift before he had to rest again. He was surprised at how well his conn officer was adjusting to his new life with only two fingers on his right hand and four on his left. Almost every one of the crew members who had survived their stint as prisoners were left with some sort of physical disfigurement. Some were adjusting well and others would never make a full physical or psychological recovery.

For the last several hours, ships from the Coalition Task Force had been jumping into the system. The ships were coming in twos or threes and then receiving positioning coordinates from the *Vanguard,* who was in charge of placing the vessels in strategic formations while they waited for further orders. The task was important, yet dull and repetitive.

"Give them their coordinates along with their companion vessels. Extend them the usual greeting and protocol instruction packet." The captain looked over the ship names for the newest trio of vessels and laughed out loud when he saw the last one. "Also tell the crew of *The Goonies* that we are ready to receive their envoy for the combined debrief. I'll tell Surgeon that his guest is about to arrive."

~

Surgeon and Cadet were training with several other members from their team. Intermixed with them were some of the more able-bodied crew members. After their ordeal, they wanted to learn to fight better in case they ever got boarded again. Most of them were doing well for swabbies and all were doing great considering what they had recently been through.

The captain approached Surgeon, who was going through weapons malfunction and reload drills with a few of the crew members. "Surgeon, I thought you'd like to know your, uh, special guest has just arrived in-system. The envoy should be on the *Vanguard* within a couple of hours."

Surgeon's eyes lit up just a little for a second before his years of combat poker face kicked in. "Thank you, sir. It's good to see you up and around lately. I really didn't like being in charge of your ship while you were still on it."

The captain smiled. "You weren't. I'll give you a heads-up when their shuttle is on its way."

"Thank you again, sir." Surgeon turned to Seth as the captain walked away. "Let's do about an hour more here before we get cleaned up for our guests."

Seth nodded in agreement and ushered a few of the crew to Joker so they could all work on some hand-to-hand combat skills.

~

It took almost four hours for the envoy to arrive. The captain was complaining to Surgeon, saying that the envoy had the Coalition president along with the Detrill and Nortes heads of state, and the security teams from the three different parties couldn't agree on anything. Not to mention the protocol officers from each party having different ideas on how things should be run. In truth, the three people in charge couldn't care less who walked through a doorway first or whose national colors were used as room decorations.

In the end, the president came up with the idea, and ultimately a direct order, that the heroes who had captured the first enemy vessel should be the ones to depart the shuttle first.

Surgeon stood with Seth and several other members of the strike team and ship's crew to welcome the special envoy. Seth was surprised at how much his hands were sweating. He had survived one of the most harrowing battles in recent Coalition history and he was more nervous than ever before. Would she remember him? Would that spark still be there? Were his feelings just drug-induced shadows from being roofied by Joker? He was about to find out and the thought almost made him throw up.

The boarding ramp lowered from the side of the shuttle and touched the deck before the first person showed their face in the doorway. Surgeon recognized the operator from his picture in the files; his name was Bloom. Bloom looked around and descended the ramp. He was closely followed by the droid they repurposed, Jeeves. The droid said something that only Bloom could hear and he gave what seemed to be a sharp reply. Interesting.

Two women came next and Surgeon could barely keep himself in one place as he looked at his wife. Daria was scanning the faces in the reception party when her eyes finally fell on Surgeon. Their eyes locked. Daria started to move down the ramp faster and saw that the way was blocked by the slow-moving Jeeves and Bloom. Without hesitation, she jumped over the side of the boarding ramp and landed six feet later in a dead run to Surgeon.

Surgeon braced himself for the oncoming woman, who flung herself into his arms and they buried their faces into each other's shoulders. Both were crying unabashedly. Daria pulled back just enough so their lips could meet and she kissed her husband as though it was the first time.

After a period of time that left most of the observers feeling a little awkward, Daria pulled away again. "You forgot to take the garbage out again. Dick."

"I love you."

"I love you, too, Mike."

"Seriously?" Seth was looking at his friend and trying not to be obvious about visually stalking Emily as she approached. "After seeing this side of you, I don't know if I can ever call you Surgeon again."

"Surgeon?" Seriously?" This was from Daria.

"Hey, we were all given our call signs by someone else, not my choice." Mike smiled. "And as long as we're talking about stupid names, *The Goonies*?!"

"Well," Daria began, "we were a group of friends who dropped down a hole and had to fight for the buried treasure."

"Yeah, I read the report. I can't wait to hear about it in person, though."

"We aren't talking later." Daria didn't care who was listening. "You'll be lucky if you can stay conscious later."

"Um, awkward..." Bloom was now standing with the group.

Seth was the first to greet him. "I've read your reports and I'm very impressed with your work. I've got a bit of a technology background and I'd love to pick your brain later." He extended his hand. "I'm Seth, but they call me Cadet."

"Ooooh, bummer." Bloom snickered. "Jeeves and I would be happy to go over the mission later. Just show me where we can grab a beer and I'm all yours."

Seth was about to say something when he felt a light tap on his shoulder. "Excuse me, Lieutenant," Emily began, "I'm not sure if you remember me or not; you weren't doing too well when we met back at your graduation."

How could I forget the love of my life? My destiny? Holy God, I didn't say that out loud, did I? Nope, still internal dialogue. Good...

"I'm sorry, I guess you don't. Well, I'm"—"

Seth didn't give her a chance to finish. "Captain Emily Riley. Of course I remember you. Thank you for being so nice to me that night. I was actually drugged by that nice gentleman over there," Seth pointed to Joker who just waved and smiled back, "so I could be kidnapped for this mission. Oh, and congratulations on your recent field promotion. Very impressive stuff."

Emily blushed. "Thank you. I didn't really do anything other than back the plays of my team." Daria gave her a little swat on the shoulder for being so humble. "I don't want to intrude, but I'd like to join your conversation with Bloom later. I'd like to hear firsthand what you've learned about the warriors."

"Of course, ma'am." Seth cringed at his own formal address. "We'd really love for you to join." He cringed again at the now excessive sense of eagerness in his voice.

"Awkward..." Bloom had his hand to his face and looked through his fingers as though he were watching a scary movie.

"Query." Jeeves spoke up in his completely out-of-place British accent. "Are you stating 'awkward' because of the obvious sexual interest this male human has in the captain and his apparent inability to function properly in her presence?"

Daria pointed to Jeeves and Bloom. "Leave. Both of you. Now."

Without a word, they both turned around and tried to find a spot farther along the reception line. The rest of the team was coming down the ramp with Davies just exiting the shuttle. Davies looked around to find Daria and when he did, he also found Mike. He was first confused because his friend was supposed to be dead. Then he was elated that his friend wasn't dead. And lastly he was ashamed as the memory and imagery of him and Daria went through his mind.

Daria saw Davies and caught the almost imperceptible change of emotion and found herself also feeling a rush of guilt. She would tell Mike. He deserved to know and she knew he would understand, given the circumstances. For now though, she hoped Davies could act natural enough to get through the moment.

Davies walked to Mike and embraced him while lifting the only slightly smaller man off his feet. "Don't ever die again, jerkface."

"I love you, too, buddy, but even my wife didn't hold me this long." Mike slapped his friend on the back as he was put on his feet again.

The small group grew as the operators from both groups mixed and were introduced to one another. By the time the president made his arrival at the door, no one was paying attention to the shuttle any more. The president laughed a little to himself as he heard the protocol officers from all three groups complaining about how their hard work had gone to waste and that no one was even paying attention. Exactly, the president thought, this is the way it should be.

~

Hours later, Daria and Mike were walking to the general debrief that had been set up in the largest conference room the ship had. The conference room was more of an auditorium with its stadium seating, monitors everywhere, and personal datapads placed on every seat waiting for their intended occupants.

The general debrief was going to be huge and necessarily time consuming. Every member of both ground teams, along with key personnel from Surgeon's infiltration ship, would be debriefing the Coalition president, Nortes empress and Detrill emperor, along with their respective staff members. After the general assembly ended, the plan was to have a much smaller briefing two days later with the key team leaders and ship commanders who would be leading the next phase of the assault.

As they walked, Daria looked to Mike. "I still don't understand what all of the faked deaths and kidnappings were for. Special Ops guys get deployed on secret missions all the time. Why all of the theatrics?"

Mike sighed. "It's been explained to me a few times, and I still don't get it myself. I was pretty angry to say the least when I found out what they were putting you through. The short story is that they were so afraid of what was going on in the outer colonies, they didn't want to risk any security leaks whatsoever. They went to extremes to ensure that nothing about this mission got out."

"Well, we all know that 'Military Intelligence' is the most profound oxymoron in the universe." Daria gripped her husband's arm a little tighter as they exited the lift and walked into the conference room and took their assigned seats.

As the rest of the team members entered the room, Daria saw that there were quite a few people she knew from the various trainings, deployments, and duty stations she'd been a part of over the many years. She also saw that Emily and Seth were paired together and looking like two pre-teens at a junior high dance.

As more operators entered the room, Daria saw one who instantly caught her eye and tugged at a very old but always prominent memory in her mind. She stood and seemed almost zombie-like as she approached the man who had already taken his seat.

The man looked up at her and squinted a bit as though he thought he should be able to place her face but was unable to. Daria reached down and placed her palm on the man's chest and whispered, "Reaper."

Reaper's mind clicked the puzzle pieces together and stood to embrace the woman who had grown up so much from the little girl he had met in the electronics store many years ago. "Your father?"

"Alive, because of you." She embraced her father's savior and her inspiration. "They told me you didn't make it!"

They separated and looked at each other. "I didn't. I died in the ambulance. Twice. Once more on the operating table. I'm kind of a glutton for punishment that way."

Mike walked over. "Holy Christ. I never put two and two together! This," he pointed to his friend, "this is THE Reaper you told me about?! I never even thought to ask after I met him. I guess there was just so much stuff going on with this mission from the get-go that I didn't think about it."

"Aren't you getting a bit old for this kind of stuff?" Daria brushed her fingers through his hair as though she were looking for gray hair.

"Whoa there, missy, I was sixteen when we met." Reaper ran his fingers through his hair in a subconsciously defensive gesture. "I was in the delayed entry program and had already gone through corpsman school on my summer break. I'm not THAT much older than you, or your husband for that matter."

"We are going to have a long talk after this debrief. I need to show you pictures of my dad and stepmom." Daria gave him another quick hug and then went back to her seat with her husband in tow.

Daria and Mike were chatting about Reaper and the coincidence of everything, when the lights dimmed a couple of times to signal the debrief was about to start. Security teams for the dignitaries came into the room and took their places in locations that seemed to be an attempt at being discreet. More than one of them looked ill at ease considering the company they were in. The security forces were no match for any one of the operators in the room, not to mention an auditorium full of the guys.

After everyone was seated and ready, the president stood. "It is nothing short of extraordinary that you are all here today. Let us take a moment to remember those who could not be here with us because they made the ultimate sacrifice so the rest of us could be."

The screens in the room all came to life with the picture of the general along with a short bio on the side of the screen. "The general." The president chuckled. "I've met with the man many times in my life and I don't think I've ever called him by any other name." The group let out a small laugh in return.

The screens continued to show images of each person lost from the ship's crew and both Special Forces teams. The president spoke every one's name and added a one or two sentence anecdote for those he personally knew, which was surprisingly quite a few of them.

When the presentation was over, the debrief started in earnest. Introductions of the VIPs were made before the dialogue began. Not everyone was expected to give a detailed account; a specifically arranged outline was followed and presented primarily by the ship's captain, Seth, Emily, Wilks, and Mike. Other operators would add bits here and there as they felt it was appropriate but none took up any more time than was necessary to make their point.

The debrief took almost five hours with four well-placed twenty-minute breaks. When it was done, the empress made a brief speech of gratitude to the men and women of the Coalition for their actions and for what they were about to do. The president allowed the empress' speech to be the last word as he stood and gave a slight bow to her before leaving the room. After the dignitaries left, the group broke up of their own accord and left in mostly the same groups they arrived in.

The rest of the night drained the ship's stock of alcohol and a shuttle was actually brought from the president's ship to resupply the crew. Daria spent the night with Mike, Emily, Seth, Bloom, Wilks, and Reaper. Jeeves had been sent to the holodeck to make friends with the computer there and go over training scenarios that would help them practice fighting the warriors; Bloom seemed a little sad that his new friend was exiled from the land of organics.

The next day was spent as an informal debrief time for the operators of both teams to get to know one another and break into specialty-related groups to go over specific information. The now much larger group of operators also scheduled workout time in the holodeck to practice old skills and learn new ones.

Daria and Reaper were kept busy that afternoon while they checked out the multitude of injuries that were going around. The two groups were testing each other, trying to push the limits but not going too far. If the injuries started to get bad, Daria would put a stop to the excessive training. But for now, everything was fine and the injuries were to be expected.

That night the alcohol stock held its own as most of the operators felt like their one night of letting loose was enough for now. It was time to get serious again and their training today was a good reminder of how you didn't want to feel on a mission after a night of too much fun.

Daria and Mike were in his cabin again. She hadn't even set foot in the one that had been assigned to her and Emily. Space was at a premium on the ship so most people bunked together, officers and enlisted alike, but Mike's position on the mission granted him his own space and Daria was thankful for that.

Daria decided to tell Mike about her and Davies. Mike's eyes welled up but not with anger or sadness; it was an emotion that even he couldn't explain.

"God, I've showered with him before."

"You are such a shit head."

"It's just, well, are you ruined now?"

"I'm seriously going to kill you if you don't stop." Daria was trying not to smile but Mike was actually making her feel better about it.

"Look, I can't be mad. I was dead. I actually thought about it once and figured if this mission took too long I'd come back to find you guys together. Given what you were going through on that mission, I can understand having a moment when you both needed that." Mike brushed her hair aside and looked into her eyes. "But in all fairness, when we get back, I'm nailing that freaky hot blonde at Starbucks who always gives me extra whipped cream for free."

Daria smiled back. "If we're trying to be fair, then you need to pick someone from your mission like I did. Maybe Joker or Cadet?"

"Shut up." Mike kissed his wife and they made love a few times before finally going to sleep.

~

The next day, the team leaders met with the VIPs and their advisors to go over new information and the analysis that had been on the debrief information.

Mike was a little distracted as he thought about Daria going to tell Davies about their conversation. He hoped his friend would believe her when she told Davies that Mike had no ill feelings about the situation. Daria and Mike agreed that unless Davies wanted to talk to Mike about it, it would be best if the two men never spoke of it with each other.

Mike was pulled back to the meeting as the Detrill emperor stood. "As you know, my people are fascinated with shipbuilding. We were the primary designers and builders of the ships from the Nortes' old empire."

The emperor touched a panel and an image, of a fleet of ships in a solar system, came up on the screens.

"These images were brought to us by the team who has been in this system for the past five months. They used their stealth craft to sneak in to our target system and obtain these photos."

As everyone looked at the images changing on the screen, Mike spoke up. "Sir, those aren't the same ships we saw departing the interrogation planet's system."

"Good eye, Surgeon."

Mike was a little surprised that the emperor used or even knew his combat call sign.

The emperor continued, "When we first saw these images, we were taken aback. We couldn't believe that the warriors had been able to design, much less build, ships of these magnitudes on their own. We thought it might have been plausible that they found another species to subjugate and take over the shipbuilding for the Detrill.

"You see, during the uprising, the ship designers were either involved with the separation or were killed back in the empire to ensure that the legacy could not continue. There were plenty of Detrill left behind to repair ships and sustain the fleet for a short period of time, but we felt confident they wouldn't have any ship designers because education among the slaves was strictly controlled and enforced. With all of the advanced designers dead, there would be no one left to teach the next generation of Detrill slaves how to do that job."

The emperor then changed the images on the screen. "Then we came across information that was gathered by Captain Riley's team at their dig site. The warriors had a war with a species called the Cherta. Ultimately the war was a draw and both sides receded back to their home territories, with very little ground gained or lost by either side.

"The interesting part is, based on the information we received from the dig site, we believe the ships we are seeing in the target system are of Cherta design."

The emperor brought up images from the history files along with the new recon images. The ships were definitely similar, though there was about six or seven hundred years between the designs.

"Though the ships are obviously different," the emperor continued, "you can see enough similarities in the design and manufacturing technologies to know they came from the same species."

The screens were now highlighting areas on the images, showing the similarities between the ships. Technical information was scrolling along, also showing similarities in design and function.

The empress now stood as the emperor took his seat. "Also from the information obtained at the dig site and through your new acquaintances, Jeeves and Fouter, we know that the warriors took a great many of the Cherta captive and created a new class of slaves for the empire. The new class became advisors to the warriors and their war council because there was no more Nortes royals to lead them."

The empress took a deep breath. "Through your briefing packets, you have learned that we had a planet dedicated to growing the warriors for the empire. You should also have all of the details we have on the security systems in place to keep unauthorized parties from accessing the planet and using the warriors for themselves."

"If I remember correctly," Emily began, "the system is supposedly hidden by natural camouflage caused by some sort of cosmic anomaly that I quite honestly couldn't understand, no matter how many times I read the technical brief."

"That's true, Captain." The empress looked directly at Emily and smiled. "I don't understand it myself. I've always been more musically inclined rather than adept in astrophysics. Regardless, we are guessing that somehow the Cherta slaves were able to obtain the planet's location and then get that information back to their people. There are other possible scenarios but we think that's the most likely one."

The president stood to address the room. "We don't know much about the Cherta other than they were also conquerors much like the warriors and the empire they served. From the information we have, they were a much more benevolent society and did not use slavery as the Nortes did.

"But slaves or not, they were the ruling class for every society they conquered and did not live as equals with those who were taken into the fold. I don't know about you, but I don't want our cooperative Coalition, even with all of its flaws, turned into a dictatorship by the Cherta or any other species, benevolent or not." The last sentence was punctuated with the president hitting the table with a closed fist.

Murmuring broke out among the gathered group with everyone agreeing with the president's statements. Mike spoke up above the murmurs. "Okay, if these are the Cherta, then where did the warrior fleet go? We saw them amassing their ships and then departing together. During our recon of the target system and surrounding areas, we never saw the warriors or their fleet."

One of the panel's analysts stood. "We don't know the answer to that question at this point. We have theories, all of which are outlined in your materials. As you may already know or have read, the warriors have a genetically created, um, firewall for lack of a better term. This firewall keeps them from knowing, finding, or going near their birthing planet. So they may be aware the Cherta have found it but they'd be powerless to stop them.

"I know that doesn't answer your question of where that fleet went; it just kinda tells us where we know it didn't go and why."

The empress stood again. "Based on our knowledge of how the warriors fight, we believe that they are staging their forces between ours and the Cherta. They will want to have a jumping-off point that will allow them to fight either enemy at any given time.

"We are putting together logical guesses as to where they might be. Once we have put together a comprehensive list of systems, we will be sending out recon groups to look for the warriors. The only good thing about the Cherta becoming involved is that it will delay the impending invasion of the Coalition we're certain the warriors were planning."

Another ship captain stood. "Is there any possible way of aligning ourselves with either side?"

The president nodded ambiguously. "Based on what we know of the Cherta, they won't be open to that because it would make us equals instead of a citizen group within their empire. However, we are definitely not ruling out the possibility. Now that we know who we are dealing with, we are working on the details to set up an envoy in an attempt to make contact with them and hopefully come to a peaceful and mutually acceptable resolution. The information we have on them is more than five hundred years old so it's completely possible they have changed the way their empire is run, just as the Nortes and Detrill did in that time."

The president was about to continue when the empress added, "The warriors have a saying: The enemy of my enemy—"

Emily allowed her inner dialogue to become external and she accidentally interrupted the foreign dignitary, "Is my friend."

"Excuse me?" was all the empress said.

"I'm so terribly sorry, Your Highness", Emily stammered. "It's just that we have the same saying: The enemy of my enemy is my friend."

"Oh young one, if that were only true." The empress smiled as Emily shrank in her seat, clearly put in her place for interrupting. "The warriors' saying, if I may finish, is unfortunately not as promising. Their saying is: The enemy of my enemy, will be torn limb from limb and their hearts eaten while they still beat, to show what will happen to anyone who does not succumb to our might."

"Yup, that's different, all right." Mike winked at Emily to try to make her feel just a little bit better.

Epilogue

Seth's heart was pounding. He was running faster than a Shirka with his fur on fire. There were no more points of cover or even concealment as he retreated to the newest skirmish line his fireteam had set up. He wasn't sure whether it was the zigzag pattern he was running in or the ineptitude of his enemy that kept him from getting shot, but he didn't really care so long as his luck held out for another twenty meters.

"Just fucking run, Cadet! Why are you dancing out there?!"

Seth could hear Surgeon's voice coming over the comlink but he didn't want to waste any oxygen on a reply, quippy or otherwise. The enemy rounds seemed to be getting closer as evidenced by the heat Seth could feel passing by his face and the exposed portions of his arms. The enemy used a metal slug that was propelled so fast that it superheated the air it traveled through. The round also tended to melt right through Coalition armor and sometimes even set their targets on fire.

Seth dove into the rock formation the rest of his fire team was using for cover, and as he did so, an enemy round grazed his right boot and melted a good portion of his boot's heel. "Damn. I just broke these in", he said through ragged breaths.

"If you're done resting over there," Joker started in on him, "we could use another rifle on our one-two corner."

Seth was about to retort that he hadn't brought one when he realized that Jenson and Boddie were lying near the one-two corner, dead. Seth had two rifles to choose from; there always seemed to be an extra rifle lying around lately—too many in fact. Seth picked up Boddie's rifle and took all of the extra ammunition he could from both of his dead friends.

Surgeon was walking the inner perimeter to check on his men and also the status of their current positions. The war was taking huge tolls on the Coalition; fighting on a multitude of fronts against two superior forces wasn't going to last very long. Today they were fighting the Cherta, or at least the Cherta forces. Surgeon had gotten a glimpse of the alien enemies earlier but he didn't recognized their species. Luckily, they were fairly horrible soldiers and couldn't aim worth a shit. Days like today sometimes gave Surgeon just a smidgen of hope that the Coalition could pull out of their funk and win a major engagement or two and turn the tide in their favor.

Surgeon opened his comlink to his wife's team. "Daria, I hate to bug you, but we're getting our asses kicked out here. Do you have any sort of time frame for me?"

Emily answered for her friend. "I wish I had an answer for you, but I don't. The fact that the Cherta forces are pushing so hard for this moon makes me even more certain that I'm right it contains something very important to them."

Surgeon had fought alongside Emily for more than eight months now and had seen her evolve from a science geek to a truly impressive combat line officer, but she still needed to be reined in once in a while. "Ma'am, I understand that it might be valuable to them, but we have no idea if it will be valuable to us. It might just be something extremely culturally important, a religious icon of some sort. Something that won't have any value to us in this war."

"I know what you're saying, and I've thought of that, but I know I'm right. I know that we can use to our benefit whatever is in this chamber. I was here when I was sixteen; I wrote a doctoral thesis on this chamber. It's important. We need it. I'd bet my life on it."

"You already are, Captain." Surgeon paused before he spoke again. "We'll back your play, Emily, but at some point we have to leave even if we don't get what we came for. Otherwise, we may get into the chamber but we'll never get back to the fleet to use it."

"Understood. I trust you to decide when we've crossed that line. Let me know when it's time to go." Emily ended her side of the conversation.

To the rest of the fire team, Surgeon said, "The captain needs more time. We need to hold this line for as long as possible. If she makes it in to the chamber, then we'll head out in our scout craft and drop a tactical nuke behind us as we leave. Our ships in orbit are still engaged with the enemy and keeping them from landing at our six, so we still can't get orbital fire support from them. I'm open to suggestions other than keep shooting and don't die."

The warrior who was on the firing line next to Fang spoke up first. "My personal shield will be fully charged up in less than five minutes. Give me four grenades and strap some explosives to me. I can make it to their center before my shield goes down and then set off the explosives. It will take a lot of them out and cause a bit of mayhem."

Surgeon looked at their newest soldier and realized that his suggestion just removed any lingering doubt Surgeon had about his allegiance to the Coalition, or at least to the soldiers he fought alongside of. This warrior had left the dogfight against Daria's team when they stole the ancient warrior ship from the dig site at the abandoned base a little over a year ago.

A month ago, the top brass had decided to put the warrior in the field with Surgeon's team to see whether he truly had changed sides. The warrior had answered every question posed to him and even gave over much more information than he had been asked for, all without any nudging or torture required. The warrior had said that there was something wrong with him, that he hadn't been grown correctly, and that defect gave him the ability to think outside of his genetic programming. He wanted to be a part of the Coalition and what it stood for. So they let him. At this point, they didn't have much to lose.

"Thanks for the suggestion, Baldylocks, but I'm not throwing away a soldier to buy us only a few minutes. Anyone else?" Surgeon turned to look at his other flank of soldiers.

The waHillsteprrior looked at Fang. "Humans."

"Tell me about it", Fang snarled. "I'd send you out there. Sounds like a good plan to me."

"Right?!" The warrior fired a few more rounds. "And I thought my new name was 'Cue Ball'? What does Baldylocks mean?"

Seth came up beside the warrior. "I'll explain that one later. For now, give me your shield. You gave me an idea."

"What have you got for me, Cadet?" Surgeon was watching his protégé hurriedly working on his idea.

"We're going to put the shield on our combat mule and load its payload wagon with explosives." Seth was moving fast on his idea, getting the pieces in place. "We run the shielded mule past their front lines, drop the wagon, send the mule on a wide return course, and blow the explosives."

Joker had started helping Cadet with his plan as soon as he saw what was being done. "Sounds good to me. The mule can run faster than any of us can so he'll get more use out of the shield than we would anyway. And, maybe he'll be able to get far enough away that the explosion doesn't rip his mechanical hide to hell. If he gets away, we'll still have the shield and mule as assets."

"Good plan. Let me know when you're ready to send it. We might be able to plow the path for the mule so it will take less shield damage." Surgeon grabbed his own rifle and got into a firing position.

The mule was released and sent downrange, much to the surprise of the enemy. It took at least thirty meters before the shielded robot began to take any fire at all. The mule ran through the front line, taking out one of the alien enemy along the way. Fifteen meters in, the mule dropped its payload wagon and began to arc away from the explosives. Once Seth thought the mule was at a good enough distance, he detonated the charges.

"Nice!" Reaper was patching up a small shrapnel wound on Fang's leg.

"Captain." Surgeon opened his comlink again. "We just bought you a little more time, but don't take it for granted."

"We just got through the door!" Emily's excitement could be heard even through the muting effects of the comlink. "We're making entry now. If it's safe, we can fall back to the chamber interior and close the door. There's no way they're getting through it."

"Copy that. We're ready to fall back, sooner rather than later would be nice." Surgeon added to himself, *They can't get through it unless they have the key. They did build it, after all.*

The mule returned a few minutes later and Seth retrieved the shield from it and gave it back to the warrior. "Here you go, Cue Ball. Thanks for the loan."

"I really don't care what you pink hairless monkeys call me, but pick one name and stick with it." The warrior fired a few more rounds from his plasma rifle, indicating he was done with the verbal exchange.

"Apes, Baldylocks. We're pink apes, not monkeys. Totally different species." Surgeon hadn't heard back from Emily yet but he wasn't going to wait any longer. "All right everyone, we're falling back to the chamber. Get your asses moving, regardless if it's primate or genetically engineered."

The fire team performed a textbook peel-off into the tunnel system behind them. With his shield back in place and mostly charged, Baldylocks was the last man through the entrance, taking rounds that harmlessly deflected off his shield as he moved backwards. Once they reached the chamber's entrance, Seth announced over the team push that friendlies were coming in.

Once inside, they were greeted by Jeeves. "Hello sirs. I was left here to close the door after your arrival. You seem to be missing three men. Shall I wait for them or will they not be joining us?"

Surgeon would never get used to losing men, and the relief he felt from not losing more during any given mission always made him feel worse. "Close it. They aren't coming."

"Yes, sir." Jeeves began to turn to carry out his orders when he paused. "And sir, if later we could discuss the tactical use of the combat mule to deliver an explosive payload..."

"No, we can't, Jeeves. And now's not the time to discuss *AGAIN* how you are different from the automatons we use in the field. I wouldn't send you out there like that, you should know that by now." Surgeon was almost at his limit with the robot. He would need to see whether Bloom could correct some of the "issues" Surgeon had been noticing lately.

"Now what?" Joker was looking around the small room they were now safely occupying.

Outside they could hear enemy gunfire hitting the chamber door. The aliens were obviously trying to shoot the door open. Based on the experimenting Emily's team had done during the several weeks prior to the Cherta attack, Surgeon knew that even the advanced enemy weapons wouldn't make a dent in the door.

"We go find the rest of our team and see if this chamber was worth it." Surgeon motioned to Seth to take point and the rest of the team to fall in and move out.

To Be Continued...

About the Author

Jay was born in California and moved to Tucson with his family when he was seven. At eighteen he joined the United States Navy and became a Hospital Corpsman. Jay worked in the Emergency Room at the Navy Medical Center San Diego (dubbed "The Starship of Navy Medicine) in California. After four years of service, HM3 Korza took his leave and went into the private medical sector, a decision he has regretted more than once.

Jay has managed a private medical practice, worked on ambulances in Tucson and Massachusetts, and has been a paramedic for the US Department of Justice Federal Bureau of Prisons. In 2000 he started his career in law enforcement and has ever since been elated with being a deputy.

Jay currently has thirteen years of law enforcement service and seven years on the SWAT Team. He is currently assigned to a specialized support operations unit as well as being a medic and sniper for the SWAT Team.

In his spare time, Jay also teaches at the local college's paramedic program and he has desperately been trying to finish this book. If you're reading this, then he finally has. For more information about the author, please visit his website at www.1393productions.com . Any and all feedback or questions are always welcomed.

And join the conversation on Twitter with the characters from *Extinction*.

@Bloom_1393 @Daria_1393 @Davies_1393
@Emily_1393 @Jeeves_1393 @Jockey_1393
@Reaper_1393 @Seth_1393 @Surgeon_1393
@Snake_1393 @Warrior_1393 @Wilks_1393
@Scan_1393

Text and Images Copyright © 2013

Jay Korza

All Rights Reserved

Made in the USA
San Bernardino, CA
16 September 2013